To my mother and her twin sister,
Aster and Ivy are not you, but you did inspire
The Masterpiecers with your amazing talent
with a needle & thread.

To my father,
thank you for raising me in a world
filled with the timeless beauty of Art.

COLD LITTLE GAMES

USA TODAY BESTSELLING AUTHOR
OLIVIA WILDENSTEIN

Our mother used to say that Ivy sucked all the good from the womb and I was left with the scraps. I hate to think she was right about anything, but my twin sister *is* exceptional.

"You're going to do so well," I tell Ivy, squeezing her hand.

"No touching," barks the guard watching over us.

It's just the two of us in the visitation room.

Ivy yanks her hand out of mine. "I don't know about *so well*, but I'm going to do my best." She links her fingers together in a business-like manner. "Has Josh come to see you yet?"

"No."

"He told me he spoke to your warden about letting you watch the show. You have his permission to look at it whenever you want."

I give her a weak smile. "That'll be the highlight of my day."

She runs her nail underneath the peeling, synthetic wood surface of the table.

"I'm happy you came to see me," I say.

Her gaze sticks to the tabletop. It's as though she doesn't

dare look up at me. I think she's afraid to cry. "Was it really an accident, Aster?" Her voice is so faint that I have to strain to make out her words.

"Yes."

"You promise me—"

"Yes," I say. "Stop worrying about this. By the time you come home, it will be ancient history."

She bites her lip.

"Now go *make* history," I tell her.

"I'll probably be disqualified after the first round."

I shake my head. "Can you stop putting yourself down? You are *so* talented. So much more than all the other contestants."

"But this isn't only about talent."

If only I could curve the outer corners of her lips into a smile like I do at work with my computer cursor.

When her eyes twitch down to my hands, I slip both inside my jumpsuit pockets. "There's something I wanted to give you before the show," I tell her.

"What?"

"Just a little present."

"What is it?"

"If I tell you, it'll ruin the surprise." I drop my voice to a whisper. "It's in my underwear drawer. Where I kept my baby teeth."

She stays silent and still for so long that I shift around on the rigid iron chair. Suddenly, she stands. "I have to go home to pack."

"Already?"

She nods. "Before I go, though, you have to sign something for me." She heads over to the guard stationed in the corner.

As I watch her, the tips of my coarse curls brush against my gray jumpsuit. Ivy's hair is much longer than mine, and much softer. She styled mine once like hers—she even tried to teach me—but I have no patience with brushes and serums and creams. Besides, as much as I love my twin, at nineteen, we're past the age where it's cute to look identical.

After a quick exchange, she returns with his pen. She digs out a folded piece of paper from the back pocket of her skinny jeans and smooths it out on the desk. "The show sent me some extra forms to fill out. They need the signature from my next of kin in case something goes wrong."

My mouth goes dry. "It's an art competition...what could go wrong?"

"It's just a formality, Asty." She sticks the pen in my hand.

"But—"

"Nothing will go wrong." Her gaze softens. She knows I can never say no to her when she looks at me like that. "I promise."

I push out the breath I'm holding and study the paper. It's all fine print.

Ivy points to the signature line. "I've already read it. It's legalese. Disclaimers. The usual."

I bite my lip, and look back up at her. She's checking the round white wall clock, so I hurry to scratch my name on the dotted line. "Here."

She tugs the sheet away from me and folds it back into her pocket. "Are you eating? You look skeletal."

I study the sharpness of my wrist bones. They do look like they're about to pierce my skin.

When she doesn't sit back down, I say, "It's time, isn't it?" I don't want her to leave, even though I encouraged her to go.

She nods.

I stand up, hoping for a hug, but instead, she lifts the pen from my hand and walks over to the guard to return it.

Over her shoulder, she calls out, "You take care, all right, Asty?" Her voice catches on my name.

I smile even though I didn't get my hug. Just like she didn't give me one yesterday when she came to visit. Maybe with the whole "no-touching-the-prisoner" rule, she doesn't know she's allowed to hug me on her way out. I keep the smile on my face long after she's gone, just in case she returns. She doesn't, but I don't hold it against her. Ivy has trouble with separation.

She was a mess when Mom was committed fifteen months ago. She was an even bigger mess when I was arrested.

TWO

Ivy

With both Mom and Aster gone, our tiny, ground floor apartment is quiet, too quiet. I toss my keys onto our Formica kitchen countertop and head to Aster's room, which we shared before I moved into Mom's. The butterfly wallpaper is yellowed in spots and peeling, but Aster doesn't want to replace it. She hates change. She also hates order. I trip over a lone sneaker, catching myself on her white wooden dresser. Swearing under my breath, I pull open the top drawer and comb through her all-black cotton underwear until my fingertips touch a piece of cool porcelain—the tiny box Mom bought her to keep her baby teeth in when she was six. I have a matching one. Something jiggles inside. I pop the tarnished latch. Among an array of tiny dead teeth lies Aster's present.

My first impulse is to stuff the box back inside the drawer, but then I think of the police. What if they search our place and find it?

"Shit, Aster, where did you get this?" I mutter.

I snap the box closed and tread back out, hopping over an old sock that didn't make it into the hamper. I grab the large red bag I'm taking to New York, empty it, and head to the adjacent veranda Mom used as her studio. It's the only room in the apartment I feel happy in, perhaps because it's filled with colorful fabric and drenched in natural light.

I find a spool of red thread, a needle, and my seam rippers, and set to work. Ten minutes later, the porcelain box has vanished inside the lining, cushioned by the foam inserts Mom used for texture in all of her quilts. A part of me feels guilty for transforming her last creation into a bag, but another part feels reassured to bring a piece of her with me on this trip.

A car honks outside, making me jump. At the window I see a forest-green cab parked in front. My ride to the airport. I knuckle the window to get the driver's attention and hold out my open hand to signal five minutes. I race back to my room, place all of my belongings inside the mended bag, check that all the lights are off, that the fridge is empty, and turning back one last time, walk off into the unknown.

INDIANAPOLIS HAS SHRUNK. The backyard pools are drops of turquoise and the vehicles are miniature toy cars rolling over looping, white-dotted highways. I strain to make out the site of Aster's jail and think I spot it when a voice crackles over the loudspeakers, focusing my attention back inside the plane.

"Hi, folks. So it looks like our trip is going to be uneventful. Just the way I like it." The pilot guffaws. "We should be touching down in Newark at around 5:30 p.m. The weather in New York City is clear and sunny and in the high eighties. You should see the city coming up on your right thirty minutes before landing. I'll be sure to remind you. Sit back, relax, and have a pleasant flight."

"What can I get you to drink?" the stewardess asks me. "Champagne, orange juice, water?"

I'm tempted to have the champagne, but she must know I'm underage. "Sparkling water would be great."

When she leaves, I flick my gaze to the compartment overhead where I stuffed my bag. I'd been worried about going through airport security, but it turned out fine. I go back to staring at the world below.

"First time on a plane?" She's already back.

"Yes."

"I can always tell when someone's a sky virgin. I'm perceptive like that." She hands me the glass of water and a small packet of cashews. "Have I seen you somewhere before? Your face looks awfully familiar."

"I'm one of the contestants on the Masterpiecers," I say so that she doesn't come to another conclusion.

The frown on her face fades. "Of course! And here I thought they chartered private jets for their contestants."

"I think they do for the winners. But flying business is—"

"Can I get your autograph?" She thrusts a cocktail napkin and a ballpoint pen at me.

"Sure," I say, and scribble my name—Ivy Redd—on the napkin before handing it back to her.

"I'll be rooting for you, Miss..." Her voice trails off as she studies my name, and the frown gusts across her face again. Thankfully, someone's call button draws her away.

When she stops by my row later, I've put my headphones on even though I'm not listening to music; I just don't want her to talk to me. To make my intentions clearer, I fasten my attention to the window and the empty sky beyond until we land.

As I step off the plane, she whispers something in the other stewardess's ear, but holds her thumbs up nonetheless. She's probably figured out whom I'm related to. It's not much of a secret, especially now that I've willingly stepped into the spotlight and splashed our family name on every tabloid in the United States. I pass by a newsstand and spot my face, alongside the other competitors' in a Brady Bunch composition on the cover of People Magazine. I don't purchase it. I'd rather not read what is being said about me and I already know everything there is to know about my adversaries.

With no suitcase to wait for, I breeze past the luggage carousels and find the person sent to pick me up. He's carrying a sign with my first name. No last name so as not to attract too much attention.

"Is this all?" He points to my duffle bag.

"Yes."

"I suppose they're going to be lending you clothes," he says.

"Yes." They mentioned it in the exhaustive packet they sent me two weeks ago.

"How was the trip?" he asks.

"Fine."

He tries to pluck my bag off my shoulder, but I hold on tight.

"It's not heavy," I tell him.

We walk through the crowded terminal toward the glass doors.

"First time in New York?" he asks.

I nod.

"You're going to love it. Supposed to be great weather all week."

"Don't think I'll be getting out much."

"Right," he says, just as his phone rings. "Yes...I'll pick him up too...okay, ma'am."

He stops and doubles back toward the terminal, signaling for me to follow him.

"Another contestant?" I ask.

He shakes his head. "Woo-hoo! Mister Jackson!"

A man in a tailored suit clutching a rolling black leather case catches sight of him and treads our way. Because he's on the phone, he greets the driver with a silent nod. He doesn't greet me, though. But I suppose that a judge can't greet a contestant, because Brook Jackson is none other than one of the Masterpiecers' judges.

Brook walks alongside the driver, crossing the car lanes. I follow close behind. We arrive in front of a big black car whose trunk pops open without anyone touching it. The driver sets Brook's wheelie case in.

"Want to put yours in the back?" he asks me.

That's when Brook realizes I'm there and finally hangs up. Dark brows pulled together, he slips the phone into the breast pocket of his jacket. "I'm sorry. I didn't realize you were with us." He looks at the driver and then down at the sign that carries my name. "Ivy," he reads out loud. His gaze snaps up to my face. His skin has gone a few shades lighter. He scans the parking lot. "Carl!"

"Yes, sir."

"Get the girl another ride," Brook says.

"On it." The driver raises his cell phone to his ear.

"Judges and contestants can't be seen together! Who was in charge of this planning?" Brook is so loud that a few people stare.

Carl covers the mouthpiece. "Mrs. Raynoir, sir. She told me to pick you up since I was already at the airport."

Brook shakes his head a great many times, yet his dark hair is gelled back so stiffly, it doesn't budge.

"Danny, buddy, I got a customer in the parking lot of terminal A," Carl says. "Needs immediate pickup. You free? Great. Usual spot."

"This could've been a disaster. If the paparazzi—"

"You better get in the car, sir," Carl says, disconnecting. He tips his head toward two men with large cameras poised in midair. "They're here."

Brook lunges into the backseat and shuts the door just as

the two men barrel across the busy car lanes toward us. They stop inches away from my face. I can nearly feel the cool glass of their lenses. I hear the *click, click* of the shutters. It mirrors the *blink, blink* of my eyelids. Carl grabs my arm and yanks me away from them just as a black sedan pulls up. He opens the door and pushes me in. Before I've even straightened upright, the door closes and the car swerves away.

The new driver is chuckling. "Never loaded up a customer so fast and I'm used to working with stars. Movie stars. Music stars. You name it, I've driven it."

I turn around to look at the paparazzi. Their cameras are aimed at the car.

"They got their money shot, sweets," he says. "Your pretty little face will be everywhere by tonight."

"It's already everywhere."

He eyes me in the rearview mirror. "Everyone's been waiting for Lucky Number Eight."

"Lucky?"

"That's what the media calls you. Lucky Number Eight. You know...because the person they picked before you was disqualified, and you got the spot."

"I suppose I did luck out," I say as we pull up next to a tollbooth.

He lowers his window and hands the woman in the booth a ten dollar bill. As he waits for his change, he turns to peer at me. His hair is gray at the temples and his eyebrows are so bushy, some hairs are curling. "You're prettier in person."

"Thank you."

He spins back toward the toll officer to pocket his change. "So which contestant are you the most worried about?"

"I'm not worried."

"Confident little thing, huh? And pretty. Got a boyfriend?"

"Not yet." I pick at a loose thread on my bag and pull on it.

It bunches up the seam and finally rips off. I'm left with a small hole which I'll have to mend...like everything else in my life.

His phone rings. "Yello," he shouts. "All good, chief. On our way to the Met...yup...ETA is forty-five minutes...you can count on me."

He pops his phone into the cup holder and shoots the car onto the highway, just missing a yellow cab. He slams on his brakes and hits his horn, insults the taxi driver, and then crosses three lanes in one go. Nauseated, I lower the window and stare out at the crackling blue city looming in the distance.

My bag is on my knees. I don't shift it to my feet. Instead, I pull it closer to me, because it smells like home, like fabric softener, like Mom. Aster never liked our mother. She reproached her everything: our lack of money, of clothes, of food. But it wasn't Mom's fault. She tried her best. Her fingers bled from trying her best.

I caress the wine-colored spot along the seam; a drop of dried blood Mom never had time to wash off.

THREE

When Ivy left, it hit me that I wouldn't see her for ten days. *Ten!* I've never been apart from my sister for that long. I must look really glum because a woman with red dreadlocks keeps staring at me in the cafeteria. In the past two days, no one has bothered talking to me...which is fine. I don't feel chatty. Besides, there's no point in making friends. I'll be gone soon.

Dreadlocks chews her food and gawks. Frankly, it's annoying. For a moment, I pretend she's not there, but it becomes unbearable. I'm about to go off on her when I hear my name called out.

"Aster Redd, you got a visitor."

A visitor? I wipe the surprise off my face before Dreadlocks can spot it. Why wouldn't I have visitors? I know people. I quickly grab my tray, dump the half-eaten contents, and set it on the shelving. Then I stride through the metal detector and past the guard who's holding the door open for me. I imagine I'm going through a portal that will lead me out of here, but I end up in a sterile corridor irradiated by zinging strips of too-bright neon.

Through the glass door of the visitation area, I can make out Josh's familiar broad shoulders. When the guard buzzes me through the door, I hurry to where he's sitting and plop down. He's dressed in his police uniform and sports dark circles beneath his green eyes.

"Hi," I say, my voice a little airy from the thrill of seeing him. Even though we're no longer together, I can't help my heart from beating faster in his presence. I've loved him since we were five and have never stopped, not even after the awful morning six months ago...not even after we decided to take a break from each other.

"Hey." He scans my face. It practically feels as though he's touching it.

I shiver. His hands were always so soft, so much softer than mine. Then again, at the pizzeria where I serve and do the dishes, I have my hands in water half the day.

"The chief okayed my involvement."

I let out a sigh of relief.

"Look"—he takes the little notepad peeking out of his shirt pocket and the tiny ballpoint pen hooked into the spiral binding. It's the one I bought him when we were still together. The ink tip comes out when you shake it—"I really don't feel like you're telling me everything, so let's go over this again."

"But I—"

"Just humor me."

"Fine." I look down at the chipped edge of the table. "I was counting up tips when this guy walked in to pick up his take-out. Everyone had left."

"You mean all the customers?"

"I mean *everyone*. I was in charge of locking up."

"What did he order?"

I fling my gaze back up to his. "A pepperoni pizza."

His eyes hover over mine. "I dropped by the pizzeria and

asked Abby for a receipt. She didn't find anything. Not even a credit card slip."

"He paid cash."

"What about the receipt?"

"It must be there. She must not have looked well."

Josh rubs the back of his short brown hair. "So he bought a pepperoni pizza...then what?"

"As he was paying, I thought I recognized him from somewhere. It took me a second to realize it was from that file you keep on your desk."

He sighs and it resonates deep inside his chest. "Which you shouldn't have seen."

"But I did. He was a wanted criminal."

"Granted, but you're not a detective, Aster."

"I know, but he was right there."

"You should've called me."

"I tried."

"No, you didn't."

"I did."

"Aster," he growls.

"Okay, fine. I didn't. But that's only because he was getting into his car. So I locked up fast and got into mine. My cell phone didn't have any more battery."

Josh fixes me so intensely that I fold my arms in front of my chest.

"I got him. Isn't that what matters?" I ask.

"He was wanted alive."

"He tried to yank me out of the car. I reacted." My heart's beating faster, pumping blood that feels like fire through my body. "I didn't think I'd killed him. It was an accident."

"Was it?" he whispers loudly.

"Yes! I'm not a murderer, Josh."

He fixes me as though trying to x-ray my scalp to peer inside my mind. "I got an anonymous tip."

"An anonymous tip?"

He nods and leans his muscular forearms onto the fake wood table. Josh spends equal time at the gym and at work. For the longest time, I thought he would become a sports coach instead of an officer. "Someone saw you that night. They called in to say a small Honda had a large, bloodied crack in the windshield, and the girl at the wheel was nervous and apparently cold. Covered in some blanket."

"I admitted I hit a man. And I'm allowed to have been cold. I was in shock."

"What did the blanket look like?"

"I don't know. Blue."

"He said it was multi-colored."

"It was dark out. He couldn't have seen."

"Was it one of Ivy's quilts?"

I shake my head.

"Where's the blanket now?"

"Probably still in my car."

"It wasn't. I checked."

"Then someone took it out. Why is this even important? Troy Mann is what's important."

He smacks his palms against the table, which makes me jump. It also makes the guard in the corner stop picking at his cuticles to stare at us. The sound reminds me of my mother's palm colliding with my face, leaving a glaring red imprint that would begin fading just in time for the next slap. "That's not the point, Aster. You can't go around killing people."

My saliva suddenly feels like plaster, thick and dry. "But he was yelling at me. He tried to strangle me."

"You should've driven away," he says, his tone more sad than angry.

"I would've lost him, Josh."

"I'd rather you lost him. Instead, I—we—might lose you, Aster."

"I'm right here," I say, wrapping my hands around his.

"No touching," the guard snaps.

I glare at him, but let go.

"What happened after you hit him?" Josh asks.

"I drove off." I smelled the blood through the shattered windshield. "I threw up, so I went home to take a shower." I swallow. "You know me, I hate blood. Especially since…" I don't mention the awful morning. Josh was there. He remembers.

He shakes the small pen. The ink tip slides back in. He shakes it again. It slides back out. He does this several more times before asking, "You didn't take anything from the crime scene, did you?"

I shoot my gaze downward. "No," I say, peering down at my cracked nails. They're all so short. Except the one on my right pinky. That one is long and sharp. It's the only one that never breaks. The one on my left hand is torn off like the others. My pinky nails are like Ivy and me—one's stronger than the other.

"The police report states there was dirt underneath your nails."

I ball my hands and burrow them underneath my armpit. "My keys fell in the potted plant by the door, because my hands were shaking. I had to dig them out."

He eyes me in silence. "Aster…"

His voice is so soft I'm expecting him to tell me he loves me, reassure me that he's going to get me out, that—

"Tell me the truth."

"That's what I'm doing!"

"I know you well enough to know when you're lying, and you're lying. I can't help you if you don't help me."

"You never believe me anyway," I say. My vision is clouding. "You didn't believe me that morning in the park and you don't believe me now." Josh's face wobbles. The entire room wobbles. There are two, three, four guards. An optical illusion. "This conversation's over." I'm about to stand, but Josh grabs my arm and squeezes it.

"It's not over."

"Take your hands off me," I say coolly, since the guard is suddenly totally useless.

"Aster, please..." His voice has dropped to a whisper. "Please...stay. I didn't mean to upset you."

"Thanks for making them approve the TV channel."

His overly tanned forehead scrunches up again. He's going to have skin cancer someday and he'll deserve it.

I shrug his hand off. Accompanied by the guard, I leave and count the number of footsteps it takes to reach the dayroom and the little screen that will make the next few days bearable.

FOUR

Ivy

I haven't been sleeping much since Aster entered the Indiana Department of Correction, so I doze off in the back of the sedan, which makes me miss my first glimpse of the city. When I wake up, I don't feel rested, but I don't feel as horrid as I've felt this past week.

I take in Manhattan. The waning sun softens the sharp edges of the buildings. Gray, white, beige, glass, and metal collide in a lovely, linear landscape. I snap a mental picture of everything to reproduce with fabric when I get home...or maybe on the show.

The car lurches to a stop at a red light. Danny spins around. "Oh, you're not sleeping! I was worried I was going to have to wake you. I hate interrupting someone's peace. Although you didn't sound too peaceful."

I frown.

"You were mumbling all these things."

"Like what?"

"I couldn't understand much. Heard the words *man* and *quilt* a couple times."

I concentrate on the outside world to forget my inside

world.

"Must be the stress from the competition," he says when I don't speak for a long time.

"Yeah."

When we pull up, there are swarms of people with flailing arms and smartphones propped in the air.

"Ready, sweets?"

"Ready."

He smiles and hops out his door to open mine. "I got your back." He extends one arm.

"I'm good," I tell him, pushing out of the car, but he keeps his arm over me anyway. The stench of wool and perspiration prickles my nostrils.

I hear my name. It's being screamed left and right. I also hear *number eight* hollered. I raise my eyes and get lost in the grand stone building before me. Voices and street noise die away. It's just me and the block-long museum I've longed to visit since my early teens.

"My wife just saw us on the news," the driver says, pocketing his phone. "She'd like an autograph. Can you do me the honor?" He already has a pen and a dollar bill out.

As we push into the museum, I sign my name across the creased green and white paper.

"Break a leg, Eight."

And then he leaves through the revolving doors and I'm alone in the mammoth entrance, underneath a row of carved columns holding up a mezzanine. I step further inside, looking up and around like Charlie when he entered Willy Wonka's chocolate factory. The walls stretch up neck-breakingly high, vaulting together into giant arches and wrapping around magnificent skylights. The octagonal desk at the center of the space has been turned into a giant vase enclosing a landscaped mound of orchids, peonies, and calla lilies.

"Thought you'd never make it." A woman in jeans, a black tee, and a headpiece is standing right in front of me.

I didn't hear her approach.

"We got to get going. The show starts in an hour. Follow me. Number Eight's in the building, Jeb." I don't see anyone else around, so I assume she's speaking into her mic. When we arrive in front of an elevator, she says, "I'm Cara, your assistant." The doors open and we step in, and then they close and we're whisked away from the beautiful lobby. "You'll be on the third floor throughout most of the competition. The other floors are off limits, unless you're escorted there. Receptions and events will take place in the Temple Room. I'll be accompanying you everywhere." She pushes her short, bottle-blonde hair behind her ear to clear her mouthpiece. Her roots are shockingly black.

The elevator pings and the doors open. Cara goes right. I follow. We continue down a short hallway toward an open doorway. The walls inside the vast room are wainscoted wood with a repetition of pale rectangular patches at eye level—probably where paintings were hung.

"They removed the artwork for insurance reasons," she explains when she notices me studying the walls. "Your prep table's over there. Number eight."

There are eight stations with the same three-sided mirrors adorned with round light bulbs. The numbers stick out above the top of the mirrors, large and gold—impossible to miss. People are milling around. Most are dressed casually and sport the same headpieces as my assistant, though I spot some sitting in front of the vanities—other contestants. Two of them turn to glance at me. The third doesn't turn, but his eyes follow me in the mirror. In spite of the light shining into them, they're dark, practically black.

"Over here will be your living quarters," Cara is saying.

We weave out of the room into a contiguous one. A long

band of beige fabric stretches from floor to ceiling, spanning the entire width of the stripped gallery. We penetrate a flap in the middle. It's a tent, but not just any tent—it's something out of Shakespeare's *A Midsummer Night's Dream*. The entrance is paved with a forest of potted trees strung up with twinkling lights. There's a white oval table on one side of the garden, and a living area made up of a long couch and plush armchairs on the other.

I trail after Cara down a grassy corridor lined with the same lit trees. Every fifteen feet or so, there's a zippered flap with a large number painted in silver. Number eight's the last one.

"Your room," Cara announces, unzipping the entrance.

We leave the garden theme behind, and enter a luxurious bedroom. It's hard to believe we're still in a tent, what with the hardwood floors, the velvet upholstered headboard, the king-size bed, and the mirrored bathroom in the back.

I must look awed, because Cara smirks. "Nice, huh?"

I nod.

"Okay...so before I go, I need your cell phone and any other electronic devices you might've brought with you."

I dig my phone from the front pocket of my duffle and give it to her.

"Nothing else?" she asks, brows drawing together over her large brown eyes.

"Can't afford anything else"—I give her a wide smile—"yet."

"You can unpack later." She eyes my bag. "Your stylists are waiting by your station. Go out in a bathrobe and slippers." She juts her chin to the bathroom wall where a white robe is hanging. "I'll pick you up and take you to the venue as soon as you're ready. See you in a few."

The second she vanishes, I drop my bag on the bed and

sprawl out on the comforter. The duvet is so soft, it molds around my body. I don't want to move; it's heaven.

A shrill, "All contestants to the dressing room!" echoes from a concealed speaker. I pry myself off the bed, wondering if someone saw me, but the zipper is shut tight and there are no cameras on the cloth ceiling—at least none that are apparent. It was probably an announcement meant for everyone. I kick off my sneakers and strip. And then I look at the mess, and it reminds me of Aster, and I don't want to be reminded of her right now, so I fold everything up and place it neatly on the wooden bench at the foot of the bed.

As I wait for the shower to heat up, I tie my hair up. In the mirror over the sink, I see Aster staring back at me with her haunted blue eyes. I fling the door of the shower open to allow the steam out. When it has completely blurred my reflection, I step inside and breathe. It feels like breathing fire and yet it's the freshest breath of air I've had since leaving Indiana.

Too soon, I get out and dry myself in the honeycomb bathrobe that is softer than cashmere. I wonder if I'll get to take it home. The number eight is stitched on the breast pocket in silver thread. The slippers are fuzzy and thin-soled. They fit a little big, but stay put. Casting one last glance around, I return to the grassy hallway and retrace my steps to the makeup room.

"About time," a woman with black hair all the way down to her waist says. "I'll be your makeup artist for the duration of the show. Amy, get your ass over here. We have thirty minutes left to get her ready!"

A twenty-something girl with pink hair and extra-wide hips scampers over with an apron full of pins and brushes. "Hi," she says, smiling warmly.

"Get to work," the makeup artist tells her as she wipes my face with a damp cotton disc.

Amy's smile evaporates. In silence, she yanks my hair, while the other one stabs at my face with brushes and pencils.

"Is this the first time you've worked this competition?" I ask.

"Look up," the makeup artist says. I still don't know her name. Then she adds, "I've been here since the beginning. I was assigned to the past two winners."

"Wow," Amy whispers.

"I only work with winners," she adds, looking straight at my reflection. "Let's hope you won't break my streak, Eight."

"I have every intention of winning."

Amy pulls on my hair as she brushes it, bringing moisture to my eyes. "This is my first time."

"And your last if you make our contestant cry and ruin my work."

"Oops...sorry, Leila. She has *a lot* of hair," Amy says.

I do. I have a proper mane, like my sister. Unlike Aster, though, I brush mine out religiously and coat my strands with gloss and softener. If I didn't, they would tangle and look like the frizzy mess she doesn't mind sporting. We assume we got our hair from our father. We never met him, gone long before we were born, but apparently he was a handsome, dark-skinned man with a strong southern accent. Although Mom wasn't a romantic, she loved our father. She never straight-out said it, but when I took an interest in stitching quilts, she unlocked the bottom drawer of her sewing table for me, and I understood...I understood so many things about my mother that day.

"Time?" Cara's right behind me. I can see her in the mirror.

"Five," Leila says.

"Okay, good. I'll go inform Jeb." She walks back out of the gallery.

The blow-dryer shuts off. Amy made my hair stick straight.

I raise my hand to feel it. It's smoother and softer than I've ever managed to achieve.

Leila rubs something into my cheekbones. It makes them shimmer like copper. "Your outfit's in the dressing room. Amy will show you."

Amy leads me to a curtained room with a purple velvet pouf and a floor-length mirror. I let the bathrobe fall to the floor, which makes Amy blush. People are so funny about nudity. We're all just flesh and bones.

"Arms up," she says, staring at the blue material she's clutching.

She pulls the gown over me, making sure her fingers don't graze my skin. The cool satin feels divine. I touch it, and it reminds me of the first quilt my mother showed me how to stitch.

"Same color as your eyes," Amy says, pulling me back into the present.

It's the exact same shade, which looks striking against my skin. Especially around the waist where there are large cutouts lined with blue stones. She hands me a pair of silver platforms. With them on, the hem of the dress barely brushes the carpeted floor.

"Jewelry," she says, plopping a big silver ring and a pair of earrings in the palm of my hand. I slip the ring on, and then hook the blue chandelier earrings through my lobes.

I swing my head from side to side to admire my reflection. "Are the stones real?"

"I think so."

Cara pops her head into the makeshift dressing room. "Good. You're dressed. Let's go."

The remaining people in the room stare at me as I traipse out. The attention gives me such a rush that I feel as though I'm walking on air. We return to the lobby, turn left, and walk by the mountain of flowers toward a wing of dimly lit corridors filled with Egyptian treasures. We tread so quickly that I don't have time to take everything in. Not that I can concentrate on much else than the imminent introduction ceremony. When I hear music and loud voices, my heart somersaults and I forget all about the artifacts and statues.

"Most of the events will take place in the Sackler wing," Cara explains.

The music is getting louder. We're getting closer.

"It's where they keep the Temple of Dendur," she continues.

"The Temple of what?"

"Dendur. A gift from Egypt to the United States in 1965."

"A real temple?" I ask.

She nods. "It's something," she says, just as we veer through a disproportionately small entranceway—disproportionate because the room stretching beyond it is majestic, rising thirty or forty feet high with a twinkling, glass-paneled ceiling that echoes the vertiginous slanted wall of windows framing Central Park. I can still make it out even though the sky is dimming.

Dominic Bacci stands on an elevated stone platform between two structures—a thick pale arch, and a larger, columned structure covered in chiseled hieroglyphs and animal carvings that crop up in the warm glow of the overhanging projectors. To his right, on a gold bench, sit Josephine and Brook, and behind him sit the other contestants. A hundred—or perhaps more—round tables dripping with candlelight, white flowers, fine china, and jewel-toned spectators girdle the stage and the sharp, U-shaped pool filled with coins.

"Go," Cara whispers, giving me a little shove into the room.

Shoulders held back, I step from obscurity into the light. Dominic spots me right away.

"Eight! Lucky number eight, you made it!" His voice erupts out of his microphone.

Everyone spins in their seat to stare. I put on my best smile and strut toward Dominic, the icy satin dancing against my naked skin. I set aside Aster and the mess that awaits me in Kokomo, and focus on this dream that has become a reality. One tiny dream bobbing in a raging sea of nightmares.

FIVE

Wow. I'm not sure if I say this out loud or not. I don't really care. The only two people in proximity are Dreadlocks, who gaped at me in the cafeteria, and another girl with a thick body and a black mullet. Most of the other inmates are busy reading or playing board games.

Dreadlocks swivels her head from the screen to me so many times that I snap at her. "What?"

After a beat she says, "You look a lot like that chick in the blue dress. What gives?"

"She's my twin," I admit, although we don't even look alike anymore. They made her into some sort of Hollywood siren while I resemble Frankenstein's daughter.

"What did I tell you, Cheyenne?" Dreadlocks scoots to the edge of the couch, bends at the waist, and holds out her hand. "Pay up."

The hefty chick—Cheyenne—digs into the top of the V-neck tee she wears beneath her prison-issue jumpsuit and slaps a hand-rolled cigarette into Dreadlocks' palm. I expect a prison guard to intervene, but the one present is too busy twirling the knobs on her walkie-talkie.

"I'm Gillian, but you can call me Gill," Dreadlocks says, settling back into the battered couch.

"Aster," I say, leaning away from her until the armrest jabs into my ribs.

"What you in for?" she asks.

"Nothing."

"That must've been some pretty ugly nothin'," Cheyenne pipes in.

"Self-defense."

One of Gill's orange eyebrows hikes up her freckled forehead. "They locked you up here for self-defense?"

"Yeah. To await my trial."

"Are you some repeat offender?" Gill asks.

"No."

"Flight risk?" Gill continues.

"No." When she pops her mouth open again, I say, "You mind? I'm trying to listen to the show."

"Thank you!" a suave voice explodes out of a microphone. "Your presence at the third annual Masterpiecers games proves that we're doing something right." The voice belongs to Dominic Bacci, art patron extraordinaire and creator of the Masterpiecers, the famed finishing school for artists, dealers, and collectors.

Dominic makes a few jokes, throwing out chalky smiles left and right. Everyone laughs, especially the women—I can tell because it's high-pitched. He's a tabloid favorite and an international celebrity. At sixty-three years old, even though his hair's turned silver and his skin's a bit creased, he attracts women of all ages.

"Before we introduce you to this year's lucky eight, Josephine and I—" He doesn't get to finish his sentence as another wave of applause ricochets against the slanted glass wall.

Josephine Raynoir, Dominic's second-in-command, stands up and waves to the room. Then she gracefully lowers herself back onto the judges' golden bench. Her silver pantsuit is as shiny as the diamond lariat that dips down the length of her bare back. She's fifty but looks thirty, with white blonde hair cut with such precision that her hairdresser must use laser beams.

"Dominic's such a sleazeball," Gill mumbles.

"I'd do him," Cheyenne says.

"You'd do anyone with a pulse."

"I wouldn't do you, Firehead."

"Good. You're not my type," Gill tells her.

"Will you two please shut up?" I say, my tone sharp.

Dominic Bacci taps his microphone to recapture everyone's attention. "Josephine and I want to welcome this year's top graduate—" Applause. Dominic raises his voice and continues, "Brook Jackson—" Hollers. Dominic smiles, out of pride or habit I'm not sure. "To this year's panel."

Brook rises and bows to either side of the room. Deep dimples crease his jaw, which is covered in an afternoon shadow.

When Brook sits back down and the audience quiets, Dominic walks over to a blonde whose face is so shiny, she looks like she has plastic skin. "Now let's begin with introductions. Lincoln Vega, please stand, my dear."

She docs, her beaded dress swooshing to her feet and gleaming like the lopsided neon sign above the pizza joint where I used to waitress.

"Lincoln is an avid art connoisseur, who, at twenty, dreams of becoming the next Picasso. I even read in your application that you recreated his *Demoiselles d'Avignon* in chalk in a subway station. Shoot us the picture, Jeb."

The stupendously huge screens dotting the room fill with the image.

"That's quite a lot of talent. I even suspect not all would be lost if you don't win. Right, Delancey?"

"Who the fuck is Delancey?" Cheyenne asks.

As though Dominic heard her, he adds, "Delancey's a talent scout. He's launched many a career. Are your parents watching us tonight?"

Lincoln is grinning so widely that I expect her to give a shout-out to her parents. She doesn't. "Mom's dead. But if my dad's alive, maybe."

Dominic cringes. "How indelicate of me."

She gives him a sweet smile. "It's fine, Mister Bacci."

The camera swirls around the room, closing in on certain spectators' faces as they utter *awws* and *poor girl*. Then it's back on Lincoln whose green-gold eyes glimmer. She's either about to cry or loving the attention. I'd put money on the latter. There's something about her that blocks my sympathy. Possibly her cool, polished exterior. She makes me think of a slab of marble and you can't feel bad for marble.

I catch Josephine inspecting her. Unlike the others, she's not gushing.

"Heard the female judge was a lesbo. Is that true, Firehead?" Cheyenne asks.

"Just because I like women doesn't mean I know all the lesbians out there," Gillian says.

I'm about to shush them when Dominic introduces the next contestant. "Herrick. That's an uncommon name," he says.

"I'm an uncommon man." He wears eyeliner and a burgundy floral scarf that he keeps petting.

"Quite true." Dominic smiles. "At the ripe old age of nine, Herrick was so taken with Michelangelo, he reproduced the Sistine Chapel fresco on his bedroom ceiling. Then, if I'm not mistaken, you redecorated your parents' entire house."

Herrick grins. His teeth are like Chiclets, large and rectangular. "You're not mistaken."

"Any pictures, Jeb?" Dominic asks. The screens flicker with a lengthy slideshow of Herrick's house.

"That's nasty," Cheyenne says, picking her nose.

I agree with her. I wonder what Ivy thinks. I wish the camera would move to her, but it stays on Herrick's smug face. He caresses his black pompadour hairstyle as he chats with Dominic about his expectations of the competition. I zone out because Cheyenne's now feeding herself the booger. I clamp my teeth together to avoid regurgitating my tasteless breakfast.

Next up, Nathan Stein. Forty-three years old. Sad eyes and shaggy brown hair. When I first saw his picture on TV the day they announced the contenders of this art competition, I thought he was some homeless man. Now, with clean clothes and a shave, he looks less unkempt. He still looks sad though. I learn he's the descendent of an art dealer whose family was robbed by the Nazis during the Second World War.

"Art. It's in my blood," he says.

"I hear you," Dominic says. "So tragic what happened to your family...to the world." Dominic's still smiling, which is totally weird. Maybe it's some nervous tic, like someone laughing at a funeral. "You know, that's one of the reasons our school was created. To protect art dealers and safeguard their collections." After a brisk shake of his head, he adds, "So tragic." Then he squeezes Nathan's shoulder. "Well, best of luck, my friend."

Applause. He walks across the stage to the next person, a boy around my age.

"We have a very special contestant this year." He pauses for effect. "Ladies and gentlemen..."

Drumroll. There's an actual live drumroll. It comes from the mammoth orchestra positioned against one of the walls.

"Brook," Dominic calls out. The youngest judge snaps to

attention, raking his hand through his shiny black hair. "You want to come and introduce your little brother?"

"No fucking way! I didn't realize they were related," Gill says.

I knew. Ivy told me. She learned everything there was to know about her competitors.

Brook grins and gets up, covering the short distance in long, fluid strides. He takes the microphone from Dominic and drapes his arm around the boy's shoulders. "As you all know, the school has a strict one-person-per-family rule. However, Chase shares my passion for art and artists. Don't you, little brother?"

Chase nods, even though it looks painful for him to do so.

"When he told our parents two years ago that he wanted to follow in the family footsteps, our father tried to dissuade him. What did he suggest you do again?"

"Investment banking," Chase answers flatly, shrugging his brother's arm off.

A flicker of emotion crosses Brook's face, betraying some underlying animosity between the brothers. I wonder if it has to do with the school's one family member policy.

"*Ooh.* Investment banking. *Bo-*ring," Dominic says, leaning over Chase to speak in the microphone that Brook is now clutching with both hands.

Chase gives a crooked smile. "It could've been worse. He could've suggested auditing."

Laughter.

Chase's face stays impassive, but he stands up a little straighter. He's shorter than Brook, and definitely not as handsome. Still, he's good-looking with his purposely-messy brown hair and dark eyes; he's just not the god his brother is. Sort of like Ivy and me.

"So," Brook continues, "he sends in his application and *bam!* Josephine insists he be a part of this year's competition."

"But it wasn't all excitement and entrechats," Dominic adds, performing a sort of hop kick before landing like a ballerina with his feet angled sideways and his knees bent. The audience laughs. "There was still the issue of no siblings," he says, panting slightly.

"Before the winners were publicly announced, there was much, much deliberation," Brook says. "But since Chase is here with us tonight, you can imagine what Dominic's answer was."

"Yes," Dominic exclaims, seizing the microphone. "I said yes!"

Chase sort of smiles but I can tell he's nervous. He keeps stretching his fingers and folding them into fists. The camera pans onto his face, so close that I notice he has long, sweeping lashes.

"Best of luck, Chase." While Brook returns to the judges' bench, Dominic reaches Maxine's side. "Now, let me introduce you to contestant number five, Maxine Specter."

She gives the audience a wave and a smile. She looks nice and bland, like Special K. Ivy will have no trouble taking her out.

"Maxine has a funny story to share with you tonight," Dominic says. "The story of how she got here."

Maxine touches the brown fuzz growing on her head. "Oh, no...I couldn't possibly—"

Dominic cuts her off. "Oh, yes, yes, yes."

Blushing, she nibbles on her lower lip, and then gulps in a big breath. "Daisy Dukes."

"Ah...Daisy Dukes. I *love* Daisy Dukes," Dominic says, which makes a bunch of people in the audience hoot.

"I mean the shots," Maxine adds.

"Of course. Me too." Big theatrical wink. I can nearly hear his eyelid open and shut.

"I had twelve of them—" she says.

"The drinks," he clarifies. I think everyone got it, but *hey*, it's his show.

"They're teeny tiny, but *really* strong. That's why—"

"What's in them?" Dominic interjects.

"Um...I'm not sure."

"Can someone find out and mix some up? I think we could all use a *tiny* Daisy Duke. Except Chase, Lincoln, and Miss Ivy over there."

The camera perches on my sister's face. I scoot closer to the edge of the couch, hungry for a glimpse of her. The armrest practically pops out one of my ribs. Too soon, they're back to filming Maxine.

"So tell us how a drink landed you on my show."

She clears her throat. "When I got home, after the bar, I was reading my emails. Among them was one my mother had forwarded me with a link to the application form. My parents are great art enthusiasts—I was raised around art. Some children have musical mobiles hanging over their cribs...I had an authentic Calder."

Subtle tittering erupts which relaxes the stiff line of Maxine's shoulder blades.

"Anyway, I thought I'd make Mom and Dad proud so I filled in the application and emailed it. I'm not really sure what I wrote in it though."

"Whatever you wrote in it got our attention, so assume it was great! Did you celebrate with a haircut?"

She winces, the corners of her large eyes crinkling. "That was a bet. I told my best friend that if you guys accepted me, I would shave off my hair. I really didn't think I'd win."

He grins. "Can I touch it?" he asks, already running his palm over her scalp. "Ooh...it's so soft."

Maxine hoists up a smile that doesn't reach her eyes.

"Can I call you Daisy from now on?"

Her face crinkles with a clumsy smile. "S-sure."

"Good luck then, Daisy."

He starts walking to the next contestant, but doubles back to stroke her cropped hair. Maxine goes crimson. Dominic winks and scampers off.

"And in this corner, we have world famous hooligan, J.J.!"

Ivy told me J.J. became famous after he spray-painted the corridor of his dorm in college. At first, he was fined, but then the principal decided it made the drab cement more attractive, so he dropped his complaint and commissioned him to repaint the rest of the hallways. After he graduated, other colleges called on him to enliven their bland atmospheres.

"How many schools have you spray-painted to this day?" Dominic asks.

"Three. I'm working on number four."

The screens around them are displaying his work. It's actually pretty neat, with all the colors and the oddball characters.

"Promise not to paint over any walls in this place or we'll get into serious trouble."

J.J. smiles. "Promise, dude."

"Shall we shake on it?" Dominic suggests, jutting out his hand.

Chuckling, J.J. shakes it.

"Josephine, do we have insurance?" Dominic asks, twisting around, still holding J.J.'s palm.

She smiles complacently.

"Phew." He lets go of J.J. and makes a big show of swiping his brow. "Best of luck to you, my friend."

"Thanks, man." J.J. is very West Coast, totally chill and totally tanned.

"And now...a woman who needs no introduction."

I think I'm about to see my sister, and my body goes as rigid as the rusty bars of my cell. *Don't bring it up, Dominic. Don't bring me up!*

SIX

Ivy

"Miss America 2000!"

People clap. The woman closest to me smiles and gives the cupped-hand pageant wave. Seriously, who invented such a pathetic gesture?

"Maria Axela," Dominic says, proffering his arm.

She latches on to it and rises, her black lace dress swinging around her knees. Even though she's in her mid-thirties, Maria exudes a voluptuous childishness with her perky breasts, flat waist, and pouty red lips.

"So tell us, Maria, what made a former beauty queen enter an art competition?"

"What made me enter?" she repeats in a thick Hispanic accent. "It's quite simple really. I'm not just nice to look at"—she winks—"I'm skilled."

"Jeb? Can you—"

Before Dominic even finishes his sentence, the screens light up with Maria's work. Sixteen paintings of pageant winners. I stare along with everyone else, thinking that whoever told her she was skilled should be shot. The oil paintings are poor renditions of chirpy girls in sequins. I scan the

36

room. Everyone seems captivated—everyone except for Brook. He's staring at me. When our eyes meet, he jerks his gaze back to the screen, a little color staining his jaw.

"I don't know what's more beautiful...the women who pose, or your execution of them," Dominic says. He tucks a few more words into her ear, which make her glossy lips pull up. "A big round of applause for the Masterpiecers' first beauty queen contestant."

Maria sits back down, while I sit up straighter.

"And last but not least, please welcome a young and extraordinarily talented girl, Miss Ivy Redd."

I grin as I stand. Dominic's already at my side. He smells like a bottle of cologne, and something stronger—stale and vinegary. Day-old Merlot?

"This girl has created something truly original. Quilts! And I'm not talking old-timey ones, but fresh, modern works inspired by cityscapes, nature, basically everything she observes around her. Jeb?"

I watch the projected images of my work, a sense of pride stirring deep within me. Blown up and bright, my pieces look magical.

"So tell us what or who inspired you?"

"My mother," I say into the mic Dominic is holding up to my mouth. "She made quilts. Incredibly colorful landscapes with silk and tassels and chiffon."

"Like yours?"

"In a way. Although, I favor abstract over figurative."

"Do you stitch them by hand?"

"Of course. I have to feel the fabric, the thread, the needle. I need complete control over the process."

I'm eager for him to ask to buy one. I think he just might, when a waiter scuttles onto the stage, rudely interrupting us. He's carrying a silver platter covered in shot glasses. The liquid inside is amber with smoke curling out of it.

"Is that what I think it is?" Dominic asks the waiter, forgetting all about me.

"Daisy Dukes, sir," the man says, extending the platter.

Dominic grabs a glass and holds it up. "Daisy, to you, my dear." He's about to drink it, but stops. "Isn't there a saying that people who drink alone are drunks?" His smile widens and he gestures for the waiter to distribute the glasses.

He starts with me. I'm about to grab a random one when he points to a small glass that isn't fuming. Frustrated, I take it.

"Everyone has a shot glass?" Dominic asks. "Bottoms up!" Just as I tip my glass toward my lips, Dominic hollers, "Wait! Ivy, no!"

I jolt and spill some juice. It trickles down my forearm and soaks into the immaculate satin.

"Hers is simply *du jus*, Dominic," Josephine says with a strong French accent. "It's not even the same color as this"—she sniffs it and her nose wrinkles—"*concoction*."

He claps his hand over his chest emphatically. "And here I thought I was going to get in trouble with the authorities." His comment receives laughs.

I stare at the expanding wet spot on my thigh. Why did Dominic single me out? Chase and Lincoln are underage too.

"Now I *really* need this." He bares his rows of pearly whites like a shark. "Ready?"

There's a hum of assent. Elbows lift, necks snap backward.

Josephine puckers her painted lips. "That's *dégoûtant*."

Dominic smiles and shakes his head. "Don't mind her, Daisy. She thinks everything's awful if it's not French."

"You're such a *baladin*, Dominic," Josephine says.

"That means *catch* in French," he ping-pongs back.

"*Non*." The corners of her mouth lift briefly. "It means comedian."

"And this, ladies and gentlemen, is why I've never gotten romantically entangled with this beautiful woman. We don't speak the same language." Dominic flings his shot glass to the waiter who just catches it. "Now, where were we?"

"The last contestant!" people answer back jovially.

"Oh, yes. The last contestant. Ivy, anything you'd like to add at this time? Perhaps you'd like to send out a greeting to a family member?"

"No." I hope Aster won't get offended, but I don't feel like bringing her up.

He tips his head to the side. "Well then, best of luck to you, *Mademoiselle* Redd!"

Luck is overrated. Relying on it would be like trying to climb a fir tree by holding on to its pinecones. Dumb.

"May the best one win!" Dominic exclaims.

The orchestra on the side of the room breaks into the Masterpiecers' anthem, a melody about beauty and emotion and vision—or so Dominic explained the first time the show aired two summers back. It's pretty, but a little too mournful.

"Thank you all for coming," Dominic announces once the music dims. "Now enjoy your dinner and don't get to bed too late. Tomorrow's event will begin at 10 a.m. sharp in the main hall. Contestants, it's picture time!"

As we file off the stage underneath expanding applause, my stomach grumbles, the packet of nuts from the plane long gone. I smell fresh baked, buttery rolls and something rich and spicy. I fill my lungs with the aroma to ward off the hunger.

I meet some curious gazes as I walk out. I smile to appear forthcoming. Cara's there when I walk out, standing next to seven other people with head mics and informal apparel—the other assistants, I suppose. They all come to join us.

"How's that stain?" she asks.

I'd nearly forgotten about *that* stain. The fabric is darker. "Should I change before the group shot?"

"No. They'll probably have you stand in the back."

I clench my jaw. "They could have me sit down. It's barely noticeable if the fabric is bunched up."

"I don't choose, but it's a possibility," Cara says as we walk back through the Egyptian artifact-filled rooms toward the grand hall with the domed skylights.

It's full of people—security guards lining the walls, the camera crew, a guy with a shaved head prepping a large camera on a tripod, and faceless others milling about, adjusting furniture, strobes, reflectors, and the angle of an enormous painting they must be using as a backdrop. I feel like I'm on a movie set. It reminds me of my childhood fantasy of becoming an actress, which I grew out of during adolescence when I discovered my talent with needles and thread.

Cara leans in as we arrive on the set, so close that her blonde bob grazes my chin. "The photographer's really famous."

I stop myself from scratching the spot her hair brushed to avoid blemishing my skin with red claw marks.

"Works for all the fashion magazines," she continues.

It still tickles, but I keep my nails at bay and focus on the photographer. He does look familiar with his smooth head and handlebar moustache.

"Patrick Veingarten," she says.

He's not just famous; he's a legend.

"Dominic, my friend, it's been ages," Patrick says. They smack kisses on each other's cheeks. "Ravishing, as always, my dear Josephine," he says, lifting one of her white hands to his lips. "And if it isn't the Masterpiecers' most beloved graduate," he tells Brook, clapping his back.

"You mean the one who stuck around." Brook smiles and his dimples appear.

Patrick chuckles.

"So what are you thinking?" Dominic asks Patrick, gesturing to eight ornate golden frames.

"You'll see," Patrick begins. His gaze scans all of our faces before perching on mine. He strides toward me and takes my elbow. "Let's start with you."

He has swirls of light green and brown in his eyes, like slow-churned, mint chocolate chip ice cream.

"I hope my camera will do you justice," he adds with a wink.

"Where would you like me?"

"Somewhere more private," he whispers inside my ear.

I replace the snort frothing up with a subtle titter, which I hope will win me a spot in the foreground of the picture.

"Why don't you sit here?" he says.

Ka-ching. I lower myself into a rose-colored velvet chair that's angled sideways, cross my legs, and straighten my back.

"Too stiff. Too stiff," he says. "Let yourself go a little, Ivy. Think languid, just pleased, but still ravenous. I'm sure you know how to do that."

I hear someone grunt, which makes everything tighten up inside of me, from my ligaments to my veins. I look for the source and find Lincoln scrutinizing me, arms crossed in front of her chest. She's just jealous I was chosen first. I breathe in deeply and do as I'm told.

"Now tilt your head to the side."

I let my eyes go unfocused to blur the ogling faces around me, then slowly, I unfold and refold my legs, lay my forearms on the stuffed armrests, and loll my head against the soft velvet imagining it's one of my mother's quilts.

"Get the oval frame in front of her," Patrick yells to one of his assistants. It's so large it encases all of me. He steps back to observe the effect. After a long minute, he breathes, "Perfect... a true work of art." He admires me for so long that my confidence skyrockets. Coupled with my roiling hunger, I feel like I'm floating, hovering over the rest of the contestants on a cloud as gilded as the frame outlining me.

"Next," he yells.

I skid off my cloud, and land with a thump in the deafening room.

Leisurely, Patrick positions the others, bestowing upon them the same admiration he afforded me. Stupid me for feeling singled out. Patrick's appreciative of his work, not of his subjects. He scatters the judges among the framed contestants and instructs them to act as though they were appraising our value. Brook, who's supposed to be assessing my worth, is looking everywhere but at me. I'm pretty sure I make him uncomfortable.

While the strobe lighting blinks on and off, making a popping sound each time, the assistants orbit around us, slanting reflectors and readjusting the frames.

Patrick steps out from behind his camera. "Perfect. No one touch anything! Brook, I'm sure your shoes are valuable, but eyes on Ivy please. Everyone else, stay in position."

With one click, we are immortalized.

I return to my cell with my head so full of my sister that I don't mind she didn't send me a verbal shout-out. We're twins—we have other ways of communicating. When she smiled, I knew it was for me.

I also don't mind all the attention I'm getting tonight. Let them stare at the new girl. Let them get an eyeful. Soon, I'll be gone. Ivy will take me to New York with her. I'll be able to quit my job at the pizzeria and focus on what I love best: graphic design.

A bell rings through the sterile hallway signaling that the cells are about to be bolted for the night. I hurry into my room just as the automated gates begin grinding against their built-in rails to lock us up like lab rats. The shrill sound reminds me of the garbage truck that used to beep every morning at five sharp while it backed into our street. Never thought I'd be nostalgic for the sound of a garbage truck.

I brush my teeth and splash cool water over my face from the sink in the room I thankfully don't need to share with anyone. As soon as my head hits the pillow, I fall asleep, but wake long before dawn. I fish out the book that I keep underneath my pillow to make it more substantial. I don't have a flashlight, so I angle the cream pages toward my barred window through which trickles the faint glow of the perimeter lighting.

I borrowed the book from the prison library. It's the story of a Southern white woman's love affair with one of her father's slaves. Sometimes, I wonder if my ancestors were slaves too. I'll never know. My mother had no stories about my father. I remember asking her how long they'd known each other before she had us. Her answer was always a huff and a flick of her wrist. Then again, my mother was no storyteller. There were no bedtime fables when we were children and no dinnertime tales. Rare were the times when we all sat around a table for a meal anyway.

I realize I've read the same paragraph three times, so I put the book away and fall back asleep. It's the shrill ringing and metal grating that rouses me. I rub the sleep out of my eyes, but it feels counterproductive, like I'm pressing fistfuls of sand into them.

I use the toilet quickly, feeling exposed now that the lights are on and the other inmates have started filing out of their cells. I stretch the T-shirt I've slept in over my knees to hide more skin. Before even washing my hands, I race to the bed and yank on my jumpsuit.

Breakfast is the usual: bland oatmeal. It goes down okay and doesn't come up, unlike some of the other stuff they serve. I take my food back to a deserted table and wolf it down because I want to go to the dayroom to see my sister. Unfortunately, Gill spots me and strides over. She sets her tray down right in front of mine.

"In a hurry, A?" she asks.

"A?"

"It's better than Ass."

I narrow my eyes. "My name's Aster. Not Ass. Not A."

"O-*kay*," she says, scrunching up her lips. "Don't get your jumpsuit in a twist. I was just trying to be friendly."

"I don't need a friend." When she smirks, I add, "I'll be out of here by next week. No point in making friends."

"Breaking out so soon?"

"No. I'll be released so soon," I say.

"Yeah. Keep thinking that if it helps you sleep at night."

"It was an accident. I'm not some criminal."

"I'm pretty sure killing a man makes you a criminal."

I glare at her. "Just shut up."

"Or what? You'll kill me too? Aster, if they thought you were the victim, you wouldn't be locked up with the likes of me. Wanna know what I did?" She's smiling. It's grotesque. Her teeth are crooked—all of them.

"I don't care what you did."

She sets her pointy elbows on the table and knots her finger together. "You're not even a little curious?"

I shake my head and gulp down the remaining cooked cereal even though it has the texture of wet cement. And then I'm on my feet, tray in hand, about to make a run for the door when one of the guards marches my way. He has rolls of fat bulging over his waistband.

"Inmate Redd."

The cafeteria goes quiet—too quiet. Sure enough, everyone's gaping.

"I'm here to escort you to your appointment with the psychiatrist," he says.

"Now?" I exclaim.

The guard lets out a thick laugh. "No, tomorrow."

There's snickering.

"Yes now. Let's go!"

"But—"

He hunches over and leans in so close that his nose is nearly against mine. "Do you want to end up in the tank instead of in your cozy little cell? Because I can make that happen."

I swallow hard. "No, sir."

His breath smells like stale cigarettes. It makes my eyes water. After a few painfully putrid seconds, he pulls away and starts for the door. Gill smirks. I would give her the finger if I weren't afraid of how she would retaliate—because isn't that what people do to each other on all those prison shows?

I peek at the clock on the wall right before going through the metal detector that checks for stolen cutlery. Eight thirty. I have another hour before the show starts, although I'll miss the preparation.

"Is this a routine appointment?" I dare ask the guard.

He turns to look at me, lips hoisted up on one side like skewed blinds. "Yeah. Your mani-pedi's right after."

Seven days. I focus on that. In one week—if the district attorney hasn't already set a court date and a bail amount—Ivy will come home and find a way to set me free. She promised and she always holds her promises.

"Here we are, princess," he says, rapping against a glazed glass door. "Have fun."

The door swings open to reveal a woman in a tweed skirt suit. She seems way too chic to work in a prison. "Hi. My name is Robyn." She holds out her hand.

I shake it quickly, barely pressing down, then stride into the room past her. There are two large windows overlooking the barbed wire fence and the dense forest beyond.

"Please take a seat." Robyn has lines around her mouth and eyes.

I sit facing the windows. She sits across from me, a dark outline against the stark light.

"Would you like a glass of water?"

"No."

"So, Aster, tell me...how are you adjusting?"

I shrug. "Fine."

"Are the other inmates treating you nicely?"

"Yeah. Whatever." The small talk is making my skin itch, so I cut to the chase. "Why am I here?"

"I'd like us to discuss how you're feeling."

"Awesome, thank you. Can I go now?"

"Sarcasm denotes distress. Are you distressed about being here or over the events of August 17th?"

"Is anyone not distressed about being locked up in prison?"

"So it isn't August 17th that has you so upset?"

"Of course I'm upset about *involuntarily* killing a man," I say with a huff. "Just like I was *distressed* when I ran over my neighbor's cat two years ago. It sucks."

"You sound more distraught about the cat."

"The cat was innocent. It didn't deserve it."

"But the man did?"

"Troy Mann had ties with the mafia. He was a bad man. He killed people. So forgive me if I sound cold, but killing him —involuntarily," I add, "is probably a good thing for humanity."

"Let's talk about that then."

"Fine."

She flicks her gaze to the folder resting on her lap. "After you saw Troy Mann at the pizzeria, you followed him back to his motel without alerting the authorities. Is this correct?"

"Yes," I say.

"Why?"

"So he wouldn't get away."

"Why didn't you call the cops?"

"They wouldn't have come in time."

"What did you think you would do once you found out where he lived?"

"I wasn't thinking that far ahead."

She scribbles in the file. "Once you got to the motel, why didn't you phone the police?"

"My cell had no more battery."

Again, she takes note of what I say. "So he got out of his car and walked over to your window?"

"Yes. He'd noticed I was following him. He threatened me."

"What were his exact words?"

"He told me he would break some bones in my body if I didn't leave straight away and forget I ever saw him. He said he would hurt Ivy if I called the cops," I say in a hushed voice, rolling the scratchy fabric of my jumpsuit between my thumb and index finger. Ivy used to do that on a frayed and yellowed piece of quilt to soothe herself. It worked for her so perhaps it'll work for me. After a few minutes, I don't feel better.

"The cops didn't find a pizza box in his car. Do you know why that is?"

"He tossed it out on his way home. From his car window."

Her already lined forehead puckers even more. I count nine wrinkles. "Into a bin or on the sidewalk?"

"In a bin."

"Do you remember where that bin was?"

I shake my head. My breathing is too shallow. I focus on dragging it out. "I was focused on not losing him."

"No cross streets come to mind? Store awnings?"

"It was ten-thirty. It was dark and everything was closed."

She shuts the folder. "How do you feel about your sister leaving for an art competition three days later?"

"I forced her to go. It's her chance, and I won't take that away from her. Plus we need the money."

Robyn holds my gaze. "But how did it make you *feel?*"

"I miss her."

"Do you feel like she abandoned you?"

"Didn't you hear what I just said? *I* forced her to go. She would've stayed if I'd asked her to."

"Are you certain about that?"

"Yes."

She stares at me, then stands up. "This was a good session, Aster."

"That's it? We're done?"

"For today. I'll see you next week. Same time?"

"I won't be here anymore."

"Is that right?" One of her eyebrows lifts. "Well then, feel free to stop by before you leave. I'm here every day from ten to four."

"Sure." *Not.*

As I rise, she extends her hand. I don't shake it, so she lowers it to the file she's clutching against her chest. A paper's sticking out. I catch the word *nervous.*

"Good-bye, Aster."

I walk out of her office on autopilot, distracted by those seven letters. If I'm nervous, then I'm in trouble.

EIGHT

Ivy

Thanks to the sleeping tablets I picked up in the pharmacy on my way to the airport, I sleep deeply and dreamlessly and wake only because I hear birds chirping. It takes me a second to remember I'm inside a museum, and then another to activate my brain and realize that tweeting birds isn't normal. But then, this is the Masterpiecers—the school defies normalcy. They very well could have actual birds. They have real grass and small trees outside our tents.

"Ten minutes to hair and makeup," I hear someone call out from the grassy hallway.

I tie up my hair and jump into the shower. Too soon, I hop out and don the bathrobe someone's already replaced. While I brush my teeth, I search for a fresh pair of underwear in my duffel, but my bag is empty. Someone unpacked it!

I throw the toothbrush on the bed, and with both hands, feel the bottom of the bag, trying to locate the lump. When I touch it, a whoosh of air tears out of my lungs. Willing my heart to quiet, I grab a thong from a drawer and tug it on underneath the bathrobe. Still agitated, I head to the prep wing, bypassing the breakfast spread.

Lincoln and Herrick are already seated. Both have people working on them. I meander toward my station where Leila and Amy are waiting, and sit, bobbing my right knee up and down, up and down.

The bright bulbs are blinding, yet I notice Cara's reflection in the mirror. She's wearing a head mic. "Cup of coffee, tea, green juice?"

"Green juice," I say.

When she leaves, Leila tapes a picture to the mirror, her long black hair swinging around her waist. "That's your look for today."

I stare at the picture. "Is the photo in black and white?"

"Nope." She smacks a piece of gum around in her mouth. "They just want your skin to be pale."

Amy leans in toward the picture and then sways back like a bamboo. "That's some serious hair teasing."

By the time they're done with me, I look spooky and electrocuted. Thankfully, I'm not the only one. Chase also resembles an albino macaque. We even wear matching outfits: white tights and white V-necks.

The others look different. Lincoln is doll-like in her polka-dot dress. She has rouge on her cheeks and cherry-colored lipgloss.

Maria, the ex-beauty queen, is literally washed out, her dark skin and clothes have been bleached, down to her clogs that are also gray.

Herrick's skin has been tinged pea green, like the hulk, and his clothes are orange.

Maxine sports a yellow wig over her buzz-cut, dark purple circles under her eyes, a red clown nose, and a pair of ripped Daisy Dukes.

Nathan's longish hair is pulled into a ponytail and he's wearing a pair of round bifocals that emphasize his sad eyes. His shirt is oddly buttoned and his tie's on crooked.

And J.J. looks like a yeti. They glued whiskers to his tanned face and stuffed him in some furry outfit.

I'm thinking that my accouterment isn't the worst when Dominic bursts into the room. "Is everyone—" He doesn't finish his sentence. "Fabulous! Now hurry and eat some breakfast. Make it substantial. You're skipping lunch." As he heads toward Jeb—who's practically as short as Aster's prison warden—he calls out, "I want you all in the main hall in fifteen for the announcement of today's episode!"

"Hey, Ivy," comes a voice from behind.

I turn to find Brook in a black suit and black shirt opened at the collar. "And here I was afraid I wasn't recognizable anymore."

He chuckles, which makes him appear somewhat kinder.

"So what are we doing today?" I ask him.

"Can't tell you."

"Really? Not even a hint?"

"Not even a hint." His dark eyes crinkle at the corners, penetrating but not as abrasive as last night.

"I should go eat something," I say.

He gestures toward the panel of fabric delineating our quarters. "After you."

My seven opponents are chatting while gobbling down plates piled high with slices of bread and golden pastries. Maxine and Nathan seem to be hitting it off. She's propped up on the arm of the couch and Nathan's standing inches away, laughing. Every so often, his eyes dart to the hem of her Daisy Dukes.

"Morning, everyone," Brook says with a smile.

As he enquires as to how they slept, I head to the buffet to pick up a piece of toast, which I slather in cream cheese and strawberry jam. There are pieces of real fruit in this jam, unlike the dollar brand Mom used to buy that was basically red goop with strawberry extract. Quickly, I load up a second slice just as someone from the camera crew arrives and barks, "Last touch-ups and we're a go. Come on, people."

I gulp it down, wishing I'd had time to grab a cinnamon roll or a banana from the buffet. Food going to waste—especially such incredibly expensive food—is a pet peeve of mine. Mom was like that too, although she took it to another level. She would skim the green fluff from expired yogurts and scrape the mold off sliced Wonderbread. Aster, on the other hand, would rather starve. Mom used to think she was anorexic, but she's just not interested in food and forgets to eat.

Once our makeup artists fix what needs fixing, we file out of the third floor and take the wide staircase down to the darkened main hall. They've covered all the windows—even the round ones on the ceiling—and turned off all the lights. Spotlights suddenly flare up and settle on each one of us, plunging the cavernous space beyond in total inky blackness. I blink, but avoid squinting because I'm being filmed. Instead, I call upon my other senses as though they were insect feelers. From the thundering applause resounding against the tall stone walls, I can tell that hundreds of people are gathered in the lobby, and from the heady scent of caffeine, I can tell that breakfast is in full swing down here as well.

"Today, we begin with a show," Dominic says. "A great, great show. In our métier, we call it performance art." He spins around to face us. "For those of you who've never heard of it, forfeit this instant!"

Is he serious?

Dominic guffaws. "I'm kidding. Who fell for it?" His eyes shine as they scan each of our faces. "Don't tell me you all knew what I was talking about?" Still no one speaks. "Well then, this should be a breeze for all of you. Music, maestro."

The orchestra plays the opening notes to the Masterpiecers' theme song.

"Lights!" Dominic exclaims over the music.

Large spotlights blaze, illuminating seven square forms cloaked in heavy emerald velvet. Dominic raises his hands, palms facing up, as though making an offering to the gods, and the velvet is pulled off, shimmying like the glossy leaves of the buttonbush shrubs bordering our ground floor apartment. The fabric pools to the side of enormous glass cubes in which various pieces of furniture have been deposited: chairs, desks, a bar, a human-sized hamster wheel. One's even filled with dirt.

"Contestants, your stages!" Dominic bellows, his voice rife with delight. "Herrick Hawk, for the next eight hours, you will be a carrot. You will stand in dirt. You will not talk. You will not move. But please, don't forget to breathe," he adds with a bark of laughter.

The green makeup does little to hide Herrick's revulsion. When he finally moves, it's in slow motion. One of the stage hands props a ladder against the side of his dirt-filled glass cage to help him scale the wall. He lands noiselessly on the thick earth. He doesn't insert himself in the hole they dug against one of the sides. He's probably waiting until he has to.

"Maria, my dear, I hope you enjoy knitting," Dominic continues, wrapping one arm around the former beauty queen's waist.

"Not especially," she says.

"Well that's too bad, because"—he shoves her toward a cube with a chair in the middle and a basket full of electric blue yarn—"you will be knitting a scarf for the next eight hours."

"*Que bueno*," she mumbles, advancing toward her box.

"Daisy. Darling Daisy," he tells Maxine. "Guess which stage I've had readied for you."

She points to the one with the bar.

"Good girl. You'll pretend to pour yourself shots and drink them."

He grins. She doesn't.

He turns to Lincoln, who's smoothing down her gold hair. "You see that stage with the wooden vat and all the wands sticking out of it?"

She nods.

"That's all yours, sweetheart. You will enchant us with bubbles of all sizes. It will be beautiful."

She smirks as she leaves. I wouldn't have minded blowing bubbles dressed as Lolita for a few hours.

I stare at what's left: the hamster wheel, a desk with a stool and a thick leather-bound book, and a glass cube with two chairs facing each other. I hope I get the desk, but I don't. It becomes Nathan's. He must read the entire book. I'm jealous until I hear it's an encyclopedia on plants and seeds.

J.J., unsurprisingly, is awarded the hamster cage. The whiskers gave it away.

"Chase and Ivy, you will look at each other for the next eight hours. You may blink, but no looking at anything or anyone else. Studies have shown it's extraordinarily intimate when it lasts for four minutes," Dominic says, which makes me grunt. "No one's ever studied the effect of eight hours, though."

I'm sure it will have the opposite effect. When I spot Lincoln toying with her bubble wands, I'm envious. Why didn't they stick her in here with Chase? I walk ahead of him, threading myself through the thick crowd, and take a seat on one of the transparent chairs, bracing myself for complete boredom.

"Can I get a countdown?" I hear Dominic ask.

I stare around me one last time before I'm stuck with Chase's pale face. The crowd starts counting down from ten to one. My gaze locks on Brook's. He's standing right outside our cube, his arms folded in front of his chest.

"*Three...two...one...show time!*" everyone chants.

Cara seals the door of our cube, and then, it's just me and Chase. There's no more noise except that of my breath whooshing past my parted lips.

The first hour is the most painful. My eyes are sore, and my bottom, in spite of relentlessly shifting around in the plastic chair, smarts. My nostrils keep flaring from Chase's oily, green smell that makes me think of muddy grass after a rainfall. But the physical agony is nothing compared to the displeasure of being scrutinized by him. His eyes feel like the sheets of icy rain that fall over Kokomo in autumn. I hope mine feel the same.

After the second hour, it gets easier because my vision has gone unfocused. I've shut down. My breathing has slowed and my soreness has receded. I stare unseeingly at Chase. My peripheral attention is on the world outside the glass cube. People point as they mill around our *stages*, and discuss our quiet showcases. One presence never shifts though: Brook.

When hour number three is announced, my stomach growls so loudly that I think Chase hears it. I will it to stop. It does by hour four. I feel light now. By hour five, I'm floating, more clear-headed than a Buddhist monk who's been meditating his entire life. At least, that's what I imagine meditating monks feel like. I have no clue.

Hour six, it gets easy. Staring into Chase's dark irises is hypnotic.

Hour seven. Something strange happens. There's shrieking. A lot of it. I'm so tempted to turn to see what's going on. Maybe it's some ploy to break us. The crowd around our box migrates to another part of the room. *Okay*...maybe it's not a test. I strain to listen to the world outside. I make out Dominic's voice and metal hitting the floor. The squealing resumes, and then it gets quiet again. Eerily so. I look at Chase —I mean really look at him—to see if he knows what's happening, but his features are set in stone.

It's finally hour eight. If I was floating three hours ago, now I have an out of body experience. I'm soaring over the glass ceiling, watching myself watch Chase. It's overwhelming and extraordinary. I'm not sure if it's my empty stomach or the silence, but this tranquil strength envelops me. It's so powerful that I shiver, and so wonderful that I smile. And for the first time in months, I feel like everything is going to be okay again.

Chase looks stiffer than he did at the beginning. There's tension in his arms and shoulders. Even his legs, which are splayed out in front of him, are as rigid as tree trunks. He hasn't stirred in the past hour, yet there's this vein on his temple that's been pumping feverishly, as though his pulse were racing. My blood, on the other hand, is syrup, sluggishly sliding underneath my skin.

Loud music suddenly fills the vaulted room. It's followed by Dominic's voice announcing that the contest has been completed. Chase's lips unbolt, and he rips his eyes off mine. I can almost feel the tear. He springs out of his chair and marches out of the glass cube without a word.

I'm offended.

"You may return to your tents and relax for an hour." Dominic's voice rings too loudly.

Chin up, I rise and thread myself through the applauding crowd, my irritation at Chase's brisk exit dissipating. I don't want to rest; I want to stay here and lap up the praise the spectators are distilling on me as I pass by them.

Someone grabs my elbow. At first, I smile, thinking it's a fan, but then I spot Cara. "Lost your way?"

"I'm not tired."

"Contestants can't mingle." She all but drags me to the stairs.

I shake her off with the energy brought on by the compliments. "That's a stupid rule."

"Yeah, but it's a rule. Up we go," she says.

I go up a few stairs, but turn back and take one last, longing look around. As my gaze surfs over the crowd, I catch sight of a man with dark hair and an orange tie. He's watching me with great interest. Too much interest. Then again, I'm sort of a star now.

NINE

I've just spent several hours in front of a tiny television screen. My eyes are raw, my legs stiff, and I'm ravenous. The oatmeal might have tasted like cement, but it wasn't, and there's now a gaping void in my stomach. The food will suck tonight, like it sucks all the time, but I'm so hungry I don't care. I could eat the polyester fill of my pillow. I head to the cafeteria along with the hordes of other inmates. I spot fiery red dreadlocks ahead of me, so I slow down. Maybe if I wait for Gill to sit first, she won't join me.

I take my time gathering my meal. Finally, Gill sits next to fat Cheyenne and two other women who do not look particularly friendly. She catches me staring, so I turn my attention to the opposite side of the room where I find a table occupied solely by a white-haired woman whose advanced age leads me to believe she's inoffensive. I place my tray next to hers and take a seat.

The mashed potatoes are lumpy, the piece of meat appears as appetizing as a shoe sole, and the boiled carrot, with its green leaf, resembles Herrick. I squash the tender orange flesh with the tines of my fork. My stomach growls, so I gobble it down along with the watery potatoes. I have more trouble with the meat. The blunt knife doesn't even pierce the steak, so I pick it up and tear off chunks with my teeth.

My least favorite time of day comes after dinner. Ironically, it used to be my favorite back home: shower time. I sorely miss the privacy of my bathroom. Tightening a tiny, scratchy towel around my body and keeping my prison-issue flip-flops on, I head to the salmon-tiled communal shower where the grout has turned a nasty shade of tobacco.

Most of the prisoners use this time to socialize. Definitely not me. I'm in and out so quickly that I don't press the shower button more than once for water. I still have foam on my thighs and calves. I sponge it up with the coarse towel and don my gray uniform.

"Can I be escorted back to the dayroom?" I ask the guard on duty.

She narrows her eyes.

"Officer Cooper got me special permission. It's in my file," I tell her.

"Is that so?"

I nod.

She holds out her palm. I stare at it so long, that she says, "A twenty will do."

"Twenty what?"

"What do you think?"

"You want me to bribe you?"

"It's called payment for services rendered."

Right. "I don't have any money on me."

"That's a shame."

"But Josh—I mean Officer Cooper got—"

She's twisting her long neck left and right. "Don't see *him* nowhere."

My nostrils flare. My first reflex is to dig through my pocket for my cell phone. Then I remember that it was confiscated because I'm in fucking prison. The guard turns her back to me to survey the palette of naked bodies on display.

Desperation hits me so hard that an idea—probably an awful one—materializes in my brain. "I have a proposition for you," I say, coming around to stand in front of her.

She cocks her head to the side. "I'm listening."

"My sister's competing in the Masterpiecers. You know, that show about—"

"I know it." She scrutinizes my face. "That's why you look familiar. You're related to that girl, Lucky Little Eight, or whatever the media calls her."

"Her name's Ivy."

"What's your offer?"

"I'll give you some of the prize money."

"She hasn't won yet."

"But she will. I know my sister. She always gets what she wants."

"How much are we talking?"

"A hundred dollars."

She snorts. "Isn't the prize a hundred thousand?"

"Yeah, but I'll need bail money, and Ivy will want to keep some—"

"Five thousand."

"Five thousand?" I choke out.

"Take it or leave it."

My bargaining skills are nil, but I can't just hand over five thousand bucks. Then again, we're talking about imaginary money. Once I'm out, I'll never see this woman again so she can hang on to her imaginary payday.

"For that price, I get permission to watch the show whenever I want."

"Aren't you a little wheeler and dealer? Fine. But—"

My mouth goes dry.

"If your sister gets disqualified," she says, "you'll still owe me the money."

Cold sweat gathers on the nape of my neck. I remind myself that it's pretend money, like the one Ivy and I bartered when we played on the faded Monopoly board my mother once brought back from the flea market. We'd had to make playdough houses and hotels, and cut and write our own chance cards and property deeds, but at least we had the board, the dice, the bills, and the metal tokens. It gave us something to do on dreary, rainy afternoons.

"Fine," I finally say.

She smiles. "Kim!"

A short woman with a long, coarse braid trots over.

"Gotta escort a prisoner. Take over."

The walk to the dayroom is quick and quiet in spite of the pointed looks the guard keeps firing my way. I wish she'd stop. I wish everyone would just stop looking at me.

She buzzes the door open. The TV's already on. I can hear two commentators rehashing the day's event.

"Hey, Redd," she calls out as I hurry in.

"Yeah?"

A crooked smile lights up her face. "I always collect."

When I nod, she leaves, and the anthem booms out of the stereo in time with the door banging shut.

"Welcome ba-ack!" Dominic singsongs. He's holding his mic so close to his lips that it looks as though he's French-kissing it. "Tonight is an unusual night, because, usually, there's a vote among the judges and among the audience to decide who gets the boot. Tonight, we didn't have to deliberate. Performance art wasn't Maria's forte. Or maybe it was the knitting..."

Laughter warbles out of the dark pit of people seated around the raised stone platform. It's scornful, which makes me angry, but my anger recedes when I spot my sister. Her face resembles burnished copper, and her lips have been painted a bright red. When they curve into a smile, I feel an overwhelming sense of pride.

"That's my sister," I say to no one, but Ivy must hear me because she winks. I wink back, and then settle down to watch.

TEN

Ivy

"You're late," Leila says when I arrive at my station the next morning, yawning and stretching.

I didn't fall asleep until really late—or maybe really early. With no windows and no clock, I couldn't tell what time it was.

"Get in the chair. We have forty minutes left. Amy!" Leila's shaking, even her slick-straight hair is vibrating.

"Herrick just arrived," I point out.

"I don't give a shit about Herrick. I give a shit about you. Why are your eyes so puffy? Didn't you sleep?" From the way she mutters this, I take it she's not asking. She pulls a little tube from her makeup trunk and rubs a dollop of its content across both my lids. It burns like ice.

"What the hell is that?" I exclaim.

"Hopefully, a miracle," she says. "Now don't move until I'm done."

While Leila brushes and stabs my face with crayons and mascara wands, Amy blasts my locks with hot air. No one talks. Chase is at the next station getting primped. Although his gaze is locked on the mirror, the line of his shoulders tightens as though he senses I'm looking. Last night, over dinner, I was tempted to ask him what his problem was, but that would exhibit insecurities, and New York Ivy has *no* insecurities. Powder wafts into my right eye and it tears up. I blink, but it still waters.

Leila grumbles as she swabs my lash line with a Q-tip. "Look up."

Finally, I'm ready. My hair has been slicked down. It reaches far below my shoulder blades and shines like spun gold. The amethyst powder on my lids makes my eyes appear bluer and hooded instead of swollen from lack of sleep.

"Tonight, six-thirty sharp. Not a minute later." And then she's gone.

"What's her problem?" I ask Amy, who's masticating her lip.

She gathers my hair in a high ponytail and wraps a ribbon around it. "Leila's a perfectionist."

"So am I. It doesn't mean you have to be nasty with people."

"Why aren't you dressed yet?" Cara exclaims, stopping by my station.

"She'll be ready in five minutes," Amy tells her.

"Just hurry. I put your clothes in the dressing area."

On the purple velvet pouf, my assistant has laid out a pair of light jeans, a pearl-colored shirt, and white sneakers. I pull on the jeans while Amy helps me with the blouse, careful that it doesn't snag on the ribbon in my hair or pick up pigment from my skin. I tie up my sneakers and reemerge after a glimpse of myself in the floor-length mirror.

Cara is checking her bulky, neon-orange rubber wristwatch, the sort of watch I drooled over as a pre-teen. Now I aspire to sleeker ones, preferably metal and preferably brand-named. If I win the prize money, I'll buy myself a diamond watch. And exotic fabrics from India. Maybe I'll even go to India.

As my mind travels to faraway destinations, my feet travel down one flight of stairs to a bright and grand hall with wall-to-wall oil paintings and statues. As I approach, the crowd parts to let me through. I hop onto a makeshift podium covered in navy fabric and join the lineup of contestants. The Master-piecers' anthem plays and quiets the straggling voices.

Once the music stops, Dominic, who's clutching a large glass jar, explains today's test: solving a riddle that will lead us to a specific work of art. "Each contestant will take a piece of paper from this container. Under no circumstance can you show anyone besides Jeb. Jeb will film your riddles, then broadcast them to our faithful viewers. Now, let's start with the girls."

Lincoln goes first, then Maxine, and then me. As soon as I unfold my paper, my gaze flies over the riddle.

"My luminaries were shaped by bees and human blood."

WHAT THE HECK ARE LUMINARIES? *Lights?*

A camera pops up in front of me, pressing down toward the paper like a dog snout. After everyone's picked a riddle, and it's been videotaped, Dominic says, "Ladies and gentle-men, please remember that you are *not* to help our contestants. You may follow them on their hunt, but do not offer clues or answer any questions, or they will be eliminated. Understood?"

A loud *yes* resounds.

Dominic grins. "The works you are looking for are on this floor and this floor only."

I'm about to pounce off the stage when Lincoln asks, "Do all our riddles lead to different ones?"

"Of course," Dominic says.

"Can we jot down thoughts?" Nathan asks.

"No pen, no paper. Use your minds," Dominic tells him, tapping his temple. "Ready?"

"Yes," I say along with the others.

"Let day number two begin," he exclaims

Lincoln leaps off the stage first and barges through the dense crowd of cocktail-attired people gathered in the long hallway, clearing a path for the rest of us. After we've all funneled through, the audience seams together and turns to follow. Heels and soles pound the floor. Most spectators keep out of our way, but some get so close, the camera crew has to corral them back. I try to ignore the rubberneckers as I move around the museum, but they're always there, gaping, pointing, and whispering. It's distracting. I remind myself that they are the people who made this competition possible with their money and their connections. Without them, I wouldn't be here. The thought makes their presence more bearable.

A painting captures my attention. It's a seascape of crimson-hued waves thrashing against a large wooden boat with a setting sun in the background. The sun is a luminary, right? And the water is red, like blood. But there are no bees, so I move on.

As I tread through the chain of galleries, I glimpse a lot of suns and stars and moons, several lampposts and light bulbs, a hefty dose of oozing blood, but not a single painting containing bees. After an hour, I collapse on a banquette. Somewhere along the way, I managed to lose the camera crew and the audience.

"My luminaries were shaped by bees and human blood," I whisper, hoping that saying it out loud will help me make sense of it. It doesn't. Checking that no one is around, I keep talking to myself, because too many ideas are playing leapfrog in my brain. "Okay. So...the light source was made by bees and blood. Maybe I'm not looking for bees and blood in the art. Maybe just light sources."

I sound silly...I sound like Mom. Always talking out loud to herself. I bat my lashes to dispel the sudden moisture caking my eyes and find myself staring right into a camera. *Shoot.* I strap on a confident mask that quickly decomposes when a rush of excitement booms out of an adjoining gallery making the camera crew race out.

I lean my head back and close my eyes. Slowly, I tap my skull against the wooden headrest, hoping I can knock the answer into my brain.

Can bees produce light?

Can honey produce light?

Or pollen? Pollen is yellow? Could pollen be considered light?

What makes some bugs light up?

"Think synonyms," I hear someone tell me.

I snap my lids up to find Brook sitting next to me.

"Trying to get me eliminated?" I ask, my heart bumping around my ribcage. The gallery is empty save for the two of us.

"No," he says quietly. "Synonyms are the foundation of a riddle. It's a fact, not a clue."

After a minute of silence, curiosity gets the better of me. "Who solved theirs?"

"Believe it or not...Daisy."

"Daisy?"

"I mean Maxine."

"No, I know who Daisy is. I'm just surprised—I thought it would be your brother."

Brook's eyes darken. "He's still searching."

"He'll get it soon enough."

"He *is* pretty obstinate," Brook continues.

"I can tell."

"This is his chance to get what he wants."

I smirk. "If he wins, will he be allowed to attend the Masterpiecers or does he just get the hundred grand?"

"He'll be allowed to attend."

"Won't that destroy the school's policy?"

"It will complicate it," he says as I stare at the Jackson Pollock in front of me. The paint splatters remind me of the last quilt I sewed. I used splatters of silk and velvet instead of paint. "Is your sister also artistic?"

"No. Not in the least."

He's looking at the Pollock too. "You don't talk about her."

"I came to compete in an art show, not to discuss my family."

"Fair enough."

"Now can you please leave so I can concentrate?"

"I'll be quiet."

I'm about to tell him that it's his presence I find troublesome, when I hear footsteps. My pulse skyrockets. I leap up and away from Brook before anyone can assume I was cheating.

Chase is standing in the large doorway.

Brook rises slowly and walks over to him. "How are you holding up?"

"I thought the contestants weren't supposed to speak with judges or people from the audience," Chase says curtly. The vein on his temple lobe throbs.

"I can ask how you're doing."

"Is that what you were asking Ivy? How she was *doing?*" His accusatory tone makes me livid.

"Yes." Brook pushes a shiny lock of black hair off his forehead. "I wasn't giving her any clues, if that's what you're worried about."

No one speaks and no one moves. The large gallery

suddenly feels oppressive. I pretend to examine a painting when I hear loud applause.

"Another winner. You two better hurry up," Brook says, brushing past his brother.

I walk off in the opposite direction. There's no way I'm spending any more time cooped up in a room with Chase. Plus my painting's not here. There are no light sources in any of the pieces hanging on the wall. As I cross the entire south wing, I start the unscrambling process anew.

Bees can't produce light.

Blood can't either.

What's synonymous with bees? Besides bugs and honey.

Pollen...honeycombs...buzz. I keep buzz in mind. *Filaments buzz.*

Or maybe it's a painting that was buzzed about.

Maybe it's a painting that was killed for!

My pulse quickens because I think I'm onto something. I commit this thought to memory then move on to the verb.

What's tantamount to shaped?

Formed. I try it out in the riddle.

My luminaries were formed by bees and blood.

Ugh! It doesn't make more sense. I think up more synonyms. My brain halts on the verb *molded.*

My luminaries were molded by bees and blood.

My nose wrinkles at the idea of a painting fashioned with blood. A few years back, a painting *was* made with excrement, so maybe there's one made with blood and dead bees. I check the label affixed to the wall in front of me. It's a Dubuffet created with plaster, oil, tar, and sand. Tar...weird. I didn't know artists used tar. The next painting is a combination of acrylic and wax. I get this niggling in my skull and read it again. *Wax.* Bees make wax.

I check the work associated with the plaque, but can't find

anything resembling a light source. It's a painting representing waves or squiggly lines. Not my painting.

A shift in the air alerts me to a presence. It's Nathan. His forehead glistens with sweat. Either he's been running or he's nervous. From the way he fidgets with his belt buckle, I decide it's the latter. Another round of applause erupts somewhere in the museum. I tick off my fingers. Three. I think of what Lincoln said, about us chasing the same painting and start wandering off toward the din. Just in case. When I get to the gallery, I find J.J. beaming in front of a Persian rug. *Yeah...I don't think our riddles are linked.*

"Ivy? Did you solve yours?" Dominic asks. He's standing right next to the graffiti artist.

Josephine and Brook watch me, and so does the audience. One of the cameras is poised on my face.

I put on a smile. "Almost."

Willing my knees not to shake, I walk out of the gallery and look at all of the paintings made with beeswax. I now understand the sneakers. The museum is a maze. I begin jogging, grazing the walls so that I can read the insignias without stopping. When I spot the word wax again, I stop to examine the subject matter: a self-portrait with no source of light. But still, I don't move. I study it and something clicks. It's textured, like the Dubuffet! *Of course.* That's what wax does. It makes my quest easier now, as I only stop in front of paintings that have relief.

A loud clamor resonates. *Four.* There are two spots left. I pick up the pace. There's a painting that takes up an entire wall. It's huge. And has tons of texture and color. I desperately try to locate something akin to luminaries or blood. But unless blood is neon pink and luminaries are dandelions, it's not it. My stomach lets out an angry growl that mirrors how my mind is feeling.

As I rip through yet another gallery, I hear a new commotion. *Five!* How is everyone done and not me? Their riddles must have been easier than mine! One spot to go. One spot. *One.* My rubber soles pound the floor. I cross Nathan's path. His eyes are as bright as his cheeks. He's running with a purpose. That's when I begin to lose hope. I'm tempted to trip him, but that's not going to help me.

I watch him disappear into the adjacent room, his footsteps ringing like a ticking time bomb. I suck in a breath and focus on the artwork around me to snuff out the ticking. Nothing resembles a freaking light source. There's a painting with a bunch of geometric shapes, there's another that looks like some blown-up Japanese calligraphy, there's a white flag, there's a—

I twist back toward the flag. It's white, but textured. And there are stars on it. Stars are light sources, right? I dash to the plaque, heart crashing against my ribcage. *Encaustic oil, newsprint, and charcoal.* Many had to die to unite America. I have my blood and my luminaries...

"What the hell is encaustic?" I say out loud.

"Wax."

The only other person around is Chase, and he's staring at another painting. Did I imagine his voice?

"Wax?" I repeat.

He doesn't answer. He doesn't even look at me. Maybe it was some ruse to make me fail. Chase would never help me. *Would he?* I stare at the flag and think that it fits my riddle.

A noise rises not far away. Nathan's stupid sweaty face pops into my mind and I sprint toward the clamor.

It has to be the flag.

"I got it!" I yell the second I enter the gallery.

I notice pity staining the onlookers' faces. And then I notice Nathan standing beside Dominic, beaming like a stop sign.

He got it before me.

ELEVEN

Every inch of skin on my body burns as though it were being doused in acid.

"Nathan. Your answer?" Dominic asks.

The camera moves off Ivy's face onto Nathan's. I don't care about his face. I care about Ivy's. Only Ivy.

"Looks like someone doesn't win after all," the long-necked guard says. Ever since I promised her the money, she's been bursting into the dayroom to catch segments of the show.

"It's not over," I tell her. It can't be. Ivy's the best.

The camera slides back to her. She's bleached all emotion from her face, but I know she's unwell. I can feel it through our twin connection.

"*The Love Letter* by Jean Honoré Fragonard," Nathan says, his face as shiny as a glazed donut.

Dominic shakes his head as though he has a fly buzzing around it. "No, Nathan. That's not it."

It takes a few seconds for the smile to tumble off Nathan's lips, as though each cell of skin is repositioning itself.

"I'm sorry." Dominic pats him on the back. "Ivy? What do you have for us?"

She doesn't move. I spring to the edge of the couch. "Come on, Ivy," I whisper.

Giraffe-neck smirks.

"What's the answer to your riddle, sweetheart?" Dominic asks.

She moves forward, carving a path toward the master of ceremony. Once next to him, she says, "*White Flag* by Jasper Johns." Her voice is steady.

Dominic hisses, hiking up his lips and baring his teeth like a hyena.

My hope shatters like the ornament Mom threw at my head during our last Christmas together.

"Is that your final answer?" he asks.

Her gaze coasts over the crowd, over me, but the rest of her face remains impassive. "Yes."

Dominic begins to clap, and then everyone claps, and I realize her answer was correct and Dominic was just being an asshole. My emotions are all over the place, like the shimmery painted glass fragments that embedded themselves in my skin. Nathan swipes his eyes. He's crying. I want to care, but I don't.

The TV switches off.

"What did you do that for?" I exclaim, twisting toward the guard. "It's not done!"

"For today, it is. Recreation time."

"I don't want to go to the yard."

The guard smirks. "And I don't want to babysit you, but I do it anyway."

"I'm paying you."

"I let you skip lunch already. Now get your ass to the yard before I do away with your little privilege."

I grind my teeth together and get up. The enclosed prison ground is full of people. Some are just hanging in groups on the grassy part; others are doing pull-ups on metal bars like caged monkeys. Half of them are crazy. I wonder if they arrived like this or if prison turned them into wackos.

The temperature is sweltering. For a second, I tilt my face up to absorb the sun, but then it's too hot. I look for shade, but there is none. Shade would be too much of a luxury. I walk over to a deserted strip of dusty pale sand and drop down. First I sit, but it's awkward just sitting there, being stared at by the entire prison population, so I roll back and close my eyes, and replay today's show.

When I don't feel the sting of the sun, I snap my lids up. Sure enough, Gill and Cheyenne are standing above me.

"The princess finally joins us," Cheyenne says.

"Tired of watching your little game show?" Gill asks.

"It's done."

"*Aww*...did your pwetty little sister lose already?" Cheyenne asks.

My jaw clenches. "No. Can you move? You're blocking the sun." I'd rather get sunburned, charred even, than endure another minute of scrutiny.

"I'm blockin' her sun," Cheyenne repeats, distorting her voice. I don't know if she thinks she sounds like me, but she doesn't. She just sounds like an idiot. "Get any darker and you'll turn black. That's Firehead's type."

Gill shoots her a look, which makes Cheyenne wobble away. I'm hoping Gill will go away too, but she doesn't. Instead, she lies down next to me. I scoot a few inches away. It disrupts the sand that floats up like a dust moat and cakes my face.

"Ever heard of personal space," I mutter.

"Chill. I'm not gonna jump you."

We don't talk for a few minutes, but I can feel she's there, her body vibrating inches away from mine. I roll up. She watches me, but doesn't move.

"You have sand in your hair," she says.

"Whatever. I'll wash it out," I say, patting it to get rid of any excess.

I scan the yard. Women hang out in racial clusters. I realize I wouldn't fit in anywhere. I'm too light for the African American group and too black for the whites. I stare at Gill, suddenly aware she must be breaking some code by hanging with a mixed girl.

I tip my chin toward the group Cheyenne has returned to. "Shouldn't you be with them?"

"Why?"

"You're white."

She snorts. "I don't believe in segregation."

For some reason, her answer makes me hate her a tiny bit less. "Because your ex was black."

She shrugs. "That's part of it."

"What happened?"

Gill turns to her side and props her head up on a bent arm. "*Now* you want to know?"

"Actually, I don't." I rub my hands together and watch as a little puff of dust disperses in the air in front of me, glimmering in the bright sun.

"She hurt me, so I hurt her," Gill says.

I stop rubbing my hands.

"I found her hooking up with another chick. In our bed. I got mad. I threw the girl out, and then we had a fight and I left."

I frown. "And then?"

"And then I went to the bar where I worked. It's in a crap neighborhood, so the owner keeps a handgun under the register. I took it and went home. She was sleeping."

"And you shot her?" I exclaim.

"No, I fucked her with the gun." She gives me a wry smile. "Of course I shot her. She hurt me. She broke my heart."

I swallow. It feels as though the dust has coated my mouth and throat. "But now she's gone."

"And she can never hurt me, or anyone else, ever again."

There's something hard and shiny in Gill's eyes, like congealed tears.

"It wasn't the first time she'd two-timed me, you know. She did it with a guy too. Said she was making sure she liked women best. I believed her." She's biting her bottom lip with her buckteeth. "You know what they say: 'Fool me once, shame on me. Fool me twice, shame on you.'"

"Isn't it the other way around?"

She narrows her eyes. "No. It's just like I said it."

I drop it because arguing a quote is pointless.

"Now you know my story. Out with yours."

Although I don't want to talk about it again, I know she won't let it go, so I tell her what I told everyone else.

I don't tell her the real story.

TWELVE

Ivy

fter bidding farewell to Nathan, who left shortly after
the evening announcement, we are sent back to our
wing for dinner. I want to skip the meal, but I don't think I
could sleep yet. I'm way too wired—probably because I tasted
the sour tang of elimination today.

I take my seat at the table that is now set for six. There's
music tonight; it's soft and throaty and fills the room. An
animation is playing in the middle of the white glass top: a
video of a graffiti artist creating deceptive murals full of
trompe-l'oeil. As I watch him, my fingers itch with the fire to
create. They long for my spools of thread and my collection of
rainbow-hued fabrics. I rub my thumb and index finger
together, feeling the slightly hardened skin, and ideas for new
panoramas spring to mind.

"So that was fun," Lincoln says, her hazel eyes gleaming.

Herrick pulls up the lapel of his purple velvet dinner
jacket. "Yes. And easy."

A waiter deposits a fancy salad in front of me. Just a few
leaves stick out from underneath a pile of cubed white cheese,
diced beets, and halved cherry tomatoes.

I sense Chase's eyes on me. After feeling them for eight hours, I could feel them anywhere—probably even in a congested subway station. I look up from my plate and glare back.

"Hey, Maxine, how'd you guess so quick?" J.J. asks, chewing with his mouth open. The salad dressing tinged pink from the beets is frothing around his neon white teeth. It's disgusting, yet fascinating—and a good distraction from Chase.

"I used to write riddles for candy companies. You know, the ones they print on the inside of the wrappers."

"How'd you get into that?" he asks.

"An ex-boyfriend. He worked in marketing and got me the job," she says, toying with the thin gold hoops hooked into her earlobes that reach her chin.

"That's cool."

"Yeah. But there's not much use for it in the real world."

"Except for today," J.J. says. He's taken another bite, and again, his mouth is wide open.

"Can you keep your mouth shut while you chew, J.J.?" Herrick asks.

J.J. wipes his mouth with his wrist. "Should I be worried that you're staring at my lips?"

"Don't flatter yourself," Herrick says.

"And here I was afraid the zipper of my tent would shoot up in the middle of the night and other zippers would shoot down."

"I wouldn't say those things if I were you, J.J.," Chase says. "You heard why contestant number eight got disqualified?"

"Ivy got disqualified?"

"Obviously not, surfer boy," Lincoln says.

"The one whose spot Ivy...took," Chase says.

"Pictures got him disqualified, not me," I counter, my voice as sharp as the pointy blade of my seamripper.

"What pictures?" J.J. asks.

Lincoln pushes a curled lock of blonde hair behind her ear. "God, what planet are you from?"

"I don't follow the news."

"Really?" Maxine says.

"If something's important, I'll hear about it."

"It's pretty ironic, though, isn't it?" Chase says, unfolding his arms.

"That I don't read the news?" J.J. asks, sponging the crumbled cheese with a piece of bread.

"No, dickhead." Lincoln rolls her eyes.

"That a white supremacist was replaced by Ivy," Chase says.

I lock eyes with him. "Why?" I ask, daring him to voice his thoughts.

He doesn't, and silence settles over the room.

After a long minute of heated glaring, I lean back. "I didn't rig the competition. I was chosen. Based on my application. On my skill. But perhaps you did, Chase. After all, your brother's a judge. How difficult could it have been for him to get Josephine and Dominic to endorse your application?"

"You don't know the first thing about me and my brother," he says, his voice low and rough.

"I know he got into the school, and you didn't."

"Because he was older. He applied first."

I lean forward, the silver sequins of my shorts digging into my bare thighs. "Is that the reason, or is he just better than you?"

Chase's eyes grow dimmer, like pieces of sky filling with rainclouds. "Is that what Brook was telling you during the riddle hunt? That he's better than me?"

"Brook?" Lincoln pipes in. "You spoke to him during the test?"

Chase nods. I'm tempted to kill him for bringing it up. I'm sure I would feel no remorse.

"Cheating, Redd?" Lincoln asks.

"Of course not!"

"Then why were you talking with my brother?" Chase asks.

And why did you give me the definition of encaustic? "We were talking about *you*," I spit out.

His thick eyebrows arch up.

"*Ooh...*this is getting interesting," Herrick says, tapping his shiny black nails on the tabletop.

"Brook was telling me how badly you wanted to get into his school. Basically, he pleaded with me to let you win," I say, stretching the truth, hoping Chase is too proud to check. "How's that for fraternal love?" I scan the faces of my enemies. "Wouldn't be surprised if he came to all of you at some point to ask you to go easy on Chase."

A hush falls over the table. Chase's complexion has gone paler. For a second, I think he's going to leave, but he doesn't. I don't know if it's because he's hungry for the second course that's just been brought out, or because he's trying to prove a point.

I spear a broccoli floret and place it on my tongue. Still looking at him, I chew. No one speaks. The clatter of forks and knives and the low music break the otherwise stifling silence. It's only after the plates are cleared that someone speaks.

"I wonder what they'll have us do tomorrow." Lincoln is plaiting her side pony, but doesn't tie the ends, so when she releases them, her hair unravels and ricochets the subdued light from the sconces mounted on the canvas walls.

"Maybe they'll have us make something! That would be so dope," J.J. says.

"Not for me and Chase," Maxine says, ever the considerate one. "Unless you know how to paint or something," she adds, her cheeks flushing.

"No," he says. "But I'm sure they'd find something else for us to do. Maybe auction off what you make."

"Ever sold anything, Chase?" Herrick asks.

He nods.

J.J.'s laminated shirt gives his black eyes a feral gleam. "What?"

"A thirty seven million dollar painting."

Intrigued, I sit up, my scratchy silver sequin shorts scraping my bare thighs again.

"Thirty seven million?" Lincoln chokes out. Either a piece of the fancy multigrain and olive cracker she's eating or the price tag went down the wrong way.

Herrick places his elbows on the table and knots his fingers underneath his chin. "What was it?"

Chase is leaning back with his arms crossed. "That's classified."

"Oh, come on, dude, you can tell us," J.J. says.

Chase shakes his head. "You can't reveal that sort of information, or you lose your clients. Confidentiality's a primal rule of art dealing."

"Good thing I don't want to deal then," J.J. says.

"How much did you make out of that sale?" I find myself asking.

He raises his eyes to mine, his incredibly dense lashes sweeping up arrogantly. "My commission was ten percent."

"Are you fucking kidding me, dude? Three and a half mill!" J.J.'s interested again. "Maybe I *should* deal."

"I'm a firm believer that if you do anything for the money, you won't do it well," Chase says.

I grunt. "That's easy for you to say when you have the money."

His dark gaze brushes mine.

"Was it a piece your family owned?" Maxine asks.

"No. Only Brook's allowed to dig into the family vault. My

dad's not even licensed to sell anymore. Masterpiecers' rules. It was a piece from Christie's. I worked there one summer."

Dessert arrives. Vanilla soufflé. "I could really get used to this place," Maxine says, picking up her fork and piercing the crisp top. It deflates slowly, the edges folding into the gooey center.

"I propose a little toast." Herrick raises his glass of wine. Maxine and J.J. follow suit while Lincoln, Chase, and I lift our glasses of sparkling water. "To fun, to knowledge, and to ambition."

Everyone's about to drink when Lincoln blurts out, "Better look into someone's eyes, Ivy, or you're going to have seven years of bad sex."

Even though I'm not superstitious, I stare into the only set of eyes looking back: Chase's.

"I need more wine," Herrick calls out, but no one comes. He spots the decanter on the buffet behind us and grabs it.

"I think I'm going to call it a night." Lincoln pushes back from the table. "Sweet dreams."

After she leaves, J.J. asks, "Anyone want her dessert?"

It's still golden and puffed.

"I'm stuffed," Maxine says.

Even though I'm not usually one to turn down food, I don't think my stomach can stretch anymore, so I shake my head.

Herrick nurses his glass of wine. "It's all yours."

As J.J. seizes Lincoln's soufflé, Maxine nudges me. "We're being filmed," she whispers. She budges her eyeballs to the left, toward a camera with a glowing red dot that's hooked into the corner of the tented ceiling.

"Duh," Herrick says. "They mentioned it in one of the files they sent us. We had to sign off on it. Didn't you read it?"

"I hate fine print," Maxine says.

Herrick shrugs. "We're on a reality TV show. It's standard."

"Does it record our conversations or just our images?" Maxine asks.

"Just our images," Herrick says, downing the last of his wine. He smiles and waves at the camera.

After a beat, I ask, "Are there cameras in our rooms?"

Herrick smirks. "You got something to hide, Ivy?"

"My body, for one."

"Suddenly modest, Redd?" Herrick asks.

I suck in an air-conditioned-loaded breath that makes my lungs flame like rayon on fire. "What's that supposed to mean?"

"My stylist told me you were quite comfortable with nudity," he says.

"And how would your stylist know that?" I ask.

"She heard it from the girl who does your hair."

"I'd be comfortable too if I had a body like hers," Maxine says, squeezing my forearm.

I snap my arm out of her grasp. Before she can fumble for an apology—because Maxine strikes me as a person who apologizes for everything—I repeat my unanswered question. "Are there cameras in our rooms?"

"No. That would be an invasion of privacy," Chase says.

Good. Then no one caught me freaking out over what I've hidden in my bag.

"Why is everyone watching me?" I ask Gill over breakfast the following morning.

Gill turns to take in the entire room. "Because you're still the new girl."

"How long do you stay the new girl?"

"Until there's a new girl," she says matter-of-factly. "Few weeks would be my guess."

"Thank God I'll be out in a few days then."

She loops one of her brassy dreads around her finger. "Still believe that?"

"Of course I still believe that!" My temper flares, which attracts more attention. I lower my voice. "I didn't do anything wrong."

The tall guard with the potbelly approaches our table. I wrap my feet around the legs of the bench, an old habit left over from school.

"Inmate Redd, the shrink wants to see you again."

Could he speak any louder? "Why?"

"'Cause she has a crush on you." He lets out a yip of laughter that reminds me of the sound of an injured dog.

When I don't laugh, he clears his throat. "I didn't ask, but I think it's because something's wrong with you. Would you like me to go find out?" He smiles.

I grumble as I get up.

"I heard your sister was almost eliminated last night." I bet he's trying to rile me up.

"Well, she wasn't."

"I'm betting Chase Jackson's going to win."

"Good for you," I say.

We tread down another hallway in silence. The walk seems endless this morning.

"You really believe your sister has a chance?"

"Of course!"

"They do call her Lucky Number Eight, don't they?"

"Apparently."

"I heard the guy—you know, the racist dude—I heard he lawyered up and everything."

"Good for him."

"Claims the photos were doctored."

"Of course he does."

"You might get a new roommate soon."

My brain attempts to make the connection between doctored photos and new roommates. When it does, I stop walking.

"Guess who suspect number one is?" He waggles his brows. One of them is slashed by an old scar, which he probably got for being an asshole.

"Ivy didn't do anything," I say, starting back up.

"She's still suspect *numero uno*."

I whirl around on my flip-flops, and my brittle hair—there's no freaking conditioner on this side of hell—flogs my cold cheek. "My sister is good. Real good. She had nothing to do with it."

"I didn't come up with it. I saw it on CNN. If you stopped

watching that show of yours and started watching the news, you'd have heard it too."

"Is everything all right out here?" Robyn asks. She's leaning against the shiny, thick crust of eggshell paint coating her doorframe.

"Fine," I say, storming past her into the office. I bet she now thinks I'm irritable on top of being nervous.

I drop down on the couch—the one facing the window—and fold my arms. Anger is ticking through me. I focus on my breathing to relax. It doesn't work, so I press my fingertips against my temples and think of the song Ivy hums to me when I'm out of sorts. That usually quiets me. When it doesn't, I let my hands fall back against my thighs.

"Tell me what's going on, Aster." She's sitting now, legs crossed neatly.

"The guard was making stupid accusations."

"What sort of accusations?" she asks. The beet-colored silk scarf tucked into the collar of her navy blouse makes her look old.

"That my sister got someone kicked off the show to take his place."

"Whose place?"

I frown. Doesn't she know anything? "That contestant who got disqualified because he was racist."

"Tell me more about this contestant."

"He attended a white supremacist meeting with swastikas inked on either side of his face."

"Do white supremacists frighten you?" she asks.

"I'm part black, so yeah."

"Have you ever been threatened because of your skin color?"

"I was insulted."

"What did they say?"

"They called us—"

"Us?"

"Ivy and me."

"I thought it was only you."

"I'm a twin," I say matter-of-factly. *How dense is this woman?* "They called us brownies, half-breeds, bounty bars."

"How did your sister react to the slander?"

"She told me not to listen to it."

"But you did?"

"It was hard not too. They were saying it to my face."

"But not to Ivy's?"

"To hers too, but she didn't care, so after a while, they stopped harassing her and just harassed me."

"So your sister wasn't treated the same way you were?"

"People respected her."

"And they didn't respect you?"

"No."

She nods, jots something down, then flips to another page in my file. "I asked to see you today because I'd like to talk about your mother."

"My mother?"

"We didn't talk about her yet."

"I hate her. She hates me. End of story."

Robyn's pen scratches the paper on her lap.

"What are you writing? That I'm delusional about my feelings for my mother? That she's really a caring person, but I'm not worth caring for?"

She looks up. "Is that how you feel? That you're not worth caring for?"

I don't want to answer this woman who keeps asking irritating questions and extrapolating.

"Aster, did you feel you weren't worth caring for?" she repeats.

"My sister loves me. Josh too."

"Josh?"

"My boyfriend."

"And your mother?"

"My mother's screwed up in the head! I don't give a crap what she thinks of me!" My nostrils flare. I can feel them expand. I stare down the bridge of my nose expecting to see smoke curling out.

"What do you mean, *screwed up in the head?*"

I wrench my gaze back up. "Isn't that in my file?"

"It is, but I don't care what's in your file. I want to know what's in your mind."

"You don't care what's in my file?"

"That's what I said. Now tell me...why do you think your mother hated you?"

"She threw stuff at me all the time. She slapped me. She even locked me in the hallway closet once...all day, and then when I peed myself because I couldn't hold it in any longer, she called me horrible things."

"Did she ever insult or hurt Ivy?"

"No. Ivy was her little princess. She taught her how to sew. Never taught me. Never even let me come into the room where she worked. But Ivy could. She could go anywhere, touch anything." I shove my parched locks behind my ears, but they don't hold and spring right back like metal coils. "I was the odd one out. She told me once she wished I were dead. She hated me. Told me I had screws loose. She was the one with the fucking loose screws. She didn't even know it. I had to schedule an intervention to have her committed. Ivy was pissed, but she didn't see how bad Mom had become. She didn't understand what stage four schizophrenia meant."

I wring my hands together, remembering that June morning perfectly. It was hot—stiflingly hot—and it wasn't even eight o'clock. Ivy had just come in from a run and was chugging orange juice from a carton in the fridge when our doorbell rang. She got to the door first. The shocked look on her face when she swung it open and found Mom's shrink flanked by a police officer brandishing a court order will forever stay ingrained in my memory. Ivy hated me then. She hated that I'd gone to see a judge behind her back. She hated that I'd shown a doctor the bruises Mom inflicted on me. She didn't understand how scared I'd become that, one day, one of those bruises would end my life.

Mom spared my sister because she held so much promise. Ivy was going to save our family, that's what Mom always said. Not me. I was going to be its downfall.

"It took my sister a long time to forgive me," I tell Robyn. "Sometimes, I think she hasn't completely forgiven me."

"Have you asked her?"

"She said it was in Mom's best interest...that I did the right thing."

"So what makes you think she hasn't forgiven you?"

"I don't know. Little things. Like she goes to visit her behind my back. She took up sewing like her. She left me here." My cheeks are dry, yet I feel like they should be wet, because my heart's been cracked open like a walnut.

The therapist scoots to the edge of her chair. The file flops open on her lap, but the pages are blank. She'll probably fill them out the second I leave. "Aster, you told me that *you* encouraged your sister to go to New York."

I suck in a sharp breath. It feels like a knife sliding down my throat. "You know I take care of her?"

Robyn frowns at the change of subject, but scoots back in her armchair. "No. I don't know."

"Yeah."

"How do you take care of her?"

"She doesn't know how to cook, so I cook for her."

"How else do you provide?"

"She's an artist, so I work two jobs."

"Is that how you paid your mother's institution bills?"

"No. The government covers those."

Her forehead creases, which makes her eyebrows arch up like furry rainbows. "The government only allocated a small amount of money to your mother."

I frown. "Then who's paying for it?"

"Do you have any other family?"

"No."

"Then my guess is that your sister took care of the bills."

"My sister? But she's never made a dime!"

"Are you sure about that?"

Am I sure? "Of course!" But I'm not. How was Ivy making money? Was she selling her quilts? Wouldn't she have told me if she were? *Oh, God, no...* My sister couldn't have been involved with Troy Mann, could she?

"Aster? Are you all right?"

"I'd like to talk to Officer Joshua Cooper," I say.

"What would you like to talk to him about?"

"Something. Can you get in contact with him?"

"I can ask the warden if he can arrange something." After a few quiet minutes, she stands. "I would like to schedule another session tomorrow. Same time?"

"Will you contact Officer Cooper?"

"Yes."

"Then okay. I'll be here tomorrow." I stand to leave. "We're done, right?"

She nods, so I start toward the frosted glass door. As I pull it open, I hear her call out, "We made good progress today."

I agree. Finding out my sister was making money behind my back is progress.

FOURTEEN

Ivy

I feel like a zombie this morning. I'm so tired that I nearly stride right into a wall of glass. Thankfully, Maxine warns me right before I face-plant. Three glass cubes have been erected in the makeup wing, similar to the ones they'd used for the performance art test. Inside each, they've set up a long glass desk and three chairs. I suspect it's for today's challenge.

As we're primped and dressed, my attention wanders to the other contestants and lingers on Chase. Even though the tents are fabric and fabric absorbs noise, I heard him move around his room last night. I even saw light flicker on and off. His makeup artist is applying concealer to his face, which leads me to believe the shadows underneath his eyes rival mine. What could keep Chase Jackson awake? I doubt it's stress. Even if he loses, it won't change much to his gilded life. I bet his parents would still be proud of him. *His parents.* Are they in the audience? Chase's gaze lands on mine, so I snap my attention to my reflection in the mirror.

Amy's humming to herself as she teases my hair and pins it into an elaborate half-up, half-down 'do. And Leila's her usual bright self—not. She snaps my chin up and pokes a black pencil into my lower lash line. I bite my lip and blink. I'd ask her to be more gentle were I not terrified she'd be even less so. Her kohl-smeared gaze shifts from one side of my face to the other to inspect her handiwork. When she puckers her lips, I brace myself for more pain.

Ten minutes later, I'm released from my torture chair and stuffed into a sleeveless, knee-length dress with a beaded collar. The high-heeled sandals I have to wear will give me blisters. The only positive aspect of the strappy heels is that they probably signify I won't be racing around the museum like some headless chicken.

Dominic checks in on us like he does each morning before we have breakfast. But this morning, it isn't to make sure we're ready. "Ivy, a word." He gestures to a glass cube.

The others all glance our way, but leave for breakfast. Dominic shuts the door behind us.

"Our school was built on an honor code, which every student swears allegiance to the day they enroll. *Inter se credimus.* Do you know what it means?"

I feel heart palpitations in my jaw. Did Chase tell him he gave me a hint yesterday? "I'm guessing something about giving credit," I say, although I know that's not it.

I try to block out the curious gazes of the crew members filming us while Dominic jiggles his head left to right.

"Not exactly. It means, *In each other we trust.* Now, I hate myself for having to ask this..." He's dropped his voice although I doubt anyone can hear us. "I wouldn't even bring this up, but it's all over the news." Despite the layer of foundation on his cheeks, Dominic's face looks like a crumpled sepia photograph.

My entire body pulses. Even my eyes have trouble focusing. I see everything double. "What's on the news?"

"That you might've had a hand in eliminating the former eighth contestant."

All at once, relief and astonishment catapult through me. The two emotions are so different that they make my body go still and throb more fiercely. "I had nothing to do with his elimination."

"You don't know how relieved I am to hear you say that. I'll have you know, I didn't believe it for a second." He lays a hand on my shoulder and squeezes it, then rubs it a little, then squeezes it again. "I'll prepare the press release and we'll go over it before you face the"—he suddenly looks around and releases my shoulder—"cameras. Okay?"

"Okay."

"And with Brook. Yesterday. During the test. Someone told us they saw you talking."

Someone. I grunt. I bet that someone is Chase. For a flimsy second, I'm tempted to tell him about the latter's unwelcomed clue, to have *him* disqualified—but then I come to my senses. I would be too. I seal my lips shut and add that information to the long list of secrets I have bottled up. If only I could just get rid of them all, throw them into some mental well and watch them sink.

"We were discussing the school," I say.

A smile appears on Dominic's face and then vanishes and then returns, like a flickering light bulb. "So not your riddle?"

"No. Not my riddle."

He exhales such a deep breath that his skin regains some of its firmness. "Good. That's what he said too. Good."

And then I'm allowed to go to breakfast, but the knot in my stomach is so tight that everything I swallow tastes like chalk. After wolfing down two croissants, I perch myself on one of the armchairs and sip scorching coffee. I don't partake in any conversations. I don't answer questions about what Dominic wanted. The only person not enquiring about my clandestine meeting—unsurprisingly—is Chase. *Bastard.*

Someone from the camera crew bursts in to inform us that

it's show time. Accompanied by our assistants, we return to the Temple Room. The anthem is already playing as we file onto the platform between the two Egyptian relics. Instead of tables, they've set up rows of tourmaline-colored velvet chairs. The audience is already seated, gold paddles dangling from their clapping hands.

Josephine and Brook are standing side by side on the far right. His face is pulled tight, a bit like Josephine's. I can tell he went through the interrogation. He'll probably keep his distance from me now. All the better. I'm done fraternizing.

"Day number three!" Dominic exclaims. "Already. Can you believe it? Could someone please stop time? Anyway. Back to day number three and test number three, which will be..." *Drumroll.* "An auction! Yes, Lincoln, you were right," he says, whipping around toward us.

When? She must have mentioned it while she was being made up into some slutty librarian. The top knot on her head, her heavy eye and lip makeup, and her tweedy shift are not flattering.

"It's a natural part of the art business," she says, smiling.

"It is," Dominic says. "Now for the rules. Each one of you will have to auction off a lot. They're all worth the same, so the person with the lowest sales total loses. Now, before you go up in front of our generous crowd"—he whirls around—"you are feeling generous, right?"

The audience laughs.

Dominic grins as he turns back to us. "You will be given information on the paintings and sculptures you are selling. You'll have to present that information in a way that makes the piece attractive, and I'm not talking about fabricating stories. I'm talking about crafting factual poetry. *Ooh...*I should coin that phrase."

Clapping rises from the pit of onlookers.

When it dies down, he continues. "The bids will increase

by the thousand until they've reached half the value of the object, then by five-thousand. Who knew art required math skills?" Dominic chuckles, along with a chunk of the audience. "When Brook comes around with the glass jar, you'll fish out one paper. On it, you'll find a number that determines your turn. The first contestant will not have less time to study the lots. Everyone gets the same thirty minutes."

Herrick's lips are arched high from the excitement of today's test. I don't feel excited about it.

Brook keeps his eyes trained on the jar as he waits for us to pick a paper. I'm the last one to go so there's only one paper left. I unfold it after he walks away with the empty jar. It reads 3. At least I'm not first. I'll get to observe the others.

"Okay. Let's rearrange you by number," Dominic says.

We weave in and out of line. The order is Herrick, Maxine, me, Chase, J.J., and Lincoln. When Chase comes to stand next to me, I angle my body away from his. I don't care if it's subtle or not. Unfortunately, I can still smell him. I breathe through my mouth until Dominic dismisses us. We return to our living area to wait for the judges. They've cleared breakfast, but there's still a basket of fruit, a jug of coffee and one of hot water. I make myself tea and go sit next to Maxine who's bouncing her folded legs.

"Nervous?" J.J. asks her.

"I was a girl scout. And for three years, I never sold a single box of cookies, so yeah."

"Not even to your parents?"

"They were gluten-intolerant."

"*Ah*...the rich people's disease," Lincoln remarks.

Maxine's legs stop joggling.

"Just sayin'. No one in the shelters I grew up in ever complained of any intolerances."

For a second, Maxine doesn't answer and I wonder if she's offended, but then she says, "You're right."

Lincoln tips her head, seemingly astounded that Maxine has agreed with her. I'm intrigued in spite of my desire to stay out of these people's lives.

"You're loaded?" J.J. asks. He's leaning forward, chomping on an apple, his mouth wide open, his teeth paler than the fruit's flesh.

Chase and Herrick, who are sitting next to each other, stop discussing art to listen in.

Her cheeks get rosy. "Dad manages a fund. Mom's a homemaker even though she's never home, nor is she ever making anything." Her fingers are curled together in her lap. She seems so uncomfortable speaking about herself, yet she rambles on. "I have a brother. He's in college. We're not very close. Do you have any siblings, Lincoln?"

"Probably. Who knows?"

I toy with the bedazzled collar of my sleeveless dress as I think of my sibling. I wonder if she's following the show.

"I don't even know who my dad is, but I can bet you anything that if I win this competition, he'll seek me out pretty quick." Lincoln's face doesn't betray the bitterness of such a remark. If anything, she looks nonplussed at the prospect. "I bet I'll have tons of dads by the end of the show."

"Okay, kids." Dominic storms into the room with Josephine, Brook, and what seems like the entire film crew. "Are you ready?"

We all nod. Not that it would change anything if we weren't.

"Chase and Lincoln, you're with me. Ivy and Daisy, with Josephine. J.J. and Herrick, follow Brook." When none of us move, Dominic adds, with a smile, "Chop chop."

I get up slowly and trail after Maxine and Josephine. She leads us to the makeup room and into one of the glass cubes.

"Your *dossiers*," she says, pointing to two thick files that have been deposited on the table. She slides gracefully into one of the transparent chairs. "Sit, girls."

As Maxine lowers herself into the chair, one of her heels slips and she ends up falling hard on her butt. There's a rip in the fabric of her dress. Her face floods with color as she clumsily latches on to the edge of the table and hoists herself back up. Josephine's eyes glow, but her face remains impassive. Considering we're in a glass box, the cameras catch her fall. Everyone catches it. Including Brook whose face goes dimply, as though Maxine's wardrobe malfunction has cracked the tension in his body.

Poor Maxine covers her cheeks with her palms, but then she remembers the tear and moves them to the gaping seam.

"I'll get started with Ivy while you change," Josephine says. Her blonde-white hair is stiff with gel and slicked back as though she's just stepped out of a swimming pool.

I flip open the beige folder and balk at the first printout. Then I gulp and look up at Josephine.

It can't be...

"An *artiste* must sell themselves," she says.

I'm too rattled to say anything. I just blink.

"We were very taken with your quilt, Ivy. It's very *originale*. However, we only required pictures of your work. So I must wonder"—she leans her flawlessly pale forearms on the glass table—"why did you send it in? Especially after you were selected..." A large oval diamond graces her narrow ring finger.

I swallow. "Um..." I swallow again. "I-uh..."

"Just so we're clear, it won't help you win...if that's the reason."

The blood drains from my face. "That wasn't the reason."

"Good. Anyway, your quilt is school property now. *Tu comprends?*" I must look utterly clueless, because she adds, "You understand?"

"Yes."

"I need you to sign this form to allow the Masterpiecers to sell your work."

"What happens if I don't sign it?"

"It gets locked up in one of the vaults, which will benefit neither you nor me. It's in your best *intérêt* to sell it. Did you see the *prix* we fixed?"

"Twenty thousand." I try not to act surprised that anything I made could be worth so much. "Is the money mine after the auction?"

The corner of her mouth lifts a fraction of an inch before dropping down. "*Non.* School property. Haven't you been listening? But you get *une commission.*"

"Ten percent?"

"Five."

The topstitched seams strain over my taut shoulder blades, slicing into my skin. "For the whole lot?"

Josephine smirks, which looks as unsightly as a crack on porcelain. "*Non.* Just for your piece. We almost gave it to one of the others to sell. You should be thankful."

That's not at all how I feel. I feel confused and shocked, but definitely not thankful. I turn to the next printout before Josephine can spot my agitation.

"Sorry. I tried to be quick," Maxine says, rushing back inside. Her dress is forest-green and stretchy now.

"*C'est bon.* You still have time," Josephine says.

In silence, we study our lots while the judge circles around us like a bird of prey.

The second item I have to sell is a plaster and copper sculpture by one of the school's students. The third are two bowls molded on Marilyn Monroe's breasts, nipple and all. The fourth piece is a fluffy cotton violin encased in a Plexiglas box. The artist, Zara Mach, is a Masterpiecers' graduate. Everyone knows her name. She's a big deal in the art world now. When I see the price tag for the violin, my lips part with a gasp. Suddenly my quilt feels like some old coverlet fit for a garage sale. Who will want to buy it when they could own a $250,000 Zara Mach?

"Two minutes left, girls," Josephine says. "*Des questions?*"

Maxine raises her hand. As Josephine walks over to her, my gaze flies over all the information on the last printout. It's a charcoal sketch by Paul Gauguin of one of his indigenous Tahitian women valued at $150,000.

"Ivy? Time's up." Josephine extends her palm.

I close the dossier and hand it to her. Once Maxine steps out of the cube, I ask her, "Is there any way I could place a phone call later today?"

"*Non*...unless it's vital. In which case, *oui*, but we'd listen in."

It's vital, but I don't want anyone besides Josh to know that. I rub the nape of my neck that is covered in goose bumps trying to come up with a better idea, but my neck isn't some magical lamp—no genie or genius thought comes out.

"Ivy, are you okay? You look pale," she says.

"I'm...I'm fine," I say, letting my hand collapse against my side.

As I walk out, I pray that Josh is watching the show. I need him to know that the quilt we've been searching for is here.

FIFTEEN

"What did I miss?" Gill asks, dropping down on the couch next to me.

"Nothing," I grumble.

"Uh-oh..." She tips her head to the side. "Does your mood have to do with the show or with the shrink?"

"Both."

"You want to tell me about it?"

"No."

Gill pouts.

"Look, I just spent the past hour talking to a shrink, so I don't want to talk anymore."

The contestants are filing in to the vacant first row of the Temple Room. Ivy sits between the aisle and that girl with the buzz cut. I study my sister, feeling like it's the first time I'm really seeing her.

I feel a hand on my thigh and I start. "Please don't do that."

Gill pulls back and burrows deeper into the couch, lips squashed together.

I focus my attention on the small monitor and pretend that everyone around me has vaporized. On the stage, they've added a golden podium that resembles a metal spider web. It's one of the pieces Maxine will sell, or so the commentator is saying.

While the contestants were studying their lots, the network was showing footage of their life off the podium. The luxury of their tents makes the correctional facility appear particularly drab. We also got to witness Maxine's dress mishap. Had I not been in a mood, it might have made me smile. It definitely tickled Cheyenne whose fat ass was already spread on one of the two couches when I stormed into the dayroom.

While Dominic goes over the rules one last time, Herrick climbs onto the stage and positions himself behind the podium. He looks confident, but appearances don't mean anything. His Elvis hair has been teased into a shiny black wave that looks like it's about to crash off his head. As I wonder how it holds, a few notes resonate, announcing the beginning of the test.

There's a flurry of activity as a scroll is brought out of the larger of the two temples. It's a religious artifact made by Tibetan monks. The bidding starts at ten thousand dollars. It ends at twenty. A flash of disappointment fires across Herrick's face. He undersold it. The scroll is rerolled and another item is brought out: a wooden chair that resembles cardboard.

"Christos Natter began wood-carving at six." Herrick's voice is trembling a little. "He began at six in his family's shed using slabs of wood his father, a carpenter, would discard. He soon entered his creations into fairs and competitions. Which brought him to the attention of Mister Delancey—"

A round of applause drowns out Herrick's voice and the camera sweeps across the room toward a seated man whose skin is shiny ebony. He gives a curt nod, which surprisingly doesn't dislodge the monocle set over his right eye that makes him look like he's snuck off the page of a nineteenth-century

British novel. After another round of applause, the camera shoots back to Herrick.

"Th-the lot consists of six chairs," he stammers. The gavel in his hand trembles. "They're all one-of-a-kind pieces. The auction will begin at twenty thousand dollars." He darts a glance at the judges' bench. Brook takes an exaggerated gulp of air, probably to remind Herrick to breathe. Herrick's jaw unclenches. He guzzles in some air and begins again.

The room goes completely quiet.

Herrick's voice explodes out of his microphone. "Twenty. Do I hear twenty? Twenty-one. Twenty-two. Gentlemen's bid at twenty-three."

And up and up he goes, attaining numbers that seem downright preposterous for a bunch of chairs.

"Thirty nine, anyone? Come on, people, have a little— We've got thirty-nine in the back." Herrick's confidence is tangible. "That's more like it. Do I hear fo—forty in the corner!"

The sound of percussion vibrates across the vaulted room. It's a reminder that he's reached half the value.

"Forty-five. Fifty to the lady in the back. Fifty-five..."

One of the neon strips on the ceiling fizzles and sputters out, casting a shadow over our half of the windowless dayroom.

"He's up to eighty-five thousand now," Gill says. "No, ninety! Shit..." she whispers, her eyes glowing in the darkness from the reflection of the monitor.

I yank my gaze back to the screen, just in time to hear Herrick say, "Going once, going twice, sold to the lady in the back!" As he slams his gavel, the black wave of suspended hair crashes against his forehead. He rakes it back and grins.

"Who the fuck has ninety thousand dollars to spend on a buncha chairs?" a skinny woman with a hairnet asks. I think she's the cook. Seeing how skinny she is, I bet she doesn't eat her own food.

"They're sculptures," Gill says. "The buyer probably won't even sit on them."

"I bet they'd crack if I sat in them," Cheyenne says.

"Canteen benches barely hold your fat ass up," the cook says.

Cheyenne shifts around on the couch. "You got a bone to pick with my ass, because I got a bunch of bones to pick with your cookin'?"

"You don't look like you got a problem with it."

"Are you insultin' me?" Cheyenne jumps to her feet, surprisingly lithely considering the mass of cellulite she needs to haul up.

The cook springs up too. Cheyenne gets in a punch and the cook's face snaps backward. Something cracks. I pray it's not her neck. It isn't. It's her nose. Blood squirts out. She starts screeching and claws at Cheyenne's face. I look around, wondering when a guard will rush in. When nobody comes, I shoot Gill a look. She's smiling, her crooked teeth overlapping her lower lip. At some point, she moves, but it isn't to break up the fight. She scoots her legs onto the couch so they're not in the way.

The cook's on the floor and Cheyenne's on top of her now.

"She's turning blue. She can't breathe," I yell.

Still no one does anything. I race to the digital box by the door and press on the call button. Seconds later, two guards vault into the room. They each grab one of Cheyenne's flabby arms and hoist her up. The cook's coughing and choking, but her face is returning to its original color.

As they take Cheyenne out of the room, kicking and screaming, the cook yells, "I put you on a diet, bitch!" She's rubbing the red patches on her throat where Cheyenne's fingers had been only seconds earlier. She takes her seat on the couch. "Crazy fat bitch," she mutters. She stares around the room. Her deep-set eyes land on me. "You the one who called security?"

I'm not sure if I should nod or deny it. Will I be considered a rat if I admit to it?

"Yeah. She's the one," Gill says. She pats my hand.

"I owe you then. What you like to eat?"

I want to say tasty food, but obviously I don't.

"What you like? What you miss in here?" she repeats.

"Chocolate. I miss chocolate."

She nods. "Hope you're not too picky on the color."

"No. I'm not picky." My stomach rumbles at the prospect.

"I see what I can get."

Gill's still patting my hand. It's weird now, so I yank it out of her reach. "Thanks."

"The name's Miss Chacha. 'Cause I'm hot like Sriracha."

Hot as in spicy, because she's definitely not pretty. "Thanks, Miss Chacha."

"Just Chacha." Still rubbing her neck, she settles back in the couch and turns her attention to the TV.

The show. *Shit!* Maxine's on stage now. The banner on the bottom of the screen shows she's on her last lot, the spider web podium. Maxine walks around it, mic in hand, puking out detail after detail on the refined metal design and intricate netting and the polishing technique. She took Dominic way too literally on his factual poetry. Finally, she begins the auction.

As the price goes up, I ask, "How did Herrick do?" I'm hoping someone was paying attention.

"He got $405,000 in total. Apparently all the lots are valued at $500,000, so I think that's pretty good." It's a girl leaning against the back wall who answers me. She's so pale she's virtually translucent.

I turn back to the screen just as Maxine pounds her gavel. Her cheeks are all rosy and she's smiling. As she skips off the stage that is being readied for my sister, the commentators launch into a detailed discussion of her performance. "She reached the price on four pieces—the Donaski podium and the gelatin print—but had some trouble with the…"

I let their voices trail off as I read her score: $435,000. Despite my mixed feelings for Ivy, I hope she'll do better than Maxine. I see her walk up on stage. She looks so beautiful in her black satin dress. And her hair is fabulous. I can't help but run my fingers through mine that is clumpy and dry like hay. Instead of chocolate, I should have asked for conditioner, but I'm reminded that I have no one to look nice for here. Might as well eat chocolate to forget.

"She your older sister?" Chacha asks me.

"She's my twin."

"Seriously?"

"Yeah."

"You don't look alike."

I'm tempted to press down on those red spots she's still nursing, but I refrain because I don't want to end up on a "diet."

"Like real *real* twins?" she asks.

"Yeah, Chacha, like real twins," Gill says. She's turned to gaze at me. The intensity in her eyes is really disconcerting. "I see it."

"I don't," Chacha says, squinting to make out my features.

Even though she discusses my resemblance with some other inmates, I zone out. Ivy's on the screen, gavel in hand. She isn't smiling, which makes me anxious. And then I understand why when the first piece she has to auction off is brought up on stage.

SIXTEEN

Ivy

"This piece is very dear to me, because, as some of you might know, it's one of mine. What you don't know, because it's not written anywhere except in here"—I tap two fingers against my heart—"is that I created it for someone I loved right before they passed away."

I pivot toward the quilt that's twice my height and strung up to an invisible clothing line hooked between two wooden beams. It resembles *The Kiss* from Klimt—at least that was my intention when I made it. The patches of gleaming gold, burgundy velvets, emerald silks, and Indian mirror work are shaped into the interlocked bodies of lovers.

"I gave it to her in the morning, and that evening, she was gone. She didn't have long with it—just a few hours, but at least she got to see it, to touch it..." I let my voice trail off and stare into the camera poised on my face, hoping that Josh is on the other side, listening in. "It's listed as 'Untitled' but it does have a name: 'Love.'"

I stroke the fabric and my nail snags on a thread. I peer at the spot more closely and realize there's a tear in the seam. Did it get damaged in the mail?

Dominic clears his throat, so I return to the podium. "I will start the auction at fifteen hundred dollars."

From fifteen hundred to thirty-five, it's a breeze. People are bidding one after the other. Thirty-five hundred to fifty-five takes longer. And then I hit a standstill at seventy-five hundred. I try to drag out the auction a little, but no one bids. "Seventy-five hundred." I wait. Still no one raises a gold paddle. The room is oppressively silent. Even though it's a lot more money than I got for it the first time around, I'm nowhere near the price Josephine fixed. "Seventy-five hundred going once, going twice, sold." I slam the gavel against the podium. I think of the commission I just earned—three hundred and seventy-five dollars—to avoid thinking of how I undersold it.

Before it's carried off the stage, I turn back toward it, toward the gaping seam that sticks out like an ink stain on a blank page. It hits me that, if it had been damaged in transit, the tear would probably not have been along the seam where the binding is sturdiest.

The wooden beams are grabbed and lifted away. As the quilt fades through one of the arches, I still can't make sense of the tear. Dominic clears his throat again. The next piece I must auction off has already been set. I gape at the copper statue. It takes me a second to remember anything about it.

Focus, Ivy. I press the image of my quilt as far away from my mind as possible and begin. Zara Mach's work goes for $260,000. I don't feel much pride at having exceeded the set price. If anything, it brings me further down. By the last lot, my voice has become robotic and I don't even try to enchant the audience. Someone buys the Gauguin for $120,000—a bargain. I undersold it, I undersold the bowls, and I undersold my quilt.

I slam the gavel for the last time, unwrap my fingers from the wooden handle, and slowly descend the stairs. On my way to my seat, I pass Chase who I know will crush this test. His confidence vibrates off of his skin, as dense as his sickening, grassy scent. I don't look at him as he begins, don't observe how comfortable he is behind the podium. Maxine and Herrick keep praising his demeanor, his poise. It drives me insane.

"Five hundred and twenty-five thousand dollars," Herrick whispers loudly. "He got more than what he was supposed to."

"I heard," I hiss.

"What's eating you?" he asks.

"I'm tired. And I have to give a freaking press conference in a few hours. I need to get out of here." I stand up, approach Dominic who's sitting at the end of our row, and tell him that my head is spinning.

The room has gone quiet around me as everyone's desperately trying to listen in.

"Let me signal your assistant," Dominic says. "She can help—"

I shake my head. "It's a short walk. I'll be okay."

"Assistants have to accompany contestants everywhere. Show rules, sweetheart."

People stare as I stride down the aisle. I bet the cameras are getting a lens full of my inelegant escape. Chase is probably snickering, reasoning that his success vexed me. I don't care though. The only thing I care about is finding out how the hell my quilt got on the show. Even though I don't want to be disqualified, returning to Kokomo to unravel this mess would do me a lot of good.

As Cara escorts me back to the third floor, I reminisce on my one and only encounter with Troy Mann the morning he rang my doorbell not long after Aster left for her day job at the ad agency. At first, I hadn't been too keen on letting him in. I'd left the chain on the door as I spoke to him. But then he told me how he'd seen my work on TV, in that feature the Master-piecers had run on its contestants, and I'd let him in, flattered that he'd even taken an interest in me. Little did I know he was a wanted criminal, embroiled with the mob. Had I known, I wouldn't have let him in. I wouldn't have sold him a single thing. I wouldn't have accepted his roll of hundred dollar bills that was surely tainted and illegal.

Two nights after Troy died, I phoned Josh and asked him to retrieve the quilt before the police could. I didn't want to get in trouble for having sold something to a mobster. Unfortunately, Josh hadn't found it; fortunately, neither had the police. But an anonymous tip came in on their hotline about my sister having a blanket on her lap. *Could it have been my quilt?* If it was, then that would mean she sent it to the show. But why? So that I would get in trouble? So that I would get locked up right alongside her? Could my sister be crazy enough to do such a thing?

I shiver. Yes, she could.

The second I step inside my room, I kick off my heels, drop my clothes on the floor, and turn the shower on. I make it hot and slip in, sidling along the mosaic wall until I'm sitting with my knees tucked underneath my chin.

Time goes by—a lot of time—and I'm still underneath the shower. I'm convinced it's Aster now, and my confusion and shock has turned to anger. Suddenly, the water stops and a towel is thrown on top of me.

"Get out," Leila snaps. "The press conference starts in an hour and you look like a drowned rat."

I glare up at her, but stand. Slowly, still sizzling, I settle on the bench by my bed next to a pair of beige pants and a white silk shirt—probably my press conference outfit. As she works on me, everything becomes blurry outside like everything is blurry inside.

"What's going on with you?" she asks, which is weird because Leila isn't the concerned type.

"Nothing that concerns you," I tell her.

She stops what she's doing and let her hands fall against

the black apron in which she stores all of her brushes. She has a ring on each finger. On her middle finger, she has two—a simple band at the base and a more ornate piece on her knuckle.

"If I didn't value my job, I would quit on you," she says, plucking the pins out of my waterlogged hair.

"Thank goodness you're such a dedicated worker then."

"It wouldn't hurt you to be kind, you know," she says.

I let out a dark laugh. She has no idea what she's talking about. Kindness doesn't breed sympathy. I was kind to my sister, and how does she repay me? She set me up.

She played me!

SEVENTEEN

"Inmate Redd, you got a visitor," Giraffe-neck tells me.

"Not now." I'm still trying to get over the shock that the recipient of the quilt was someone on the Masterpiecers. Either Ivy isn't safe or she's involved.

"Let me reschedule." Giraffe-neck's poised next to me like some root vegetable. Her lower body doesn't shift but her lengthy neck curves and tips as she pretends to push on the walkie-talkie strapped to her shoulder.

I sigh and look up. "Who is it?"

"A police officer."

I hop off the couch. It must be Josh. Robyn kept her word.

"Never seen an outlaw so excited to meet up with a police officer," she remarks.

I don't bother explaining my relationship with Josh to Giraffe-neck. It's none of her business.

When we get to the visitation area, I realize it's pouring outside. There are no windows in the dayroom, but here there are three. The light is dull gray and the glass is sprinkled with raindrops. That's probably why they let the entire prison population stay indoors today.

When the door clicks, I go straight toward the table he's sitting at. "I need you to check my sister's bank account," I say, dropping into the chair opposite him.

"Hello to you too, Aster."

Josh's brown hair is matted with rain and his short-sleeved, navy shirt sticks to his skin. Serves him right for not wearing a coat. He says it's because coats are cut too narrow, but I know it's because he loves to put his muscular forearms on display.

"I think Ivy was paying Mom's bills."

"That's swell. Means you don't have to pay them."

"That's not swell! She lied to me, Josh."

"How?"

"She never told me about the money."

"Why are you so worked up about it?"

"Because—" *Ivy might be entangled with the mob.* Even though I've known Josh forever, I can't confess my terrible intuition.

"Aster, I came to talk to you about something really important."

God, if she is, then my present will give her quite a shock.

"How did Ivy's quilt end up on the show?" Josh asks.

I startle. "Ivy's quilt? I have no idea."

"Want to know what I think? I think you have an idea...a very good one. I believe you found it next to Troy's body and sent it there. I believe it's the one you used as a *blanket*."

The blood drains from my face.

He jolts so far forward I can see all the different shades of green around his black pupil. "You're not denying this," he whispers loudly.

I drop my gaze to my nails and the thin white crescents that are reappearing at the tips. "No. It was a blanket."

"Aster," he growls. "You're lying. Just like you lied about the pizza. Troy Mann was a vegetarian. He wouldn't order pepperoni! I have a freakishly detailed file on him. Did he even come to the pizzeria, or did you just follow him from your house?"

"I...he...maybe it wasn't pepperoni. I don't remember."

"Sure." He snorts.

"Okay fine. He didn't stop by the pizzeria. I saw him at our house. I saw him go inside, and then I followed him back to the motel."

"Finally! The truth comes out," he says, slapping the desk. "Why are you always lying to me, Aster?"

I look up. "Always lying?"

"You know what I'm referring to," he says.

"The baby?"

He nods.

"I never lied about the baby," I say.

"Your doctor told me everything."

"My doctor told you what I asked her to tell you. I was trying to protect you."

"Bullshit."

I shake my head. "I didn't make it up. I felt it move. I saw it move. I was throwing up every morning."

Josh's fingers crawl over my shaky forearm like a spider. "It was all in your head."

I swipe them off. "No, it wasn't."

"Aster..."

I can't stop shaking at the memory of the blood pouring out of me the morning I lost the baby. "It was real," I croak.

"Let's not talk about it anymore."

I push my chair back and jerk up. "I need to go."

He sighs. "Don't be like that."

"Be like what?" I say, sniffling.

"Just stay."

"And be interrogated and mocked? No, thank you. I'd rather go hang out with people who don't think I'm crazy."

"I never said you were crazy."

"You didn't have to say it." I keep my gaze leveled on his. "Don't bother coming back here anymore."

"I'm going to come back. I'm in charge of the case."

It would have been too much to hope that he come back for me. Slowly, his face fragments, and I'm left with the one of the dead man. Every night, I see it. Every day, I think of it. The chin-length dark hair muddied with sweat, the crooked nose, the olive skin tinted red with blood. I blink and he's gone, and Josh is back, still looking contrite. He claps his hand around my wrist. I let his touch warm me for a second, and then I don't.

"Before you go, can you tell the warden to inform the guards that I *am* allowed to watch the show whenever I want?"

"The warden would never listen to me."

"He did the first time around."

"What are you talking about? What first time?"

"Ivy told me you got me that privilege."

"The warden? I've never even met the man."

"If *you* didn't talk to him, then who did?"

"Are you sure someone did? Are you sure you didn't convince yourself that—"

I give him such a glacial stare that he shuts up, and then I plant both my palms on the table and lean across it. "I'm not crazy." I don't scream this, but I do make sure each word rings out loud and clear. "Got it?"

His eyes have gone wide. I whirl around and make my way back to the secure door. I expect him to call me back, maybe even apologize, but he doesn't.

"I want to see the commander," I tell the guard.

"Did you request it on your digital box?"

"No."

"No, ma'am."

Seriously? "No, *ma'am.*"

"What is the nature of your request?"

"A complaint, *ma'am.*"

"Against the police officer?"

"No." After a beat, I remember to add, "Ma'am."

"We can stop by his office, but if he's busy—"

"If he's busy, I'll make an appointment."

She leads me down a new corridor, her long, thick braid swinging across her podgy back. I haven't met the warden yet. I didn't think I would need to, what with my stay in this prison being transitory. I'm not sure what sort of man I'm expecting, but definitely not one who's half my size and watering a plant.

"What may I do for you?" he asks when he spots me in the doorway.

I snap my gaze to another part of the room until I think I've got my gawking under control. Then I look back at him. "It's about my sister, Ivy."

Something flashes across his face, as though the name is familiar to him. Then again, everyone in America is familiar with my sister's name now.

"You may leave," he says.

I think he's dismissing me and I'm about to lose it, because I've reached my breaking point, but then the guard steps out and closes the door.

"Take a seat." He gestures to the free chair in front of his desk.

Stunned, I sit.

"What about your sister?" he asks, setting down his watering can next to a framed picture of a little girl with a big dog posing against a colorful background. I suppose it's his daughter. I check his left hand and, sure enough, find a ring.

"She's on a show, but you must know that."

"I do."

"Ivy told me that Officer Cooper spoke to you about letting

me watch it whenever it was on, but he swears he never spoke to you."

"Officer Cooper didn't ask me." His skin tone has lightened. "Your sister did."

"Ivy came to speak to you?"

Gradually, his color returns to normal. It's so gradual that I can actually see it come back in patches across his face. "Yes. She was worried about you."

Something warm replaces the chill I've carried around all day. "Well, the guards aren't letting me watch the show whenever I want."

"This is a department of corrections, not a country club." His tone is kind. "My orders only go so far. There *is* a schedule, and even though the guards can be lenient, they must still enforce it."

I want to tell him about Giraffe-neck's bribe, but ratting out a guard probably won't win me popularity points around here.

"I'm happy Ivy's doing so well," he adds.

"She didn't do well today." I chew on the inside of my cheek.

"She's not disqualified."

My teeth release my cheek. "She's not? She's still in?"

"Yes. That's what the commentators were saying, although Dominic Bacci hasn't made the official announcement."

"Who's out?"

"The graffiti artist, I think."

"J.J.?"

"Yeah, that's the one."

Happiness fills my chest like helium. I believe I'll take flight any second.

"Aster, since you're here, I'd like to discuss your medication," he says.

The balloon pops. "What about my medication?"

"A guard told me you've been refusing to take your pills."

"I don't need them. I haven't taken them in months."

"I was told you did need them."

"By whom?"

"Mental illness doesn't just go away. I had a sister—"

"And I have a crazy mother! I know what crazy is. I'm *not* crazy."

He doesn't speak, which is worse than if he did.

"Did Robyn put you up to this?" I ask.

"Robyn?"

"The shrink."

"No. Miss Pierce and I haven't discussed you yet."

"Yet?"

"You're bound to come up in our weekly debriefs."

"I'll be gone by then."

"Gone? And where will you be going?"

"Home. The DA will set my court date soon, and I'll be able to prove it was self-defense."

He blinks. Three times. "Self-defense?"

I nod as I stare at the picture of his daughter again. Our mother had a picture like that on her sewing table. One child sitting in front of one of her quilts. I wasn't the child. I know because I have a small mole next to my mouth and Ivy doesn't. The girl in her picture didn't have a mole.

"Is she yours, Commander Collins?" I point to the picture.

He does a belly-flop onto his desk to grab the frame. Is he afraid I'm going to blackmail him or something?

Frame still rattling between his fingers, he says, "Yes. She's my daughter."

"Be nice to her. That's the best thing you can do for a child."

He seems to relax when he realizes I mean her no harm, and sets the frame back down, but angles it away from me. I have to admit I'm a little offended that he would jump to that conclusion. As I stand, my gaze is drawn back to the picture. There was something about it...something familiar. I wonder if it's the little girl. Maybe I served her pizza. I have the nagging feeling that's not it.

Ivy

I'm sitting down with two lawyers, Dominic, and Josephine in one of the glass rooms we used earlier to study our lots. The crew has dismantled the other two rooms. Around us, there are no cameras and no assistants.

"So I've prepared a few words that we'd like you to learn by heart," one of the lawyers tells me. She hands me a printout, which I read over quickly.

After I set it down, they begin explaining that journalists are going to try to rile me up to get a reaction. I am not to lose my calm—like I did earlier, at the auction.

I glare at the male lawyer who's just interjected that bit. "I was feeling faint."

He doesn't respond. He just plays with his lacquered fountain pen, spinning it like a top on the glass table.

The female lawyer breaks the silence. "They're going to bring up your sister—"

"My sister? Why would they bring her up?"

All four exchange a look.

Then Dominic skews up his lips and says, "Because she's in jail. They've been trying to get a statement from you about her since the day you arrived. Anyway, they've dug up everything they could find. But not just about you. About all the contestants," he adds as though it will make me feel better. It doesn't.

"They'll bring up the murder," the woman lawyer says.

"It was self-defense."

She glances at Dominic.

"It was," I insist.

"Well, it still might come up."

"It's none of their business, right? I don't have to respond."

She shakes her oblong head. Her eyes are set so wide apart, she reminds me of a goat. "No. You don't. We'd rather you don't."

Dominic's complexion is a little ashen. "The only thing that matters today is proving you didn't doctor the images of Kevin Martin."

"Doctor images? Is that what he's saying I did?"

"He's not saying *you* did it," the male lawyer explains, "but he is claiming the images were doctored. He's even provided the originals. They've extracted the IP address from the PNG metadata and—"

"In English?" I ask.

He stops spinning his pen. "The originals date back three years and were taken in his town, but three years ago Kevin was serving in Afghanistan."

My eyes go wide. "So the images really are fake?"

"Unless his entire platoon is lying about his whereabouts, then yes," Dominic says.

"Does this mean I'm disqualified?"

Dominic gasps as though surprised I've come to that conclusion. "Of course not. But it does mean there's been some rigging, and since you're the only one who benefited from it—"

"Mister Bacci, with all due respect, *you* selected me. I

couldn't have been your only runner-up. Plus, I don't know the first thing about computers or IP addresses or metadata."

"Do you know somebody who does?" Josephine asks.

"I don't think so."

"It's time," the woman lawyer announces.

I skim over my rehearsed lines, then hand the paper back. "I'm ready."

Dominic squeezes my shoulder. "It'll be quick and painless. Don't worry." That's easy for him to say.

As we file out of the room and take the elevator down to the main entrance, the lawyer with the goat face makes me repeat the lines. I recite them by heart. She's pleased, impressed even. We cross the lobby and go out the revolving glass doors. I breathe in a gust of city air, hot and humid and full of car exhaust, but at least it's fresher than the recycled air of the museum. I shade my face from the bright sun and then I dare look down. The stairs are carpeted with reporters, and beyond them, spilling out onto the street which has been closed off by blue police barricades, there is a crowd so huge that it reminds me of the computerized battle scenes Aster created for a designer launching a toga-inspired clothing line.

I've always wanted to be famous, but for my talent. No one came today to see me stitch beautiful fabrics together. They came to see me hang. I check for a pillar and a noose as I attempt to keep track of what is being said. Everything's too loud, too bright. At some point, the lawyer nudges me, and I recite my lines. I must do a good job, because she nods and turns back to the frenzied crowd. In the haze of my brain, in the fog of camera flashes, I hear my sister's name being yelled.

"Isn't Aster a Photoshop wiz?" a sweaty-faced reporter asks. Spittle flies out from his thick lips and lands on my forehead.

Mechanically, I wipe it off.

The question is repeated, distorted, distended. It's as

though the entire crowd below roars it as one. The chilling truth is that my sister *is* a Photoshop wiz.

What sort of Machiavellian scheme has Aster planned? And what the hell is her endgame? To trap me in some chaotic maze to make me pay for being the sane one?

NINETEEN

I throw up when I enter my cell.

"What the hell?" mutters the guard who escorted me back. "What did you do to your pillow?"

I smell the air and heave again. And again. The third time, nothing comes out. My stomach is empty, yet the hollow contracts. The guard yells for some assistance. I slink against the cement wall and drop, forcing myself to breathe through my mouth.

"Inmate Redd, if you have a nose bleed during the night, you are asked to take your dirty linens to the laundry room. We're not your maids," Giraffe-neck bellows.

With the back of my hand pressed against my lips, I say, "It's not my blood." I hate the sight of blood. I hate the smell of it. I hate everything about it.

Blood is death.

She splays her hands on her hips. "Whose is it then?"

"I don't know."

"Well, grab your pillow. I grant you special permission to go to the laundry room."

The perspective of touching the dark stain makes the spasms flare up again.

"If you don't care to clean it, then sweet dreams."

I push my palms against the cold concrete floor and rise. Finding a stain-free spot, I pinch the pillow and avoid looking at it as I walk down the hallway. All the prisoners are in their bunks, lazing around and chatting. Their conversations stop as I traipse by. I commit those who are snickering to memory. I'll know to stay away from them. Gill, Chacha, and Translucent-girl don't smile. The really old woman with the turban also doesn't react, but then she's talking to the ceiling, so she's probably oblivious to the revolting joke that's been played on me.

I get another metallic whiff and swallow hard.

When I was eleven, I jerked awake in the middle of the night. Something warm had seeped through my pink cotton nightgown and drenched my sheets. I didn't know about periods, so my first thought was that I was bleeding out. I remember racing to my mother's room in tears and turning on her bedside lamp to show her the blood because I was too frightened to form words. She'd opened her eyes, taken one look at me, and flipped over grumbling, "If you get yourself knocked up, you're out of my house. And turn off the fucking light!"

I pass the last cell and catch Cheyenne smiling. It makes her face resemble a slab of veal loin laced in butcher twine. I don't feel shame anymore, just pure anger, and anger sharpens my senses, and I know, with perfect certainty, that she did it. I slow down when I arrive in front of her. My gaze is drawn to her hands, which rest against her side like little bloated stumps. Something's dangling from them, a half-open book, my book, the story of my ancestors. I match her syrupy smile, and then I swing the pillow into her face. The still-wet blood leaves a satisfying orangey smear on her forehead. She bellows like a wounded cow.

"Inmate Redd!" Giraffe-neck's voice is shrill. "Do you want me to take away your *privileges*?"

"I slipped," I say sweetly. "I'm so, *so* sorry, Cheyenne."

There's great silence at first, and then the dormitory erupts with laughter. The officer grabs my upper arm and drags me all the way to the laundry room where she instructs a young officer—he barely looks a day over eighteen—to pay close attention to me.

I let the water flow over the foreign stain. As the crimson turns to salmon-pink, I feel cleansed, pure again, no longer a martyr, almost a virgin. I rub the fabric together to remove the last of it. Soon, my pillow is white, but my nail beds are red, roughed up by the friction. I place the pillow in the dryer and sink to the floor to watch it spin as though it were a television monitor. It's hypnotic. I find my thoughts straying back to my sister and to her breakdown this afternoon. I wish I could syphon away her pain, but from here, with no means of communication—I'm allowed a phone call but she isn't—it's impossible.

"Did she pass?" I ask the young guard.

"Who?"

I stand up. "My sister. She's competing on the Master-piecers."

"I don't know what that is."

"Really? Where are you from?"

He doesn't pick up on my sarcasm. "Ambia."

I'm not even sure where Ambia is on a map and I don't really care, so I go back to watching my pillow spin. But then I get an idea. "Do you have a phone by any chance?"

"Only for emergencies."

I take a step closer to him. He takes a step back. "Does it have an Internet connection?"

"Don't come any closer or I'll call for b-backup," he stutters, raising his hand to his walkie-talkie.

I stop moving. "Look, the commander gave me permission to watch TV. Because of *this*"—I tip my chin toward the rotating pillow—"I wasn't able to catch the end of the show. Could you type in Masterpiecers and just read out the results?" I add a, "Please, sir," to help my case.

He fumbles for the phone in his uniform pocket. His eyes flick from the screen to me. And then his fingers tap on the digital keyboard.

I wait with bated breath for the announcement. Finally, it comes.

"'J.J. Fails to Score,'" he reads nervously.

A breath escapes from my parted lips like a gush of steam. Ivy really is still in!

He darts his gaze to me. When he's satisfied that I haven't shifted, he looks back down. "'Ivy Not Caught Redd-Handed.'" His voice rings out in the cement laundry block. "'Jackson the Auction King.'"

"Go back," I say. "To the 'Redd-Handed' headline."

He reads out an article about how my sister swore in a press release that she had nothing to do with the doctored photos of former contestant number eight. "While police follow a new lead, Dominic Bacci and Josephine Raynoir have announced their generous offer of letting Kevin Martin enter the competition. Kevin has accepted and will arrive at the Metropolitan Museum tomorrow. The show will take a one-day break and resume on Friday." The guard glances up. "Doctored photos? Police investigation? What sort of show is this?"

The sort that will either make or break my sister.

TWENTY

Ivy

"Everyone to the prep room!" comes a voice from the concealed speaker in my tent. I still haven't located it.

I stick the pillow over my head. If only I could stay buried underneath my comforter for the rest of the evening and for our day off tomorrow. I can't stop thinking about what the reporter implied. I don't *want* to believe him, but a big part of me does.

"Everyone to the prep room!"

This time, I throw the pillow off and peel the covers away. I stop by the bathroom to splash cool water against the nape of my neck and rinse away the sour taste in my mouth. I'm still fully dressed and made up, but my clothes are wrinkled and my mascara is smudged. I carefully swipe the dark smear with my fingertips and head out.

In the hallway, I come face to face with Chase. It's the first time this has happened even though our rooms are across from each other. He clearly looks as surprised as I am from the near collision, but he gets over it quicker than I do. He steps back and tips his head in a gesture meant for me to go ahead of him. I don't want to walk in front of him—not that I believe he's going to stab me in the back—so I pretend to have forgotten something in my room. Behind the taut fabric walls, my heart bangs like thunder. I strain to hear his footsteps crush the soft grass. I count to thirty slowly, then I count back down to zero, and then I cautiously lift the tent flap. The sharp green scent of him lingers, but he's gone.

Dominic, Josephine, and Brook are waiting for us, dressed down from their usual suits and silks. Josephine sports a pair of narrow jeans and a batwing cotton sweater that makes her seem more human; Dominic, a red-checkered shirt that brings out the warm hue of his skin; and Brook, black jeans and a blue shirt.

"So, in light of these strange events, we thought we'd take you out on the town for dinner. And tomorrow"—Dominic grins—"since it's supposed to be in the nineties, Brook has graciously suggested to host you in his penthouse for a pool party. I'll organize transportation and bathing suits for noon, which will give you ample time to sleep in."

"That sounds amazing," Lincoln says, flapping her eyelashes that are so laden with mascara they look like crow wings.

"Also," Dominic continues, "as some of you might already know, we've invited Mister Martin to compete."

"But I thought—" Maxine glances at me and then back at Dominic. "I thought he wasn't *fit* for the show."

"It's come to our attention that *les photos* have been doctored," Josephine explains.

Gazes automatically land on me.

"He will arrive tomorrow," she continues. "Which is why you get a break. *Fantastique, non?*"

I'm wondering what part of it is fantastic, the break or Kevin joining us.

Dominic's lips press into a taut smile. "I'm truly sorry for all this."

"Why couldn't you have offered Kevin a spot on next year's show?" Herrick asks.

"Because there wouldn't have been a 'next year's show.' His lawyers were threatening to have it canceled altogether. You have Josephine to thank for keeping it running." His hand rises to her forearm, but instead of settling there, it continues its upward ascent toward his silver hair. Although it's rigid with gel, he rakes his fingers through it.

Maxine gives a small clap, but since she's the only one, she stops and her cheeks turn crimson.

Dominic gestures to the curtained area. "Your stylists have laid out some outfits in your dressing rooms."

Just as we're all about to head off, J.J. arrives in a pair of baggy jeans that show too much of his yellow boxers. He's rolling a small canvas case.

"Is that your doggy bag for the restaurant?" Herrick's joke is lost on J.J. In truth, it's sort of lost on me too.

"I'm not going to the restaurant." He stops in front of me as he says this; as though it were my fault that he was voted off.

Granted, I was the closest to failing, but I didn't. *He* did. I fold my arms, which doesn't prevent him from doing something totally unexpected. He hugs me. I keep my arms locked from sheer surprise, and because I don't do hugs.

"Good luck, Redd," he says.

And then he moves to Maxine and Lincoln, and repeats the hug-luck combo. He high-fives Chase and attempts to do the same with Herrick, but the latter doesn't lift his hand, so J.J. slings one arm around him and squeezes him.

"Are you sure you don't want to stay for dinner?" Dominic asks.

"Got a new paint job for a school in Harlem. Your show gives good exposure, Mister B." He's bobbing his head or pecking the air—it's hard to tell.

Dominic nods. "Glad you got something out of it. Send us a picture once you're done vandalizing public property."

"Sure thing." J.J. shakes Dominic's hand, and then Brook's. "They're documenting the whole thing for Vanity Fair so you'll definitely get an eyeful of *moi*." He winks at Josephine, who rolls her eyes. "Miss Raynoir. A pleasure."

Instead of shaking her hand, he lifts it to his mouth and gives it a languorous kiss. She surprisingly doesn't slap him, but she does wipe her hand on her jeans the minute he turns around.

"*Bonsoir*, dear friends. May the best one win!" And then his assistant walks him back to freedom.

I must watch the doorway a long time, because Brook clears his throat. "You need to get ready."

"I'm going," I murmur distractedly.

"Always hard to see someone lose," Brook continues.

"Actually, I was thinking the opposite."

Brook lifts one thick eyebrow. He probably thinks I'm cold, but that's not how I meant it. I don't care enough to explain that J.J.'s departure gives me hope, hope for doors opening in spite of losing the competition. I hadn't thought about the exposure. I hadn't thought there was any way into the art world if I didn't win this competition or attend the Master-piecers. For the first time since I arrived, I'm not worried about losing. The treacherous tunnel I'm walking through will lead back into the light whether through a gilded doorway or a pothole in the road.

DINNER'S A BIG PRODUCTION. There are paparazzi lurking outside the museum when the gleaming black minivan emerges from the underground parking lot. Their lenses suck at the car's tinted windows like leeches. It takes nearly running them over to dislodge them. When we pull up in front of an Italian restaurant downtown, there are more of them. They swarm toward the vehicle before we're even parked.

Along with three other broad-backed, suit-clad men, Danny, my driver from the airport, fends them off to create a safe passage for us. He shoots me this strange look, the sort of look Mom would give me when my stitching was sub-par. I wonder if it's because of the press conference today. Even though I'm not a suspect, Aster is, and her actions reflect on me.

The restaurant is a hole-in-the-wall that's been reserved exclusively for us. The other tables have been pushed against the flower-papered walls and covered in overflowing baskets of fruit and dripping wax candles. The effect is lovely and romantic. I must gape around too long because when I move toward our table, the only vacant seat is between the Jackson brothers. "Fun," I mutter under my breath as I slide into the chair. Lincoln is on Brook's other side. She's lassoed him into a conversation about pasta making. And here I thought that the only thing she knew how to cook was Meth.

"So Kevin's coming on the show," Chase says.

At first I think he's talking to Maxine, who's sitting on his other side, but then I realize she's deep in conversation with Dominic.

"Apparently." I grab a breadstick from the basket in front of me and munch on it without looking at him.

He angles his torso toward me. "Why do you dislike me so much?"

I squeeze the breadstick so hard it snaps in two. One end falls right into the hand-painted presentation plate. "Let me see...you implied that I had a hand in Kevin's elimination *and* that I cheated during the riddle hunt. Are those good reasons, because they sound like pretty good ones to me?"

"I admit, I wasn't the friendliest—"

"No shit," I say sarcastically.

"But that's because I know nothing about you."

"So you assume things."

"Yes. Just like you have your own assumptions about me."

I do.

"Today, what you said during the auction, that you made the quilt for a dying friend. Was it true?"

"It wasn't for a friend."

"Who was it for? A boyfriend?"

"I don't want to talk about it."

He leans back in his chair. "This is me trying to get to know you so I can stop assuming things."

"What's the point? Soon one of us will be gone," I say.

Chase's dark eyes keep studying me.

When I can't take his scrutiny anymore, I turn toward Brook. "There was a rip in the seam of my quilt. Was it damaged in transit?"

Brook's thick lashes sweep down over his eyes, which he's trained on the platter of paper-thin cold cuts and salty chunks of Parmesan. "I wouldn't know."

"Who would?" I ask.

He shrugs.

"Didn't you see the tear?" I ask.

He finally looks away from the appetizers. "Doesn't matter, does it? It's no longer yours."

"It matters to me. I don't want the buyer to be disappointed. Could I work on it before it's sent off?"

"It's already been sent."

"What if the buyer returns it?" I ask.

"He won't."

"How can you be sure?"

"Ivy, relax." He lays his hand on my forearm. His fingers are cold. "It was a small hole. No one will see it."

"So you *did* notice it!"

"What did Brook notice?" Josephine asks.

"Nothing," Brook says, removing his hand.

"The rip in my quilt," I say.

"I thought it was intentional," Josephine says, spinning the large diamond ring around her thin finger.

"Why would I intentionally put a hole in my quilt?" I ask.

"Modern art," Maxine says, as the waiters place gold-rimmed plates topped with an assortment of pasta in front of us. "You could shred one. I'm sure it would sell well."

"That's an idea," I say.

I look down at the mounds of pasta on my plate. The raviolis are large and beet-colored; the linguine, green and deliciously fragrant; the gnocchi, ridged and glistening with a melted butter and herb mixture; and the square of lasagna, still bubbling with cheese.

Not only was Aster trying to sabotage me, but she damaged my work. The guilt that has gnawed at me since I made her sign that paper giving me power of attorney over her vanishes. Aster can no longer be left to her own devices. She is lost in the debris of her mind. I'm angry because she's my twin, and I love her more than anything, but I also hate her more than anyone. I crumple the napkin in my lap and set it on the linen tablecloth. Wordlessly, I rise and head to the bathroom before my wet eyes can expel the tears.

Lincoln walks in moments after me. She disappears into one of the stalls and emerges before I have time to escape. Over the sound of running water, she asks, "How did the press conference go?"

"Fine," I say, tossing the embroidered hand towel into the wicker basket below the sink.

"No one really believes you got him disqualified." She turns off the water and dries her hands against her eggplant suede skirt. I'm about to tell her that she shouldn't wet suede when she adds, "You didn't, right?"

"Of course not."

"And your sister?"

"What is it you heard, Lincoln?"

"That she's talented with computers."

"A lot of people are talented with computers," I counter.

She shrugs. "Chill, Ives. I wasn't accusing her of anything." She rests her hands on her flat belly. "I'm stuffed. The food was so delish, wasn't it?"

I nod and brush past her.

When I get back to the table, Josephine's gone and Dominic resembles my iced water. Tiny drops of perspiration drip down the sides of his face.

"What did I miss?" I ask Brook.

"The usual...Dom and Josephine had a disagreement."

"Over what?"

"God only knows. Josephine's been acting strange for a while now. I think she might be pregnant."

"Pregnant?"

"I know, right? Not really the maternal type—"

"Is she married?"

"Engaged."

"I didn't know."

"Not many people know."

"Is he in the art world?"

"No. He's some big shot businessman." He takes a sip of wine. "What about you? Any boyfriend back in Kokomo?"

"No."

"That's surprising," he says with a brazen smile.

Heat smears my cheeks. I grab my glass of water and take a gulp that goes down the wrong hole when Brook's hand grazes my thigh. I cross my legs to shift it off because Chase is staring. I'm the source of enough gossip already.

No need to add fuel to the fire my sister has kindled.

TWENTY-ONE

I scoop up oatmeal and let it plop back down unceremoniously into my plastic bowl. It's lumpier than usual, and settles in clumps on the filmy surface.

"You look like you didn't sleep," Gill says. Her gaze vacillates between my porridge and my face.

"I have to go do meditation. Want to come with me?"

"To meditate?"

"Yes."

"I don't know how to meditate," she says.

"I don't either, but the shrink thinks it can help me. I'm bored just thinking about it."

"Well, now *that* really makes me want to go."

I smile, and then catch sight of a black mullet. "Hey, Cheyenne," I say sweetly.

She wobbles to a dead stop.

"Got something for you." I chuck a tampon at her. Over dinner, I asked Chacha for a box of them instead of chocolate. "It's more absorbent than a pillow." I make sure my voice carries even though the cafeteria is totally quiet.

Cheyenne blushes so hard that all three hundred pounds of her turns cherry red.

Gill's face splits into a wide grin, as do many others. The only ones not partaking in the contagious glee are Cheyenne—for obvious reasons—and the ladies sitting at her table. They're all firing me vile looks, which will surely be accompanied by some form of retaliation.

"So, meditation?" I ask Gill again as though Cheyenne had never walked by and I hadn't just embarrassed the shit out of her.

"Can't believe you just did that. You have some serious balls, Aster."

I can't believe it either. "I met the warden yesterday."

Gill bites her lower lip with her buckteeth. "What did you think of him?"

"Seems nice enough." I play around with my porridge again. "He knows my sister."

"He does? How?"

"She paid him a visit when I was booked. Asked him to be nice to me."

"That's chill of her."

I nod, inspecting my nails.

"I have some cream in my room. It's real hydrating." She tips her chin toward my hands. "If you want some."

"Um...sure."

"Do you garden?"

"Garden?"

"You know, plant flowers and shit."

"No. Why?"

"Because when you got here, your nails were all torn and dirty. My aunt—she raised me—well, her nails were always ripped from growing vegetables outside our motor home."

I drop the spoon. The rounded part sticks to the porridge for a second before toppling off the side of the bowl and clattering onto the steel tabletop. "I'm just not good at taking care of my nails."

"I'd be glad to take care of them, Aster," Gill says. "If you'll let me."

I blink.

"Sorry to interrupt your moment, Inmates, but you got a visitor, Redd," the potbellied guard says.

One of Gill's tawny eyebrow lifts.

"I thought I needed to go meditate?" I tell him.

"After," he says.

"Gill will join me for the meditation."

"Does she have permission?"

"Miss Pierce suggested creating a meditation circle. Hard to create a circle with only two people. Unless you plan on joining, sir?" *Where is this cockiness coming from? The despair of lockup?*

His face colors a little. Only his scar stays white. "Get your skinny ass off the bench, Inmate. I don't like to wait."

I shoot up. "See you later, Gill."

A smile floats across her face. I wonder if giving her hope is wise. She's sort of a wacko.

Driscoll leads me to an area I haven't been to yet. There are four identical rooms with glass walls on the hallway side, and brushed cement everywhere else. Each contains one table with two iron chairs.

When I spot Josh, I swivel toward the sergeant. "I don't want to see him."

He just grunts, beeps the door open, and shoves me through. "You got fifteen minutes, Officer Cooper, then I need to take her to her shrink appointment."

Josh looks up. His expression is so grave that my mind somersaults to my twin.

The door slams shut behind me and I jump. "Wh-what's going on? Is it Ivy?"

"Sit down."

Legs trembling, I take a seat across from him.

"Aster, did you doctor the photos of Kevin Martin?"

"Who?"

"The contestant who was eliminated. Did you do it?"

"No. Why?"

"Because the media is claiming you might be behind the fake pictures."

"They're fake?"

"Are you playing dumb?"

"No!"

"Isn't Photoshopping part of your job at the ad agency?"

I snort. "Yes, but I didn't do it."

"You promise?"

"Yes! Anything else you came to accuse me of?"

He rubs his neck, or more precisely a spot that's purple and swollen.

"Is that a hickey?" I exclaim.

"What?"

"On your neck."

"Oh that...I cut myself shaving." His jaw reddens so quickly that I know he's lying.

"Are you seeing someone?"

He inhales deeply. "Do you really want to know?"

I bite my lip because it's started to wobble. "Since when?"

"Let's not talk about this—"

"Since when?"

"A month."

"Is it serious?"

"Aster," he whispers.

"Well, is it?" My voice is surprisingly steady.

"I don't know."

"Do I know her?"

He rubs the hickey again, and then he nods.

"Who is it?"

"Heidi."

"The floozy from Dairy Queen?"

"Don't call her that."

"You're the one who told me she slept around. She's going to give you HIV."

He widens his eyes. "Goddammit, Aster! You and I are no longer together."

I recoil as though he's slapped me. And then I start bobbing in my chair, forward and backward, like a reed caught in a tempest. I need Ivy. I want her to come home. She's the only one who gives a shit about me.

TWENTY-TWO

Ivy

I wake up sweating. Without windows or a watch, I have no idea what time it is. For a second, I think it's the middle of the night, but I hear noise—chatter—so I assume it's not. I throw the covers off my legs and head toward the shower. I've had the nightmare again—the one where my sister comes at me with a kitchen knife while I'm sleeping, but it's not my sister, it's my reflection, and I stab a mirror. It shatters, but then it mends back together.

Trembling, I twist my damp hair up into a bun and step into the warm spray. I let the water tumble over my forehead and drip into my open eyes, hoping it will blur the dream and wipe my mind. It doesn't, so I get out and don the khaki shorts and white tank I brought with me, then head for breakfast where they're serving pancakes and waffles topped with real maple syrup, not the imitation corn syrup that's dyed brown. It's a true feast. As I ask for a second serving, Herrick's assistant walks in and hands each one of us a fabric bag with the Masterpiecers' logo. Inside, I find a beaded turquoise bikini, a pair of silver sunglasses, and a bottle of sunscreen.

While Lincoln, Herrick, and Maxine return to their rooms

to change, Chase and I remain in the living room.

"Excited to go home?" I ask.

"Home?"

"Don't you live with your brother?"

He looks like the orange juice he's chugging has turned sour. "Hell no. Whatever gave you that idea?"

"I don't know. I just assumed. Do you live with your parents?"

"At twenty-one, that would be a little sad, don't you think?"

I bristle. "*I* still live at home."

"By choice?"

I say, "Yes," even though it's not a choice. I wouldn't be able to afford paying my own rent. "Mom's not there anymore and Dad...well, he doesn't live there either."

"Where is he?"

"I don't know. He left before we were born. I don't think he ever knew Mom was pregnant."

"So you've never met him?"

I shake my head.

"And you're okay with that?"

"How could I not be okay with it? I don't know his last name. How could I find him?"

"Your mom never told you his full name? Was it a one-night stand?"

"Of course not. They dated a few months, but he was always in and out of town because of his job."

"What did he do?"

"Sold fabric. It took him all over the world." Mom told me his favorite country was India. He regaled her with stories of textile factories in which women would plunge silks and linens in vats of dye, then hand bead intricate motifs along the seams. He promised to take her there someday, but that day never dawned. "So, where *do* you live?"

"I have an apartment by Washington Square Park. Close to NYU. Still have a year left, unless I get into the Master-piecers."

"I thought you were so sure you were going to win."

"Only idiots don't doubt themselves. But I'm still planning on crushing you, and the others." There's a glimmer in his brown eyes. In some other life, he must've been a bloodthirsty revolutionary. I can just picture him running across a field, armed with a rifle and a ferocious will to kill. "Shouldn't you go get changed?"

"I'm not planning on swimming."

"Why not?"

"Because."

"Because what?"

"I just don't feel like it, okay?" I stab the last piece of waffle and stuff it inside my mouth just as Maxine walks back in, telling us just how excited she is to get out of the museum. And then the rest of the group follows, and an assistant walks us down to the underground parking lot.

Except for the sleek black minivan, the garage is deserted. Unlike Fifth Avenue. Clouds of people and clusters of news vans swarm the street. The second our ride emerges, the paparazzi start shooting. Considering the windows are tinted, I doubt their pictures will be worth anything, but they click away nonetheless. Some even trail us all the way downtown, to what Maxine tells me is the Meatpacking District. It seems like we've left the city. The streets aren't grid-like anymore. Instead, they jut out in all directions, and the buildings are squatter and wider, like warehouses.

Brook's building is entirely covered with black glass that shimmers in the light of the midday sun. I count seven stories, which is not tall for New York, but high enough that the paparazzi won't be able to hound us. I would hope.

When we get up to the penthouse, Brook gives us a tour.

His gigantic bachelor pad is filled with priceless art and sharp-edged furniture in muted colors of gray and beige. Even the satin and velvet throw pillows are sleek and puffed up, resembling something Jeff Koons would've crafted out of stainless steel.

"Can I use your bedroom to change?" I ask Brook after the others file out on the deck.

"You didn't put on your bathing suit back at the museum?"

"I didn't have time," I say.

"I would rather—You know what, go ahead." He tips his head toward his bedroom. "You can even leave your stuff in there."

"Thanks," I say, clutching my little fabric bag as I walk quickly down the hallway. Once inside, I lock the door and race to his nightstand where I spotted an electronic tablet earlier.

I press on the screen that flares to life without prompting me for a code. With shaky fingers, I pull up an Internet page, log in to my account, and write an email.

JOSH—

The quilt is here...was here. It's the one I auctioned off. There was a rip in it. I think Aster did it. Can you find out why?

AFTER PRESSING SEND, I start researching my sister's case. A knock resounds on the door, making me jump.

"Everything okay?"

"Y-yes," I say. "Almost ready."

Fingers trembling, I clear the browser history, return the tablet to the nightstand, throw off my clothes, and wriggle into my bathing suit. When I open the door, I come nose-to-chest with Brook.

"That's a nice color on you," he says.

I can smell his breath, minty and cool on the tip of my nose. "Thanks."

He peers behind me. For a second, I wonder if I turned off the tablet. Or maybe I put it in the wrong spot.

My heart thumps so loudly that I'm afraid it'll give me away. I try to sidestep him, but he claps his hands on my upper arms. "I'm going back to the museum to greet Kevin." His eyes are on me again. "Save me a swim, okay?"

"Brook? Your phone keeps—" Chase's words die off when he turns the corner and spots us.

I bounce away from Brook and mumble something about seeing them outside. I try to walk at a normal speed even though I'm tempted to run. Not so much from Brook, but from Chase. I know he's not a mind reader—I'm well aware they don't exist, unlike Mom who never took a decision without consulting the bald tarot card reader on Buckeye—but still, I worry he'll see the guilt rifling through me. I broke a show rule. I could be eliminated if anyone found out I established communication with the outside world.

Keeping my face as blank as possible, I walk past Jeb whose camera is poised in my direction, past the sliding glass doors, past Herrick and Maxine who are floating on inflatable rafts while Lincoln does laps, and straight toward the over-stuffed, orange lounge chairs.

"You should come in. The water's delicious," Maxine says, readjusting the floppy brim of her hat.

"Maybe later," I lie. I'm not going in the pool. I can't.

I close my eyes against the bright heat and try to relax, but my muscles are tense and my mind is buzzing with the email I wrote Josh. I hope he replies before we're carted back to the museum because I need answers.

TWENTY-THREE

"Why did you buy it?" I ask Troy.

"Have you been following me?"

"Why did you buy it?" I repeat, this time with more authority.

Troy places his hand on my half-open car window. A large gold pinkie ring reflects the orange Vacancy sign overhead. His nails are buffed and trimmed, and his fingers are long and golden. Feminine hands. That's what they strike me as. Shouldn't a mobster have dried blood underneath his nails and bruises on his knuckles? "As a pretty investment."

"Redecorating your underground office, are you?"

He combs his fingers through his greasy, chin-length black hair. "My underground office?"

"Isn't that where the mafia conducts their business?"

"The mafia?"

"Don't play dumb. I know who you are...I know what you do."

"Really? And who am I then?"

"Troy Mann. A wanted criminal."

He straightens up, but keeps his hand on the window. "Where would you get that sort of idea?"

"I read your file. You're wanted for money laundering and arms trafficking."

His pupils pulse against the yellowish iris. "I have no clue what you're talking about," he says, but I can tell he does.

"I'm not sure why you bought the quilt, but you leave my sister out of this."

"Your sister? I don't even know your sister."

"You bought the quilt from her."

Slow...that's what he is, because he repeats, "Your sister?"

"Just give me the quilt and I'll pretend we never met."

Thick fumes from my eighties Honda drift through my open window and fill the car.

His lips lift in a wide smile. "Are you trying to con me, Ivy? Because that's not a wise idea."

"I'm not Ivy."

"Sure. And I'm part robot." He chuckles and taps on the window. "Now get out of here."

"I'm not leaving without the quilt."

"I'm starting to lose patience. You don't want me to lose patience, Ivy."

"My name's Aster."

His hand is back on the windowsill. He's squeezing it so hard that his knuckles have turned white. "Go...now," he says, his voice low and threatening.

"Not without the quilt."

As a deep growl leaks out of his mouth, his hand shoots inside the car and comes at my throat like a claw, cutting off my air supply. I eye the lever to bring up the window, but it'll take too long to wind up. Keeping my gaze on his, my fingers crawl over to the stick shift. Holding down the clutch, I back up. It rips his fingers from my throat. And then I spin the wheel and ram into him. His body hits the hood and his head smashes against the windshield, which cracks from the impact. For a second, his cheek stays glued to the glass, but then the thick blood that's oozing out of his ear and forehead makes him slide off and thump to the ground.

I yelp, my gaze darting over the two floors of motel rooms. There's no movement and no light.

"Nobody saw you, Aster," I whisper to myself. "Nobody." Yet my entire body rumbles like the Honda's crap engine. "Besides, you didn't hit him that hard. You just stunned him. That's all. He's just stunned." I grip the window's lever and wind it up, but my palm is so slick that my hand skids off three times. I abandon the third time.

I ought to drive away, but I need the quilt, so I wait two minutes, five, ten. Still Troy doesn't stand. The keys to his room will be in that messenger bag he was carrying. Breathing hard, I open my door, take my seatbelt off, and get out. His outstretched hand is the first thing I spot. I watch his slender fingers, expecting them to curl, but they remain flat against the asphalt. I creep closer, and closer, and closer until I can see all of him, as flat and lifeless as his hand. Unconscious, not lifeless, I correct myself.

The bag rests a few feet away from him. I hop over his outstretched arm and bend to grab it, but he grabs me first, squeezing my ankle and twisting it with his dainty hand. I catch myself on the dented hood and kick as hard as I can, just managing to dislodge his fingers. And then I run, faster than I've ever run before, and spring into the car. Without bothering to close my door, I put the car in drive. It lurches forward, then up, then down. My ears buzz like after that awful rave Ivy dragged me to a few months back.

"I killed a criminal," I reassure myself. "A bad guy. A very bad guy. Very very bad."

I peer at the bag on the passenger seat, expecting some bomb to detonate, but it isn't rigged. But what about a tracking device? Maybe there's one inside. I jam my foot on the brake pedal and the edge of the steering wheel bites into my abdomen.

With shaky fingers, I pluck the bag off the seat and set it on my lap, and then I flip it open. Inside, there's a bulky package. I take it out to search the rest of it for keys, but my fingers don't come in contact with metal...they don't come in contact with anything. No keycard, no phone, no wallet. I turn it over and shake it, but still nothing falls out.

The key must have been on him. My forehead throbs. I rub it, trying to think. If I don't go back and search his body, then his death will have been for nothing. But if I go back, and someone sees me—No, I can't go back. I spot a trashcan. I open the car door and fling the bag into the bin. I'm about to do the same with the package, but curiosity gets the better of me and I tear it open. I blink because what I see can't be real...what I see is what my mind wants to see.

Ivy's quilt.

I touch it. It feels real. I pull it out and unfold it. Gold and satin glimmers, and this fabric covered in tiny mirrored-beads speckles the drab gray interior of the Honda with tinsels. I gather it in my arms and hug it to me as though it were my own sister. She's going to be so thankful, so so thankful.

Something crunches underneath my fingers. I frown and pull the quilt back. I press down on the spot and again it crackles. I prod other parts of the quilt, but there is no noise. I go back to the spot and turn on the car light to inspect it. Something catches my eye along the seam—on about three inches, the thread is of a different color. I tug on it with my sharp pinky nail until it breaks, then carefully, I pull apart the two sides of the quilt and extricate a folded piece of wax paper.

Why in the world would Ivy place a sheet of—I don't finish my thought when I glimpse what's inside. I fold it up and stuff it back in. And then I just breathe. The empty street beyond goes in and out of focus.

I cough from sucking in too much air. I pick up the torn package and read the mailing address. It's going to New York.

"New York?"

"Yes," *I say, looking at the passenger seat. It's empty. I'm talking to myself. I rub my corded neck, trying to ease my nerves.*

Headlights appear from behind, blinding and bright. I yank out the wax paper and stick it in my bra just in case it's the cops, but the car is a black pickup. It sidles in next to mine.

The automated window slides down. "Having car trouble, miss?"

"Uh...no. Everything's fine."

"Redd?"

I start. I'm about to ask him how he knows my last name when he stares at my windshield, at the bloodied crack. He must be referring to the blood.

"Your ride looks pretty banged up." He's wearing a green cap with a pine tree and a deer on it.

"I hit a deer."

"Not many of those in Kokomo."

"I hit it back in Vermont."

He eyes me, then the windshield. "I got a guy who could fix that for you cheap."

"I was going to get rid of the car. It stalls half the time."

"He sells some too."

"I'm good. Thanks. My dad's waiting up for me. I should get home."

"I suppose you should."

I grip the stick shift. "You mind backing up a little?" I ask.

"You reported the deer to the police?"

My fingers tighten around the knob. "Yeah. Can you please move?"

He doesn't. Cold sweat gathers on the nape of my neck, gluing my springy curls to my skin. A hand lifts them, squeezes my shoulder blades. I jump and shiver. It's just my imagination. The guy's still in his truck, still next to me.

"What's up with the blanket?"

"My heater's broken," I lie.

"It's August."

"Well, I'm cold."

I'm about to push my car up onto the sidewalk to maneuver out of the tight spot when he taps the brim of his cap like an army salute and pulls his truck back. A swirly tattoo of barbed wire decorates his entire forearm.

The Honda springs into action so fast, it sputters and stalls. I glance into my rearview mirror. The pickup is still behind me. Praying that the guy won't follow me, I step on the clutch, then on the gas, and then I drive in the wrong direction until I'm sure I've lost him.

Even though my attention is on the dark road, my mind is on the quilt and the diamonds. If I keep the quilt here and the police find it, Ivy will get in trouble. I think of throwing it out, but I can't do that to my sister, to her beautiful work. Without braking, I grab the torn package and stuff the quilt back inside. I need something to close it. The bakery box! Bending my arm at a strange angle, I seize it from the backseat and peel the long piece of scotch tape used to keep it shut. I swerve in next to a mailbox, come to an abrupt halt, and stick the piece of tape on the tear. It doesn't quite cover it all, but enough so that the content doesn't fall out. And if it does, then so be it.

"Better lost than found," I murmur.

"Is she confessing?"

"I don't know."

I snap my lids up and blink from the harsh lighting. Large tawny eyes stare down at me. Gill's. I sit up quickly.

"What was in the package?" Driscoll is standing next to Gill.

"Wh-what?" I stutter.

"You were talking in your sleep," Gill says.

I dig the heels of my palm into my eyes, but stop when she combs a piece of hair behind my ear.

Driscoll folds his arms together and leans against my cell's open gate. "What package were you talking about?"

"Huh?"

"Can't you see she's not even awake yet?" Gill exclaims.

"She looks pretty awake to me."

Driscoll's walkie-talkie buzzes. "Sergeant, you're needed in the cafeteria."

He grumbles that he'll be right there. "Oh...Robyn wants you to go meditate again, Redd. You can go during yard time since you're no longer allowed out."

"I'm not?"

"Nope. Too many reporters out back."

"Reporters?"

"Yeah. You're real notorious."

I blanch.

"Miss Pierce said I could come back with her."

"You got yard time, Swanson."

"I think you can find it in your heart"—she taps her pelvic bone—"to allow me a free pass."

Driscoll's face turns beet red; only the diagonal piece of pink skin, on which no brow hair will ever grow back, remains pale. "Fine," he grumbles.

"What was that about?" I ask her once he's gone.

"I waxed him. Down there," she says with a smirk.

I gag.

"Yeah. Gross. I know." She plops down on my bed. "Bad dream?"

I nod even though it wasn't a dream. It was a memory.

TWENTY-FOUR

Ivy

"You're going to get a sunburn," Chase tells me.

My eyes are closed but I know his voice by heart now. "Why do you care?" I ask, looking up at him. He hovers over me, casting a shadow over the top half of my body.

"I don't. Just thought I'd mention it," he says, sitting on the fluffy orange cushions of the lounge chair next to mine.

"Thanks for your concern."

While he settles back, cradling his head on his bent arms, I peek around the deck.

"Where's the camera crew?" I ask.

"On their lunch break. I think they're waiting for Brook to return with Kevin. Stir up some drama."

I eye him, wondering if he thinks I'm going to make a scene, because I'm not. He stares right back. Even through his dark aviators, I can tell that's what he believes.

"Talking about drama, what's up between you and your brother?" I ask.

Chase's eyebrows, which look more copper than brown, draw together in a frown. "We don't get along."

"Why not?"

He flicks his gaze back up to the sky. "You get along with your sister?"

"Most of the time. But we're very different."

"I read somewhere you were Miss Popular in high school, but not her."

"That's because she never tried to make friends."

"Maybe she didn't want to compete with you."

"Huh?"

"It's hard to have an all-star sibling."

"Why would you compare yourself to your sibling?"

"You don't; the world does."

"Is that how you feel about Brook?"

His biceps tighten. I hit a nerve.

I turn over onto my side to face him. "If you feel like that, why didn't you choose another line of work?"

"Art is my passion. Life's too short to do something you're not passionate about." After a beat, he adds, "Could *you* see yourself doing something else?"

I look at the pool, at Herrick and Lincoln splashing a giggling Maxine. "I'd hope to be able to do only that."

"You sold your quilt well."

"No, I didn't."

He frowns—he probably thinks I'm conceited. "I bet your next piece will go for three times as much. You have a name now."

"That's associated with murder. Super name," I mutter.

Chase reaches over and touches my arm, which makes my breath hitch. "Ivy, you're not the one who killed a man."

I stare at my skin, so he pulls his hand back. "I know that." The spot he touched feels a few degrees warmer than the rest of my body. I lift my eyes back to his face. "What's your girl-friend up to this week?" I ask, to change the subject. And also, because I am slightly curious about the blonde who posed with him in that People Magazine shoot.

"Don't know and don't care."

"Really? I thought—I thought you were practically engaged."

"The journalist wrote that to sell more copies."

"Weren't you dating since you were toddlers?"

"Not toddlers, but yeah, we were together a long time."

"What happened?"

Chase's jaw tightens. "Brook happened."

"What do you mean?"

"He screwed my ex." I must look horrified because he snorts. "Lost some of his appeal now?"

"I'm not interested in him."

"That's not what it looked like in the hallway, or at the restaurant for that matter."

"*He* came on to me. Besides, you were so pleasant to talk with last night."

He smiles, but there are the layers of hurt behind that smile. "I was trying to be. I think I'm going to jump in. You're sure you don't want to join me?"

"Yeah. I'm sure."

After he gets up, he waits as though hoping I'll change my mind.

"I think I'll take a nap," I say. "I slept badly last night."

"You better get out of the sun then."

"I will."

Just as he leaps into the pool, I move to a shaded part of the terrace where the crew has set up a drink stand and some finger food. I pour myself a glass of icy lemonade and sit in a padded armchair with my legs curled underneath me. As I sip the chilled drink, I watch the city skyline. It's all at once mesmerizing and boring. So much so that, between the view and the lounge music playing on the deck, my lids eventually droop close.

I wake up to Chase nudging my shoulder. I uncoil my legs

that prickle, and wipe the sleep out of my eyes. "How long have I been out?"

"About an hour. We have to get inside," he says, tipping his chin toward the building next to us.

A guy with a massive camera is standing on the roof, clinging to the ledge to snap pictures of us.

"He's going to fall off!" I say.

"Jeb phoned the police," he says, his gaze running over my legs. "They'll get him down." He extends his hand. "Come on." I must debate to take it for too long, because he pulls it back and walks away.

I rise and head inside. Maxine, Lincoln, and Herrick are all sitting on the couch, chatting about how persistent the paparazzi are and how they can't believe the police are getting involved. As I'm about to sit next to Chase, the front door opens. It's Brook and Kevin.

Kevin who still thinks I got him eliminated. Kevin who hates my guts. Kevin who was in the army.

Kevin's eyes lock on mine, and I drop into the seat, hitting Chase's thigh on my way down. When I stare back up, the sergeant is watching me. Palms moist, ears zinging, I peel myself away from Chase.

Kevin's flip-flops flap against the stone floor as he cuts across the room toward Maxine. Trailed by one of the cameramen, he introduces himself and shakes her hand, then Lincoln's and Herrick's and Chase's. He doesn't shake mine. Probably because he thinks Aster was involved in getting him eliminated. And maybe he's right. Maybe she did doctor those photos. But just maybe, it wasn't to sabotage him. Maybe it was to sabotage me.

S itting on the floor of the shrink's office, I try to relax, but the memory is still raw.

"Aster, you're shaking," Robyn says. "You want a blanket?"

I nod. Gill is watching me. She's always watching me. Everyone's always watching me.

Robyn drapes a polar fleece throw over my shoulders, then takes a seat on the floor next to me. "Let's link hands," she says as she shuts her eyes and starts humming.

Gill grins.

"I want to hear you hum, girls," Robyn says, eyes still closed. "Like yesterday."

So I do, but not Gill. She's smiling too much to hum. I nearly don't see her crooked teeth anymore. Ivy and I both inherited our mother's straight teeth. It's not much of a legacy, but at least she passed on something valuable. We would have been a hell of a lot less thankful for the bump on her nose or her freckled Irish skin.

For some reason, thinking about my mother makes me think of when I was pregnant. My mind flutters to my flat stomach, which is more concave than flat now. I remember feeling the baby move, how it had filled me with purpose. I wouldn't have had much to offer, but the pregnancy proved I wasn't as messed up or weak as Ivy, my mother, and Josh all thought.

Anyway, considering all that's happened, I realize that my loss was a blessing. I wouldn't have wanted to be pregnant in jail. I do want a child someday, though. Not now. Not in the next five years. But one day. I want to love a being like I was never loved. I want to preserve that being's innocence like I was never allowed to preserve mine.

My heart is so deeply lacerated that it will never beat like a normal heart, yet it beats. This is why I don't want to keep poisoning it with medication and toxins. As I hum, as time passes, my chest vibrates and a warm current flows through my veins.

"Now open your eyes and savor the sensations in your body," Robyn says.

My lids don't snap up. They lift gradually, like motorized garage doors.

"Let's take a moment to thank our mind for the respite it has offered our body."

I don't thank my mind. There are limits I will not cross and talking to oneself is one of them. Robyn slips her hand out of mine, but not Gill. I have to release hers. She smiles at me so luminously that I become uncomfortable. I don't mind the fact that she has a crush on me. I don't even mind her company. But her touch, her attention, her intent...it's overwhelming.

"How do you feel?" Robyn asks.

"Swell," Gill says, all toothy and bright-eyed.

"And you, Aster?"

"Fine."

"Just fine?"

"It was good," I say, "for me. For my head." I tap my temple to convince her I got the point of the exercise.

She looks pleased. "Glad to hear that."

We start toward the door, but Robyn calls me back.

"Save me a seat at lunch, okay?" I tell Gill.

She nods happily, her red dreadlocks frolicking against her gray jumpsuit.

After the door closes, Robyn states the obvious, "You made a friend."

"You seem surprised."

She avoids responding. "It's healthy to have friends."

"Even if those friends are murderers?" I say, thinking of Gill's ex. Another reason I should discourage her interest in me.

"'Every saint has a past and every sinner has a future.'"

I'm astounded a prison shrink would think so quixotically. "What was it you wanted to talk to me about?"

"When he dropped you off, Sergeant Driscoll mentioned you had a vivid dream."

"Yeah. So?"

She narrows her eyes. "You want to discuss it?"

"No."

"Was it about the hit and run?"

"Maybe."

"Have you been having a lot of dreams about it?"

"Yes."

"I know something that could help. There's this new drug the FDA just approved."

I shake my head. "Drugs can make me sterile."

"Are you thinking about having children?"

"Doesn't every woman think about that?"

"You're only nineteen."

"I know, but as you said, everyone has a future."

"Do you consider yourself a sinner?"

I frown. "No."

She studies my face in silence for a bit, then walks over to her desk, grabs a pamphlet, and returns to me, brandishing it. There's a white-haired woman on the front who's smiling so widely I can see the gold fillings in her molars. "Check it out okay?"

I grumble a *yes* and shove the glossy foldout into my pocket. "Is that all?"

"I don't know. Is it?"

"Yes."

"Then you are free to leave."

If only she meant this hellhole.

JOSH RETURNS THE FOLLOWING MORNING. And not to see how I'm doing. He's back because he has questions. "Why did you send your sister's quilt to the show?" He's leaning his forearms on the metal desk of the visitation room, hands firmly clasped together. His skin is brown, but there's a thin white line visible beneath the hem of his short-sleeved police shirt.

"I didn't send it to the Masterpiecers. I—"

"You did."

"Let me finish." I shoot my gaze up to his, trying to ignore the hickey. "I left it in the package I found it in. It was already stamped and addressed."

"To the Masterpiecers?"

"To some place in New York. I didn't make the connection until I saw it on the show."

"You swear you're not making this up?" Josh asks.

"On Ivy's life."

"Why would a mobster send a quilt to the show?" Suddenly his green eyes go wide. "Ivy mentioned a tear. He was using it as a vessel!"

"You spoke to her?"

"Got an email yesterday."

I look up at the black, dome-shaped camera over the table. "Are we being recorded?"

"No. I asked them not to. Shit, Aster... Troy Mann was using it to transport something! If there was tear, then the person who received it must've taken it out. And if it's someone from the show—Shit," he adds in a low voice.

I glimpse a red dot on the black dome, but it blinks off as quickly as it appeared. I keep looking at it, just in case it returns. "I think we're being watched," I whisper.

Josh glances up. "We're not. I promise."

"I don't believe your promises anymore."

Silence hangs between us, as thick as the Indiana snowstorm that blew the night I lost the baby...the night Josh and Ivy found me curled up on a bench underneath a casing of snow. My lips were purple, or so they told me.

"What could've been inside that quilt?" Josh muses.

"Diamonds."

"Diamonds?" He's so stunned his voice squeaks. "How— You took them out?"

"Do you think Ivy was in on it?" I ask suddenly.

"Huh?"

"Isn't it a big coincidence that both she and her quilt were headed to the Masterpiecers? Do you think that's how she got on the show?"

He shakes his head.

"It would explain how she paid Mom's bills."

"What? Are you insane?" he snaps.

I bristle. "You have a better explanation as to where she found the money?"

"Yes. I do actually. She took out a loan on the apartment."

"She couldn't have. I didn't sign any paper. Unless she forged my signature..." I stare away from the camera and straight into Josh's face that has paled a little. "She forged my signature?"

"No."

"Then how—"

"Your mother put the deed in Ivy's name."

"In both our names."

He shakes his head. "Just in Ivy's."

"But Ivy told me—"

"She was trying to protect you."

My eyesight goes blurry. "Mom disowned me?"

He nods. "I'm sorry, Aster. You weren't supposed to find out."

"Of course not," I snap. "*Keep everything from Aster since she's too unstable.* I should have a T-shirt printed with that."

"That's not why we kept it from you."

"Whatever."

"Ivy didn't want to hurt you."

"I said, whatever." My tone is so shrill that Josh shifts in his seat.

"I should warn Ivy about the diamonds."

I think of the porcelain box with the gift I left her—the diamond that escaped the wax paper and landed in my bra. It had plopped on my bathroom tiles after I'd finished burying the others underneath the buttonbush shrub by our front door. "Oh...she's going to find out soon enough."

"Why? Did you leave them in the quilt?" he asks.

"Yes."

"Shit." The chair legs scrape against the cement floor as Josh pushes back from the table. "Why would you do that? How the fuck am I supposed to find them now?"

I lounge back and cross my arms. "Use your super badge power."

"This isn't a joke, Aster."

"Then you should really get going," I say.

He stands and heads toward the door. Before leaving, he glances back. I don't break. I don't tell him the truth because he doesn't deserve it, and neither does my sister. They're both liars.

Driscoll drags open the door of the cement box to let Josh out, and then holds it for me. "I don't got all day, Redd," he says, so I head out too.

My rubber soles flap over the linoleum floor like soggy fish tails.

In the dayroom, I spot Gill on one of the couches. She pats the spot next to her, and I drop down into it. Her hand crawls to mine. "Your skin's freezing."

I pull my fingers out of hers, pretending that my intention was to comb through my frizzy hair. I get a few inches off my scalp when a rope of knots hinders me. Since Gill's lips are still turned down, I pick up her hand and squeeze it. A crooked smile lights up the freckles on her face.

The show starts and I snap my attention to the TV screen. Dominic stands on top of a pyramid of trash. At least, that's what it looks like at first. He explains it's components of today's test. Each contestant will have to create a collection using ten pieces from the mound below him. And then he proceeds to explain that a collection isn't just a bunch of objects displayed next to each other, but a carefully thought-out continuum of pieces that are linked together by minute details.

He begins a countdown. The camera slides over the six contestants' faces. Kevin, whose bushy eyebrows are slanted over his high forehead, cracks his thick neck. Herrick, who's hooked the rucksack they've given each contestant on his forearm, is rubbing his hands together as though he's about to dive in. Chase looks calm whereas Maxine seems spooked by the mess. Lincoln scans the pile, eyes pinched in concentration.

And then I see Ivy whose skin glows as though she's gotten a suntan.

The sound of a whistle rings out. The contestants fly off toward the pile. Some scale it, others circle it, sifting through the mess like a bunch of homeless people. Ivy comes up with a strand of pearls. She chucks them into her bag and keeps tilling the mess. Chase grabs a plastic sword. The commentators are going crazy keeping track of everyone's findings.

When the camera swings back to my sister, she's holding a bouquet of paper roses. She looks at it a second, but then pitches it back into the pile. The roses land a foot away from Maxine who grabs them like an eager bridesmaid. My sister lunges for something, as does Chase. The same thing: a gun.

One of the commentators chuckles. "A gun! Shouldn't they be fighting over that paper bouquet?" There's something about the way he says this that makes my ears prick up. What does he mean? Did something happen between Chase and Ivy?

Slowly, Chase relinquishes the weapon. A flicker of hesitation crosses Ivy's clear blue eyes, but it zips off her face as quickly as it appeared, and she shoves the pistol into her bag. As she turns away from him, her light green dress billows around her knees like an ocean wave. The camera shifts to Herrick who's collecting nails and wooden boards. He's even found a chalice-like cup. Lincoln's stockpiling tin cans and glass jars, and flattened cardboard. I can imagine her narrative: 'Containers Through the Ages,' or something of the sort. Kevin's bag bulges with large objects. He's found an old rusty pipe, which I wouldn't have touched with rubber gloves. He stuffs it into his rucksack. When the camera finally moves back to Ivy, she's studying a fur bunny attached to a magician hat. She punches the bunny and it vanishes inside. She keeps it. The pile of crap is dwindling.

Ivy stares down at her feet, bends, and rises again

clutching a broken umbrella. It goes into the bag, along with a brass trumpet. Then she runs toward an old liquor bottle tipped on its side on the outskirts of the thinning pile. Lincoln's hand is already arcing toward it, so Ivy dives to get it. Stunned, Lincoln quickens her gesture, but she's not quick enough. The bottle vanishes in the depths of my sister's bag.

"I was expecting a catfight," one of the commentators says, his deep voice rattling with excitement.

"No, you were *hoping* for one," a feminine voice answers.

The man chuckles as Ivy whirls away from a steaming Lincoln. I don't know how many items she still needs, but her bag looks like it's about to burst. She races toward one of the last three items. Only Chase, Lincoln, and Ivy are left scouring the floor. The others are all off to their mini galleries to begin arranging their loot. The camera returns to the center of the room, where my sister's unrolling a scroll. When her face lights up with a smile, and her feet carry her away to her own white box, a giddy breath puffs out of my mouth.

"Someone's excited," Gill says.

I think she's talking about Ivy, but she's watching our linked hands. I'm crushing her fingers. I let go.

"I don't mind," she says.

But *I* do, because there are other people around, and they're gawking and whispering things. I stand up and stretch. My body feels stiff. Then I pace the threadbare rug because they've gone to commercial break.

"Ladies," Sergeant Driscoll says. "Yard time."

Everyone grumbles as they stop whatever games they were playing and file out through the secure door that Giraffe-neck is holding open.

"But it's raining," Gill says.

"You won't melt, Firehead," Driscoll tells her. "Only sweet girls melt, which ain't your case."

Gill glares at him.

Giraffe-neck yells, "Hey, Redd, I'm not a door stop. Get your ass over here."

"No yard time for her. Commander's orders," Driscoll informs her.

Gill cocks an orange brow. Before she can ask why, Driscoll shoves her into the hallway.

Giraffe-neck lingers in the doorjamb. "Did you blow him?"

"Huh?"

"Kim told me the warden closed the door the other day. He usually never conducts a meeting without a guard present. Unless he's receiving special—"

"I didn't touch him," I tell her.

She eyes me a long time. "He's into that shit. Just so you know."

"Thanks for the warning."

"You still owe me."

"I know."

She lets the door swish shut behind her, leaving me with repugnant images of the warden. I think of his daughter, and how angelic she looked in that picture. If she found out about her father, it would break her heart.

The Masterpiecers' theme song erupts in the quiet room. The camera broadcasting the show lifts, as though attached to a drone—which it probably is—and films the six contestants milling around their mini-galleries from above. It looks like the Pac-Man-inspired video game I designed my first week of junior high. I'd helped Ivy out with hers—perhaps more than helped—and gotten in trouble for it: a visit to the principal's office and a low mark on my project.

Helping Ivy seems to bring me nothing but trouble.

TWENTY-SIX

Ivy

Kevin reminds me of a fairytale ogre, the sort who eats children for breakfast. Threatening and huge. We haven't talked yet. Not one word, not even hello. We avoided each other all afternoon. At some point, I even faked a headache to burrow in Brook's bedroom, which earned me a strange look from Chase. I don't know what he imagines. Even before what he told me about Brook and his ex, I wasn't interested in his brother. The only reason I wanted to go in the bedroom was to check my email. Of course, I couldn't tell him that.

When I'd stepped inside the bedroom, two things struck me. First that Brook or someone else had touched my clothes because I'd left them folded on the seat of the large armchair in the corner and they weren't folded anymore, and second, that he'd removed the tablet. I was too preoccupied with wondering if he suspected I'd used it, to worry much about him manipulating my clothes.

I feel something cold touch my lips, and realize it's the microphone. Dominic's holding it close to my mouth, waiting. "Ivy? Your collection?"

"The roaring twenties," I say.

He nods to egg me on.

"But it didn't start that way. When I found the pearl necklace and the top hat with the bunny, I thought about doing a collection around costumes. But then I realized I had more than just stage props...I had an era. The gun, the smoking pipe print—"

"For those of you who don't know, Magritte is a surrealistic painter, and surrealism started in the 1920s. This particular work—the original one—was painted in 1929," Dominic says. "So, Ivy, what would you name your collection?"

"A Time."

"Can't get more straight to the point," Dominic says. "Nicely done."

I inhale the praise. I'm lucky, really lucky, because my choice of the print was based on the popularity of pipes in the twenties. I had no clue when the surrealistic period started. Dominic has given me way more credit than I deserve.

"So, Chase, tell us about your collection," Dominic says.

"I built it around the Dutch painter, Rembrandt." He proceeds to explain how all the objects he gathered—from the horse figurine to the long brown feather—were featured in his paintings. Plus, he names each painting and explains the symbolism of the objects. Thankfully this competition isn't about knowledge. If it were, none of us would stand a chance to Chase.

The audience claps loudly for him—louder than they clapped for the rest of us. I bet they're rooting for him. When everyone falls quiet, Dominic moves to the last contestant, Kevin. His voice explodes out of the microphone and echoes through the cavernous stone lobby. His collection is about pipe dreams—illusions—thus the big rusty pipe, the paper bouquet that I thought Maxine had taken, and the magnifying glass. I hate to admit that it all makes sense. I so wish it hadn't.

After we've all defended our collections, we are dismissed until the evening show. Our assistants lead us back to the large staircase under dense waves of applause. My heart beats fast as I wonder how I did. I know that on TV, there's a running commentary, but we are not privy to it. As we reach the first-floor landing, the applause stops and a commotion erupts. It's followed by heavy footsteps on the stone stairs. Police officers dressed in plainclothes flash shiny badges as they jog up.

"Ivy Redd?" one of them barks.

The contestants and assistants part around me. I feel like I'm having that dream where I'm walking down Highway 31 in Kokomo, naked, while everyone is clothed, even the girls from the Hip-Hugger strip club.

A woman walks up to me. "I'm Detective Clancy. You need to come with us."

My mouth goes as dry as a sunbaked cornhusk. "Wh-why?"

"We need to ask you some questions."

"About what?"

"About your sister."

"What *about* my sister?" This time, my tone is a bit snappier.

"Do you really want us to discuss this in front of the cameras?" She gestures to Jeb and his crew whose devices are aimed on us.

"Just tell me if she's okay."

"Depends what you mean by okay."

"Physically?"

"Yes. Now, are you coming or do we have to cuff and drag you out of here?"

Although it's painfully embarrassing, I follow her and pretend everyone is not staring at me. As I start down the stairs, Dominic arrives. His neck is bright red, as must be the rest of his face underneath his thick layer of foundation.

"What in God's name is this about?" His usually suave voice is slightly shrill.

Detective Clancy sticks her hand on her very narrow hips. They're like man hips. "Nothing that concerns you or your show, Mister Bacci."

"With all due respect," he says, "Ivy is part of my show, so it does concern me."

"We have a few questions for your contestant regarding her sister's murder case. We'll have her back to you in no time."

I'm praying that Dominic will tell her that she has no jurisdiction here, but that would create a messier scene, so I place my hand on Dominic's forearm and put on a brave face. "It's okay, Mister Bacci. I'll get this over with quickly, in time for the announcement tonight." I turn to the detective. "I'll be back by then, right?"

She nods.

I let my hand drop and follow her across the lobby where the audience parts around me like the Red Sea. People whisper, point, gasp. It's just as shameful as the press conference. My heart is blasting against my ribcage, making my seafoam bodice vibrate. I pray no one can see it.

The early afternoon sun is blinding. I keep my eyes on it long enough to create a glare that erases the rest of the world around me. Blood gushes behind my eardrums, dimming the ambient clamor. The detective mutters something, but I don't hear her words. I doubt she's talking to me anyway. She opens the door of an unmarked vehicle and waits for me to settle in the backseat before slamming it shut and sinking into the front seat.

"Fucking move, people," yells the young guy with silver hair, slapping the steering wheel. He starts nosing the car through the crowd. Surprisingly, he doesn't roll anyone over. "I don't get this show," he adds, spinning the wheel so abruptly that I'm thrown against the door.

I gather the soft hem of my dress in my fingers and roll the material between my calloused thumb and forefinger. The softness reminds me of the rolls of cloth in Mom's locked drawer. While they dated, my father would gift her rolls of exotic fabric after each of his trips. She'd kept them all intact, never once cutting a strip to use in her quilts. Every time I'd visit her in the psychiatric hospital she'd been relocated to last spring, she'd ask me if I'd kept my promise not to tell Aster about them. She was afraid my twin would trash them out of spite for her. I don't think Aster would ever do such a thing, but what do I know? My sister's mind works in mysterious ways.

The precinct is teeming with visitors and cops and ringing phones. Detective Clancy takes the lead once inside and guides me toward an elevator. We exit on a high floor and head down a hallway of closed doors. She knocks on the one emblazoned with the number two, and then she pushes through and points me to a chair. While I sit, the silver-haired detective comes in with a folder tucked underneath his arm. He closes the door behind him and they both take a seat across the desk from me.

"So," Detective Clancy begins, clicking on a small device in the middle of the table. "This interview is being recorded. I'm Leah Clancy and this is my partner, Austin McEnvoy. Could you state your full name and date of birth?"

"Ivy Redd, born December 21st, 1996."

"Thank you. May we call you Ivy?"

I shrug.

She tips her head to the recording device on the table.

"Yes," I say.

"The date is August 25, 2016 and the time is 3:13 p.m. The interview is being conducted at the Midtown North

Precinct in New York City. The purpose of your presence here today, Ivy, is to shed light on your involvement with the deceased mobster Troy Mann."

"My involvement?"

Detective Clancy holds up her finger. "One of your neighbors saw Mister Mann leave your apartment on the morning of August 17th. Could you tell us what he came to see you about?"

On cue, Austin flips open the folder. There's a picture of Troy and me standing by my open apartment door. I know exactly who took it: Mister Mancini, nosiest neighbor in all of Kokomo.

"He bought a quilt from me," I say.

"We'll give you a chance to explain yourself in a second, but first I'd like to state that this is an out-of-custody interview."

"Meaning?" I ask.

"Meaning you are not under arrest and you are free to leave anytime," she says.

"Like now?"

Austin gives me a challenging look. "We wouldn't advise you to leave now."

I narrow my eyes.

"You are entitled to free and legal representation—"

"I don't need a lawyer."

"But you are entitled to one."

"Great," I say.

"You don't have to confess to anything, but it will harm your defense if you willingly withhold or falsify information. Do you understand?"

"I do."

"Okay. So, with that in mind, if you decide not to answer a question today and that question later comes up in court, and you decide to answer the question then, you may be found liable of aiding the commission of a crime."

"I'm here of my own free will, am I not?" I snap.

Leah Clancy presses her pale lips together. They're practically the same shade as the rest of her skin, a sharp contrast to her dark brown hair and eyes. "Ivy, who is the man in the picture?"

"Troy Mann."

"So you knew him?" Austin asks, leaning back.

"*Knew* is a big word."

He taps the tip of his thick finger on the picture. "You're talking with him."

"Yeah. I am, but I didn't know him. He discovered me through the feature the Masterpiecers—"

"The Masterpiecers is the reality TV show Ivy is competing on," Leah states for the digital recorder. "Go on."

"He saw me on TV and tracked me down to purchase one of my quilts."

"Could you describe the quilt he purchased?"

"Why is that relevant?" I ask.

"Because we didn't find the quilt," Detective Clancy says.

"Maybe he sold it to someone else."

"Just describe it already," Austin says.

I glare at him. "The quilt represented two people kissing."

Thankfully, there's no flare of recognition on either detective's faces.

"How much did he pay for you for it?" Austin asks.

"That's confidential."

Detective Clancy eyes me in silence for a second, and then she says, "Then we'll have to subpoena your bank records."

"He gave me cash."

"Did you declare the sale?" Austin asks.

"I didn't have time to," I lie. Hell, I'm not going to tell the police I had no intention of paying taxes on it.

Austin snorts. "Sure."

"Ivy, did you know you were dealing with the mafia?" Detective Clancy asks.

"No."

"Yeah, right." Austin grunts and crosses his feet on the table.

"It's true. I had no idea."

"Your sister knew he was part of the mob. Said it in her testimony," Austin remarks.

"We don't tell each other everything."

"I still have trouble believing you didn't know who you were dealing with."

"Are you accusing me of something, Detective McEnvoy?"

"Not yet," he says.

Detective Clancy gives him a pointed stare. "Was your sister aware that you sold him a quilt?"

"No."

"We received an anonymous tip that your sister had a blanket on her lap the night of the murder. Could that be the quilt which you sold to Mister Mann?"

"She keeps one of my quilts with her in the car because her heater doesn't work."

"It was August!" Austin says.

"She's always cold."

"The Honda was searched and it wasn't in there," Detective Clancy says.

"Then maybe she took it out."

"You want to know what I think, Ivy?" Austin says. "I think you sold a quilt to Mister Mann, then once you found out he was part of the mob, you asked your sister to retrieve it so that you wouldn't be associated with him."

I try to suppress my increasing urge to punch him by folding my arms together. "I don't know how you treat your siblings, Mister McEnvoy, but I actually respect my sister. I wouldn't send her to do my dirty work. If I'd found out Mister Mann was part of the mafia, I would've attempted to contact him myself to cancel the transaction."

"*Attempted* to contact him?" Austin asks, tipping one of his eyebrows up.

"It's not like he left me a business card." I fix my gaze on the cigarette butt wedged in the sole of McEnvoy's work boot.

"Now, about the hit and run." Detective Clancy shuffles through the folder and takes out a picture of a dead body annotated in red pen. "Are you aware that according to the coroner, your sister hit Mister Mann, then proceeded to back up the car and roll over him?"

I swallow as a bitter taste fills my mouth. "No."

"Does your sister have a history of violence?" she asks.

"No." I shake my head. "She's not violent, but she's not always...there." I drop my voice on the last word, hoping it's so faint the recorder won't pick it up. If Aster ever hears what I think of her, it will break more than her heart. It will break *her*.

"What do you mean by that?" Detective Clancy asks.

"She suffers from mental illness," I murmur.

"What sort of mental illness?"

"Schizophrenia."

A wave of silence swells through the room. It hovers and finally comes crashing over me when McEnvoy asks, "Are you saying that your sister's actions on the night of August 17th could've been prompted by a bout of craziness?"

"No! That's not what I'm saying. Not at all."

"But you just said that your sister's not always," Austin continues, "what was the word you used? Oh, yes, *there*."

"He threatened her."

"No kidding. She tracked him all the way to where he was staying," he counters.

"Because she was trying to be a good Samaritan."

"Good Samaritans don't crush people under their car tires."

"He tried to strangle her. That must be in the police file. She had red marks on her neck."

Austin shrugs. "Could've done it to herself."

"She wouldn't do that."

"Are you sure?"

"Are we done here? Because I have to get back to the show." I make to get up.

"Whoa there, Ivy," McEnvoy says, "you didn't tell us where *you* were on the night of August 17th."

"Where *I* was?"

"What my colleague is asking is how do we know you're not the twin in the car?"

The blood drains from my face. "What?"

"You have motive. More motive than your sister."

"What?" I repeat, too stunned to think of anything else to say.

"We just want to check your alibi," Leah says.

"I was at home. Working."

"Anyone can attest to that?"

"I work alone, so no."

"So you have no alibi?" Austin states.

"I *have* an alibi. I just have no one to confirm it."

"That could prove problematic." He slips his feet off the table and plops his forearms on the metal surface.

"My sister confessed to the crime," I say.

"Perhaps she's covering for you so that you could go on that little show of yours."

My heart is pounding so loudly that it feels like it's trying to kick its way out of my ribcage. "I'd like a ride back to the museum now." When neither gets up, I repeat, "Now."

Detective Clancy holds up a finger to her lips. "In conclusion, Ivy Redd attests to not knowing Troy Mann was involved with the mafia. She also states to having sold him a quilt. And she says that Aster may not have been *herself* on the night of August 17th. Is this all correct, Ivy?"

"Yes."

"Okay. Thank you. The time is 3:25 p.m. and the day is August 25th. This was Leah Clancy and Austin McEnvoy." She presses down on a button to click off the recorder, then rises and leads me back down to the lobby and out of the police station.

The paparazzi haven't wasted a second to find out where I was taken. They probably followed the black sedan Dominic sent to fetch me. Danny, the driver with the tangled eyebrows, doesn't address me once during the ride back, but he does peek at me several times in his rearview mirror, disappointment and curiosity warring on his face. It's the same look everyone on the show gives me the second I step back into the museum, from Cara to the film crew.

As I get into the elevator, eyes cast downward to avoid the stares, a hand slides between the closing doors and presses them back open. And then Brook steps in and dismisses my assistant and the doors shut. When the elevator starts rising, he tugs the red emergency lever. It stops and the lights dim.

His Adam's apple bobs up and down, but he remains silent. Then his lips part and close, and then they part again.

"What?" I ask when I can no longer take it.

"Dominic's worried about you. He's worried you have a lot on your plate. Perhaps too much. He thinks that maybe you should..."

"Maybe I should what?"

His shadowy gaze drifts over the floor, then over the wall behind me, and finally perches on my face. "He thinks that maybe you should drop out." He speaks quickly, as if saying the words fast will dampen their sting.

"Drop out? Of the Masterpiecers? No...no way. I want to stay. I *need* to stay."

"Ivy, you're doing well, but—"

"But what?"

"But there's a lot to think about. Between the media, and Kevin, and your sister. You should see what's being written up in the newspapers."

I snort because it finally dawns on me where he's going with this. "I'm bringing the show bad press. Is that what you're getting at?"

"Well...not exactly."

I narrow my eyes.

He scrapes his hand through his perfect black hair. "Yes."

"Don't you know journalists love scandals?"

"I know that, but—"

"They don't intimidate me, Brook. And neither does Dominic. I'm sorry about the bad press, but I'm not leaving the show. This is my one chance. Maybe you don't understand because you've never had to worry about where your next meal came from, but I *can't* drop out. And I'll say this again however many times I need to, but I had *nothing* to do with Kevin's pictures." I shake my head, and my hair flutters against my bare shoulders. "You know, for a second there, when you cornered me, I thought you were going to ask me how I was doing. I thought you were worried about me. But I guess people like you, like Dominic, like Josephine, only worry about themselves."

"Don't say that," he says, stepping forward. He's close enough to touch me. Thankfully he doesn't. "I *am* worried about you. The situation sucks, Ivy. Really, it does."

"I'm still not leaving. If you want me out, you'll have to disqualify me."

From the regretful look he gives me, I realize that must be exactly what they're planning, and my mood, already soured by the precinct and the interview, spoils like bad milk.

"That wouldn't be fair," I say in a raspy voice.

Brook doesn't respond. The silence hangs heavily between us. It fills the small space like steam, thinning the breathable air.

"The public's vote counts for something," I add, mostly to reassure myself. "Now, can you please switch the elevator back on?"

His fingers hover over the lever. "Could Aster have had anything to do with Kevin's pictures?"

"I doubt it."

"But you're not sure? She's your sister—"

"If I remember correctly, you had no clue your brother entered the competition," I snap back.

He frowns, and it leaves a deep vertical groove between his dark eyebrows. "I did know. His girlfriend told me."

"The one you screwed?"

"You know about that?"

"Yeah."

After a long bout of silence, he says, "I have a great lawyer."

"Are you threatening me?"

His forehead smooths out. "I meant for your sister, Ivy."

"Oh."

"And he'd be free."

"Really?" Suspicion creeps into my brain. "Is he free even if I decide to stay on the show?"

"Yes."

"Does he work pro bono?"

"No. He's a friend."

"Why would you do that?"

"So you can forgive me for being disrespectful toward you."

"I don't know what to say."

"Just say yes, and I'll make the call."

His offer feels too good to be true, yet I find myself accepting. "Okay."

The elevator jerks to life and the lights snap back on, bright, blinding. Soon, the doors are opening. Brook brushes a strand of hair off my cheek and whispers that he's going to call his lawyer friend right away. I thank him in a muted voice before stiffly walking out, past Chase and Lincoln who are standing by the door of the makeup room, past the myriad of assistants and camera crew on their coffee break, past the tree-lined hallway, and into my tented safe haven.

TWENTY-SEVEN

I gaze at the television screen long after the afternoon test has ended, but I don't see anything.

"Male deodorant has a real fascinating effect on women," Driscoll says, tipping his head to the commercial on the television. "Want a whiff of my armpits, Redd?"

Mechanically, I look up at the guard. "I'm allergic to male stench."

His smile drops and so does his voice. "I forget. You're one of *them* now."

"One of them?" I ask.

"Lawn grazers."

"Huh?" When it dawns on me what he's inferring, I feel a sharp desire to slap him. I curl my fingers into fists against my stiff jumpsuit. "What is it you want, Sergeant?"

"What is it I want? Now let me see...a lightweight dome tent, a Harley Davidson, a set of fancy steak knives—"

"I mean with me. I doubt you came for small talk."

"You doubt right." He shifts on his spindly legs. "Turns out you're a popular girl, Redd. You got someone waiting for you in the visitation area."

I'm betting it's Josh. He probably made a U-turn on the freeway. "Officer Cooper?"

"Nope."

"It's not?"

"Just said it wasn't."

For a moment, I think it's Ivy, but she's in New York being questioned by some detectives.

"You better hurry. Fancy man like him probably has elsewhere to be."

"Fancy man? I don't know any fancy men."

"Quit stalling. I gotta go train the *yobwoc*."

I frown as I stand up and trail him to the door.

He glances back at me. "Gotta go explain that giving prisoners access to Internet on cell phones doesn't fly with me. You knew that, right, Redd? That you ain't allowed to ask guards for their phones?" As I walk past him, he adds in a low voice, "At least not for free?" He falls in stride with me. "In the future, if you ever need a phone, I got one." He pats his pant pocket, and then his hand crawls to his crotch, which he pats in turn.

Asshole, I think but don't say. My eyes must be pretty expressive though, because Driscoll's cocky grin dissolves. When he buzzes me into the attorney visitation area, a suit-clad man pushes his chair back, rises, and extends his hand. "Hi, Aster. I'm Dean Kane, your lawyer."

"My lawyer?"

"Yes."

His dark suit and pink tie held flat against his dress shirt by a gleaming gold bar makes him look too elegant to be state-appointed. His retainer alone must equal what I make in a year.

Sure enough, he adds, "You're my pro bono case of the year." Then he props his briefcase on the table and gestures toward the chair opposite him.

"So"—he takes out a folder—"I familiarized myself with your case, Aster. You're being charged with first-degree murder for running over—"

"First-degree murder?" I yelp. "It was self-defense."

"You hit a man, *then* you ran him over. You're facing forty years to life imprisonment."

"What?" I pinch the skin on my arm to make sure I'm awake. Unfortunately, I am. "But he threatened me."

"That'll be the base of our defense. But there are aggravating circumstances that aren't going to work in our favor. For one, your psych report." He takes out a paper from the file. "It says here you were diagnosed with schizophrenia at the age of twelve and that your condition has progressively worsened."

I feel like I've been punched...hard. Spasms erupt in my extremities and then move to my muscles...to my teeth...to my bones.

He shuts the file. "Also, a witness informed me that you took something from the crime scene, which gives you motive for the assault."

"A...A witness?"

"Yes."

I choke on my saliva, which makes me cough.

Dean nods. "What was worth killing a man for?"

I blanch.

He leans across the table. "I'm on your side, Aster."

"I didn't take anything."

"Did you *not* hear me say I was on your side?" When I keep quiet, he drums his fingers on the table. His large gold pinkie ring draws my attention. I try to make out the insignia. Suddenly, he stops tapping and grumbles loudly. "Look, I have several other cases I need to oversee. Either you cooperate and give me something I can work with, or I'll leave you to some newbie public defender who'll ensure that the only way you leave this place is in a casket. Now, I strongly suggest option number one as I've never lost a case in the past, and without me, judging from your file, you're not getting out of here alive."

I don't want to die. And I don't want to stay in here forever. "My sister's quilt."

It takes him a second to register that I'm speaking about the case. "What did you do with the quilt?"

"I destroyed it."

"Really?"

"Yes."

"So it's not the quilt that your sister auctioned on the Masterpiecers?"

"No."

"Did you tell anyone else about the quilt?"

"Just—No."

"Just whom?"

"Just a friend," I say.

"Which friend?"

"Why do you need to know that?"

"To make sure they don't go telling anyone else that you took a quilt from a dead man."

"He won't say anything."

"And how would you know that?"

"Because I trust him."

"From now on, you shouldn't trust anyone but me. And you shouldn't talk to anyone else. Okay?" Dean asks.

"Okay."

"Was there anything else in the bag?"

"No." I bite my lip. "Why did the cops interview my sister?"

"You're changing the subject."

"Please...I need to know."

"They wanted to make sure she wasn't the one behind the wheel of the Honda."

"Huh?"

He sighs. "That she wasn't the one who ran Troy Mann over."

"Of course she wasn't! It was me in the car."

"Don't worry, she told them that. She also told them about your affliction."

"My what?"

"The schizophrenia."

I bite down on my tongue to avoid sobbing or screaming—whichever comes first. "She told the detectives I was crazy?"

"Yes, but that'll work in our favor. It'll explain why you ran him over *after* you rammed into him. You'll get sent to an institution."

"I'm not crazy."

He eyes me in silence as he gets up and tucks the file back into his fancy leather briefcase. "Would you rather stay here?"

"No, but—"

"Then make it work, and I'll make it work."

"How am I supposed to make it work?"

He swoops down and drops his voice. "Act like your mother used to."

"You mean *does*. She's still nuts."

His lips perk into a bright smile. "You're a quick study."

I'm not sure what he means, but don't have time to ask as he's already standing and knuckling the door for the guard to open it. "Before I forget, I found out who was behind those doctored photos of the contestant."

"Who?"

"I'll tell you as soon as I inform Mister Martin," he says, before flying down the hallway, the bottom of his pink tie flapping against his shiny belt buckle.

TWENTY-EIGHT

Ivy

While prepping me for the evening ceremony, Amy doesn't dare look straight into my eyes, but Leila does. Her kohl-lined gaze is blacker than usual, and tighter. She's still mad at me. When Amy leaves to gather more pins, she says, "You're throwing everything away."

"I'm not throwing anything away."

"Oh, come on, Ivy. You're all broken and hopeless. I can feel it. I can see it. And if I can see it, I know that you can too. Snap out of it."

"Snap out of it? My life outside these walls is crumbling and you're telling me to snap out of it?"

"Yes."

"You have *no* idea what it feels like to be trampled by the world, scrutinized by everyone. No idea!" My voice trembles. "So don't you dare tell me to snap out of it!"

Leila's face shutters up just as Amy returns. Her head swings from Leila to me. She can tell something has gone down, but thankfully, she doesn't get involved.

Leila undoes the black apron tied around her waist and

sticks it on the counter in front of me. "My hand's cramping," she says. "I'll see you tomorrow."

"But—" Amy's mouth is gaping.

Leila's already gone.

"But—she—half your face," Amy stutters.

"Are you done with my hair?" I ask in a toneless voice.

"Almost." Her hands tremble as she sticks a bunch more pins in. "Um...do you want me to get another makeup artist? I'm sure—"

"Don't bother. I'll do it myself."

As she packs up her tools, I take the black liner and some violet powder, and finish what Leila started. One of my eyes looks smaller than the other, but I don't care. I just want to get this night over with. I toss the brushes and pencils onto the black apron and walk into the dressing room just as Maxine and Lincoln wiggle into their outfits.

"Could these be any shorter?" Maxine asks, attempting to tug the skirt on her cocktail waitress-like dress further down.

"At least we have tights on," Lincoln says, her green-gold eyes on me as I pull my outfit off the hanger.

"They're so sheer," Maxine complains. "Everyone will see my cellulite."

"Oh, stop it," Lincoln says. "You don't have any."

"I do. Look." Maxine pinches the back of her thighs.

The discussion makes me want to hit something. How can they talk about stupid butt dimples in front of me? My sister's in a correctional facility for killing a man, and I'm being accused of setting up a fucking contestant.

"Oh...well," Maxine says with a sigh. As she turns away from the mirror, she notices me. "I'm sorry about your sister."

"Sorry about what?" I ask.

Maxine's face colors. "Oh...uh...well, Kevin...he uh, told us what's going on."

"What did he say that makes you *sorry about my sister?*"

"Um...just that she...that the man...that she's being charged with first-degree murder."

"You shouldn't believe everything you hear," I tell her.

"I'm sorry, Ivy. I didn't mean—"

I pull off my bathrobe and tug on the tight satin number. "Just drop it, okay?"

She nods a great many times before finally rushing out of the dressing room.

"So...what's up between you and Brook?" Lincoln asks. They brushed her blonde hair to one side like a fifties actress and strapped a crawling diamond earring to the ridge of her exposed ear.

"Why don't you ask Kevin? He seems to know everything around here," I say as I yank on smoke-colored tights.

"Funny"—she snorts—"seriously though, you were in that elevator a long time."

"How do you know how long I was in there?"

"Because your assistant came huffing and puffing up the stairs, carping into her mouthpiece about Mister Jackson not letting her do her job. So"—she bats her eyelashes—"what happened?"

"He told me I should quit the show and I told him to go screw himself." I leave out the part about the lawyer.

"No you didn't."

"Not in those exact words, but yeah, I did."

"It would've been pretty cool if you'd forfeited."

I flip her the middle finger, which makes her laugh.

"You know, I'm pretty sure that if we weren't competing against each other, we'd get along well, you and I."

I slide my feet into a pair of pointy yellow heels, and stand up. "I guess we'll never know."

Lincoln's looking at my charcoal dress without really looking at it. "Kevin freaks me out," she says suddenly. "The way he looks at us...like we're part of the Taliban. Ever since he arrived, the atmosphere's changed. His tent is right in front of mine, and last night, I swear I could hear him pace around his room. And then outside on the grass, there was definitely noise. I don't feel safe. That's what I was telling Chase this afternoon."

"And what did Chase say?"

"He told me to come and sleep in his room if I needed to."

"How gallant of him," I say mockingly.

She cocks her head to the side. "Are you jealous?"

"Jealous? No."

"You sounded jealous."

"Well, I'm not. I don't care about Chase."

"He cares about you, you know?"

"Yeah right," I say, heading toward the curtain.

"He was pissed when he saw you in the elevator with Brook."

A little bit of warmth seeps through the armor I've wrapped around my body since the interrogation. But then I remind myself that Chase basically propositioned Lincoln. "If you do sleep in his room, keep the noise down."

She smiles. "I'll try my best."

I walk out, banishing thoughts of Lincoln and Chase together, but some still creep into my mind during the evening segment. I'm so distracted that I almost clap when Dominic announces that Maxine received the lowest score. To prevent any further mishaps, I tuck my hands together until we are released—which doesn't come soon enough.

"We need a bottle of champagne," Lincoln announces once we've been returned to our tent.

"You're underage," one of the waiters tells her.

"No shit, Sherlock. The champagne's not for me," Lincoln says.

"Are you staying for dinner or are you leaving right away?" Herrick asks.

Maxine sniffles. "I...I..."

Lincoln, who has her arm draped over Maxine's shoulder, squeezes her tightly. I strongly believe that her amiability and exuberance come from the fact that she hasn't been kicked off the show. "She'll stay for dinner."

"I don't...don't want to...to eat," Maxine sobs.

I'm not cruel. I feel bad for her. Maxine is genuinely nice...annoyingly nice. But I'm not that surprised she's leaving. To be honest, I'm more surprised she's made it this far.

"You don't look too shook up to see her go," Chase says quietly, sidling up next to me against the back of the couch.

The scent of pine needles is everywhere. "I thought I was the one who would get voted off the show, so call me selfish, but I'm relieved." With my heels on, I'm not far off from his height.

"Hey, Jackson, considering your birthday's in two days, here," Herrick says, holding out a glass of champagne.

"Considering there's a camera right there"—Chase tips his head toward the ceiling—"I'll pass."

"Give it here," Lincoln says, sticking it in Maxine's free hand.

"Bottoms up, Daisy," she says with a wink.

Maxine quits sniffling long enough to smile. Then she tips the glass up and finishes it off in four long swallows. Lincoln seizes it from her fingers and holds it out for a refill. The waiter obliges. She hands it back to Maxine, who guzzles it down. This time, swiping her mouth with the back of her hand, Maxine asks for a refill herself. Herrick and Lincoln begin chanting her name. She shoots back the glass.

"Dinner's ready," another waiter announces.

I press off the back of the couch and take a seat along with everyone else. Maxine's eyes are all shiny and her nose is tinged red. At the table, she drinks another two glasses.

"Better slow down, there, G.I. Jane," Herrick says, "or you're going to pass out before the main course."

Maxine breaks out into an uncontrollable fit of giggles.

"That's the plan," Lincoln says. "Isn't it, Maxine?"

She bobs her head and lifts her glass. "Screw you, Dominic!" She tips her head back and drinks. "Screw you, Josephine!" She takes another sip. "Screw you, Brook!" She's about to take another sip when she starts laughing hysterically. "Sorry, Chase."

"Oh. I don't mind. I'll even drink to that." He raises his glass of water. The ice cubes clink inside.

I don't cheer, because I don't want to get in trouble. The cameras might not pick up sound, but the waiters might relate our dinner chat.

At some point, the conversation switches to actual screwing. We get way too many details on Herrick and Maxine's personal lives. Kevin squirms in his chair, which looks odd for someone of his size.

"What about you, Kev?" Herrick suddenly asks.

He goes stiff as a log. "Been with one woman only."

"You never strayed while you were in Afghanistan?" Herrick continues.

"No. Never."

Herrick combs his fingers through his pompadour. "That's pretty impressive. I don't think I've ever met a monogamous person. Unless I'm in the presence of two more...Chase? Ivy?"

"Hey! You forgot me," Lincoln says, sticking out her bottom lip.

"Oh, come on, honey, you're so *not* monogamous."

Her pout turns into a smile. "Fine. You got me. Monogamy's boring." She suddenly whips her gaze toward Kevin. "To me," she adds. "Monogamy's boring to me. But maybe it's because I haven't met the right person like you have."

He stares at her, but doesn't react, which makes her feline eyes grow wide in apprehension. A stiff awkwardness ensues. Even Maxine seems sobered up by it.

"I think there's no right or wrong relationship," Chase says, which loosens the tension.

Herrick, who's had about half a bottle of champagne, asks, "What's your style, Jackson? Faithful or unfaithful?"

"Faithful," he says without hesitation.

For some reason, the rope of muscles in Kevin's shoulders loosens, as though being in the presence of a fellow monogamist is comforting.

"And you, Ivy?" Herrick asks.

"Faithful."

Chase studies me as he usually does, while Kevin snorts.

"What?" I ask him.

"You don't look the type. I know women and—"

"You know women?" I ask. "I think you stand to be corrected. You know *a* woman, Kevin. *One*. Your wife. I don't know what she's like and I don't really care. But don't go assuming you know what I'm like."

Kevin leans his beefy forearms on the white glass tabletop. "I know more about you than you think. My lawyer's connected. Did you know he's originally from Kokomo?"

"A lot of people are from Kokomo," I say, leaning my own forearms across the table. "So if you have something to say to me, say it." My voice is strong, but the rest of me isn't. Each one of my nerves feels like it's toppling over the next one, like a long line of dominoes.

"My lawyer told me not to engage with you."

"Did he tell you I bite?"

His eyes turn a forbidding shade of brown. "You'll know soon what he told me."

"It's my last night with all of you. Can we talk about something else?" Maxine asks, staring at me, pupils throbbing.

"Yes, let's," Herrick says. "I say we talk about me again."

"I say we don't," Lincoln answers.

I stand up. "I'm sorry, Maxine, but I've had a really long day. I think I'm going to try to get some sleep."

"Oh. Okay."

She looks so disappointed that for a second, I reconsider, but then I see Kevin and my resolve strengthens.

"Will you give me your phone number?" she asks.

"You want my number?"

"Yes. I want your number," she says. She stands up on wobbly legs and stumbles toward me like a newly birthed foal. "I want to throw a party for the winner after the show's over." She grabs a pen and notecard off the living room table, and gives them to me.

I write down my number, and then, before I can get away, she locks me in a big hug. I go stiff, but it doesn't bother Maxine.

"Good luck, Ivy," she says, patting my back, and then she adds in a low voice—I'm surprised she can exert that much control over her vocal cords—"You're going to win. I can feel it."

I can't, but I hope she's right.

"Inmate Redd, out of your bunk. It's breakfast time," Giraffe-neck yells from my doorway.

At 7 a.m. sharp, all the cell gates open and all the lights snap on.

"I don't want breakfast," I say, head buried in a new book I borrowed from the prison library.

"No breakfast, no show."

"I don't want to see the show." My sister told the cops I was crazy, so I'm snubbing her stupid show.

The guard stays quiet for a long second. "I still get my money, Redd, whether you watch it or not. Understood?"

I nod. God, will she ever stop talking about her money?

"And don't think you get to lounge around your cell, reading all day. If you don't go watch the show, I'll line up some chores for you."

"Sure."

She just stands there, with this idiotic look on her face. "I'll pick you up in an hour, then," she says, finally leaving.

I'm grateful to have another hour to mope around and dive back into my book. It's about a mother who loses her child. It's nice to know that I'm not alone. Especially these days, when I feel more alone than ever. Part of me wishes I could call Ivy, ask her why she told the cops I was crazy. I've never gone this long without hearing her voice, and I don't mean her voice on TV, I mean her voice in my ear. They're not the same voices.

After several minutes, I close the book and toss it at my feet. I can't concentrate on anything. My brain is filled with my sister, as is my heart. They say twins are two halves of a person, but that's not true. We are not two halves. She's a whole person and I am her shadow, and a shadow disappears when there's no body left to silhouette.

"There you are." Gill treads into my cell.

I sigh. "Here I am."

She frowns at my sigh, but then she gets sidetracked by the book at my feet. She picks it up and studies the cover. Before she can read the summary on the back, I roll myself up and yank it out of her hands.

"You want kids?" she asks.

Too late. "Maybe."

"You'll make a good mother."

"Doubt it. Anyway I'm stuck here indefinitely. Haven't you heard that they upgraded my charge to first-degree murder?"

"I didn't hear."

"Well, they did." Those gates I entered eight days ago feel like they're on another continent. I stick the book underneath my mattress instead of underneath my pillow so that Cheyenne doesn't find it. "What's Cheyenne up to these days?"

"I don't know. You want me to find out?"

"Can you?"

"I can do anything, Aster. Especially for you." She steps closer to me. My gaze darts around looking for something to do...anything. She takes another step and wraps her small hands around my neck and then leans in. I just manage to swing my face away. Her mouth pecks my cheek.

"I-I can't, Gill." I shrug her hands off. "I'm not stable, emotionally."

Her freckled cheeks glow red.

If I don't find a solid excuse, I'm going to have to watch my back around both her *and* Cheyenne. "I just lost a baby," I blurt out.

The flush recedes from her cheeks. "Oh. I didn't know. I'm sorry." She sits down on my bed and looks up at me. "I like children. I'd like to have one someday. Well, not me, but I'd like for my partner to carry them. But I got thirty years, Aster. I served two, and I'm thirty-seven. When I'm out, I'll be sixty-five."

"Sixty-five-year-olds can still be mothers. Especially if you don't carry the baby."

"Out there"—she points at the brick wall—"normal women...they'll be scared of me. They won't understand me like the people in here do. I'll probably end up homeless with no job. Who wants to hire a woman in her sixties who did time behind bars?"

Tears snake down her pale cheeks, so many of them that I sit on the bed next to her and drape my arm around her shoulders. She cries for a long time. When she stops, my collar is soaked.

"You're so good. You're an angel," she whispers. "That's what I thought that first day you walked in. That you had to be an angel because I'd never seen a person with such a kind, beautiful face."

"It must have been my hair. I was told the frizz makes it look like a halo."

She laughs, but then she gets up, grabs my hand, and tugs me off the bed. "I have an idea."

"I feel I'm not going to like it."

"You will! Trust me." She pulls me into the cell she shares with two other bunkmates. Underneath her bed, she has a cardboard box filled with an assortment of knickknacks, mostly hair products and creams and makeup.

"You could open a beauty parlor."

"How do you think I make a couple bucks around here?" she asks. "Here, sit on the floor."

"I don't have any money."

"Your money's no good with me."

"Gill—"

"Just sit."

Biting my lip, I lower myself to the floor and cross my legs. She takes a fine-tooth comb out of the box.

"You'll never get that through," I warn her.

"Will you please let me do my job?"

I shut up and let her work on me because after refusing her kiss, I can't refuse her offer.

An hour or so later, Giraffe-neck returns. "What do we have here? Cloning yourself, Firehead?"

Gill doesn't answer, much too preoccupied with finishing off the sections of hair she hasn't twisted and teased into dreads yet.

"Redd, get your ass up. Chacha needs you in the kitchen."

"I'll finish later," Gill says. "Don't take the rubber bands out okay? You need to keep them in until the dreads mature."

"Redd?" Giraffe-neck taps her foot. "Now."

I walk out past her.

"Firehead, yard time. It's supposed to rain again, so we're taking you out early."

It sounds like she's talking to a dog. That must not be too far from what she thinks of us.

THIRTY

Ivy

A day on the beach. That's today's competition or at least that's where it will take place.

"On Fire Island, our five remaining contestants will have to gather anything and everything they can find to create a work of art. This will test their creativity and their resourcefulness." He grins so widely that his teeth look blinding in the bright camera lights. "Although we encourage them to take their time, it would be nice if they were finished with their pieces before the evening celebrations." Dominic rubs his palms together. "We've got a wonderful, wonderful evening in store for you."

My head feels like a geyser, filled with vapor and about to blow because I had a shit night. Barely slept. And when I did manage to fall asleep, I heard the zipper of my tent lift, but when I clicked my bedside lamp on, it was shut, so I must have dreamt it.

"Without further ado, we will head out. Don't forget your hats and sunscreen. The weatherman said it will be hot. Low nineties. This ought to be good," he says, rubbing his hands together. "See all of you on the beach in two hours."

As we walk out of the lobby toward the black minivan that's parked in front of the museum, Lincoln leans in, "Sit next to me on the bus? I have something to tell you."

I nod and put on the sunglasses the show has lent me. They're big and black, with gold branches and large rims, exactly what I need to cover up the red tinge of my eyes and the dark circles Leila did a sloppy job concealing. When she showed up this morning, I was surprised, but then again, she'd be out of a job if she hadn't.

"Let's go to the back," Lincoln says, sticking her sunglasses on top of her head.

Kevin's sitting all the way in the front, right behind the driver. Chase and Herrick are on either side of the middle aisle, which leaves the backseat vacant.

As we settle down, she says, "Maxine would've loved this test. I wish she were still here." She drops her voice, "Instead of *him*."

"So what did you have to tell me?"

Her green-gold eyes, that look more green than gold in the sunlight, glisten. "Last night...I went to sleep in Chase's room."

I stiffen, which makes a small smile cock her lips up.

"Anyway, I went to sleep there with Maxine who was drunk as shit. We were going to sleep together in her room, but she was freaking out about you-know-who"—she tips her head toward Kevin—"so we asked Chase if we could squeeze in next to him." She toys with the fringes of her see-through beach dress. "He gave us his bed and slept on the rug."

"How nice of him."

She releases the fringes. With her voice barely above a whisper, she says, "Guess who was out on a midnight stroll?"

Goose bumps scurry over my bare arms.

"He was right outside your tent," she whispers. "Chase went out and asked what he was doing. He pretended he was sleepwalking." She doesn't yell this, but it feels like she does. I can hear her words echo inside my skull, adding to the throbbing ache.

"Chase is going to talk to Brook about getting a camera installed in the hallway. One that picks up sound," she adds in a low whisper.

"Is he going to tell him why?"

She nods.

After a beat, I ask, "Do you think he was coming for me?"

She raises her shoulders. "Honestly, I have no clue. He seems nuts enough to do that. Herrick was telling me he has PTSD."

My skin feels clammy. I press the blades of the air vent overhead shut, even though, deep down, I know the A/C isn't to blame.

"Last night he said he had stuff on you. Does he?"

I think of the quilt Troy Mann bought from me. "We all have skeletons in our closet, don't we?"

"I don't."

"Really?"

"I smoked pot. Still do sometimes. But that's the worst drug I ever used 'cause I don't want to end up like the low-lives who brought me into this world. Why do you think I'm on this show?"

Perhaps I misjudged Lincoln.

Her gaze settles on the bridge we're crossing to reach Long Island.

"How did you get into chalk drawings?" I ask her.

"By accident. One of the guys I was dating—he was a teacher—decorated the wall of his kitchen with blackboard paint. One night, we smoked up a lot, and I mean a lot. So much that by the time we tried to have sex, he passed out on me. I couldn't sleep, so I got out of bed and grabbed a piece of chalk from the kitchen counter and drew...all night."

"What did you draw?"

"A landscape with swirly clouds and swirly hills and a swirly sun. A little like Van Gogh. I curled up in front of it, thinking it was the most beautiful thing in the world."

"Let me guess...when you woke up the next day, you thought it was horrible."

She shakes her head and her ponytail swishes. "No. I still thought it was beautiful, but I had no recollection of having done it. I wanted to erase everything and see if my hands could really master chalk like that, but my boyfriend forbade me to touch it. He told me to go down in the courtyard behind the apartment complex and train there."

"Under the influence?"

She smiles. "If you call coffee an influence, then yes. But no weed this time. I needed to see if I could really do it."

"And?"

"And a few of the people who lived in the building came down and sat with me while I worked. This dude practiced his saxophone and this old lady made me a sandwich."

"How did your drawing turn out?"

She grimaces. "Eh. Wasn't of the caliber of the night before. But it was good enough to make me go down and practice every morning for a month. Some of my boyfriend's students came to film me. They were working on a documentary for school. You saw some of the footage on the first night."

"Picasso's *Demoiselles d'Avignon*?"

"Yup. That was my best one. That was the day my boyfriend told me to sign up for the competition." She gets this distant gleam in her eyes.

"Are you still together?" I venture.

"Nah."

"Why'd you break up?"

"Life."

"That's vague."

Her cheek dimples. She's probably chewing on the inside

of it. I do that sometimes when I'm sewing. "He wasn't ambitious like I was. It drove a wedge between us. Plus, as I said last night, I'm not really into monogamy and he was," she says with a smile. "But it ended well. We're still friends."

"You're lucky."

"Lucky?" she asks, lifting a dark brow. The contrast with her light hair makes her eyes really pop.

"To have stayed friends."

"You didn't stay friends with your exes?"

"I only had one. And no."

"I'd ask if you want to talk about it, but you don't seem like the sort of girl who likes to share."

"There's nothing worth sharing. I was fourteen; he was fifteen. All we ever did was kiss and hold hands."

"You're a virgin?" she basically shouts.

Widening my eyes, I shush her, but unfortunately it's too late. From the chuckle that escapes Herrick's mouth, I know he heard Lincoln, which surely means that everyone in the van is now aware of my...inexperience.

In the middle of scouring an enormous soup pot with a stainless steel scrubby, I see it! That thing in the warden's picture that called out to me. I see it so clearly that the pot, which I'd tipped to the side to conquer the burned bits, slips from my wet hands. It makes a loud banging noise against the sink.

"Hey! Watch it! I'm already half-deaf," Chacha says. She sticks her index fingers in her ears and rotates them as though trying to clear the wax. "Now my head is going to be ringing all day."

"Sorry." I tip the pot back on its side and scrub it with renewed vigor. When it's clean enough to reflect my face, I set it to dry and wash the metal prep counters. An entire layer of grease comes off. I would have found that revolting if I hadn't been so rattled by my discovery.

"Lunch is ready so I go," she says. "I like to shower after I cook. You take the ice off the shelves, okay?" She points to the steel door in the middle of the white ceramic wall.

I nod, but then ask, "Isn't shower time before dinner?"

"You're not the only one with privileges, Redd. Stick around long enough here, and you get special treatment. Been here twelve years." She takes off her apron and hangs it on a hook. "Beat that."

Before she leaves, I ask her, "Where's the ice pick?"

She smiles. She's missing her left canine. "No ice pick. That's a weapon."

"Don't you use knives?"

"Yeah, but only when a guard's around. They're locked up if not."

"Well, how am I supposed to de-ice the freezer then?"

She claws at the air between us like a rabid cat. She even hisses. "Use your nails, Redd." She laughs at my shocked face, and keeps cackling long after she's vanished from sight.

I stare down at my nails, which are soft from the warm tap water and chipped from the metal sponge. I won't have any left by the end of this chore. I'm not vain or anything, but ripped and bleeding nails hurt. I crush them into my hand at the memory of the dark closet and the wooden door I clawed at for hours. *And Ivy doesn't get why I despise our mother.*

I look around for something to use and my gaze falls on the steel scrub. I pick it up and walk to the freezer door, which I prop open with a rollaway metal island. I lock the wheels in place, turn on the lights, and step in. The coolness feels divine against my balmy skin. It must be close to ninety degrees in the kitchen, what with the stove and halogen bulbs on.

There are four rows of shelves, each coated with several inches of snow-like ice. I start by taking down all the packages and boxes from the shelves before getting around to scrubbing. After several grueling minutes, the only thing I've managed is to scrape off a few flurries. I return to the kitchen, check around for something else, anything else. When I spot the clean soup pot, I get an idea—not brilliant but worth trying.

I fill it with water and heat it on the stove. Once it simmers, I bring it into the freezer and splash the shelf. The water instantly melts the ice. It's magical. I'm so proud of my ingenuity, that I head back out and repeat the process. After thirty minutes, half of the freezer is defrosted. For a proud second, I gape at my handiwork, but then my pride vaporizes when the lights turn off and the door bangs shut. I race toward it and grope for the indoor latch—because I assume there is one. The second my fingers close over it, I expel a deep breath. I twist it and push against the door, but it doesn't budge. I do it again. Still nothing. Again. Nothing. And again. Nothing. The latch is broken.

I yell at the top of my lungs, hoping someone, anyone will hear me, but it's midmorning and everyone's still out in the yard. I slam my fists against the door out of frustration and then stick my forehead against it and focus on breathing.

I need to stay calm. Chacha will be back soon. She's only taking a shower. How long can a shower last? And then there's lunch to be served. I'll be here for an hour max, maybe two. I can't freeze to death in that amount of time...*can I?* How long was I at the park that day after I lost the baby? It was really cold too. I didn't die however deeply I wished to.

I lower my sleeves, find a spot on the floor still warmed by the boiling water and hook my arms around my knees to conserve energy. But it's a mistake, because soon the bottom of my pants is soaking wet and cold. The dampness has even penetrated my underwear, all the way to my skin.

I start humming that song Ivy hums to me. I don't know how many times I sing it, but my teeth are clattering. I clamp my mouth shut before the enamel shatters. Suddenly, I hear voices outside and I leap from my spot on the floor. I pummel the door and scream. My heart pounds in time with my fists. I'm not going to freeze to death after all.

But the door doesn't open. And no one answers me. Or rather there is an answer to my loud plea—laughter. Not the cackling sort. It's a laugh I've never heard before, yet I know exactly whom it belongs to.

Cheyenne.

Suddenly, the rage I felt the night she soiled my pillow fires through me and I shake. I'm going to kill her. I scream until my voice becomes hoarse, and still I yell. I don't tremble anymore. To say the truth, I'm so angry that I don't feel the cold. I don't feel much of anything except the thrashing in my ribcage. My heart's going to fracture one of my ribs if I don't calm down.

I hear more noise outside. I pound my fists harder and scream louder, but my voice no longer carries much sound and my arms are tired and frozen. My hope dissolves as quickly as the ice earlier. I walk to the back of the freezer, pick up the soup pot, and throw it against the door. It makes a loud clatter. Someone must have heard that. Still no one comes.

The noise beyond the door is deafening. It's lunchtime, which means that I've been in here for at least two hours. I pick up the soup pot and throw it again. Uselessly, it clangs to the floor. I try to do it a third time, but my arms are too stiff and it crashes before reaching the door. It still makes noise though. So I do it again. I lift it, drop it, lift it, drop it. Over and over, until my arms feel like they're about to rip from their sockets.

I sink down and tug my arms through my sleeves to rest them against my bare skin. I need to keep my extremities warm. For the first time in my life, I'm thankful for the amount of hair on my head. I curl my toes, in and out. At some point they stop moving. I try to jiggle my legs, but they feel heavy... so heavy.

Maybe I should get up and walk to keep my body temperature up, but then I'll breathe a lot and might deplete the air of oxygen. I try to get up anyway, but I stumble. I can't lift my heavy, rigid body off the cold, steel floor...and I'm so tired...my lids feel like iron shutters...my forehead tingles...everything's very black...black like molasses...thick like molasses...shiny like molasses...sticky like...

THIRTY-TWO

Ivy

The beach is a wide strip of creamy sand bordered on one side by the Atlantic Ocean and on the other by tufts of long, wild grass. Even though the sky is light, the sea is deep cobalt, the same shade as one of the fabric rolls in Mom's secret drawer. Small waves lap the shore, dragging along broken shells, slimy algae, pale rocks, and sticks of all sizes. It's wild and briny—not the sort of beach I dream about with turquoise water and white sand—but it's a beach nonetheless. As I watch the landscape with its swooping, loud gulls, an idea for a quilt flourishes in my mind. I snap my lids to store the image in the depth of my imagination.

The show has set up a row of striped tents that resemble vintage popcorn boxes to house port-o-potties and changing rooms. Further down the beach, there is a pleated organza big top underneath which several long wooden tables are being decorated with copper pots overflowing with rosemary and lavender, and ceramic bowls piled high with yellow lemons. Acoustic music trickles out of speakers. It mirrors the land-scape, sounding like breaking waves and the balmy breeze.

Our assistants come toward us to take our shoes and spray

us with sunscreen. Then they hand us the mesh bags we used yesterday and lead us to the cleared spaces on the sand destined for our works of art.

The camera crew is in place. They wait for Dominic's signal to begin taping. In front of Dominic, amidst the packed crowd, I spot the star-maker, Delancey. In spite of the sweltering heat, he's wearing a white pin-stripe suit with shortened pant legs. I haven't seen him since the first day, but I bet he's been here all along, meandering around us like the rest of the audience. To say the truth, I've been so focused on competing that I've barely looked at anyone. I scan the faces surrounding us. Some look vaguely familiar—either from the silver screen or from the tabloids.

A photographer has his camera ready on a tripod. It takes me a second to recognize Patrick Veingarten. He waits for Dominic's signal like everyone else. It comes in the form of a launching of white helium balloons. There are five of them just like there are five of us. I tip my face up and watch them sail away, chalky dots against the bright blue.

I hoist my bag onto my shoulder and set out. I'm still not sure what I'm going to make, but I know something will catch my eye and jumpstart my creative juices. I tug my fingers through the swaying tall grass that looks bluish-lilac up close. I break off a piece and inspect its elasticity and strength by tying a knot. It's sturdy, so I grab a bunch and place them into my bag. I spot Kevin not far from me. He's pulling out bundles of the grass, so many handfuls that his piece will surely consist of only that, which spurs me to find some other material to use.

I walk further away from the water line, kicking branches and twigs off my route. A broken slab of wood calls out to me. I bend over and pick it up. When I stand up, I find myself nose-to-nose with Patrick. Well, maybe not nose-to-nose, but nose-to-camera. His index finger is poised on the shutter release.

"Hi," he says. His bald head shines in the sun.

"You shaved your mustache."

He smiles. "I shaved my mustache." He snaps another picture of my face, then one of my hands wrapped around the piece of wood.

"Wasn't it your trademark?" I ask.

"It was, but I turned a page in my life, and in this new chapter, I don't have a mustache."

I raise a skeptic eyebrow, which he captures on camera. Still smiling, he winks and walks toward the other contestants. If I cut off my hair, would I be starting a new chapter also? At least, I would no longer be mistaken for Aster. No one would ask if I was the twin at the wheel of the Honda.

I stick the plank in my bag and meander back down to the beach, fingering the curled tip of my ponytail. I'm not careful and trample a twig. A sharp, stabbing pain makes me curse and sink to the ground to inspect my sole. Sure enough, it's punctured, and blood beads over the surface. I look for Cara, and see her chatting with another assistant. I wave. She doesn't see me, but a middle-aged man in a pink polo shirt and checkered shorts does, and waves back.

Idiot, I grumble. Since he's the only person whose attention I've managed to grab, I gesture him over. He races toward me.

"I don't think I'm supposed to talk to you," he says, swiveling his face around like an alarmed puppy.

"Can you just get my assistant? I need a Band-Aid."

He catches sight of the trickling flow on my foot. "Right away." He jogs back toward the shore, but does a U-turn. "Which one is she?" He runs in place, which just looks odd.

"The peroxide blonde with the short hair," I say, pointing her out.

"Righty-o," he pants, and runs toward her. Still running in place, he taps her shoulder and aims his entire right arm toward me.

Cara disappears into one of the popcorn tents, reappears, and trots toward me. The first aid box in her hands reassures me that the guy wasn't a total idiot.

She kneels beside me and takes my feet in her hands. "It's not too bad."

"It hurts like a bitch," I say.

When she sprays antiseptic on my skin, a shrill scream jerks out of my throat. She eyes my sole more carefully. "Actually, the shard is pretty big."

"No kidding," I mutter.

She grabs a pair of tweezers from the medical kit and proceeds to dig through my skin for the sharp piece of wood. I clamp my teeth shut to avoid yelling again.

There's sweat on her brow. "I don't know if I can get it out. Maybe—"

"Give me that," I say, wrenching the tweezers out of her hands.

Trying not to flinch, I press my thumbnail against the butt of the shard to coax it out. Slowly, it moves back the way it came, and soon, the end of it appears like a baby squeezing out of its mother. I snap the tweezers around the shard and pull it out. It's no longer than my smallest nail, but it's sharp as a stake.

Cara, who's turned a little pale, soaks a fresh piece of cotton with antiseptic and applies it to my small wound, then she dabs some cream and covers the area with a large waterproof bandage. My foot throbs, but I stand up and walk on it. That's when inspiration hits. I pick up every piece of wood I can find, from twigs to branches.

When the mesh bag is about to burst, I return to the beach and dump out the contents in the space I was allotted. Lincoln is kneeling, a small piece of wood clasped in her hand. She's drawing or writing. Herrick is building a wall out of seashells. It's intricate, but doesn't look stable. Chase has been digging:

inside an enormous hole, he's sculpted hills and towers. He's building a sand castle. I smile to myself. Good dealers don't make great artists. But my amusement fades when I see the beginnings of Kevin's work. He's weaving the tall grass together and it's starting to pool at his feet like a rope.

Forgetting all about my foot, I commence, praying that the structured piece I'm planning will hold. I take two twigs and weave a stalk of grass around the ends to keep them together at an angle. Surprisingly, it works. I take another stick and then another, positioning them this way and that until I have something that resembles a small web. I keep at it until I run out of wood. I lay my piece down and pick up my bag. Fueled with excitement, I race back toward the long grass and tear more stalks and replenish my stock of wood. I step on a small seashell on my way back, and my foot pulses with pain, but I push on. The sun is no longer high in the sky and Lincoln and Chase are no longer crouched on the sand. Both are finished, and are being interviewed by Josephine in front of one of the cameras.

I kneel down, flip my bag over, and start again on my wooden spider web. I use longer sticks, which airs out the piece and makes it grow quicker. I can feel a crowd building around me, curious, but I don't waste time looking up. Spinning the web, I tie and angle, tie and angle, until the disk is larger than I am. Then I get up and study it. Against the pale sand, it resembles a trap.

My gaze lands on the large plank. I decide to strap my piece to it so that I can stand it up. I don't know if the long grass will suffice in maintaining it upright, but it's worth a shot. Inspired by Kevin's rope, I create a large plait with the grass, which I then wrap through the bottom rung of my web and tie around the plank. I craft five more fat braids to hold the plank base in place.

And then I pull my piece up. If it holds, it will be the most magnificent and complex work achieved today. If it collapses, it will very possibly get me eliminated.

213

THIRTY-THREE

"What the hell, Redd?"

I try to tip my head up, but it's as heavy as a bowling ball. It lolls right back to the floor where I've collapsed. I'm hoisted up. I try to pry my lids open, but they're glued shut.

"What the hell?" Chacha mutters again. "Get her some blankets. Anything in wool. Socks."

Light burns my lids. Warm hands rub my skin. I'm being moved from one side to the other. They're going to hurt the baby, but then I remember the baby's gone.

My clothes come off, or is it my skin? There's more rubbing. It feels like they're massaging bruises. It hurts. I want to tell them to stop, but my lips can't shape words. Besides, my mouth is too weak to expel them.

"I'm here, Aster," I hear.

*Ivy...*Ivy came back.

Sluggishly, painfully, I crack open my lids; it feels like cracking thick ice. I look for my sister, but can only see blurred shapes and blobs of color. I blink, but still, nothing is sharp, which pains my eyes, so I close them.

"Stay with me, Aster."

You *stay with me.* My heart moves delicately, like an eyelash flutter. *Choose* me *this time, not the show.*

"Don't cry. You're going to be all right." The voice is clearer, clear enough for me to realize that it doesn't belong to Ivy, but to Gill. "They sounded the air horn an hour ago. They thought you'd broken out. Didn't you hear it?"

I try to shake my head, but my neck is frozen.

Chacha grumbles, "Said she would take my shift so I could rest. Shoulda known. Shoulda known. Going to tell Driscoll. Stay with her."

I grab her arm but can't hold on. "On't," I whisper, unable to sound out the *D.*

"What did she say?" Chacha asks.

"I didn't hear anything."

The light goes gray behind my clasped lids.

Something soft touches my lips, like peach fuzz. "Say it again, Aster." Gill's voice is so close that it sounds like it's inside my head.

"On't," I whisper faintly. My throat is scratchy, like the fabric bunched around my hand.

The light turns gold again.

"She says *don't.* I don't think she wants you to tell Driscoll."

I part my lips and swallow a long sip of hot air. It stings my throat. And then I try to talk again, but my teeth keep clattering. Still, I manage, "Acci...acci...ent."

"Accident my ass," Chacha says.

"P-pease," I murmur.

"Maybe she's right. Maybe don't say anything."

"Cheyenne is a mean bitch. She—"

"It's Aster's choice."

"My kitchen. My rules."

"Then talk to Cheyenne, but don't involve the guards. Would that be okay, Aster?"

I manage a minuscule nod.

"What the—" It's a man's voice. "Where was she?"

"In the freezer," Chacha says. "It was an *accident*." I can tell from her intonation that she's pissed I've chosen to lie.

"I've got two patrols canvasing the area and she's in a fucking freezer? You got to be kidding me," Driscoll says. I hear him yap orders—probably calling the cavalry back. "Can she walk?"

"Keep her horizontal!" Chacha says. "Don't you know nothin'?" She grumbles something in a language I don't understand.

"*Yobwoc*, get in here! Carry her to the infirmary," the sergeant snaps.

Hands lift me. They're not very big, but I can tell they're not Gill's. They're calloused. How can I feel callouses through wool? Am I naked?

"I'll get her feet," Gill says.

"Keep her wrapped. Like a burrito. She needs to stay warm."

As I'm carried down the bright hallway, I squeeze my lids tighter, trying to block out the glare. I don't know where the infirmary is, but the trip there seems endless. Once we arrive, I'm deposited on a sheet of paper that crinkles underneath my weight.

Gill's explaining that I was locked inside the walk-in freezer for close to five hours. Fingers probe the vein on my neck. The blanket is removed. My hands are inspected. My toes, which feel like they are being pricked by a million needles, are probed. Something goes in my ear. It beeps.

"Ninety-one point five," the nurse reads out. "Mild hypothermia."

My lids are pressed up. A flashlight blinds me. I blink them back shut.

"Responsive eyes. Good. What's your name?"

"She's conscious," I hear Gill say.

"Did I ask you something?" the nurse snaps. She has a sturdy and authoritative voice. "What's your name?"

"Aaas...ssser," I murmur. My teeth are still chattering.

"Last name?"

"Rehh..."

"Inmate Swanson, can you get a bowl of broth from the kitchen?" she orders.

"Right away," Gill says.

Drawers open and close. Paper crinkles.

"Officer Landry, help me roll this under her," the nurse says.

I'm unwrapped, exposed again, and then squashed between something brittle and cool that turns hot in seconds. It crunches like paper, but it's not. *Foil.* That's what it must be.

"You can leave. I got it from here," the nurse says.

Silence.

"She'll be awhile."

"The sergeant will want to know how long," the young guard says.

"I don't know," she huffs. "First I need to stabilize her temperature, and then I need to get her to stop shivering."

"What should I tell him? He's going to want to know when he should pick her up."

"*When he should pick her up?*" she says. "Tell the sergeant he should *not* pick her up, because if he puts even a single toe in my infirmary, I'll cut off his tiny testicles and string them around my neck. Tell him that, will you?"

I wonder if my muddled mind has just made that up.

After a very long minute of silence, he says, "I-I can't tell him th—"

"Just tell him I'm keeping her overnight," she says. "Got it?"

"Yes."

"Now get."

After he's gone, she bustles around her infirmary. Gill returns. Together, they try to tilt my head up and slide some broth down my throat. I cough and gag. After another failed attempt, they release me. My head rolls to the side, and my cheek meets the pillow. The skin on my face has thawed out enough to feel the soft firmness. It reminds me of my pillow, the one I don't have to prop up with a book.

God, I miss my pillow. I miss my home.

I'M startled awake by the clicking sound of a keyboard.

"Good. You're up."

I jerk up on my elbows. Sweat coats my brow as my eyes dart from the white room to the middle-aged blonde shutting her laptop screen and coming toward me. I don't know who she is. Nothing looks familiar. Paper crunches beneath me and foil crackles. Why am I wrapped like the garlic bread we serve at the pizzeria?

The woman gently coaxes me back into a horizontal position and takes my pulse. It's late. I'm not sure how late, but there's barely any light outside.

"Do you remember what happened to you?" she asks, fastening a blood pressure monitor around my bicep.

I blink. Like feathers, fragmented memories drift into my mind. *Chacha. The basin of boiling water. The walk-in freezer. The cold.* Slowly, I nod.

"Being disoriented is a normal symptom. It's also a side effect of shock. But you'll be pleased to know your vitals are back to normal and your temperature's up. You're good as new."

She begins peeling the foil off my body. My skin is slick with perspiration, yet I don't feel particularly warm. I shiver when the air hits the sweat. The nurse catches my tremor, stops what she's doing, opens a cabinet, and extricates a folded towel. She lays it on top of me, and then proceeds to remove the rest of the foil.

"I heard talk it wasn't an accident," she says, peering at my face through a pair of canary-yellow bifocals.

I don't answer. I just stare at her boy-cut hair as it swishes around her face.

"You missed a good show today."

I raise an eyebrow.

"The Masterpiecers," she says, balling the foil and chucking it into the bin at the foot of the exam table. "It's my guilty pleasure, but don't tell anyone, okay?"

The pillow is soft and takes the shape of my cheek. "I won't," I whisper. But I don't want to talk about Ivy because, even though she didn't lock me up in the freezer, she told the cops I was crazy.

"You okay, hun?"

"Yeah," I croak, even though I'm not okay.

"Your sister's real talented."

Don't talk about her, I scream inside my head.

Unfortunately, she forges on. "I wish I could've bought something of hers before she got on the show, but it was already too expensive then. I got a stack of bills this high." She holds her palms apart as though there was an invisible accordion in between them. "And a mortgage and—"

I'm startled she knows the price of my sister's quilts.

"What?" She glances at the door. When she sees no movement behind the frosted glass, she peers back down at me. "Are you okay?"

I'm about to nod, but I find myself asking instead, "How do you know how much her quilts are worth?"

"Oh. Harry told me...I mean Commander Collins. He has one."

My brain catapults the picture on his desk to the forefront of my mind. That was what I'd realized when I was scouring Chacha's soup pot! His daughter was posing in front of one of Ivy's quilts. "The warden owns one of my sister's quilts."

It's not a question, yet the nurse treats it as such. "Yes. And it's *gor*-geous."

She smiles because she attributes my astonishment to sibling pride or awe when in fact, it stems from confusion. Did he buy it, or did she bribe him with it?

The nurse tucks me under the towel. "You can be really proud of your sister."

I don't answer.

"You want to watch some reruns of today's show on my laptop?"

"Do I have time?"

"Time? Hun, you're not going back to your cell tonight, and it's only seven thirty. Before they announce the winners, they'll show a recap of the day's highlights. I missed a bit when you came in." Since I'm not very enthusiastic, she adds, "But if you're too tired, I'll just listen to it on my headphones and let you rest."

"No. I want to see it."

"Great. Here, let me raise the backrest up a notch." She adjusts it so that I'm propped up. Then she sits on her wheelie chair, places her computer on her lap, and drags herself back over to my cot. She logs in to the TV network's website and pulls up the first and most popular tab: *The Masterpiecers*.

Her screen goes momentarily dark and then the image of a bright shore fills the blackness. How ironic that while I was freezing, Ivy was on a warm beach. The commentators launch into vivid descriptions of the day's test, from Lincoln's intricate drawing, to Chase's sand city, to Kevin's wild grass rope, to Ivy's magnificent stick spider web, to Herrick's transitory seashell wall. They're making prognostics as to who will get eliminated tonight. After seeing my sister's piece, I'm a hundred percent sure it won't be her. Nevertheless, I'm not enthusiastic because her talent has brought me nothing but pain.

As the recaps stop and the show goes live, I look for my sister. I find her sandwiched between Lincoln and Herrick, dressed in a flowy, Grecian gown that billows around her ankles. All the competitors are in white tonight. They're standing a few feet away from a massive bonfire like warlocks and witches about to leap into the pyre to burn for their sins. The flames dance across their tense faces. I search my sister's expression for emotion and spot nervousness. I wonder if she knows what happened to me today.

"I don't see how she would," the nurse tells me, her gaze taped to the screen.

"What?"

She swings her gaze toward me. "You asked if she knew what happened to you today."

I said it out loud. *Wow*, my brain must not have thawed out completely. "Right."

The video montage people have divided the screen into six equal parts. Five of them show the artworks, and the last show Dominic raising the microphone to his lips to announce the loser.

"This is my least favorite part of the show," he begins by saying. "Especially now that we—Josephine, Brook, and I— have discovered how talented you all are. Please remember that disqualification doesn't mean you lack talent or intelligence. Disqualification just means you didn't score well on this particular test."

He studies them, offering each a pearly smile. But then his smile fades as his gaze settles on one particular contestant. I can't tell if he's looking at Ivy or Herrick.

"Herrick Hawk, your piece was inspired, but not thought out enough. One puff of wind, and it buckled. Even though some art is as transient as a butterfly, at the Masterpiecers, we believe in creating something perennial." Dominic walks toward him and puts his hand on the twenty-three-year-old's shoulder. "We will miss you deeply. And on behalf of everyone here on the show, I wish you the best of luck with all of your future endeavors."

As Herrick's face decomposes, the image switches to flashbacks of his journey on the show: snippets of interviews and slow motion highlights of Herrick competing, laced with pretty music. The nurse sniffs next to me, lifting her glasses to blot the tears from her eyes. I don't feel particularly sad for him. It's just a stupid show. He's not going to rot away in a cell for having rid the Earth of a bad person.

THIRTY-FOUR

Ivy

"I really didn't think I'd be sticking around after my sand castle exploit," Chase tells me as we are led to the banquet underneath the white big top.

I laugh because I'm in a good mood. Not only am I still on the show, but my work has been touted as the most magnificent piece of the day. I felt it would be, but a gut feeling isn't worth as much as spoken compliments. I spy Herrick in my peripheral vision. His cheeks are blotchy red and his nose is running, and his big hair, which is usually so perfectly slick, is standing on end. He's a mess. If I lose, I won't make such a miserable display of myself in front of the cameras. I'll keep it together.

"By the way, Chase, thank you for last night."

"Last night?" Brook says, appearing beside us. "What happened last night?" Brook eyes his brother, then me, but thankfully doesn't insinuate anything.

"Kevin was out late," I tell him. "And since we don't have locks on our tents—"

"You have nothing to worry about," Chase says.

I frown. "Have you seen the size of him? Plus he hates my

guts. Brook, would it be possible to get an extra camera to monitor our hallway?"

"I'll see what I can do. Anyway, congratulations, you two."

"It's Ivy you should congratulate. My work was pretty pathetic," Chase says.

"Maybe, but you're still here," he says.

The vein in Chase's temple throbs. I don't think he wanted Brook to validate his comment, I'm pretty sure he wanted him to tell him how crafty it was. Brook's gaze is focused on me, so he's oblivious to his brother's soured mood.

"I'm going to grab something to drink," Chase mutters. "You want anything, Ivy?"

"I'm fine, thanks."

"Nothing alcoholic," Brook says with a grin. "At least not for the next"—he checks his expensive wristwatch—"three hours and forty seven minutes."

Chase doesn't return his smile. He just leaves.

"What happens in three hours and forty seven minutes?" I ask.

"He's going to be legal."

"Oh, right." I glance at Chase. The white linen shirt is stretched tight across his shoulder blades and his dark copper hair gleams in the firelight. "He doesn't seem very excited about it."

"Oh, he will be. I've organized fireworks and s'mores and a champagne fountain."

I don't think a big celebration will thrill Chase.

"I wanted to tell you something." Brook's voice has dropped so much that I think he's going to bring up the elevator conversation again. "Kevin's lawyer is here."

"Really?" I squeak.

"He scored an invite without us knowing. Jeb was reviewing the raw footage earlier and recognized him. Anyway, I've told Dominic, who's asked him to leave, but he says he didn't come here as Kevin's lawyer, but as Madame Babanina's guest."

"Madame who?"

"Madame Babanina. One of the show's biggest sponsors. Cleaned her husband out in a divorce, and then donated half his money to the school to annoy him. Anyway, Kevin's lawyer was her lawyer and—"

"Can you point him out?" I ask.

Brook turns and inspects the beach. After a few seconds, he tips his chin toward a man sitting to the right of a woman sporting tight black lace and exaggeratedly curved bangs— Madame Babanina. "If he talks to you, you come straight to me, okay?"

I nod.

"On another note..."

"Yes?"

"Would you consider selling me your web?"

"You want to buy my web?"

"Yes. I'd like to buy it."

"Can you?"

"I have money." He gives me a big smile.

"No, I mean, doesn't that break some show rule?"

"There's no rule against purchasing art from an artist. Didn't you see the Zara Mach accordion over my bed?"

My heart's vaulting against the walls of my chest at being called an artist by a real connoisseur. I take a deep breath and try to think of something to say besides yelling, *hell, yes.* "I wasn't going to sell it..." My voice shakes. I suddenly wish Chase were here. He'd get me a hell of a price.

"Okay, but now that I'm offering, how much would you find fair?"

I pretend to think about it. When enough time has passed, I say, "Thirty thousand."

"That's reasonable," he says.

Reasonable? It's outrageous! I made the piece out of twigs and grass. I keep my cool and fold my arms. "Cash."

"No. I need to write you a check. For tax and insurance reasons."

"Oh. Right."

"Trust me, you don't want to get acquainted with the IRS."

I run through mental calculations of how much I'll be left with.

"Don't worry, you're still going to make a bunch of money, Ivy."

He's right, but it probably won't be enough to cover the amount of Aster's bail now that she's being charged with first-degree murder. If she can even make bail. I shiver and look down at my bare feet. They replaced the Band-Aid with a sturdier one, so that I can go into the sea, but the inky darkness doesn't inspire me.

"So do we have a deal?" he asks.

I crane my neck to look at Brook. "Yes."

He extends his hand. I lift mine and feed my fingers around his.

"What are we shaking hands to?" the photographer asks.

I yank my hand away.

"I've just bought my first Ivy Redd piece," Brook says with a smile.

Patrick's brown eyes grow rounder. He snaps a picture of my face, and then finally lowers his camera. "The web?"

"The Web," Brook says, grinning. He glances at me, the smile growing on his lips. "Shall we call it that?"

"Sure."

I spot Kevin a few feet away, hard to miss considering how sunburnt his large forehead has become. He's talking with his lawyer and another man sporting a wool suit and a cherry-red tie. Something about him strikes me as familiar. I'm sure I've seen him before, but where?

"I might not be the first owner of a Redd original, but I'm certainly the luckiest because I saw it come to life under my very own eyes. How many collectors can claim that?" Brook is telling the photographer. Suddenly, his hand closes over my arm. "Excuse us, Patrick. I have someone I'd like to introduce to my contestant." We walk straight toward Kevin and the two men. "Ivy, I'd like you to meet Dean Kane, my dear friend and the lawyer who will be defending your sister."

Frowning, I shake hands with the man with the bright tie. And then it hits me where I saw him. After the performance art test.

"And this is Mister Kelley," Brook says, gesturing to Kevin's lawyer.

I shake his hand too, even though I really don't want to.

"I should get back to Madame Babanina. She doesn't like to be left alone," he says. "Mister Martin, I am deeply sor—"

Kevin, whose chin is tucked into his neck, doesn't wait for him to finish his sentence before traipsing away.

"Brook, may I speak to Ivy privately? I'd like to discuss her sister's case," Dean says.

"Sure, but don't bore her with too many details."

He nods and we set out along the beach, toward the obscurity beyond the big top.

Once we cross over into the darkness, I ask, "What were you talking about with Kevin and his lawyer?"

"His press release. I told him to cancel it."

"Did he agree?"

"He did."

"Really?"

Dean nods.

"How? Why?"

"I have proof that your sister didn't doctor those photos."

"Who did, then?"

"I can't disclose that information."

"I won't tell anyone."

He shakes his head. "Sorry, Ivy, but you'll find out if Kevin decides to go public with it. Now, about your sister's case. I'm unclear about something. How well did *you* know Troy Mann?"

"Me?"

He nods.

"I sold him a quilt, but that's it."

"Your sister told me you spent a long time in the apartment with him."

"What? How would she know? She was at work."

"No. She was leaving for work. Got in late. I checked with the receptionist at the ad agency."

"She was spying on me?"

"What did you talk about with Mister Mann when he came to your place?"

"I just showed him the different quilts I'd made, and then we discussed prices."

"Which one did he purchase?"

"A quilt depicting a city skyline."

"I'd appreciate if you told me the truth, Ivy. I might be your sister's lawyer, but I'm also working on your behalf."

"I-I am."

He cocks his head to the side. His hair is so slick with gel that it reflects the moonlight. "Aster sent the quilt he bought to the show, so I assume it's the one you auctioned off."

I freeze and look beyond him, at the lavish, prattling crowd. "Fine...yes...that's the one. Did she tell you why she sent it?"

"No."

"Could you ask her?"

My gaze drifts to the red tie hooked around Dean's collar that's held tight against his dress shirt by a large gold bar. He fingers it. "Sure, but that wouldn't do much for her case."

"It would do a lot for my state of mind."

"Apparently, the quilt was torn," he says, obviously not caring much about my morale.

"Did *she* tell you that?"

"No. Brook did. Would you know why?"

"Either Aster ripped it because she was angry with me or it was damaged in transit," I mutter.

He narrows his eyes, and I bristle. I don't like him. I bet Aster doesn't either.

"What? You have another theory?" I ask.

"We're dealing with a mobster, so yes, I do have another theory. I think he was using the quilt to transport something."

I blink.

"Any thoughts as to what that might be?" he asks.

"No," I whisper.

"Well, if you think of anything, let Brook know and he'll convey your message to me. Now, about your sister's case. The DA upgraded it to first-degree murder, which means that she's facing forty years to life."

"I heard, but it was self-defense."

"Your sister followed Troy Mann back to the motel he was staying in, thus instigating the threatening situation, so pleading self-defense would work as well as an apology."

"But she didn't mean to."

"I beg to differ. From the coroner's transcript, she hit him a first time, then backed up and rolled over him. I'm building my defense upon the fact that she's schizophrenic."

"She what?"

He repeats what he's just said, padding the account with such vivid details that I think I'm going to throw up.

"So I'll have her plead insanity," he tells me.

"She's going to hate that," I say in a small voice that's almost swallowed by the sound of the waves lapping at my feet.

"It's her only hope of getting out."

After a long moment, I nod.

"You'll have to testify—"

"No."

"Do you want to save your sister or not?"

"I do."

"Then you'll have to give a testimony."

"I have a paper."

"What sort of paper?"

"One she signed to give me power of attorney over her. If you show it to the judge, then I won't need to testify, right?"

The ocean fills the night with its briny, wild scent.

"I'll need that paper."

"You won't tell her about it, will you?"

"She signed it, didn't she?" he asks.

"She didn't read it."

"Oh." Dean tips his head to the side and observes me. "To use it in court, she'll have to swear she signed it of her own free will."

I dig my feet into the cold, wet sand. "There's no way around Aster finding out what I think about her?"

"If I were you, I'd be less worried about offending your sister and more worried about convincing a judge that her actions stemmed solely from her...how should I put it? *Bewildered* mind."

"Where else would they stem from?"

"Did you ever think that perhaps your sister knew there was something in the quilt...something extremely valuable? And that's why she killed Troy Mann."

My jaw slackens because I hadn't considered that. And suddenly it all makes sense. And I understand how my sister—who barely can afford food and gas—managed to give me a diamond as big as one of my nails. She found it inside the quilt.

THIRTY-FIVE

When my burger arrives, my appetite vanishes. Or maybe it vanished when the nurse confirmed the warden owned one of my sister's works. It's not so much the fact that he possesses one that bothers me, but the fact that he hid it from me. I've been trying to come up with reasons. I have two. My sister sold it to him, and then asked him to keep quiet about it so that I wouldn't know she'd made money and ask her for some. Not that I would ever grovel. Or, she gave it to him so that he would treat me well.

If she gave it to him, then I should be ashamed of all the bad thoughts I've been harboring about my sister. If she sold it to him, then my bad thoughts are founded.

"I have some fresh clothes for you to change into," the nurse says, handing me a folded gray jumpsuit, a white T-shirt, a white bra, and a pair of cotton panties.

I loosen the towel, but keep it over me as I pull on the underwear. The nurse surely has seen me naked, but that was when I was unconscious.

"I'm going to head home, but I'll be back first thing tomorrow morning. I've organized for Officer Landry to move you to a cell in the medical unit. Another nurse will come in for the night shift. If you feel ill or anything, just let her know."

"Okay."

She slings her roomy handbag over her shoulder. Her laptop peeps out of it. "I hope you have a good night."

"Nurse—"

"Celia," she finishes.

"Nurse Celia, thank you."

"Just doing my job." She smiles and draws open the door, and her yellow bifocals that hang on a chain around her neck bounce against her double Ds. "Sweet dreams, Miss Redd." *Miss Redd*...not Inmate Redd or Redd...*Miss*. Never thought I'd appreciate the title as much.

The young officer—the one Driscoll bosses around—is standing right outside. She clicks off the light and leaves me with him.

"Can you walk?" he asks.

"I think so. Is it far?"

"No."

I lower myself off the exam table and take wobbly steps to the open doorway and past the guard. He leads me to a cell two doors down and unlocks a gate. The windowless room is entirely padded and contains a single iron bed. No toilet. No sink. A chill races over my skin because it looks fit for a crazy person. He waits until I'm inside, then bolts the gate shut behind me. I sit on the bed. The springs creak and the mattress feels like a slab of wood.

"You sleep now," he says, settling on a chair outside.

"I'm not tired."

"Well, you have to sleep. The nurse—"

"Okay. Okay." I lean back and close my eyes just to please him.

I hear paper rustle. I crack one lid up. He's pulled out a small paperback from his jacket pocket. From the cover, I can tell it's a spy novel. Spy novels always look the same: dark woods with just a faint source of light. His gaze lifts toward me and I snap my lids shut again.

I try to sleep, but I just can't. "Actually, I'm hungry," I say, sitting up. "My dinner's on Nurse Celia's desk. You mind bringing it over?"

He looks perplexed, as though I've asked him to fetch me the moon.

"I promise I'll sleep right after."

"Fine." He stuffs the book back into his pocket, leaves and returns seconds later with my tray. He unbolts the gate, slides the tray in, and locks it up again. Then he just stands there, arms crossed.

I hope he's not planning on staring at me while I eat. "You mind?"

"Unwrap the foil and open the bun."

"Are you serious?"

"Very. I need to check for weapons."

I grumble, but do as I'm told. The beef patty is squashed and overcooked, the single leaf of salad wilted and wet with ketchup, and the bun mushy from having stayed wrapped in the foil. "No razorblade. Happy?"

He nods and sits back down while I reassemble my burger and take a bite. It turns out to be the best thing I've eaten since getting sent to prison. My mouth literally waters as I shove bite after bite down my throat. Too soon, not a crumb remains, yet my stomach rumbles for more.

I ball up the foil and place it on the tray. "How old are you?" I ask him.

"Why do you want to know?"

"Geez, it's just a question."

"Nineteen," he says.

"Shouldn't you be in college?"

"I'm trying to earn some money to pay for college."

"And then what?"

"I'd like to become a lawyer."

"A lawyer?"

"I'm studying already."

"Let me guess…you're going to specialize in criminal law."

"Maybe. I don't know yet."

"What does *yobwoc* mean?" I ask him.

"It's cowboy spelled backwards. That's what Driscoll calls the new officers."

I stretch out on the hard mattress and turn on my side, but I can't get comfortable, so I turn on the other. I stare at the cream-colored padding that's ochre in places and try to even out my breathing. There's a particularly gross spot on one of the seams that's more brown than orange. I stare at it until my vision blurs and I see double, and then triple. But still, I don't sleep.

"Can you read the story out loud?" I ask the nineteen-year-old officer.

Surprisingly, he does. And even more surprising, the story's enthralling. It's about a detective who unscrambles a prostitution ring. And, lo and behold, discovers his wife belongs to it. At some point, the brown stain fades, and the officer's voice lulls, and I finally fall asleep. And I dream.

THIRTY-SIX

Ivy

"Who was that?" Lincoln asks me after I've returned from my stroll down the beach with Dean.

"My sister's lawyer," I say.

"He's hot."

I shrug as I roam around the buffet, my plate still empty.

"Is he single?"

"Don't know. He's Brook's friend. Ask *him*," I say, just as I spot the two of them in conversation.

"Are you going to eat anything?"

"Yeah. But I don't know what."

"The smoked salmon's really good."

"Okay." I scoop some onto my plate, ladle a dollop of cream, and select some bread that looks like a pancake, which I assume goes with it since it's on the same platter. "Where are we sitting?"

"Over there." She pokes her chin to the table closest to the water. "I'm going to get a refill and be right over. I got the bartender to add some rum inside. Want one?"

I'm about to say no, but end up saying yes. I want alcohol. I want to cloud my brain so I can stop thinking about Aster deliberately flattening a man's skull with her car to steal his diamonds. There are two empty seats: one next to Kevin and one next to Chase. It's a no-brainer. I'm sitting next to Kevin. I want to know why he canceled his press release.

"Can I get an apology?" I ask, sliding in next to him.

He's staring at the bouquet of lavender in front of him. His neck is larger than my thigh and marked with thin white lines as though he repeatedly cut himself with his razor blade. "For what?"

"For wrongfully accusing my sister."

He turns toward me and I notice that his eyes are red-rimmed.

"Have you been crying?"

"It's none of your business," he mumbles.

"I didn't know sergeants were such sensitive beings."

His eyes taper dangerously close to his crooked nose. "Shut up," he murmurs.

"I'll shut up if you stop lurking in the hallway at night."

"What are you talking about?"

"Lincoln told me all about it."

"All about what?" he asks.

"About Chase finding you just outside my tent," I say.

"What?"

"Are you going to deny it?"

He shakes his head and gives a mean laugh. "I wasn't stalking you."

"I heard you! Just outside—"

He presses his chair back and shoots up.

"Is the big, mean soldier angry?" I tease as he hurries away.

I must have said it louder than I intended because both Herrick and Chase glare at me like I'm the callous one.

"What?" I say.

"You're a bitch, Ivy," Herrick says.

I frown. Lincoln's on her way back from the bar. When

she walks, her hips roll from side to side. "Hey, kiddies," she says, and swoops down next to Chase. She places a glass in front of me and winks. "What did I miss?"

Herrick pushes out of his chair and heads in the direction Kevin disappeared in.

"*O-kay*? Did I say something?" she asks, taking a huge gulp of her drink. Some of it dribbles down her chin.

"Chase, can I talk to you a sec?" I ask.

Lincoln waggles her dark brows.

"I'm good here," he says.

"Ouch," Lincoln says.

I try to catch his attention, but he's purposely looking away.

"By the way"—Lincoln raises her glass—"I heard we have something to celebrate." I think she's about to mention Chase's birthday, which I'm not in the mood to celebrate, when she says, "To your big sale!"

"What big sale?" Chase asks.

"Oh...you didn't hear? Your brother bought the piece she made today. For a *lot* of money," she adds, with a sly grin. She knocks back her drink. "Ivy, why aren't you drinking?" Her voice is really loud, and in spite of the music blasting out of the loudspeakers dotting the beach, some people have turned to stare. "One teeny sip. Come on, Redd. Don't leave me hanging."

I pick up the glass. Instead of taking a sip, I down the entire thing. Just to get her off my case.

"Good girl," she says.

The second the alcohol hits my empty stomach, I feel it bubble in my veins, irrigate my organs, and froth upward. I grab the salty pancake and stuff it inside my mouth, barely chewing it. My head spins a little and my face feels bloated. I touch it to make sure it isn't. Maybe I'm having an allergic reaction. Maybe—

The drink rises. I fling myself away from the table and cross the beach toward the port-o-potties. I'm going to throw up any second. I focus on keeping my lips sealed so I don't spout vomit. I try the first door but it's locked. The second door opens. I just have time to kneel before my stomach drains itself. Tears surge up and drip down my cheeks, plopping inside the toilet bowl. I'm not sure if I'm crying because I threw up or because of my sister's crime.

When I feel steady enough, I get up and wobble over to the glass sink. I rinse my mouth and splash cool water over my face. I take one last gulp of tap water, spit it out, then leave. I don't want to return to the table, so I wander away from the festivities. I hear hushed voices nearby belonging to two dark bodies pressed against each other. One is unmistakable—Brook—the other is a woman in black lace. Madame Babanina, the notorious divorcée. I scurry away before either of them can spot me and run smack into Chase, who steadies me. Before he can talk and have us discovered, I place my finger against my lips, point to the couple behind me, and walk to the water's edge, my footsteps muffled by the soft sand.

"Ivy?"

I turn around, surprised that Chase followed me.

"Why are you talking to me?" A gust of wind kicks up my hair and swirls it. "I thought I was a bitch."

"I didn't say that."

"But you were thinking it."

"You have no idea what I was thinking."

I take a small step into the water, not bothering to lift my flowy skirt. It's cool and prickles my ankles. "Kevin was outside my tent last night. Apparently, you saw him."

"I did."

"Then why am I the bad one?" I ask him.

Chase's eyes gleam, dark and shiny like the ocean. "He didn't come to see you. He came to see me."

"You? Why?"

Chase stares at me long and hard, as though trying to decide whether to confide in me. "He's...confused."

"About how to kill me?" I say with a snort.

"About how he feels about men."

My stomach, which is still unsettled, now feels as though it's been sucker-punched. "Oh." As I attempt to link the beefy sergeant to his sexuality, I ask, "Why didn't he go see Herrick then?"

"Were you attracted to J.J.?"

"No."

"Well, he's not attracted to every man either."

"He has feelings for *you?*"

"I know, right? Unbelievable...someone actually has feelings for me."

"That's not what I meant."

"It's fine," he says. "But we're unfortunately not wired to automatically return an admirer's affection, so I had to turn him down. I promised to keep his secret, though."

"Yet you told me..."

"So you'd stop hating him. He's not a bad guy, Ivy."

"He hasn't been very nice to me," I say.

"And you haven't been very nice to him. Now, you can start being nicer."

"But Lincoln told me—"

"Don't listen to her. Listen to *me.*"

I'm not sure whether I should listen to anyone. "Why was he crying?"

"I think it has to do with those pictures."

A high-pitch screech makes my heart pitch. I spin around and notice that people have jumped into the water and are squealing with delight. I feel a hand close over mine and tug on my fingers.

"Swim with me?" Chase says.

"I—I, uh...don't know how to swim."

"You don't?" When I stay mute, he adds, "Is that why you didn't want to go inside Brook's pool?"

I nod.

He smiles. He's very handsome when he smiles.

"I can teach you."

I swallow. "I don't feel like learning tonight."

"Then let's not swim. But let's go in a little deeper."

"What if a wave knocks me over?"

"I'll catch you," he says softly.

Perhaps it would help me get over what happened to Mom. "Okay." When my skirt floats up around me, I stop. "That's far enough."

His eyebrows quirk up.

"Don't swim away, okay?"

"I won't," he says, inspecting my face. He must notice the tension thrashing inside of me, because he adds, "There's a simple way of keeping me close."

Even though the water's cold, I can't feel it. The only thing I can feel is an increasing amount of blood pumping through my body. "Promising to let you win?"

"Not everything is about this competition." With his free hand, he touches my jaw, brushes his palm over my cheek, runs a finger along the ridge of my creased brow, and then he inches closer to me and moves his mouth over mine. His lips are soft and warm, as soft and warm as his hands that he's wrapped around my waist. As he nudges my mouth open, one of his hands travels up my spine, while the other pulls me closer. When his tongue touches mine, tremors and tingles explode everywhere in my body.

"We shouldn't," I whisper into his mouth, before pulling away.

"Why?"

"Because. There are a lot of people around. And cameras. And—"

He kisses me again.

I press him back. "Chase, I'm serious."

He frowns this time.

"People will gossip," I say.

"Let them."

"But—"

"Ivy, in four days, all of these people"—he motions to the big top—"will be gone."

"And so will one of us." My voice is muffled by an explosion overhead.

The fireworks have started. Is it already midnight? The sky glistens white and blue and gold.

"It's your birthday. You should go celebrate," I say, stroking the foamy surface of the water.

"I am celebrating. By being with you," he whispers. His breath is warm and makes goose bumps appear along my lobe and jaw.

"I thought you didn't like me."

"Well, you thought wrong."

My pulse pounds in my ears, rivaling the multicolored thunder overhead.

Suddenly a loud "Happy Birthday" chant erupts from the speakers and a spotlight falls over us. I spring away from him, but he reins me in.

"Stay with me," he whispers.

So I do. Because it's his birthday, and because I like the feel of his arm wrapped around my waist. But then I spot something behind him, a shape floating on the inky surface, a human shape, face down, moonlit and motionless. I tear my hand out of Chase's and fling myself into the cold surf, my arms cutting through the water.

I'm the first to reach the body.

THIRTY-SEVEN

I gasp awake and press a clammy palm against my lungs. It was just a nightmare...just a nightmare. As I spot Celia trundling inside the padded cell, I recall the horrid dream. I was in a water tank with no air, and this dead body was floating next to me with shimmery straight teeth and long blonde hair twisting like seaweed. At first, I thought it was Ivy, but then I saw my sister standing just outside the tank, sad but resigned, mouth opening and closing as though trying to tell me something. Something I couldn't make out. I force the nightmare into a dusky recess of my mind, but it clings to me like an insect trapped in jam.

"I'm taking Miss Redd back to the infirmary." Celia hoists me up. She's breathless, and a rivulet of sweat snakes down her neck between her large breasts.

Officer Landry rubs his eyes, which makes me think he was on duty all night.

"You'll never believe what happened," she whispers as we walk past him.

"Has there been a breakout?" Officer Landry blinks

rapidly and repeatedly, like a caffeine addict before their first morning cup.

Nurse Celia flaps her hand at him. "No, no. Settle down. There's a world outside prison, you know?"

He stops blinking.

It takes me a second to get my bearings. As she leads me back to her blindingly white office, yesterday dribbles back into my muddled brain.

She orders me to lie down on the exam table. "Last night, during the fireworks, Martin was found dead."

"Who?" I ask.

"Kevin. You know, on the Masterpiecers! He drowned! Can you believe it? I can't. It's chaos in New York, and it's all over the news, and when I stopped by Starbucks this morning, everyone was talking about it. It's crazy. Pure insanity." She has her hand over her heart as though trying to squish her excitement.

My own heart is bouncing inside its cavity, not from excitement, but from dread. And from the nightmare that still feels too real. "Was he killed?" I think of those forms my sister made me sign before leaving. Perhaps the show *is* dangerous.

"Oh, no. No foul play. He committed suicide. Apparently he was crying most of the night. Can you believe it?" she asks me again.

I shiver, which makes my dreadlocks tickle my shoulder blades.

"That photographer on the show...what's his name...you know, the famous one? Anyway he snapped some pictures of the evening and he caught one of Kevin running into the water."

"Didn't he know how to swim?" I ask.

"Are there soldiers who don't know how to swim?"

"I don't know."

"Landry?" she says loudly, spinning around. "Are there soldiers who don't know how to swim?"

"It's not a requirement to join the army, ma'am, but usually people are taught during training."

Then she asks, "What are you still doing here?"

"Uh...I'm waiting to take Inmate Redd back."

"That won't be for a while. I need to run some blood pressure tests and monitor her temperature. And then Robyn wants to see her."

"I'll wait outside then."

"No, no. Just go. I'm sure you have better things to do. Wouldn't want Driscoll to get his panties in a twist, now would we?" She flashes him a brazen smile, which deepens the small lines on the outer corner of her eyes.

After he nods, she shuts the door and locks it. Then she goes to her desk, yanks her laptop out of her slouchy bag.

"I'll show you," she whispers, putting on her yellow glasses.

As she clicks here and there, she rambles on, "Barely slept all night I was so darn agitated. I think it's because it feels like I know one of the contestants personally this year. What with Ivy being your identical twin and all."

Just as she mentions Ivy, a picture of her appears: she's standing alone, on the beach, her profile illuminated by a burst of firework. Her dress is entirely transparent, and her blonde hair is pasted to her forehead and breasts.

Nurse Celia clicks through the rest of the pictures available on the website. One of them makes me grip her wrist to stop her from snapping to the next. I let go right away.

"Could you zoom in?" I ask.

She does. Two darkened figures stand by the water line.

"Who's that?" she asks.

"My new lawyer."

"He's dreamy. Is he single?"

"I don't know." *But he's a good two decades younger than you.*

Someone knuckles the door. It makes us both jump. Nurse Celia shuts her laptop and leaps off the exam table. "One second," she yells, grabbing some keys from her bag and unlocking one of the closets. She grabs her lab coat off a hanger and throws it on before opening up. "Oh. It's you. You don't take orders real well, now do you?" She snaps the press-studs of her white coat closed. "Aster's not ready."

She's about to shut the door in Driscoll's red face, but he presses it open and barges in. "She has a visitor."

"Who?"

"Her lawyer."

"Why?"

"I don't think that concerns you, Celia."

Celia folds her arms in front of her chest.

The sergeant's gaze travels to the crest of her bosom and lingers there. "Is she well enough to see him?"

She turns toward me. "Aster, you well enough to see your lawyer?"

"Yes," I say, hopping off the exam table.

"Okay then." She snatches the keys off her desk and walks over to me, extending her arm. "Lean on me, okay?" Even though I don't feel the need for a crutch, I hang on.

"Where are *you* going?" Driscoll asks Celia, as we step out of the office.

"I'm walking her to the attorney visitation area," she says, locking her door.

"That's my job."

"She's *my* patient," Celia counters, even though I doubt that's the reason she's accompanying me.

"You are impossible," he grumbles, tailing us down the hallway.

"Don't you have some young guard to annoy?"

"I'm training him."

"He's not a dog," she says. "Then again, that's how you treat everyone."

Ouch.

"Don't you go pretending you're some saint, 'cause you're not, Cee! Saints don't sock their boyfriends with their keys." He's pointing to the scar on his eyebrow.

She whirls around, jerking me with her. "You got blown by a fucking convict while we were dating," she hisses. "You deserved it!" Then she spins back and marches me down the hallway. "Sorry, Aster. Didn't mean to stick you in the middle. Men are such a-holes."

Dean's already inside the visitation room. He's looking over some papers and drumming his fingers against the desk. When the door clicks open, he looks up. His eyes travel first to me, then to the nurse's flushed face. He stands up, extends his hand, and introduces himself. Celia does the same.

"*Nurse?*" He raises an eyebrow. "What happened?"

"An incident. Terrible what these girls do to each other in here. Just terrible." Obviously, she's decided not to believe in the accident theory.

"What did they do?" he asks.

Celia's shaking her head; her short hair wisps around her heart-shaped face. "Locked her in the freezer for hours."

I shrug away from Celia. "Why did you go to New York?" I ask, redirecting the conversation.

He gestures to the table. "Let's sit. Celia"—he fishes a business card from his pebbled black wallet and gives it to her—"it was a pleasure meeting you. Can you keep me informed of any more incidents?"

Celia smiles widely, takes the card, and slips it into her lab coat's breast pocket. He's going to regret giving it to her. "Of course. You can count on me. I'll leave you two to it. Aster, come see me after your appointment with Robyn...to run all your tests."

When she leaves, Dean and I both sit. I knot my fingers together on the table. "What were you doing in New York?"

"I went to see Kevin and his lawyer."

"He's dead."

"I heard. Suicide." There's no emotion in his voice.

"Why?"

"His wife claims it resulted from his PTSD."

"It's crazy. Just yesterday he was threatening Ivy and now...now he's gone. Is she okay?"

"Who? His wife?"

"No. My sister."

He shrugs. "She seemed all right. Maybe a little shaken, but considering she's the one who fished him out, it's understandable."

My water nightmare. I dreamt of drowning because of Ivy. They say that one twin is the receiver and the other, the transmitter. I've always felt Ivy's fears, joys, melancholy, but she's never sensed mine.

"I updated her about your case," Dean's saying. He plays with his tie. Today, it's sky blue with geometric motifs. "What was inside the quilt, Aster?"

"Inside?" I whisper, my voice catching. "Inside what quilt?"

"Don't play dumb with me. Your sister told me the quilt you stole from Troy Mann is the one that ended up on the show. I know you didn't destroy it."

"I-I..."

"She also told me there was a tear in it, which I assume was used as a makeshift pocket to transport something. Now the question is, what?"

I look down at my overlapping fingers. I'm squeezing them so hard, the tips are red and the knuckles are white.

"Any ideas?"

I shake my head.

"You were the first person to handle it after Troy Mann," he says.

"There was no tear when I had it."

Dean watches me for so long that I shift in my seat.

"I have to go meet with the prison psychologist now," I tell him.

He sighs. "Fine. Don't answer. You're the one losing out. Not me."

As I get up and walk toward the door, he slaps his papers back into his briefcase.

"I have an appointment with Officer Cooper this after-noon," Dean says.

I whirl around. "You do? Why?"

"As a character witness. I heard he was a friend. A close friend."

My palms become moist. "He doesn't know anything."

"He doesn't know anything about you, or about the quilt?"

"About nothing." I wipe my hands against my jumpsuit. "I'd like to see him. Can you tell him I'd like to see him?"

"Didn't I make it clear that the only person you should be in contact with is me from now on?"

"I won't discuss the case."

He fixes me for a long moment, as though attempting to decide whether to believe me.

"He's my only friend."

"I'm not surprised."

I frown. "Why would you say that?"

"I'm good at reading people, and you don't strike me as a social butterfly."

"Well, it's not true. I made friends here. Gill's my friend."

"Gill who?"

"Swanson. You can use her as a character witness."

"Noted."

I press on the buzzer to signal the guard I want out.

"Oh...before you go, Ivy entrusted me with this." He digs something from the front pocket of his briefcase and plops it onto the table so indelicately that the porcelain practically shatters.

I stare at it without moving for so long that Dean picks it up and walks it over to me. He yanks my limp hand open, places the box on my palm, and rolls my fingers over it.

And then he gives me an oily smile. "She also told me to tell you that she's terribly angry with you. Disappointed were her exact words. She said you would know why."

I blanch.

He glances down at his gold wristwatch. "Shouldn't you be going? I wouldn't want you to be late."

THIRTY-EIGHT

Ivy

The ride back from Fire Island to the Metropolitan Museum was quiet and the night even quieter. We all retreated to our rooms, stunned into silence at Kevin's fate. I didn't sleep, and after close inspection of the faces around the breakfast table, I'm pretty sure no one else did either. We weren't woken up this morning, yet we all converged in the dining room at approximately the same time. It's Herrick's last meal with us. I can't bring myself to say anything to him after he called me a bitch. I know it's petty of me to hold on to that after what happened, but I can't help it.

"It'll be weird being just the three of us," Lincoln says.

"I have to admit, I'm sort of glad I'm leaving. It's going to be such a fiasco around here," Herrick says, spooning scrambled eggs into his mouth.

Lincoln smirks. "More than it was already?"

Chase picks at his blueberry muffin, turning it into crumbs. He doesn't eat the crumbs. He just stares at them as though trying to divine his future from their pattern. He hasn't spoken a word to me since I dragged Kevin's body back to the beach. I don't know if he blames me for his death or if he's angry I lied to him about not knowing how to swim.

"That was the first dead body I ever saw," Lincoln says. "It's weird how colorless we become in death."

"Please stop. I'm trying to eat," Chase says.

Lincoln checks his plate. "No, you're not."

He shakes his head. He hasn't combed his hair, and it's spiky in places.

"Morning." It's Brook and Josephine. "Herrick, Dominic apologizes for not being here to see you off. He's in negotiations with the network. They want a guarantee that the show will wrap up and not be abandoned mid-competition."

"So it really will go on?" Lincoln says. There's a hopeful undertone to her voice.

Brook gives a grave nod.

"*Demain*," Josephine says. "Tomorrow. We start again tomorrow."

"Chase, Mom and Dad would like to spend the day with you. To celebrate your birthday. I'll try to meet you for lunch. Lincoln, Ivy, I would suggest you girls take it easy today, but I'd understand if you want to go out. Is there any attraction you'd like to see? A Broadway show maybe?"

"I wouldn't mind doing some sightseeing," I say, thinking about the diamond in my bag. I need to get rid of it. I'm tempted to pawn it off, but what if the salesman recognizes that it's stolen? I'd get arrested. *No, I'll have to toss it out* somewhere.

"I'll take you," Lincoln offers.

He nods. "I'll get one of the drivers to accompany you. Just in case."

"In case what?" I ask.

"In case journalists spot you. They know the show's been canceled for the day, so they'll be on the lookout. If you meet any, *please* refrain from saying anything. Herrick, the same goes to you. You are off the show, but it would mean a lot to the rest of us if you don't talk about Kevin."

"It was written in his *contrat*," Josephine says. "In all of their contracts."

Herrick mimics zipping his lips anyway.

"It was really great to have you with us," Brook says, hugging Herrick. "Really. You have a lot of talent." He pats his back and then lets go.

Josephine extends her hand and Herrick shakes it.

"Thank you. All of you. You've made this competition challenging and memorable." Herrick smiles.

"Ivy, Lincoln, someone will fetch you when the car's downstairs. We'll all reconvene at my place tonight for a quiet dinner. Have a nice day, guys." Our faces must be grim, because he adds, "At least, try to."

Along with Lincoln and Chase, I withdraw down the grassy hallway. I wait until she's in her room before following Chase into his.

"You've got the wrong tent," he says.

"No. I got the right one. Why are you angry with me?"

"You lied. I don't like liars."

"I lied because—"

He doesn't let me finish my sentence. "My ex was a liar."

"If you'll just let me explain."

"Don't bother."

"Chase—"

"Really, Ivy. You don't owe me an explanation."

"So that's it? You're just going to push me away because I pretended not to know how to swim?"

"I wasn't thinking straight last night. As you said, one of us will be gone soon, so there's no point in starting anything."

For some reason, even though he's throwing my words back at me, it stings.

When I don't move, he adds, "Is that all?"

Swallowing hard, I turn around and escape through the zippered opening, running right into Lincoln. Her eyes glow like a cat's among the twinkling tree lights.

"I was looking for you. The car's downstairs," she says. "Oh. You're not dressed."

My cheeks flame. "I will be in a minute."

"I'll wait in the living room," she says.

I walk into my room and yank on the outfit laid out on the bed. I should have stuck to my gut feeling about Chase instead of getting whisked away in the heat of the moment. I trace my steps to the red duffel bag to fish out the diamond and the paper I made Aster sign, the paper that will destroy her trust in me. For a moment, I'm tempted to throw it away, but Dean said it was her only way out, so instead, I stuff it inside the back pocket of my shorts. And then I reach further down, prepared to rip the seam. But it's already been ripped. And the box is gone!

A chill discharges up my spine. I check the zippered compartment for my money. It's all there. All three hundred dollars, but the porcelain box is definitely gone. Someone knew about the diamond. I drop down on the bed. What am I supposed to do now? Signal the theft of a diamond that most probably was already stolen? *Ugh!*

I think about going into Kevin's room and turning it upside down. He must have taken it. What if he gave it to his lawyer last night though? I pound my palms against the duvet and groan.

"Are you ready yet?" Lincoln asks, sticking her head inside my tent.

I roll up.

"What's eating you?" she asks. "Trouble in paradise?"

"Yeah," I say, because it beats explaining the whole diamond debacle. I stand up, stick the cash in my pocket, and join her in the hallway where her assistant is waiting to escort us to the underground parking lot.

"Hi, Miss Redd, Miss Vega," Danny says, holding the door of a sedan open. He seems shy—or repentant.

I don't answer him. He doesn't deserve an answer after the aversion he showed me when he believed I'd doctored Kevin's pictures. I slide in next to Lincoln, who takes out a huge pair of leopard sunglasses from her tiny purse. I didn't look for sunglasses and regret it because it's bright out.

"You like bargains?" Lincoln asks me.

"Sure," I mumble, even though I'm in no mood to shop.

She leans forward. "Century 21," she says, then lounges back and crosses her legs. "You'll see Times Square on the way downtown. And the store isn't far from the Brooklyn Bridge. We can have lunch in Brooklyn Heights. There's a little organic restaurant I used to work in. They still give me free meals."

She's extra chatty during the drive, telling me all about her city. She shows me the school where her ex taught, and the subway station where she recreated the Picasso painting in chalk. She points out the club where she waitressed to pay for her sixth-floor attic studio.

Hordes of shoppers are out, dappling the sidewalks with their colorful plastic and paper bags. Cars honk, people shout into their cell phones, garbage trucks beep, drills shatter asphalt, and kids squeal. It makes for a deafening, lovely cacophony.

"I would've liked to live here," I say.

Her elbow is bent against the built-in armrest in the door, and her fist cushions her head that's angled toward me. "Kokomo was no fun?"

"It was okay. It's a small town, though, so everyone knew everyone else's business, which can be suffocating," I whisper, watching the billboards stretching several stories high, the enormous, wrap-around screens displaying bright ads, and the cowboy in tighty-whities and lizard boots playing the guitar in the middle of all that. New York looks like some futuristic civilization.

"Why do you think Kevin took his life?" she asks. "Because he was"—she mouths the word *gay*.

"I think it's because of the doctored photos."

"Do you know who doctored them?"

I shake my head.

"So much intrigue," she whispers. "Do you remember how I joked my parents would probably come out of the woodwork if I won? Well, guess what? I got a letter."

"You did?"

"The person sent it to the show. This guy claiming to be my long-lost father. He seems way too young, though, so I don't know."

"How old is he?"

"Thirty-six. Which would have made him sixteen when I was born. Then again, teen pregnancies happen, right?"

"Did he send a picture?"

"Yeah."

"And? Do you look like him?"

"You tell me." She digs a picture out of her bag.

The man is quite handsome, with large green eyes like Lincoln's, and the same mouth with the plumper upper lip.

"I see a resemblance," I say.

She studies it too. "What if we don't have anything in common?"

"I have a twin sister, and we couldn't be more different."

"Like how?"

She's a thief and a liar. "She's a loner," I finally say.

"How's she coping behind bars?"

"I'm sure she's fine."

"You don't know?"

"No communication, remember?"

"Wasn't her lawyer there last night?"

I bite my lip, ashamed I didn't ask Dean how Aster was doing. "She's fine, apparently," I lie.

Danny clears his throat.

"Sick of being locked up, but fine," I repeat.

He does it again.

"What?" I snap.

"I read on the Internet that she was almost killed. Locked in a freezer by another inmate."

All the blood flows out of my face.

"Jail's harsh," he adds.

I'm so perplexed by the news that I let the city go in and out of focus. I do the same for Lincoln's ensuing conversation with the driver about the atrocities in prisons. Sickened by the news, I lower the window.

"We're here," Lincoln says.

We've finally stopped in front of a block-long store.

"I don't feel like shopping anymore," I tell her.

"Why not?"

"I just don't. But go ahead. I'll wait in the car." As Lincoln clicks off her seat belt, I ask the driver, "Could I use your phone?"

"No can do. Show rules."

"Please. It's to call my sister. Please."

His eyes travel over my face, then dart to Lincoln's. Maybe if I'd asked once she was gone, he would've accepted. Stupid me. "I'm real sorry."

"On second thought"—she straps herself back in—"I don't need to buy anything. Let's go to the bridge."

By the time we park next to an overhanging walkway that rises above the murky waters of the East River, I feel so sullen that I want to yell and cry. I do neither. I get out and slam my door. Danny tails us, conspicuous in his black suit and aviators. If anything, he makes people gawk and whisper.

When we're halfway across the bridge, he says, "We should head back to the car. You've been made."

Lincoln flaps her hand in the air. "Relax."

"Mister Bacci made it clear to keep you away from crowds."

"I'm not agoraphobic." Lincoln's smiling for the raised smartphones. She even waves.

I keep my face angled down. "He's right. We should head back."

"Oh, stop it, you two. They're harmless. They just want some pictures," Lincoln says. "They love us."

They love us so much that they close in on us, asking for autographs on their water bottles, their bags, even on an unused diaper. At first, Danny fends them off, but the crowd grows so deep that he is rendered powerless. He takes out his cell phone and calls for backup.

A large video camera pushes past the crowd, along with a woman holding a microphone. The reporters have found us. My breathing becomes shallow and my heart pounds harder. I look around like a crazed animal, trying to locate an escape hatch, but I can't even see the bridge railing.

I feel hands stroke my back, my bottom, my chest, and my stomach. Fabric and skin brush my bare legs and arms. The stench of armpits, of un-brushed teeth, and pungent perfumes slap me. I scramble backward, taking shelter between Danny and Lincoln, using their bodies to shield my own. An arm drapes around my stiff shoulders. Lincoln's. She's chatting with the reporter.

"Ivy was the first to find him," she says.

My breath hitches.

"Did you have anything to do with Mister Martin's death, Miss Redd?" the reporter asks.

"I said she was the first on the scene. I didn't say she killed him. Right, Ivy? You didn't kill Kevin?" Lincoln asks sweetly.

I gape at her bright teeth as she squeezes my shoulder. And then I step away, because I finally see her for the viper she is. She wants me out of the running, and by implying I could have had a hand in Kevin's death, she just might get her way.

"If you were to commit suicide in here, how would you do it?" I ask the women sitting at my table in the middle of our breaded chicken and mushy corn dinner.

"I'd hang myself," Gill says.

"With what?" Chacha asks, readjusting her hairnet.

"I'd roll up my bed sheets," Gill says. "Tie a noose."

"Okay. And where would you attach them? It's not like there's a hook on the ceiling of our cells." The woman who speaks is one of Chacha's relatives apparently—a distant cousin. She sort of looks like her even though her eyes are much lighter, almost honey-colored, and her hair's dyed blonde. Her name's Gracie.

"I dunno. Maybe on the upper railing of our bunk beds. And then I'd have to keep my knees bent until my neck broke," Gill says.

"I would use a knife," Chacha says.

"Yeah, but you have access to knives. That's too easy," Gill says.

"Then I'd drink a cleaning product. A toxic one."

"What about you?" I ask the translucent-skinned girl

sitting alone a few spaces down. She's been listening to our conversation. I can tell by the way her clear eyes keep darting our way.

She sits up straighter. "I'd cut my wrists with a shiv."

"A shiv? What's that?" I ask.

"Homemade blade, dumb-dumb," Chacha says.

"You can make it out of a toothbrush," Gracie adds. "I even heard of a prisoner making a shiv in papier-mâché out of a toilet paper roll."

"How would *you* do it, Gracie?" I ask her, pushing the corn kernels around with my fork. Chacha looks at my plate, so I scoop some up and shovel them inside my mouth.

Gracie spins a small container of creamer between her index and middle fingers. "I'd light this baby up. It becomes a flamethrower." She drops her voice. "But don't tell anyone or we'll be forced to drink our coffees black." She sets it back down and fixes me with her yellow eyes. "How 'bout you? How would you do it, Aster?"

"I think I'd just lock myself in the freezer again. At least you pass out before you die."

Chacha wrinkles her wide nose. "You're morbid."

"Why are we talking about suicide?" Gill asks, her red dreads swinging past her shoulder blades. "You aren't planning on killing yourself now, are you?"

"No," I say, even though the thought crossed my mind after Dean left. I spear a piece of soggy, breaded chicken and eat it.

Gill's brown eyes stay narrowed; she doesn't believe me. Suddenly another tray slides in next to mine. It's Translucent-girl. I wasn't sure what part of my question was an invitation for her to sit closer.

"Was that what happened yesterday? You tried to off yourself?" the girl asks. She smells like water, mineral and tinny.

"Yesterday was an accident," I say.

Chacha leans over the table to see past me. "What you in for, Sofia?"

"I killed my professor," Sofia says. "He gave me bad grades. He would've ruined my future."

Gracie snorts. "And killing him didn't fuck it up?"

Sofia shrugs. "At least I was in control of my fate."

"Ever killed anyone else?" Gill asks.

"No, but I did kill an animal once. My grandma's parakeet. I plucked it, hoping it would shut up. It just screeched louder, so I had to snap its neck." She forks another big bite of chicken into her mouth.

"Ouch," Chacha says. She scoots back, probably to put some space between herself and the pallid nutcase next to me.

"If I hadn't killed him, someone else would've. The man had it coming," Sofia says.

"How did you kill him?" I find myself asking.

"Followed one of his recipes to make acid, and then splashed it all over his body. Worked really well."

"You're real fucked up." Chacha readjusts her hairnet and then swings her bony bowlegs off the bench. "I need to get back to the kitchen. Gracie, you coming?"

Her cousin stands and follows her out. No longer under the cook's scrutiny, I push my tray away.

"Can I have the rest?" Sofia asks. "I love chicken."

I nod.

"Parakeet tastes a little the same."

"You ate the fucking bird?" Gill asks.

"I wasn't going to let it rot."

"Did you eat your teacher too?" Gill asks.

"That's sick. I'm not some cannibal. Yuck." After sticking my chicken on her plate, she asks, "Have *you* ever eaten human flesh?"

"Hell no," Gill and I say at the same time.

"Did you hear about your sister, Aster?" Sofia asks out of the blue.

"Hear about what?"

"That she might be connected to Kevin's death."

Every muscle in my body coils. "She had nothing to do with it."

"Apparently she was in the water, next to his body and—"

"What?" I say.

"Apparently she was in—"

"I heard you!" I've raised my voice. "A lot of people were in the water."

"It's Lincoln who suggested it. She said your sister was trashed last night. She could've lost control—"

"Ivy doesn't lose control."

"Are you sure about that?"

"Yes."

"But—"

Gill wraps her hands around her freckled elbows. "Drop it, Sofia."

Sofia's talc-pink lips open, but close immediately. She scrapes the remainder of my plate onto hers, and then moves back to her original seat. I get another strong whiff of her boggy scent.

Neither Gill nor I say anything for a while. After several long minutes of me staring daggers at the cup of green Jell-O on my tray, Gill speaks up, "Why were you asking about suicide?"

"It was just a topic of conversation."

"My ass. You're not the sort of person who comes up with *just a topic* of conversation. Everything you say and do, you think about...a lot."

I hoist up my shoulders, then let them slump. "Maybe I've been feeling down."

"Well let's bring you back up then," she says. "What makes you happy?"

"Popcorn and a movie."

Gill jumps off the bench. "Consider it done."

"Really?"

"Yes. I hope you're not too picky about the movie," she says. "We'll have to see what's on cable."

"I'll watch anything."

"Good."

She walks over to Officer Landry and, after a brief conversation, she's granted access to the kitchen.

A movie and popcorn sound surreal.

"She your girlfriend?" Sofia asks mid-bite.

"She's my friend."

"You sure she's clear on that?"

"I'm sure."

"Can I have your Jell-O?"

"You can have my Jell-O." I slide it over so she doesn't come near me again.

"Thanks." As I make to get up, she adds, "Another good way to get killed is messing with the wrong person." She tips her head toward Cheyenne. "But it could backfire. You could become that person's bitch, although I don't think she swings that way." After a spoonful of the wobbly green stuff, she adds, "She's probably your best bet. That is, if you're serious about leaving the DOC in a body bag."

"I'm not suicidal."

"I thought you were down."

"Eavesdrop much," I grumble.

"I don't eavesdrop. I'm just aware. Some friendly advice: no one can hurt you if you're aware 'cause you can figure their next move before they make it. I was a grandmaster when I was a kid."

"A what?"

"A professional chess player." She winks at me, her see-through eyelashes grazing her diaphanous cheek.

I've never seen anything coming. In the past, it was because I was so focused on Ivy. Now, it's because I'm so focused on my predicament. Or perhaps those are excuses. Perhaps I don't want to see things coming. Who wants to keep their eyes on the headlights of a truck that's barreling straight for you?

"We're all set," Gill says.

She's crept up so quietly that I jump.

"Already?" I ask.

She nods and extends her hand to help me up. I pretend not to see it and rise on my own. Underneath her arm, I spot a brown bag with grease smudges that make the air smell divine. Together, we walk over to Landry, who signals the squat guard in the opposite corner, the one who always sports her hair in a thick braid.

"Kim, could you take Inmates Redd and Swanson to the dayroom and stay with them. Sergeant Driscoll granted them one hour of television."

Kim frowns, but leads the way.

"How did you swing that?" I whisper to Gill. "Another free wax?"

She smiles. "Yup."

"Thanks," I say.

"Anything for you."

Her eyes sparkle like the diamond in the porcelain box. The one that's no longer there.

FORTY

Ivy

"Do not come near me!" I yell at Lincoln, grabbing fistfuls of the dove-gray sham.

After the bridge incident, Danny and two cops escorted us back to Brook's apartment where I burrowed in his guest bedroom. I haven't spoken a word to anyone since the revolting accusation. I've just lain on my side, facing the cloudless sky and wondering how I could have been so shortsighted.

"I never meant to accuse you of anything."

"Leave me alone, Lincoln."

She sticks one hand on her hip. "You think the world is out to get you, don't you? Well, you're wrong. And the only reason I mentioned you were in the water was because you were."

"And the alcohol? My vomiting? Why did you mention that?"

"The reporter brought it up. I didn't. Besides, it works to your advantage. If you were buzzed, then it looks less suspicious."

"*Suspicious?* Are you hearing yourself, Lincoln? Just get out," I growl.

I turn my gaze back to the dazzling slice of city visible

through the panoramic window. The building across the street is entirely made of glass. It reflects Brook's penthouse, down to the bodies stirring around the pool deck, setting up dinner. A hubbub erupts in the hallway.

"She's in here," Lincoln calls out.

"Ivy, we tried to come as quickly as possible but the negotiations with the network took longer than expected," Dominic says. He steps around the bed. His perma-tanned skin looks a little orange and wrinkled. "I don't like these new accusations. *And* I don't believe them." He shifts my feet to the side to sit. "Tell me what happened, sweetheart." When I don't, he looks toward the door. "Lincoln, go get ready. Your stylists are in the living room. Brook, shut the door, please." Once it's closed, he says, "It's just us now. Tell me what happened."

"Haven't you seen the news, Mister Bacci? I was accused of murdering Kevin," I say bluntly.

"And did you?"

I sit up so quickly that my head spins. "Of course not."

"Then why are you so worked up?"

"Because it's all lies." I gather my knees against me. "Just like the doctored photos."

"Then you have nothing to worry about. When the detectives get here, just—"

"The detectives?" I yelp.

He nods. "The show's lawyer—the one you met—she'll be here too. You have our total support, Ivy." He pats my knee. "You know," he adds, "last night, on the beach, I spoke to Kevin's lawyer. He told me about the sergeant's wife. About what she did...I even have a copy of her letter." He pats the breast pocket of his beige linen jacket.

"What did she do?"

"You don't know?"

"No."

His pupils pulse.

"Did *she* doctor the photos?" I ask.

"I shouldn't—"

"I was wrongfully accused—twice now. I think I deserve to get some answers."

He fixes me for a long time. "Kevin was going to leave her. So she destroyed his dream of getting on our show."

"By doctoring those photos," I say in a shocked whisper.

Winded by this discovery, I barely react when Brook, the female lawyer with the goat face, and the two detectives file into the room. McEnvoy, without asking the ladies if they'd like a seat, sinks into the leather desk chair. Combing his fingers through his prematurely graying hair, he crosses an ankle over his knee. He's wearing his black work boots again—in ninety-degree weather. They must stink.

"Good evening, everyone. I will be acting as Miss Ivy Redd's council this evening," the lawyer says, taking out a massive number of files. She thumbs through them until she finds a particular sheet of paper. "I believe this meeting will only take a minute. Here." She gives the paper to the female detective who glances down at it. I can't see what it says, but it looks like a photocopy of a ripped note.

"This only proves that Miss Redd didn't tamper with Mister Martin's pictures," Clancy says, wetting her ultra-pale lower lip. I'd forgotten how her mouth blended right into her face. "It doesn't prove she didn't kill him."

"Nor that she wasn't under the influence," McEnvoy adds.

"Oh, come on!" Dominic throws his arms in the air. "What is your obsession with our contestant?"

The lawyer holds out her hand to calm him down. "I've spoken to the bartenders catering the event and to each waiter working last night. They've all testified to never having come in contact with Miss Redd. Underage drinking might be punishable by law, but I do believe it's below your pay grade to worry about Miss Redd's alcoholic intake."

"Maybe someone gave it to her," McEnvoy says. "The gift of alcohol is illegal."

"Could we return to the matter at hand? Miss Redd's alleged involvement in Mister Martin's death."

McEnvoy's mouth opens, but Clancy speaks before he can. "Ivy, a source tells us you got in a fight with Mister Martin shortly before his death. Is that true?"

"You don't need to answer that," the lawyer tells me. She glances at the door, then at her watch.

"I have nothing to hide," I say. "Yes. We had a fight."

"What about?" McEnvoy asks, bobbing in the chair.

I don't tell them I made fun of his sensitivity; I don't think it would look too good for me. "He stole something from my room."

Dominic blinks. "Are you sure?"

I nod.

"What was it?" he asks.

"A piece of jewelry." I don't clarify it was a diamond, because if it surfaces, and it really is *dirty*, I can always say that I was talking about a ring or a necklace.

"Why didn't you come to me with that? Or to Brook?"

Brook's eye twitches.

"Can you pull the camera footage?" Dominic asks him.

"There's no camera in the hallway."

"The angle of the one in the living room should be wide enough to see if anyone went into her room." Dominic's forehead glistens with a thin layer of sweat. "This is just absurd! I swear, the show's cursed this year."

"Can we get back—" Leah begins, but Dominic interrupts her.

"When did you notice the theft, Ivy?"

"The night Kevin arrived," I lie.

"And you're sure it couldn't have happened before he got there."

"I'm sure. It was still in my bag when I left for the pool party."

Dominic slaps his thigh. "Absurd, I tell you. Brook, pull the footage of that day."

Brook's Adam's apple bobs up and down in his throat. "I'll phone Jeb."

"What were you doing in the ocean last night?" Leah asks me, her voice sharp.

"In case you didn't notice, there were a lot of people in the water," I say.

"Yes, but what were *you* doing?" McEnvoy asks.

I'm about to tell him I was swimming when a knock echoes on the door.

"Come in," Dominic says.

The door opens, and Chase comes in.

Detective Clancy frowns. "Why is this boy here?"

"Mister Jackson is here because he's Miss Redd's alibi," Dominic says. "And since you don't seem to believe a word that comes out of my contestant's mouth, I asked him to testify. Chase?"

He heaves a deep breath. "Ivy was in the water last night because I asked her to come in with me."

"And why should we believe you?" McEnvoy asks.

"Because I brought proof." Chase fishes a picture from the back pocket of his khakis. "Here." He gives it to the female detective first.

She studies it.

"Will that do, Detective? Can I be dismissed?" he asks.

She lifts her gaze back up to his face. Her eyes are as round as billiard balls.

McEnvoy rips the picture out of her hand and ogles it. Then he repeatedly flicks his index finger against it. "How do we know this hasn't been doctored?"

The vein in Chase's forehead throbs.

"Shut up, Austin," Detective Clancy mumbles, eyes flashing over the room. "Thank you for your time, Council, Mister Bacci, Mister Jackson. Miss Redd, I'm sure we'll see each other again soon."

"Why would we?" I ask.

"Just a hunch," she says.

Goose bumps scatter over my skin, because I can tell it isn't "just a hunch."

"Let me walk you out," Dominic suggests, ushering the lawyer and the two detectives out of the bedroom.

Chase leaves right after them. Before Brook can follow them out, I call him back. He seems reluctant to stay behind.

"I have a paper to give to Dean. It's for Aster's trial." I fish the signed form from my pocket and hand it over.

"Okay," he says, stuffing it in his pocket. "So you and my brother, huh?"

"There is no *me and your brother*."

"But the picture—"

"Pictures lie." I think of Kevin and the picture that got him disqualified.

"Kevin's personal effects are being packed up as we speak. I'll have the cleaners check for jewelry. What was it exactly that was stolen?"

"A necklace," I finally say.

"Can you describe it for me?"

"It was a diamond pendant. I kept it in a porcelain box."

"Why weren't you wearing it?"

"Because the show lends the jewelry. I thought my stylist would make me take it off."

"You should've left it at home then."

"I don't have a safe at home."

Brook stares at me, but then his eye twitches again, and he lowers his gaze.

"Sorry to interrupt, Mister Jackson, but we need to get Ivy ready for dinner," Leila says.

"Already?" Sure enough, the light has softened outside.

Brook gives a jerky nod.

After he leaves, Leila shuts the door and points to the chair McEnvoy occupied just minutes ago. "Sit."

Even though she makes up my face, her kohl-lined gaze never once grazes mine. Perhaps I owe her an apology—or rather I owed her an apology. Now, it's too late. Amy feels like she needs to fill the silence with chatter. She talks about everything, from the latest clothing trends to the newest weight loss cleanse. She switches from one topic to the next so swiftly that her skin purples from lack of oxygen. Strangely, I find her babbling soothing.

Leila puts the final coat of gloss on my lips and repacks her stuff. Once she's left the room, Amy unhooks the rollers from my hair and brushes them out to soften the rich curls. The effect is beautiful. I pull off my T-shirt and shorts, and yank on the electric blue frock laid out on the bed. The top is loose and gauzy, unlike the bottom, which is made of tight, overlapping bands of fabric.

"If I could keep one outfit, it would be this one," I tell Amy as she folds the garment bag.

"I'm sure Mister Bacci would allow it. You should ask him," she says. "It looks really pretty on you. Then again, is there anything that doesn't?"

"That zombie get-up," I say. It feels like it was a lifetime ago that I wore it.

"Even *that* you pulled off."

"You're way too kind, Amy. And very talented," I tell her. "You'll have to leave me your card."

Her cheeks turn as pink as her hair. "Of course! Here."

She fishes a business card from her box of pins and elastics.

It's totally tacky: gold with swirly pink lettering. "Can you leave it in my room?"

She nods so many times that it looks as though she's pecking the air.

As I walk out of the bedroom, I feel lightheaded—perhaps because my stomach is near empty, or perhaps because of how resilient I've grown since arriving in New York. The Master-piecers has transformed me. I think of Aster and wonder if prison has changed her too. I hope it's hardened her, made her more able to cope with life in society, to deal with her insecuri-ties without having to fabricate stories about aborted pregnan-cies. And then, I think about the dead man and the tear in my quilt, and my sympathy for her dries up.

When I step out onto the terrace, the sky is streaked peach and pink and gold, like a Monet painting.

"Ivy, you're here, next to me," Dominic says, pulling out my chair.

To my right, I have Brook and in front of me, Chase. Lincoln and Josephine are on either side of him. I glance at Lincoln, pleased that I foiled her plan. Her face is blank, like a child who's been reprimanded.

Dominic starts dinner off with a toast. He closes his eyes and lifts his glass. "To Kevin, who we hope has finally found peace."

"Amen," Josephine and Brook say.

"*And*, to the most eventful, and surely the most memo-rable, competition." He says this with a soft smile. "And to the last two tests! We're raising the stakes."

"Sh...Dom," Josephine says, setting her glass of white wine down. "Don't give it away."

"And to Chase's birthday...a happy one this time," Dominic adds as servers bring out little glass bowls of chilled tomato soup topped with teeny, golden croutons.

"I'd also like to propose a toast. *Plus de drame.* No more

drama. Okay, Brook?" Josephine asks, giving him an oblique smile that doesn't create a single crease on her face. Even her forehead stays perfectly smooth.

Brook's smile washes off his lips, and as dinner progresses, he becomes more and more restless, jostling his knees, toying with his fork, drinking more than he should. I count five refills. When Josephine excuses herself, telling us she needs an early night, Dominic pulls Brook aside. They talk quietly and then Dominic leaves and Brook returns. He sits down even though the table has been cleared and the camera crew is packing up.

"Dom has agreed to let all of you hang out a while longer. To decompress," Brook says.

Chase eyes his brother. "Is that what *you're* doing?"

"If you were under the stress I was under, little brother, you'd—"

"I just think you should quit while you're ahead."

"Why don't you mind your own business?" Brook answers dryly.

Chase presses away from the table and walks over to the opposite side of the terrace to lie on one of the lounge chairs.

"Well, this isn't awkward," Lincoln says. "I'm going to go powder my nose." She rises and heads inside Brook's bachelor pad.

"I feel like I'm missing something," I tell Brook once it's just the two of us.

He twirls his glass of wine between his long fingers. "Josephine doesn't like me."

"I don't think she likes anyone."

"Yeah, but she really has it in for me."

"Why?"

He glances at his brother who's staring up at the starless night sky. "Because she's afraid Dominic's going to promote me."

"So what if he does?"

"I'd be taking her place."

"Ah. I can see how that would be a problem."

"Remember that day at the airport, when you arrived at the same time I did?"

"Hard to forget when someone treats you like dirt," I say.

He doesn't react to my comment. "Josephine orchestrated that."

"If you have proof, then she can't use it against you."

He leans in closer. "Exactly."

Plumes of stale alcohol hit my nose. Before leaning back, he tucks a strand of hair behind my ear.

"You shouldn't do that," I say.

"Do what?"

"Touch me. I'm a contestant."

He drops his hand back to his lap. "Right."

In the corner of my eye, I spot Lincoln. She smiles her dark, bright smile.

"Crap. Now she's going to tell the press that you and I are hooking up," I whisper in his ear.

His dimples appear as a grin spreads across his face. "Watch me take care of that." He stands, walks over to her, and tells her something. At first, she looks startled, but then she nods. "Anyone else up for a midnight dip?" Brook asks loudly, so that his words reach his brother, the only other person on the terrace.

"I think I'm over midnight dips," I say, thinking of Kevin.

Brook winks at me before tugging Lincoln into the apartment to change into swimsuits.

I stroll over toward Chase, shake off my shoes, and lay down on the lounge chair next to his. His cologne is faint tonight, yet I can still smell the pine needles and the grass in the dark air. "At some point, you're going to have to talk to me," I say.

"Why?"

"Because we're on the same show. Anyway, I just came over to say thank you," I tell him.

"For what?"

"For stepping up for me earlier with the detectives."

The ligaments in his neck stretch and tauten. "I didn't have a choice. Dominic was going to show them the picture." His words sting. I'm about to leave, when he adds, "I've been meaning to ask how you knew Dean Kane."

"Your brother introduced us last night on the beach."

"Why?"

"For my sister. Brook offered to have him defend her."

"You should pass up on his offer."

"Why?"

"He's famous for getting some of the worst people off death row."

"That'll work in my sister's favor."

"I wouldn't trust him, Ivy."

"You don't trust anyone."

He turns to look at me. His eyes are dark, yet I can detect emotion in them, grief, disappointment, anguish. I feel the urge to stroke his cheek and comfort him, and begin lifting my hand when he turns away.

"Don't look at me like that," he says.

"Like what?"

"Like I'm some hurt little kid."

I let my arm drop back to my side just as Lincoln and Brook cannonball inside the pool.

"Are you going to join them?" he asks. "Or are you going to pretend you don't know how to swim?"

Tears laminate my eyes and blur his pale profile. "You're a dick," I murmur, turning my face upward, toward the blackness, to guide the stupid, wasted emotion back into my eyes. I'm about to ask Brook if I can return to the museum when I see him locking lips with Lincoln. As I walk by, he catches me staring and winks.

Inside the dark and deserted apartment, I find the house phone on the marble kitchen counter. I swipe it from its base and carry it into the bathroom. I lock the door and dial a number I know by heart.

When I hear a click, I whisper, "Josh?" but it goes straight to voicemail. I'm tempted to empty my heart, tell him that I think Aster didn't kill Troy for my quilt, that I think she killed him for what was inside, but I don't want there to be yet another trace of my suspicion.

Especially if I'm wrong.

FORTY-ONE

I was sick all night. When I spot Sofia scarfing down her bowl of porridge the next morning, I deduce it's not salmonella poisoning.

"Hi," Gill says, a smile stretching from one side of her face to the other. All of her teeth point in different directions like those strings of square, paper lanterns people loop around their porches in the summer.

She swoops down to plant a kiss on my cheek, but I hold her back. "I'm sick. I don't want to infect you."

Grin still intact, she says, "I'm probably already infected." She tries to peck my face again when I slap my hand over my mouth and jump off the bench to run toward the bin. I just make it.

Cool fingers stroke my neck, gather my dreads. *God, she's everywhere.* What have I gotten myself into?

"Sergeant Driscoll, can I go to the infirmary? I'm not feeling too well."

"Morning sickness?" he asks. His potbelly shakes with a chuckle while my cheeks flame.

"I'll walk her over. To spare you an uncomfortable run-in with Nurse Celia," Gill says, repaying his snarky comment.

The laughter dries in his throat. "*Yobwoc*," he yells. "Get your ass over here."

"Inmate Redd needs some medical attention," he says, glaring at Gill. "Walk her to the infirmary."

He nods. Gill hooks her arm through mine and begins to follow him, but Driscoll stops her. "Swanson, you're needed in the laundry room. Got some linens to press."

Gill sucks in a breath and releases my arm. "Asshole," she murmurs. "I'll try to stop by later, okay?"

I nod, and the movement angers my throbbing head. I hold on to the walls as I trail Officer Landry. He turns around a few times, and although he seems concerned, he doesn't offer me support. He's probably worried that touching an inmate will look bad. Or that I'll give him what I have.

The hallway floor shifts like in a funhouse. The ground goes forward and back and side to side. I trip at some point and one of my flip-flops flies off, but I catch myself before I hit the floor. Landry stops, casts another worried glance my way, but still doesn't help. My fingers tremble as they slip the flip-flop back on. My feet are white and as stiff as when Chacha extracted me from the freezer. The world spins again and suddenly I'm flat on my back and Officer Landry is upside down. Nurse Celia's face pops into my line of sight. I think I hear her call out my name but I'm not sure.

She hoists me up with the help of Landry, and together, they carry me to the cot in her office. Drawers slam, metal clangs, wheels spin. A sharp pain explodes in my wrist. I peer down and see she's stuck a catheter inside my vein and is hooking it up to an IV bag.

"When was the last time you ate something, Aster?" she asks. It sounds like she's at the bottom of a well.

"Last night."

"I mean really ate?" she repeats. "Like a proper meal."

"The burger," I croak.

"That was two days ago! Landry, get me a bottle of Coke."

While he's gone, she takes my blood pressure, inspects my eyes with a small flashlight, and prods my abdomen.

"I'm going to keep you a few hours. You're completely dehydrated."

"Sure," I say, as my head lolls to the side and my lids slam shut like magnets. "Nowhere else to go."

WHEN I WAKE UP, the nausea has receded and my vein, the one with the catheter in it, is cold from the drip. Slowly, I drum my fingers and shift my legs. The paper crinkles under me, alerting Nurse Celia of my wakefulness.

She simultaneously prods my free wrist for a pulse and keeps an eye on her watch. "That's a better rhythm," she says, and proceeds to remove the needle taped to my opposite arm. The IV bag hangs limply on a pole, near empty. "Can you sit up?"

I nod and do as I'm asked.

"I've requested they add two granola bars to your diet every day. Please eat them." She returns to her desk and grabs a glass filled with brown liquid. "Now, drink this. It'll get your blood sugar zinging."

I take a sip. When I realize it's Coke—even though it's room temperature and most of the bubbles have fizzed out—I gulp it down. "What time is it?"

"It's ten."

"My sister's show must be starting."

The nurse's eyes light up. "Want to watch it?"

"Yes," I say, because I need to see my sister's face. I need to know if she's truly angry with me. "But I can go to the dayroom if you've got other patients to see."

"No other patients. Just you." Her door is already shut, but she moves toward it to test the handle. "Don't want to be disturbed."

More like caught.

Keeping her laptop on the desk, she turns it toward the exam table. It's already broadcasting the show. She wheels over her chair and plops down. Her gaze glued to the monitor, she says, "I called Dean"—a faint linear flush extends from the bridge of her nose to her hairline—"to tell him that you fainted, but that you were okay now."

I doubt he'd care much.

Dominic's on the screen, microphone in hand. He's not smiling today. "Ladies and gentlemen, after a strange few days, and after hours of discussions, Josephine, Brook, and I feel we cannot disappoint our faithful audience, nor can we rob our remaining contestants of the chance of a lifetime. We offer our deepest condolences to Mrs. Martin and Kevin's parents and siblings, and hope that the magnificent rope Kevin wove on his last day has reached them. Also, I wish to take a moment to clear up certain assumptions that seem to have sprouted since my contestants' run-in with the press yesterday on the Brooklyn Bridge. Miss Ivy Redd had nothing to do with Mister Martin's death. Miss Lincoln Vega would like to say a few words to that effect."

The camera perches on Lincoln's face. She is sitting behind Dominic, legs folded and back rigid. When he approaches her with the microphone, her green gaze turns to Ivy whose face is impassible.

"Ivy, I regret the terrible confusion my words created. I didn't mean you any harm," she says.

Her apology sounds rehearsed.

My sister nods and her straightened hair ripples. I wonder

if she's gotten highlights. It's more golden than I remember. Perhaps it's because she's tanned so her eyes and hair look paler. I touch my own hair, coarse with dreads that, according to Gill, are maturing nicely. Ivy will hate them and tell me they're ugly and I'll get them raked out.

"Now, for today's test. We are going to attach a small camera and recording device to our contestants' chests and give them a list. That list will be for their eyes only and will contain the instructions of today's tournament. And that is all I will reveal to you, dear audience." He shoots the crowd a white smile. "No camera crew will follow them. The only footage you will be privy to will be the one that will be recorded by their personal devices. However, it will only be broadcasted once they've safely returned to the museum. We do have to keep you guessing." His smile stretches all the way to his silver sideburns.

"What?" Nurse Celia's voice is so strident that I jump. "They're horrible! They can't do that to us!"

"Lincoln, Ivy, Chase," Dominic continues, "are you ready?"

Lincoln's knee shakes; she's the only one who seems anxious.

"Brook, you may hand them their instructions," Dominic says.

The camera shifts over to him. He stands, walks to the contenders, and distributes three scrolls, each tied with a shimmery bow. They tug off the binding and unroll the thick, crackling paper.

My sister's knuckles turn white as she reads. Without even realizing it, I've jumped off the exam table and approached the computer. Ivy's expression quickly turns cool again, but the surprise and—*distress?*—are still there, etched deep into the blueness of her irises. To the world, she may seem confident, but I know she's frightened.

FORTY-TWO

Ivy

I read over the paper again. And again. The instructions are succinct and easy, but the task...God, the task sucks! I try to take a calming breath, but the air in the Temple room is stale and doesn't do crap to calm down my riled nerves. And Dominic's beaming teeth make me want to slap him. If he's so excited, why doesn't he do it himself? What he's asking of us is insane, impossible...illegal!

I go over the list one more time.

1. Corinne Bally's wooden *Babylonian Idol* at the Guggenheim Museum.
2. Otto Milo's *Painted Tissues* installation at the Museum of Modern Art.
3. Zara Mach's *Fuzzy Castanets* at Christie's Auction House.
4. Annabelle Wyatt's lithograph, *Life Dream,* at the Whitney Museum of American Art.
5. Sue Ling's turquoise and bone, *Tusk Goddess,* at the Rubin Museum of Art.

6. Christos Natter's *Miniature Barrel Chair* at the
   Wilde Gallery of Modern Art.

"CONTESTANTS, you must choose a number and say it out loud. Just the number. Obviously, don't choose the same one." Dominic guffaws, which elicits chuckles from the audience.

I swallow as Chase rolls up his paper and says, without hesitation, "Three."

I stare at the list. Of course...*Christie's*. He must know the auction house inside and out, having worked there. He probably still has an employee key card. Just the thought slices the threads of hope I'm clinging to as I dangle over the bottomless precipice Dominic has excavated beneath me.

"Six," Lincoln says. Her voice is steady even though she's bouncing her knee.

I go over the remaining four objects. They've left me with only museums. There's so much security in a museum I'm going to fail.

"Ivy? Have you made your choice?"

My lips have gone dry. I swipe my tongue over them and blink into the camera. *Shit, shit, shit.*

"Ivy?"

"Two," I say, just like I could have said any other number.

"Have you memorized your choices?"

My gaze flits over the words again. *Milo, painted tissues, Museum of Modern Art.* I'm the last to nod.

"Okay. You may leave to get outfitted with your recording devices and *other* equipment." Dominic winks, as gleeful as a kid on a merry-freaking-go-round. "Good luck."

Even though I've never believed in luck, today I want to. I also want to bang my head against one of the Met's wainscoted walls and shout, but I iron out my composure. As I stand up to leave under the audience's applause, I wave and flash a fake smile. Quietly, we take the elevator back up to our quarters. Neither Lincoln nor Chase speaks to me—or to each other for that matter. Everyone is focused on the task at hand.

As someone from the film crew hooks the audiovisual recording devices into our clothes, our assistants hand us nondescript black backpacks.

Milo, tissues, MoMA.

"How are we getting there?" Lincoln asks her assistant.

"On motorbikes. We have three waiting for you downstairs."

"I've never driven one," I say.

Cara smiles. "Good thing you won't have to, then," she says, finger-combing her peroxide-blonde hair. "Riders have been assigned to each one of you. They know where to take you so don't speak your locations." She taps the miniature gadget peeping through the ruffles of my wisteria-colored shirt.

"Why not cars?" Lincoln asks.

"So you can go faster...that's what I heard at least," Cara continues, her eyes drifting over our faces.

"They're all set. Run the test!" the person from the film crew yells.

"Ivy's a go. Chase is a go too. Got audio for Lincoln, but not visual. Bring her over."

"Turning off all mics!" someone else shouts as Lincoln is led over to the tech person.

The assistants disperse, leaving me to stand awkwardly next to Chase. Even though my mic is off, I cover it with my palm and drop my voice to a whisper, "Can't the show get in trouble?"

Chase doesn't bother covering up his device. "They have insurance. Plus it's all former students of theirs."

"Yeah, but still..."

"Just don't blow your nose in the tissues," he says. His lips don't quiver, yet there's a tangible hint of humor in his voice.

"Funny," I mutter. After a beat, I add, "This is going to be so easy for you, isn't it? You'll just strut in there with your keycard and—"

"Easy?" he says. "Don't delude yourself, Ivy. It's not going to be easy...for any of us."

"Why did you choose Christie's then?"

"Because it's small, so I'm not going to be hounded by hundreds of curious people like in a museum. I'm not a big fan of crowds." He stares down at me, his gaze devoid of yesterday's animosity. If anything he looks drained, even underneath the thin coat of foundation they've brushed over his skin. "How's your sister?"

"Aster?" I ask.

"Do you have another sister?"

I shake my head dumbly.

"My parents told me yesterday that she'd been hurt in prison."

"I haven't heard from her. No communication, remember?"

"Right." He studies me. "You must miss her."

I feel freer without her, but I can't admit that to anyone. I'd sound cruel. As Lincoln and the two other assistants walk back toward us, I say, "Yeah."

Cara readjusts my device, tests it again, and then leads us down to the underground parking entrance where three gleaming motorbikes are waiting for us. The drivers hand us bulky black helmets, which we strap on.

"Ready?" mine asks, his question muffled by his impressive handlebar mustache.

I nod and hop on, black backpack in place. And then we're off, and warm air blows into my face and blends into my hair and makes my shirt frills flutter and tickle my collarbone. I close my eyes, not from fear but from delight. The ride is exactly what I need, albeit too short.

As soon as we're parked, I take off the helmet and shake out my hair. Amy must have drenched it in leave-in conditioner because it hasn't tangled.

"I was told to give you this," he says.

It's a ticket for the museum. Dominic has thought of everything.

"I'll wait right here for you," he adds.

Gripping the tiny piece of paper, I step through the revolving doors of the Museum of Modern Art, as prepared as I'll get for the outrageous task. *Steal a work of art. Don't get caught. Don't damage it.*

"What do you think they're going to do?" the nurse asks me for the tenth time as though I could somehow have divined it from Ivy's facial expression.

"I don't know," I tell her again. "But it's something she's not looking forward to."

The nurse heaves a sharp sigh. "Man oh man, my blood pressure must be through the roof."

There's a knock on her door. She springs out of her wheelie chair and shuts her laptop. "Lay down," she mouths.

I return to the exam table just as another knock resounds.

She flings the door open and adopts a disgruntled look to mask the flush brightening her cheeks. "This better be important," she grumbles, "because you woke up my patient."

Landry shifts on his work boots and his skin colors. "I'm sorry, Nurse Celia, but I was told to check up on Inmate Redd."

"By whom?"

"Um...by—"

"Let me guess. Driscoll?" she hisses.

"No. Actually by Mrs. Pierce. She wants to see Aster. Something about her trial."

I perk up at those last words, not mood wise, but physically. I lift myself up on my elbows. "My trial?"

Landry nods.

"Am I okay to leave?" I ask Celia.

"I suppose."

"Thank you."

"For what?"

"For treating me like a human being."

Her eyes get this sheen about them. "You *are* a human being. Don't ever forget that."

I follow the young guard down the maze of hallways. The shrink's door is already open.

"Come right in," Robyn says, before exchanging a few quiet words with Landry and shutting the door.

"I've heard you've had a strenuous day," she says, lowering herself into her big armchair and folding one leg over the other. "I also heard that you've been asking about suicide."

"Who told you?"

"It doesn't matter. Is it true?"

"I've been discussing it, not asking about it."

"Are you thinking about killing yourself?" She holds her pen over her paper, waiting for my answer.

"No."

She sets the meaty part of her hand against the paper.

"You wanted to discuss my trial?" I ask.

"I did." A long pause. "But before we get to that, I have a question for you. Are you aware that your mother is dead?"

"Excuse me?"

"Your mother. She's dead. She drowned in the pond by the psychiatric home this spring."

"On purpose?" I've scooted so far forward that I'm teetering on the edge of the cushion.

"It says she slipped."

I snort. "She probably did it on purpose. To get some attention."

"Did you know?"

My eyes burn from the bright sun streaming in. "She's really gone?"

"In your file, it says you didn't attend her funeral."

I stare at her face unseeingly. "Why would I attend her funeral?"

"To say good-bye."

"I said good-bye when she was committed. Besides, she wanted to be cremated. Not buried. Ivy had her buried," I find myself telling her.

Robyn rises and moves around her office, then returns with a tissue. She dangles it in the air between us. I stare at it. She brings it closer to me. I still don't take it. "It's okay to grieve, Aster."

"I'm not grieving."

She cocks her head to the side and studies my face.

"Why would I cry for a woman who made me think I was worthless?" I ask her. My eyes are really hot. I shade them with my hand. "Can you draw the blinds? The sun's in my face."

Robyn doesn't budge for a while.

"Can you please close the blinds?" I repeat.

Carefully, she lays the tissue on the couch, shuts the blinds, and switches on her desk lamp. "Better?"

There's a lump in my throat. I must be coming down with a cold. I massage the back of my neck. My tendons feel like they've been swapped for metal cords.

Robyn returns to her chair and flips through my folder. "This arrived on my email this morning." She holds up a print-out. "Is this your signature?"

"I can't see from here."

She comes to sit next to me, places the paper on her lap, and points to the bottom of the page.

My eyesight is still blurry, so I have to squint to make it out. "Yes."

"Why did you sign it?"

"Why wouldn't I sign it?"

"Did you read it?"

"Why?"

"It's a yes or no answer, Aster. Did you read it?"

"No."

"So you don't know what you signed?"

I bristle. "I do. Ivy explained everything. It's a waiver form. In case anything happened to her while she was on the show."

"It's not a waiver." She clears her throat. "Let's read it together, shall we?"

As she begins, my knees and elbows lock. Then my fingers clench into fists and my lungs close and my veins constrict and my throat clogs up. The only part of me that doesn't shut down is the only part I wish would: my heart. Instead, each word cleaves it open a little wider. When I start crying, Robyn hands me the tissue.

Ivy doesn't care about me.

Just like my mother never cared about me.

FORTY-FOUR

Ivy

Unlike the Metropolitan, the Museum of Modern Art is a temple of sleekness and design, all white and glass. For a moment, I forget my mission and stare up and around while hordes of people enter and exit beside me at dizzying speed. No one notices me. They just walk by, their conversations contributing to the din that already resonates against the sharp, smooth surfaces.

When some teenager bumps into me, I get moving. Keeping my head bowed, I grab a museum map and head over to the ticket entrance. The woman scanning the tickets asks me to unzip my bag. She hooks one long vinyl nail inside and angles a small flashlight to view the contents. Only then does it hit me that I should have stuck something in there...anything. Walking around with an empty backpack is sure to arouse suspicion. Sweat beads on my upper lip. I don't dare swipe it off. I just hold my breath until she lets go.

As I start walking away, she says, "Hey, you."

Surely she doesn't mean me. I take a few more steps.

"Hey, I'm talking to you."

She *does* mean me. I freeze and close my eyes. I'm going to get disqualified because of an empty backpack. I don't know whether to be embarrassed or depressed. In slow motion, I turn around.

"Wear the bag on your stomach." She pats her belly. Maybe she thinks I'm foreign...or stupid. I do feel stupid.

I switch the straps to the front as she moves on to the next person. The absurdity of the whole situation exacerbates the anxiety rising within me, to the point where I let out a bark of laughter. I slap my palm in front my mouth to stifle the giggling that ensues while I check my museum map.

The second floor is the one allocated to temporary exhibitions, so I head up the escalators, still smiling like an idiot. I walk through three galleries before I find the one with the painted silk tissues. They're larger than I thought, but also wispier, practically transparent in spite of the splashes of paint. When I see that they're just lying there, haphazardly on the floor with no barriers around them, I am filled with renewed hope. This is going to be a breeze. I walk around them first, scanning the room to locate the security guards. There's only one in this gallery, and he's sitting in a folding chair by the entrance, looking bored out of his mind. I turn sideways and pretend to be captivated by a painting on the wall.

Still facing the painting, I pull one arm out of my backpack so that it hangs off one of my shoulders, then I pivot around and approach the silk tissues. Earlier, I counted five, but there are only four on the ground. I find the fifth wedged in some man's hand. I'm expecting an alarm to resound or the guard to yell, but nothing happens. When I glimpse a second person doing the exact same thing, I realize that handling them is permitted. So I bend over and pick one up too. As I twirl it around in false admiration, a man snaps a picture of me.

"You're that girl," he says way too loudly.

A woman jumps in front of him and screams, "It's Ivy

Redd! In the flesh! Oh...my...God!" She fans her face, which is flushed all the way to her hairline.

Her exclamation and hyperventilation attract more attention. Soon the entire room gapes at me, while more people pour in from adjacent galleries. The security guard jolts out of his chair and begins weaving himself through the gathering crowd.

"Back off," he says, arms fanned out wide as though the rubberneckers were dry leaves he could just rake away.

Arms shoot up with cell phones. Everyone is trying to snap a picture of me.

"Let me get you out of here," the guard tells me, after warning onlookers to step back...again.

I can't leave with him. "I'm okay," I say, as my hand drops to my side and gathers the tissue in a ball. I discreetly coax the zipper up with my thumbnail to create a small opening and stuff my fist inside. Trembling, I release the fabric along with the breath I'm holding. No one has noticed anything since I'm standing behind the guard. I strap on a wide smile and raise my voice, "Who wants an autograph?"

A chorus of *me* rings through the small gallery.

"I don't think that's a good idea," the guard says, but I brush past him and grab an outstretched pen and notebook.

I hadn't planned on a mob, but now that there is one, I'll use it to my advantage. As I sign my name, I scan the ground. I spot bright silk just a foot away. I make the pen slide out of my clammy hand. Before anyone else can retrieve it, I squat to grab it and seize the tissue.

"Who's next?" I ask, making sure my grin stays intact in spite of my galloping heartbeat.

While I sign my name, the fingers of my other hand gather the silk in a tight ball. A woman approaches me with her phone.

"So what's the test?" she asks me. I guess she must be filming.

"Aha," I say, with a giant smile. I approach the camera so it won't pick up on my hand snaking into my bag. "It's a secret." I raise a steady finger to my lips and add a theatrical wink.

The crowd goes absolutely wild.

Amid the anarchy, a little girl pulls on the frayed hem of my shorts, large eyes raised toward me. "Can I get your auto-graph, ma'am?" she asks, extending a Barbie diary.

"Of course," I say.

I glimpse another square of blue-green sticking out from underneath a teenager's sneakers. Praying it isn't damaged, I make my way toward it. Sandwiched between so many people, bending over is impossible, so I pretend to stumble. I catch my balance on the teenager, making her shift off the silk.

"Sorry," I say as I pull one foot out of my crystallized loafer and hook my toes around the silk. I deposit it in my shoe, then jam my foot back inside.

"That's fine," she says, flushed with excitement. "More than fine. I don't think I'll ever wash again."

As she gushes to all of her friends about our run-in, I locate my fourth target. I repeat my circus act with the right foot. When it's safely stuffed inside my shoe, I exhale again.

One to go.

More security guards have arrived and are pushing their way through the crowd toward me. My heart pumps so fren-ziedly that my veins bulge with blood. The one zigzagging down my arm sticks out abnormally. I snap my gaze away from my skin and desperately search the ground for the last tissue. My luck is going to run out. I can feel it like you can feel ants crawling over your skin. Sweat bleeds down my neck into my shirt collar, gluing it to my rapidly rising chest.

"Move," one of the guards orders.

Thankfully, no one listens to him. He begins to shove

people backward. That's when I see it...the last tissue. It's still clutched in the man's fist—the one who sighted me—and rests limply against his thigh. I lunge over to him. With one hand, I wheedle the tissue out; with the other, I pry his fingers open and move the pen over his palm to draw my name in loopy letters. He's so stunned, he doesn't notice the handkerchief is gone, just like he didn't notice he was still holding it.

I raise the pen in the air real high. "Whose is this?" I exclaim.

Three people shout, "Mine!"

The silk bunched in my shoes makes it hard to walk normally, so I choose the person closest to me, a pimply-faced middle-schooler surrounded by two other nerdy boys. As I stick the pen behind his ear, I drop a kiss on his suppurating cheek. Our two bodies' proximity hides my fist rocketing into the backpack. I don't bother tugging the zipper closed because the opening isn't gaping and the bag is black—no one can see the colorful installation nestled inside.

One of the guards grips my upper arm. His expression is so stern that I think I've been made. I'm sure of it, actually.

"That's it. You're a security risk. I can't even believe you were allowed to come here! The museum director is going to give Mister Bacci hell!" He's livid now. "You're going to go back to your little competition and tell him he's to expect a phone call. And if any artwork has been damaged, he should expect a bill along with that call."

As he drags me back to the escalator, I realize he has no clue what I was sent here to do and find myself grinning.

"You think it's funny?" he growls.

"No. Of course not. I'm sorry it got out of hand."

"Sorry?" He snorts while shaking his big head.

He hauls me across the lobby. At one point, my foot begins to slip out of my shoe, so I shove the rubber toecap into the ground. I nearly trip, but at least my foot shoots back into place.

When we're out on the pavement, the guard stares around. "What the—?" he mutters, releasing me. The crowd is denser out here than it was inside, as though the whole city was alerted to my whereabouts.

"Back inside," the security guard says. "We'll go out another entrance."

He grabs my arm again, but I shrug him off, scanning the crowd more intently. If only I knew my driver's name. Like a mirage, he materializes in front of me, elbowing his way through the mass of bodies.

"Grab on to my waist," he says, and I do, and I don't let go until we've reached his gleaming black bike.

I plop the helmet on my head and straddle the motorcycle, the backpack flush against my stomach.

"Hang on," he says, revving up the engine.

The euphoria swirling through me is so great that I squeeze the roaring, sun-warmed frame between my thighs and experience the high of a lifetime. That's not to say I'm changing profession to become a world-class crook, but I understand the thrill. It feels as though I've cheated death.

Is that why Aster stole the diamond? The thought unfortunately sobers me up.

FORTY-FIVE

Ashes

fter she finishes reading the document I signed giving my sister power of attorney over my life, Robyn accompanies me back to my cell and instructs the guard on duty to let me rest unperturbed. Although I would never have expected to sleep, the second my head touches the pillow, all of me shuts down. When I wake up some time later, my forehead throbs. Since I can't stop visualizing my hand signing the destructive paper, I force my eyes open. I stare at the ceiling for a long while, and then I roll onto my side and study the closed door and the quiet hallway.

I spot a cardboard box inside my cell. I sit up and plod toward it. It's already sliced open, so I lift the flaps. Inside are rows and rows of granola bars. My stomach growls so I reach in and rip one open, then another. As I chew, my mind returns to the form and my throat tightens. A clump of oat flakes goes down the wrong hole and I cough so many times and so hard that I think blood will sputter out. It doesn't. I keep coughing; I'm going to choke. I suddenly clamp my lips shut and will that death-by-granola be quick, but it doesn't happen.

It reminds me of one of my mother's exes who choked on a

piece of steak. He was standing by the kitchen counter, picking large pieces of meat from a Tupperware container with his grubby fingers and shoving them inside his mouth. I was doing my homework on the kitchen table. Although I knew what to do to clear his airway, I couldn't get myself to move and hug his torso. I feared it would make him hug me back and I didn't want him to touch me. The man survived by heaving himself against the back of a chair. The meat rocketed out of his mouth and onto my calculus notebook. It looked like a piece of his own flesh. He broke up with my mother soon after, telling her how insensitive I was. Mom, who already blamed me for everything that went wrong in her life, hated me even more after that.

"Aster," a soft voice calls out through the bars of my gate. It's Gill. Her forehead is creased with worry lines. "How are you?"

"Better. Much better."

"I've been going crazy. No one wanted to tell me what was going on."

I don't approach the door for fear she will try to kiss me. "I've been sleeping."

"Good. That must have been what you needed. You look better. Not that you ever looked bad, but you have color in your cheeks again."

I'm tempted to snort, because deep down, I feel more awful now than I did this morning.

"I saw a bit of the show. It was crazy," she says.

I don't want to talk about the show, but I can't tell her that without explaining, so I listen quietly.

"The test was stealing art! Crazy, huh? I'm not sure what sort of message that sends out to the world."

"Did Ivy make it?"

Her eyes glow like two pieces of amber. "Yes! She was in the MoMA and this mob of people..." As Gill rambles on about my sister's prowess, I swallow thickly. "She's really resourceful," she concludes.

I sigh. "That she is."

"I don't know if she's a finalist, though. I just caught her bit and a few minutes of Chase's. I don't know how Lincoln did. Do you want me to go find out? Or we could go together…I'm sure they'll grant you permission to go to the dayroom—"

"I can't. Robyn wants me to meditate in her office."

"Can I come? I really enjoyed it last time."

"I should go alone."

The enthusiasm, which made her eyes sparkle, wilts off her face. "Oh."

"I can't concentrate when you're around," I add, attempting to cheer Gill up.

"I have that effect on women." She winks at me.

"I should get going."

"Do you want me to call a guard?"

"No, I'll do it," I say, before realizing that to do so, I must walk over to the gate to enter my request on the digital box.

Gill moistens her lips with her tongue. Taking a breath, I move forward, like a criminal headed for the gallows. After I've pressed on the call button, she grips my wrist and spreads my fingers with hers, and then she tugs me close. Her lips come at me like a freight train. I don't move. I don't breathe. She cares about me, unlike Ivy. I let her kiss me even though I feel the granola bar rise. Her mouth opens a little and her tongue prods mine. For a second, I'm disgusted. But then, I get this overwhelming urge to feel something other than misery.

In my peripheral vision, I spot black boots. I jolt away from Gill.

"You called, Inmate?" Officer Landry says. His face is stoplight-red.

"Miss Pierce is waiting for me."

Gill backs up so he can open my gate. As soon as I step out

of the cell, she skims my ear with her lips. "I'll catch you later," she murmurs. "I'm not done with you."

Swallowing hard, I tread past the rigid officer. Gill doesn't know this was our one and only kiss, but she'll figure it out before the day ends.

WHEN I LEAVE Robyn's office later that evening, I know exactly what I must do to crush Gill's interest in me.

"I'd like to go to the dayroom, please," I tell Kim.

"I need to run this past the warden," she says, her long fish-tail braid swishing from one side of her back to the other.

"He's on board."

She turns and bunches up her eyebrows that are in dire need of plucking. "I need to run this past the warden," she repeats.

"Fine. Let's go to his office now, so that he can confirm what I've just told you."

"Don't be snarky with me, Inmate, or we won't pass by his office."

I don't apologize, but I also don't speak the rest of the way.

When we arrive in front of his door, Kim knocks. "Commander Collins?"

"Come in."

She cracks the door open, but doesn't step in. Neither do I, but I make sure he can see me.

"Inmate Redd is asking for permission to go to the dayroom," she says.

His gaze meets mine. "Okay."

Kim blinks back in surprise. Even though I warned her he would accept, she clearly thought I was bluffing. "How long, sir, may she stay?"

"'Till her sister's show's over. Right? That's why you want to go, Aster, correct?"

I nod.

"Really?" Kim asks.

"Yes, Officer, really." His tone is sharp. "Anything else?"

"No," she says quietly.

Right before she closes the door, I say, "I've been meaning to tell you what great taste you have in art."

From the way his eyes jut out, I fathom he's realized that my compliment isn't directed at the print in the plastic frame hanging by his window.

FORTY-SIX

Ivy

L eila is jubilant tonight, probably because I accomplished the heist. She smiles as she brushes shimmery powder onto my cheeks and lines my eyes with black kohl. She doesn't lay it on as thick as on herself, but she does use quite a bit more than usual. She keeps the rest of my face neutral, down to my lips and nails that she paints a nude color.

Amy twists my silky hair into a sleek knot that suits the simple black sheath I am to wear to the ceremony tonight. I'm no longer as confident as I was on my way back to the Met, because we all succeeded. Who passes to the next round is a mystery. Possibly, it will depend on how long it took us to accomplish the theft—which would not work in my favor considering I was the last to return—or possibly they will base their assessment on our creativity. I'm hoping for the latter.

Lincoln and Chase look like they've walked off some glamorous fifties movie set, what with her pinned curls and his open collared tux. When his eyes touch mine, I look down at the crosshatched floorboards and will my pulse to decelerate. No point in wasting heartbeats on someone who doesn't care about me.

Cara leads the way down to the Temple room. Tonight, burgundy candles rise from massive bronze candelabrums and red roses, in various stages of bloom, dangle from transparent threads attached to the glass ceiling. The effect is sumptuous.

"Don't you feel like we should be wearing masks and nothing else?" Lincoln tells both Chase and me with a brazen smile.

Chase's facial expression tightens. "It's an art show, Lincoln, not an orgy."

"Geez, Jackson, lighten up. It was just a joke," she says. When she spots Brook a few paces ahead of us, she scampers off to join him.

Although smiling, he shifts away from her when she tries to touch him. I wonder if it's because there are cameras around, or if it's because, last night, he kissed her to get her off my case.

"You look very pretty tonight," Chase says, drawing my attention away from them.

"As opposed to all the other nights?" I ask, attempting humor.

"Why would you say that?"

"I'm weird about personal compliments."

Chase smiles.

For a second, I forget how rude he was to me last night. But only for a second. "I'm not into games, Chase. Maybe you get off on toying with women, and good for you if that's your thing, but it isn't mine."

The smile drops off his lips.

"We should get on stage," I say and walk away, toward the Egyptian stone temples to take my place on one of the three chairs.

Lincoln sashays up the steps to sit next to me. Her cheeks are flushed and her eyes sparkle with excitement. Has Brook told her she was still in the running or did he promise her a repeat of last night's performance?

Chase arrives and takes his seat just as Dominic hops onto the platform in a great flourish that reminds me of the first night. Brook joins him, debonair in his burgundy tuxedo that matches the silk scarf wrapped around Dominic's neck. I don't see Josephine, but can only imagine she's still working the crowd. The audience quiets down and settles around the tables as the anthem resounds.

Dominic raises the microphone to his mouth. "Lift up your hands if you guessed today's challenge?"

Arms shoot up left and right. Dominic leaps off the platform and walks over to the first table. He holds the microphone in front of a set of heavily botoxed lips.

"I'm listening, Arabella," he says.

Smiling, the woman says, "An art heist."

"Yes! However did you guess?" He moves away before she can answer and dashes back onto his stage. "They were given some rules though: don't get caught *and* don't damage the pieces. Without further ado, our first winner is..."

There's a drumroll from the orchestra along the far wall. I bite my lip, but quickly release it so I don't spoil my lipstick.

"Jeb, shoot us the image," Dominic says.

The lights dim and the surrounding screens light up with Chase's face. It's the portrait of him they used the night they announced the contestants on national television. Aster had made popcorn, which I'd nervously noshed on as Dominic revealed the eight winners. When my name failed to appear on the screen, I'd gone to get a tub of pistachio ice cream from the freezer.

"Don't be sad," she'd said.

"Sad? Why would I be sad?"

Aster had seemed pleased I hadn't won. I tried not to let it get to me. A few weeks later, there had been this news brief about Kevin's disqualification, followed by the judges' new pick—*me*.

As Chase's face fades off the screen, so does the memory of that fateful day. Jeb has assembled scenes from his hidden camera. They've even added some spy movie soundtrack that makes the wobbly, amateurish images resemble a Hollywood feature. His performance is excellent. He banters with a young, overly made-up intern and swipes her keycard without her noticing. Then he makes his way toward the vault, greeting people left and right, stopping to ask them about their children, dogs, girlfriends. Everyone—and I'm not blowing this out of proportion—is thrilled to see him. He gets smiles and hugs and pats on the back and flirtatious winks. It's insane how much people are drawn to him. Either he's a great actor, or he's nice to everyone but me.

Finally, Chase enters the safe and searches for the Zara Mach piece. It takes him a few minutes to locate the Plexiglas box. When he does, he seizes it and strolls through the auction house with it in the crook of his arm. Once outside, he places it inside his backpack. The screen goes dark.

"You just walked out with it?" Lincoln whispers, voicing my own thoughts.

He nods, just as Dominic says, "How come no one stopped you?"

"I told them my mother wanted to see what the cotton castanets would look like on her chimney mantle before she went ahead and bid on them."

"Was it true?" Dominic asks.

A corner of his lips curves up. "No. I just thought that hiding in plain sight would work best."

Dominic grins so widely it slants his eyes. "And work best it did," he exclaims. "Your brother's a genius, Brook."

Brook nods stiffly.

"Before we announce the second, and last, finalist, we will show you the footage. Girls, are you ready?"

Lincoln smiles while I clasp my hands on my lap to keep them from shaking.

Jeb has split the screens in half: on the right side, I'm entering the MoMA; on the left, Lincoln is entering a private gallery. Since I know what I did, I watch Lincoln's footage. I watch her flirt with the young salesperson, introduce herself as a contestant on *The Masterpiecers*, explain how she's gathering inspiration for today's test. So he shows her around, unlocking the basement in which there's a special room designed for viewing art pieces. She asks him to see the miniature chair collection and he obliges. He sets everything on the Corian table and adjusts the lighting. She handles each piece with great care, oohing and aahing profusely, while he launches into painstaking details on the manufacturing process of each piece.

The camera angle shifts to an empty white wall and the man stops talking. It takes me a second to understand what's happening, but when the screen goes dark, I can only imagine she's undone the buttons on her blouse and has pressed herself against him. I look at Dominic and Brook for condemnation, but both seem amused by Lincoln's audacity.

Suddenly, the camera angle changes again—probably from her blouse flopping open. Her hands grope the brushed white surface, closing around the barrel chair. Once she's swiped it, she presses the guy back and the camera shakes as she buttons up her blouse, her hands empty. She must have already placed it in her backpack.

The man is flushed. She asks him for a pen, rolls up his sleeve, and etches her phone number on his forearm. She ends the interlude with a flirtatious, "Don't wash that arm until you call me." And then she just climbs back up the stairs and strolls out of the gallery.

The dim room becomes darker now that all of the screens are black, and two spotlights fall on Lincoln and me.

"Girls, you were both great, and your performances deserve a round of applause," Dominic says.

The room breaks out into loud clapping and shrill whistles.

"But only one of you managed to bring back your plunder undamaged."

I play the relinquishment of the five tissues over in my mind, attempting to remember their state. Maybe I irreparably wrinkled one. Or maybe one had a tread mark on it. My pulse thrashes so wildly that I think I'm going to be sick. The only thing that's keeping me from hurling is the fact that Lincoln's grin has vanished.

"Ladies and gentlemen, this year's second finalist is..." Dominic begins.

A drumroll resounds. I feel it echo inside my body, reverberate against my organs, resonate inside my skull. I don't breathe until the black screens flash back to life.

FORTY-SEVEN

Of course my sister wins. She always wins. She's draped this surprised look over her face, but I know it's just for show. Ivy never doubts herself.

Chacha's slow-clapping, having paused her card game against Gracie to marvel at my sister's achievement. "Your sister, she's a finalist now. You gonna be rich soon."

"*She*'s going to be rich," I correct her.

The door of the dayroom flies open and in file a bunch of the inmates. Gill isn't among them.

"Hey," Sofia says, coming to sit next to me. "How was your day?"

I shrug. "Does any day in here not suck?"

"Some are better than others. Heard you and Gill are a couple now."

"Where did you hear that?"

"From her. She was telling everyone during yard time."

"Everyone?"

"Whoever would listen."

"We're not."

Chacha raises one of her over-plucked eyebrows.

"Me and Gill are *not* together," I exclaim.

"Told you, Gracie," Chacha says. "Pay up."

"I saw them making out," Gracie says.

"It wasn't real," I say.

"Looked real to me."

"She forced herself on me."

Sofia's see-through eyes grow wide.

"What? You don't believe me?" I say.

She tips her head to the side.

I frown. "What?"

"I forced myself on you?" a voice thunders. Gill is standing by the door, hands on her hips.

"Shit's about to hit the fan," Chacha says, slinging one skinny arm over the back of her chair to better take in the room.

"Yeah. You did," I say. I can't back down now.

A deep blush crawls up Gill's collarbone, her neck, her jaw. It floods her face and darkens her freckles. It even seems to stain her eyes. "How dare you," she hisses. "After everything I did for you."

I point to the dreads. "You mean this?"

She tramples over the scratchy rug that's threadbare in spots and slaps me so hard my neck snaps to the side.

"What the hell?" I screech, nursing my stinging cheek. I haven't been slapped since Mom.

Mom who's gone. For a second, when I look into Gill's face, I see Mom. I see the hatred and the disappointment and the disgust.

"You really are insane," she whispers.

"I am *not* crazy."

"You fucking think everyone's always watching you. That everyone's always after you!"

"Everyone *is* always watching me!"

"I bet you locked yourself in the freezer to get us to pity

you."

"I did not!"

"What's that?" Cheyenne asks, looking up from a magazine she's been flipping through.

"Nothing," I mumble.

She cracks her knuckles. "I didn't hear real well from where I was sittin'."

"Aster told us it was you," Gill says.

I glare at her. She glares right back.

"She heard your voice, but it was probably in her head. I bet she hears a lot of voices in her head."

"Shut up," I yell.

Gill smirks. "Are you talking to your head or to me, Aster?"

I bound off the couch. "Shut up," I yell again. Tears run into my mouth. They taste like salt water.

"Aw...did I hit a nerve?"

I'm shaking. "You don't know anything about me."

"I know you're not as innocent as you claim. I saw the news. After slamming that dude with your car, you backed up and ran him over. That takes a special kind of crazy to crush someone's bones."

"You shot your girlfriend," I counter.

"Because she hurt me. What did he do to you, huh? Nothing. You killed someone for no reason."

"He was a criminal!"

From the corner of my eye, I see Chacha rising, and Gracie too. They're creeping closer to me, as is Giraffe-neck. I back up and my calves knock into Sofia's kneecaps.

"He was a mean man," I say.

"A mean man," Gill mimics in a high-pitched voice that doesn't sound a bit like me. "And you're a mean girl."

"Am I going to need to stick you in a strait jacket, Redd?" Giraffe-neck hisses, collecting my hands against my back.

Josh is standing next to Chacha. I don't know how or when

he arrived, but I don't care...I'm so relieved to see him. "Help me, Josh."

Chacha looks from me to Josh and then back to me.

"Please," I whisper.

"Who's Josh?" Chacha asks.

"My boyfriend," I tell her, staring at Gill. "He's my boyfriend."

"Josh, can you please leave?" Giraffe-neck asks, eliciting chuckles from the rapt assembly.

"No! Don't."

Josh gives me a pained look.

"What is it? Is Ivy okay?" I ask, trying to elbow my way out of the guard's grip.

She just squeezes harder. "I need another officer in the dayroom. Prisoner not cooperating."

"Josh? What's going on?"

Chacha's staring at Josh. "What's happening to her?"

"Oh, God. Something *is* happening to Ivy." My pulse skyrockets. I whip my face toward the television screen. Brook is standing next to my sister, guiding her off the stage. And that's when it hits me. "It was *his* name on the package! I remember!"

Josh's green eyes glow like alien spaceships.

"He's going to hurt her, Josh! You need to—"

The door of the dayroom swings shut. He probably ran out to warn her.

Ponytail swishing, Kim jogs through the space Josh's body occupied only moments earlier.

"Brook Jackson is mixed up with the mafia," I tell Chacha who's gaping at me.

"Mafia?" Chacha asks.

Gracie shrugs.

Kim hands Giraffe-neck a pair of cuffs, which the latter proceeds to snap around my wrists.

"Told you she was nuts," Gill says.

"I'm not nuts," I yell.

"Take her to the pink tank," Giraffe-neck tells Kim.

"What's the pink tank?" I ask.

"A place for people like you," she says, long neck curving to the side.

Cheyenne grins, as do several other inmates. Gill doesn't, but I'm sure she's pleased to see me leave in handcuffs. I bet she would have been even more pleased to see me leave in a body bag.

"People like me? What's that supposed to mean?"

Cheyenne twirls a fat finger over her temple just as I'm shoved out of the room.

FORTY-EIGHT

Ivy

I still can't believe it was my face up there.

My neighbor at the dinner table has angled his body toward me and his mouth is moving like a fish sucking in plankton. "You can imagine how difficult it was not to inform my staff about Dominic's test," the man, who happens to be the curator of the museum I robbed earlier, tells me.

I smile politely. "I didn't know you were in on it."

"Can you imagine the scandal if I weren't?" He chuckles.

"Am I blacklisted from the MoMA or will I be able to come back for a visit?"

"You may return, but only in flip-flops."

"Deal," I say with a smile.

I spot Lincoln halfway across the room. I can tell she's pissed all the way from here. And I understand. One of the toothpick-like pieces from the miniature chair splintered in her backpack. When she catches me staring, I look toward Chase, my last adversary. He's deep in conversation with Delancey, who's wearing his usual monocle and pinstripe suit—brown tonight.

Hands settle on my shoulders. I tip my face up to find

Brook grinning down at me. "How many special orders have you received already?"

"None yet," I say.

"What?" He seems genuinely astonished. "What's wrong with you people? Grab her while you still can."

"We were waiting until dessert to ask such forward questions," the curator says with a chuckle.

The man sitting across the table from me—a thirty-something blond art dealer and Masterpiecers alumni—leans back in his chair and folds his arms over his chest. "I'd like to buy your entire collection, Ivy."

Brook laughs. He probably thinks it's a joke. I sort of think it's a joke too. I smile so as not to appear stupid.

"I'm serious. All of the pieces you've made."

My smile falters and Brook stops laughing. His fingers tighten around my skin.

"Have you signed with anyone yet?" the man asks.

"Signed? You mean with a gallery?"

"Yes."

I shake my head.

"But if she wins tomorrow, she'll automatically be represented by the school," Brook says.

"And if she loses?" the guys asks.

"She'll be represented by me."

I start at Brook's avowal.

"Are you allowed to take on private clients, Brook?"

Brook's fingers are so tight now that they're probably going to leave red imprints on my skin. "Why don't you call me tomorrow and we can discuss this matter in private?"

"With pleasure. You have my number. Call me at your convenience."

The conversation has created tension, which doesn't disappear when Brook leaves to work the other tables. When dessert is cleared away, I thank the people around me for the pleasure of their company, then thread myself through the room, determined to reach the exit quickly. I don't. I can see the glass door that will lead me out. I can even see Cara, and yet I can't get to either because so many people stop me.

"Excuse me." Brook interrupts one of my fans who smells so strongly of musk, it's making my head spin. "I need a word with my contestant." He waits for her to leave before saying, "Don't sign with that guy, okay?"

"Are you really going to offer me representation?"

"I've been considering it."

"Are you allowed?"

"It's one of the clauses I've asked the show's lawyer to implement in my contract. I just need to get it past Dom."

"And past Josephine."

"Josephine's opinion won't matter."

"It won't?"

"No. Soon it won't."

"Is she leaving the show?"

"I wouldn't use the word *leaving*, but yes. Something like that."

"Was she fired?"

His eyes grow wide with a silent warning. "The heist was all Dom's idea," he says, his eyes darting to a space behind me. I imagine that either someone is coming or that we're being filmed.

"What an idea," I say, playing along. "Anyway, I should get to bed. Larceny is exhausting, isn't it?"

Brook stares at me with this bizarre expression on his face.

"Goodnight," I say since he's still just gaping.

As I join Cara, I wonder if I said something wrong, but by the time we exit the Egyptian wing, I decide that it doesn't matter if I did. The only thing that matters now is getting through the next twenty-four hours and emerging victorious.

Once I'm alone in my tented room, I untie my hair,

clean off my makeup, and slip out of my dress. As I brush my teeth, I catch movement behind me. I grab a towel and wrap it around my bare chest, then turn around, half-expecting Cara to have forgotten to tell me something.

It's not Cara.

"What do you want?" I ask Chase, narrowing my eyes.

"I came to tell you I was sorry."

"For being an asshole?"

"Yes."

At first, I bite my lip, but then I raise an eyebrow. "You admit you were an asshole yesterday?"

"I do."

"Why?"

"Because I was."

"I mean why did you say those things to me?"

"Because I was angry."

"Angry at me? Because of the whole swimming thing?"

"Because I like you...a lot...and when you lied to me, it reminded me of my ex. And I panicked." He tucks his hands inside the pockets of his tuxedo pants and looks at my red bag that sticks out in the beige-colored room like a bloodstain on a rug. "Ivy, tonight, during dinner, they were discussing your family. I heard how your mother died." He studies his feet, which he's shuffling. "That's why you told me you didn't know how to swim, isn't it?"

"I haven't been in the water since. At least not until the other night." I shiver at the memory of Kevin's body. "I don't think I'll ever be able to go in the water again now."

Chase lays a warm hand on my arm. When he sees me glance at it, he lets it fall back alongside his body. "I'm really sorry I called you a liar."

"I did lie."

"But you didn't do it to hurt me," he says.

I toy with the herringbone pattern on the hem of the towel. "Why did you help me, that day with the riddle?"

His lips perk up in a smile. "Because you're an intimidating girl, and I've never felt intimidated before." His eyes grind into mine. "I thought that if I helped you, somehow I'd stop feeling threatened."

"Did it work?"

"It did. But it wasn't until our conversation at Brook's place that I managed to humanize you."

"Humanize me? What did I say that made me so *human*?"

"You told me about your dream of living off your quilts, about your imperfect relationship with your sister, and I understood that you had all these insecurities, and for some reason, that reassured me."

"And it made you like me?"

A corner of his mouth lifts. "Oh, I already liked you. It just made me think I stood a chance."

I tilt my head to the side to observe him. "This isn't some ploy to distract me so that I lose tomorrow?"

Laughter ripples out of his mouth. "No. No ploy."

"Oopsy"—Lincoln hiccups—"did I interrupt something?" She's standing by the opening of my tent, clutching a bottle of champagne.

"Please go away, Lincoln, and take your bottle of champagne with you," I tell her.

She sticks out her lower lip. "I'll be leaving tomorrow. I didn't want to spend my last night in here alone."

"Why don't you go find my brother?"

"Your brother's the reason it's my last night."

"Huh?"

"Someone caught us making out on camera and leaked it on the Internet. Probably someone from the film crew."

"But your chair broke," I say.

"No it didn't. They just said it did to eliminate me."

I blink.

"Yeah, Ivy, you didn't win tonight because you were better than me—because you're not—you won because Dom said it was conflictual or conflicting or something like that." She takes a swig of the champagne.

Chase walks toward her. I think he's about to leave, but instead he stops in front of her and squares his shoulders. "You should go back to your room, Lincoln."

She pokes his chest. "You're not my mommy, Chase."

He swipes her finger off. "And give me the bottle before you get yourself sick."

She swings her hand out of his reach. "Okay, Mommy," she teases.

He tries to grab it from her, but she lifts her arm higher. The bottle slips and falls on the floor, but doesn't shatter. Instead, it spills champagne everywhere. She bends over and grabs it.

"Goodnight, you two," she singsongs as she finally turns to leave. "And congratulations in advance, Chase, for your win tomorrow."

Once my tent flap settles, I ask, "Is it true?"

"You deserved to win. Your performance was—"

"But is it true?"

"Is anything she says true?" he asks, grabbing some tissues from the nightstand to clean up the spilled champagne.

"Don't worry. I'll do it," I say, crouching down beside him. The towel begins unraveling, but I catch it.

Chase sits back on his heels, his eyes stuck to the flash of thigh he's just gotten. "I never thought I'd be thankful toward Lincoln for anything," he says, his tone light.

I shove him and the towel comes undone again. This time, *he* catches it. Instead of peeling it off my body, he tucks the hem back between my breasts, letting his fingers linger there. Then he leans forward and deposits the sweetest kiss on my lips. And I forget about the bad blood between us, but I don't forget that he's still my opponent, and that tomorrow—like Lincoln said—he'll most probably defeat me and that'll be the end of us...

Of this...

Of me.

FORTY-NINE

The pink tank is a padded cell painted bright pink. It's supposed to be soothing. It's not. I hate pink. The color gives me hives and I begin scratching my skin. Soon, it glows brighter than the walls. And not long after, I manage to draw blood.

I pace the cell and think of my sister and Brook and Josh and Troy and the package. Why couldn't I remember the name sooner?

"What happened to your arms?" I hear someone ask. It's Landry.

I rush to the gate and wrap my fingers around the bars. "I need to get out of here. Please."

"I, uh...I'll go get the nurse."

I nod enthusiastically. Celia will help me. She'll take pity on me. After he leaves, I strain to hear footsteps resound through the narrow hallways, but the minutes tick by and still no one shows.

I begin pacing again. And scratching. The blood under my jagged nails has turned a rusty shade of brown by the time the nurse arrives. Instead of flashing me a kind smile, Celia's face contorts into a grimace.

"Landry, walk her to my office," she says. "I need to bandage her arms."

Landry cuffs me.

"Why—I don't need these. Nurse Celia, can you please tell him I don't need to be restrained?"

She doesn't.

In silence, we make our way to her office. There's a spot of blood on the paper covering her exam table. That's why she was late. She was treating another patient. She gathers the soiled sheet, balls it up, and chucks it into the bin, then rolls out a fresh one. Landry removes the cuffs so I can climb onto the exam table. I'm half-expecting Celia to kick him out, but she doesn't. She brings over a metal kidney tray filled with cotton swabs, antiseptic, and a roll of gauze.

"Right arm," she says.

I give it to her. Gaze cast downward, she cleans it and assesses the damage, trades the gauze for a few Band-Aids, and pastes them on.

"Left arm."

"Are you mad at me?" I ask her.

She peers up at me through her yellow bifocals, but still doesn't speak.

My breath hitches. "You are."

Landry stares out the window, but I know he's listening.

"Why?" I ask.

Still she doesn't say anything. At least not to me. "Landry, you may bring her back wherever she needs to go."

"Not to the pink tank...please." My voice comes out as a hoarse whisper as the officer approaches the exam table. "Can I go to the dayroom? It's my sister's last day."

"I'm not sure you deserve to go watch TV right now," Celia says.

I gasp. "Why are you being so mean to me?"

"Me? Mean? I'm not the one blaming some poor girl of forcing herself on me. Gill tried to take her life. She was so embarrassed by your accusations that she cut her wrist on the prison fence," she says. "I tried to see the good in you, Aster, but in here"—she pounds her fist against her heart—"there's too much bad."

I squash my lips together to stop them from quivering.

"Take Inmate Redd away. I have work to do."

The handcuffs dangle from his hands.

"I'll cooperate, but no cuffs," I say.

Landry glances at Celia who's wheeled herself behind her desk and is typing something on her laptop. "Okay," he says softly. "But don't try anything."

I lower myself to the ground, and, hunched over, walk docilely out of the infirmary and away from the only person who didn't hate me in this prison.

"Where are you taking me?"

"Back to your cell."

I stop in my tracks. "No. To the dayroom...I need to see my sister."

He freezes and turns sideways. "I-I don't think that's a good idea."

"Please. Everybody hates me around here. Everybody thinks I'm crazy, and that I'm a liar. The only thing keeping my head above water is watching my sister." I take a breath. "In some ways, it feels like I'm watching myself, like I'm getting a chance to live again, and be someone...someone people respect and admire. I've never had that."

Landry rubs the back of his neck.

"Do you know what it feels like when your future contains no pigment, no sparkle? Because that's what mine looks like. I have nothing...no one besides my sister."

I think he's about to say yes when the radio strapped to his shoulder buzzes. "*Yobwoc*, you copy?"

"Copy," Landry says.

"What's the status on Inmate Redd? Is she stable?"

Landry's round face colors.

"*Yobwoc?*" Driscoll barks again when Landry remains quiet for too long. I don't like what his silence implies.

"She's okay, sir," he finally says.

"Well, she got a caller in visitation room two. Escort her there, will ya?"

"On it, sir."

As we walk down the string of hallways toward the visitation area, I take mental bets as to whether it's Josh or Dean. I'm hoping for the first, because I need to know why he didn't defend me back in the dayroom.

Unfortunately, it's Dean.

"Inmate Redd's just been released from the pink tank," Landry tells him.

Dean doesn't ask what it is. He must know. "What happened to your arms?"

I flop down in the chair across the table from him.

"Were you attacked?" he asks.

"She scratched her arms."

"Because I had a rash," I add.

Dean raises an eyebrow, but drops the topic. "I can take it from here, Officer Landry."

As soon as the young guard shuts the glass door, I say, "Thanks for sending Josh over."

The gray in his eyes looks silver in the bright concrete room, like the reflective tape on running shoes. "Officer Cooper stopped by to see you?"

"Yes. This morning. He left quickly though."

"Where did he go?" Dean's frowning.

"New York."

"He left for New York?"

I nod. "Yeah."

"That's odd."

"Why?"

"I met with his chief the other day who told me that your boyfriend was never authorized to investigate your case because of your relationship. Last I heard, he was on probation for disregarding direct orders."

"You must have heard wrong, because the chief okayed it. Josh told me so."

"I'm going to have to report him then."

My eyes widen. "No!" I shake my head. The dreads whip my collarbone. "You can't report him! He needs to save Ivy."

"Save Ivy? From what?"

"From Brook."

"Excuse me."

"Brook's name was on the package. The one that was addressed to the show with my sister's quilt in it. I remembered it when I was watching the show."

He drums his fingers against the metal table. My gaze sticks to his pinky, the one with the heavy gold ring. I've seen it before, on someone else's hand...I'm certain of it. But whose? The person had long fingers with buffed nails, feminine fingers. Was it a woman? Dean stops tapping the table. Instead, he flattens both his palms on the table and stands up. And that's when it hits me. Where I've seen it before. I jump away from him, knocking over my chair that crashes against the cement floor. As I cower against the wall, Landry races into the room.

"What? What's going on?" he yells, hand on his Taser gun.

"He knew Troy Mann! He knew Troy," I exclaim, pointing to Dean. "They have the same ring!"

Landry's face swings between me and Dean.

"You have to arrest him. He's in on it," I yelp.

"On what?" Landry asks, head still swinging back and forth. "What is she talking about?"

"I think she needs to return to the pink tank. She's obviously not stable yet," Dean says.

"The hell I'm not stable!"

More voices buzz around me. "What the fuck is the matter in here?" Giraffe-neck asks, face flushed. She must have run.

"Your prisoner is making baseless accusations," Dean says with a snort. He's so calm—too calm.

"They're not baseless. They have the same ring. Take his ring. Compare it to Troy Mann's! They're the same!"

"A lot of men have rings." He snorts again.

"I know what I saw," I say, trying to catch my breath. "You have to believe me."

For a second, I think she does, but then her mouth contorts into a smirk when someone behind her says, "Just like you saw Officer Cooper this morning?" Gill is leaning against the glass wall of the room, arms folded.

"What's she doing here?" I ask, eyeing the gauze wrapped around her wrist.

"You told me I should interview her for a character witness," Dean says, stroking the gold bar hooked into his yellow tie.

"No," I yell. "She's not my friend anymore."

"You don't have any more friends around here, Aster," Gill says. "But that's your own fault."

"I'm sorry, Mister Kane. We shouldn't have been so hasty to release her from the tank." There is no more smile on Giraffe-neck's face. "Landry, cuff her."

"What?" I roar. "No! No! I'm telling the truth—"

"Shut it, Redd," she snaps. "Or we'll have to Taser you."

"No! Don't let him get away! Don't—" Two copper wires latch on to the skin below my collarbone, delivering a jolt of electricity so great it sets my organs on fire, paralyzes my muscles, and darkens my mind.

FIFTY

Ivy

"Authenticity!" Dominic's voice booms out of his microphone. "You will be shown to a gallery in which we have arranged six of the Met's most celebrated treasures. Amidst those six, one is fake. Ivy, Chase, to win, not only must you uncover the fake, but you must also explain how you've arrived at this conclusion, because, although luck exists in the art business, expertise is still key."

The screens around the Temple room switch to visuals of the nominated pieces. The first one is a Monet representing a bridge overhanging a pastel water lily pond. The second is a swirly Van Gogh landscape with a tall cypress tree and a tumultuous summer sky. A bronze Degas statue of a fourteen-year-old ballerina is object three. Then an epic-looking painting of Washington crossing the Delaware River is number four. The fifth piece is a terracotta-hued bust of a man by Pablo Picasso. And the last is a marble statue of a mythological hero holding Medusa's severed head.

The slideshow of works dissolves back to the Master-piecers' logo.

"Contestants, you will be given all the tools afforded to

professional appraisers and you will be shown how to use them. As always, have fun, and good luck."

Bodies parallel but not touching, Chase and I descend the stairs and ford across the standing audience. I don't glance at him, afraid to spot the confidence I'm lacking...and afraid that my glance will give away my growing feelings for him. His pinkie grazes the side of my hand and I shiver. I stare into the cameras that are being wheeled in front of us, then over my shoulder at the audience marching like a disciplined army behind us.

This is it. The last day. The last contest. The last chance to win a hundred thousand dollars and an entry into the school.

Too soon, we're in the herringbone-planked gallery with the masterpieces. Dominic is standing before us and the cameras are circling us, while the audience presses up against the velvet ropes erected at each entrance. Only Josephine and the orchestra are missing.

"And now, I'd like you to meet our wonderful experts," Dominic says, gesturing to two women. Both wear simple black pantsuits. The younger one sports a pair of glasses with thick purple frames and has her hair up in a bun, while the other wears it down to her shoulders. "Chase and Ivy, meet Genevieve and Larissa. Both have trained at the Masterpiecers and still consult for us. However, Genevieve now works for the Metropolitan as their art specialist and Larissa is the woman the auction houses call upon in case of doubt."

Both women nod. Neither smiles.

"They will be assisting you today with each tool. They will, however, not be answering any questions. It will be up to you to figure out the results." Dominic pauses to make the moment more dramatic. "Finalists, it is time to begin. Ready...set...go!"

Chase pounces toward the woman who works at the Metropolitan. Smart. As I watch him move to the table covered in appraisal tools, the other woman comes up to me and sticks out a manicured hand.

"Hi, Ivy," she says as I shake it. "Shall we get started?"

When I release her hand, my fingers fall back against my thighs, cold and stiff. I nod.

"Let's go to this side of the room." She indicates the Washington painting since Chase is studying the Monet.

I walk on autopilot alongside her and stop in front of the monstrous oil painting. I read the small plaque on the wall, take in the year and the dimensions. The painting has been presented without its frame.

"Is there a measuring tape?" I ask.

Larissa smiles, which convinces me that my approach is smart. "I will get one right away."

She returns with a coiled ruler, which she holds in place while I pull it the length of the canvas, then the width. All the dimensions check out, to the fraction of an inch. I decide it must be real.

"Let's go to the next," I say, clutching the measuring tape.

Her wide, bright red lips curve up. Does she smile because I'm right? Or is it mocking? Chase is still studying the Monet, using some tool that resembles a supermarket scanner. Maybe my assessment was too rushed.

"Can I touch the paintings?" I ask.

She nods. "Lightly, though."

So I run the tips of my fingers over the subtle, sloping oil reliefs and close my eyes. If only paint could talk, tell me who brushed it atop the canvas.

"Is there another tool you'd like to use?" she asks me.

My lids snap up, and I find Chase handing back the scanner. "That," I say, pointing to it.

"Let me get it."

She crosses the room and takes it from Genevieve. Chase's gaze lifts to mine, all at once intense and gentle, and my brain becomes fuzzy. I shake my head. I need to concentrate.

Larissa's on her way back. "Here's the Proscope," she says, handing it to me.

"How...um...does it work?"

"You hold it up to the signature and it acts as a microscope. It'll show you each pixel with a clarity the human eye cannot discern. Let me just plug it into this tablet for a visual."

She holds the screen up to me as I take the small apparatus and hover it over the signature. I'm not sure what I'm looking for, but I move it over the word *Leutze* slowly. There's a feathery quality to the second letter and a sort of break in the *t* that makes me study the letter more closely. I look up from the tablet screen. As Larissa said, I don't spot any discrepancy with my naked eye. But I didn't imagine it. On the screen, it's there, unmistakable.

"Can I get a pen and paper?"

She frowns, but obliges.

I hand her the tablet and handheld microscope and take the pen and paper. I sign my name, and then take the device and run it over my autograph. I watch the screen, satisfied. There isn't a single crack in my writing, which leads me to believe that whoever signed the Delaware River painting is not Leutze.

Excitement bubbles through me, but I squelch it down as I walk over to the table laid out with all the tools. There's some handheld electric torch that dispenses black light.

"What's that used for?" I ask Larissa.

"Detecting lead in pigments."

I can't see the use of analyzing lead content.

"There was more lead in paints before the turn of the twentieth century," she explains.

I seize the tool and bring it over to the Monet. I shine the black light inches away from the pretty paint smudges. I don't see any variations and am about to let the torch fall to my side when the light touches a smear of white. The white turns blue and gray.

"Does that mean a high lead concentration?" I ask Larissa.

Her lips press together. "Yes."

So it must be real. Dominic mentioned spotting the fake. The Leutze is fake. On second thought, maybe it's just hard to sign in paint. "Can you still buy lead-heavy paint today?" I find myself wondering out loud.

Her bottom lip drops in surprise. "Yes."

So lead content isn't going to help me age the painting. I check the dimensions on the plaque and pull out the measuring tape to size up the water lily canvas. They match. I'm racking my mind for other ways of telling if something is old. On humans, wrinkles or gray hair are a good sign. Billboards fade and book pages turn yellow. "Can we pull it off the wall?"

"We can't," Larissa says, and my hope plummets. "But *they* can." She points to the guards stationed on either side of the wall. "We need help here," she calls out.

As I turn, my forehead knocks into the large camera that's been filming my every move since the day I arrived at the Metropolitan. Improbably, it's become part of my landscape, and I usually don't even notice it anymore, but I also usually don't collide into it.

"Sorry," the woman filming says. She gets a stern look from Jeb who's handling the camera aimed on Chase.

The guards flip the canvas over. I look for a yellowing of the fibers. There is none. "Can canvas be bleached without it affecting the paint?" I ask Larissa.

She tips her head to the side and her shiny black hair brushes the sharp shoulders of her suit. "No."

I catch Chase's eyes, but too briefly to read anything. He shifts back to the ballerina, leaving me to ponder the Monet.

Why in the world would someone spend time cleaning the back of a painting anyway?

Could the Leutze be real and the Monet be fake? I move on to the Van Gogh. I shine the black light on the swirly clouds. Like on the pale water lily pads, the white takes on hues of blue and gray indicating that the paint is from Van Gogh's era.

I switch off the torch. "What other tools are available?"

"The Oculus Aperture. They're x-ray binoculars that reveal the different layers of paint so you can see if the artist intended to put a mouse in the corner of his creation or if he changed the angle of a limb."

That's exactly what I need. I walk to the table in the middle of the room, where Chase is perusing what's available. As I reach out for the pair of silver binoculars, our hands collide. I snap my fingers back to my side, while his continue their trajectory. He seizes the binoculars and I think I'll have to wait, but he says, "Ladies first."

Startled, I don't take them from him, so he grasps my hand and unbolts my fingers, then places the instrument in my palm and presses my fingers closed.

"Bring them back to me when you're done."

I stare up at him, forgetting there's anyone else in the room. As the deep brown of his irises eddy around his pupils, his hand slowly releases mine. I should swim against the tide sweeping me toward Chase. It's too strong and too quick, flooding me with too many emotions.

I will drown if I'm not careful.

Aster

I vy is so beautiful in her red dress and sleek hairdo, whereas I'm so ugly. I long to yank out the dreads, but they're as resilient as the rope Ivy and I tied to a tree branch one summer, to attach a castoff tire. How we would swing on that old piece of rubber!

The memory tugs on my fraying heartstrings. *Ivy and me.* There should have been a song written about us, one with a sweet, plucky melody. Two stick-thin girls with bushy curls swinging on a craggy tire, making forts out of branches and blue Ikea bags, and rolling in tall, tickling grass until their bellies hurt from laughing. But no one will ever write a song about us. They might compose one about Ivy, though, now that she's a celebrity.

I'm propelled into the dayroom, staring at myself pulling on my ratty tresses. From inside the TV, Ivy sees me too. Her eyes are wide and expectant and scared. She needs me, but I can't help her, I can't leap through the screen. The dyed fibers of her dress tremble as her heart beats quicker. My pulse hastens in turn, making the stiff gray shroud that ensconces me vibrate too.

"Aster," she whispers. "Aster..."

"I'm here, Ivy! Right here." My voice sounds foreign to my ears, yet it's my voice. It vibrates in my chest, making it ache. "Ouch," I murmur as I shift. Paper crackles. I try to lift my wrists, but I can't. "I can't get to you. I can't move."

"No shit. You're attached to a gurney, you fucking bitch."

My lids snap up and light bounces into my eyes. Too much light and too much red. So much red, I squeeze them shut again. I pretend that I'm unconscious.

"Wakey, wakey," Gill says, digging something into my palm.

I scream out in pain, but she stifles my scream with her hand.

FIFTY-TWO

Ivy

Larissa plucks the Oculus Aperture from my hand like a child reaching into a bucket of popcorn for their first handful. "It's brand new technology," she explains. "Before, you had to take x-rays like in the dentist's office. But now, we have these! They're amazing, aren't they?" Her dark eyes glitter with excitement as she finally hands them back.

There are a few straps that go around the top of the head to stabilize them. Once they're in place, all I have to do is press a button and the binoculars flood to life and self-adjust to my vision. I focus them on the Van Gogh.

After a long surveillance, I say, "I don't see anything."

"What do you mean?" Larissa asks. "Did you turn them on?"

"Of course I turned them on," I tell her. "I just don't see any layers. Is there something I'm not pressing on?"

Without glancing away from me, she says, "Don't look for something that isn't there."

I make mistakes when I create quilts and often have to unstitch what I've sewn. But maybe Van Gogh doesn't. Maybe he's some genius who gets it right from the beginning.

With the Oculus still on, I walk to the Monet and scrutinize it through the computerized lenses. No layers. I stride over to the Leutze, stumbling into one of the guards. Large hands steady me and then I'm on my way again. I study the scene from top to bottom and side to side. There isn't a single hesitation, no soldier out of place, no fishtail sticking out from the icy river, no musket covered by a new layer of paint. Could all three be fakes? With the interactive glasses still on, I circle the room, stopping in front of the small terracotta-hued Picasso. I almost zip past it when I spot something that makes me stop and stare: the shadow of another face, a woman's face. I lift the binoculars. The woman's face vanishes. I place them back on, and the rough sketch returns.

What the hell does it mean? That it's real and the rest are fakes? I pull the Oculus off and cross the room toward Chase who's studying the Van Gogh with the black light.

"Here," I say.

He takes the binoculars from me. "You okay?"

"Just confused."

He frowns.

Dominic's arms are folded against his double-breasted navy suit, head tipped toward Brook in a quiet exchange. When they see me watching them, they fall silent. I return to Larissa who's rearranging the gauging instruments on the table. Without a word, I grab the measuring tape and head to the Picasso. The width and length match up. I'm still convinced it's real. I check the signature with the Proscope. I'm expecting solid letters, but most resemble thread ends unraveling. I turn the device off, my earlier conviction smashed to pulp. I add the Picasso to the list of fakes and move to the statues.

I start with the bronze and measure it. The dimensions check out. Degas's signature is etched in the square base by the dancer's feet. I wouldn't know if it was real or fake though.

The plaque says the skirt is made of cotton and satin hair ribbons. Delicately, I run the tips of my fingers through them. Although browned with age, I don't feel the cool, filmy texture of satin.

Frowning, I move to the other statue—the white marble one. I need a chair to measure it and ask a guard for one. He returns with a stool and insists on helping me up and holding me as I reach past Medusa's severed head to Perseus's winged helmet. Just shy of eight feet tall, as it says on the plaque. As I descend from the stool, I lose my balance. Although the guard bares most of my weight, my hand flails out toward the statue. The second I touch it, I know it's fake. Although veined like marble, it isn't cold and silken like stone. It feels like plaster. I scramble back onto the stool and swipe my index finger in the hollow of Medusa's head. A dusty white residue remains on my skin.

I take in the room from my vantage point and feel a sense of smugness and pleasure at not having been outsmarted by Dominic and Brook. I spot Chase in front of the Picasso, running his last tests. Has he come to the same conclusion?

Could we both win?

I hop down from the stool and amble toward Dominic. "I'm done."

"Are you now? You still have plenty of time—"

"I don't need more time."

"Are you certain? There's no revising your answer once you give it to us."

My certainty momentarily flounders. I feel a presence behind me and don't need to whirl around to know it's Chase. I can smell the pine needles in the small space separating our bodies.

"You have your answer too, Chase?" Brook asks.

"Yes."

"Okay, then. Ivy, you come with me, Chase, you go with…" Brook's voice dies off as his eyes settle on the entryway behind us.

"Hello, *finalistes*," comes a sharp, accented voice. "I hope I did not miss the big reveal."

"I don't like spending hours on people who screw me over." Gill's twirling something shiny between her fingers. She sees me looking at it and smirks. "Makes me discontent."

"What is that?"

"Oh, this? Something I was offered for my flowery character assessment. Something I sharpened."

My palm throbs. I shift my head to the side to glance at it. Blood trickles down my shackled wrist and along the pale skin of my forearm.

"It's worth a lot apparently. It's real gold," she says. "Slices real well too." She juts her chin toward my palm. "Now, Aster, *I'd* like my dreads back, and *Mister Kane* would like to know what you did with the *rest of them.*"

"The rest of what?"

"He said you would play dumb."

How I ever felt anything but alarm toward Gill is beyond me. As her hands move toward my head, I eye the door of the infirmary. It's sealed shut.

"Nurse Cee—"

Gill stuffs a wad of gauze inside my mouth. For some reason I think of Sofia and her prowess for chess, wishing I possessed even an ounce of it. Then I'd be two moves ahead of Gill instead of strapped down and defenseless.

"While you think, I'm taking my hard work back." Her breath whistles in my ear as the shiv saws through my hair. At some point, the serrated metal bites into my skin. "Oopsy," she says, delight lilting her tone.

She hacks through more dreads. My scalp throbs as something warm oozes down my neck. I'm not sure if it's blood or perspiration. My lashes become wet.

"You've been a bad girl, Aster. Very bad."

The right side of my head feels light and cold now.

"You've hurt a lot of people. Especially me. I should've known you would screw me over, but I was hoping...hoping we could become something. But we couldn't, could we? You were just using me. You never liked me. And I liked you so"— her tongue glides across my jaw—"so much."

I gag and spin my head so abruptly that the sharp blade saws into my neck, tearing my flesh. I whimper.

"Shit," she says as a cascade of heat gushes down my collarbone. "I think I hit your artery...*shit*."

Instinctively, I lift my hand but the metal cuff holds it back. Gill jumps up and looks around, eyes wide, spooked. She grabs on to stuff then scrambles back toward me.

"I'm going to get it under control! Don't worry."

She presses a wad of cotton against the gash in my neck. Since I can't see or touch it, I gauge the state of my wound from the roundness of her eyes. It must be bad because the amber irises float on the white.

"Shit!" She throws the cotton on the floor. It's so full of blood it doesn't even arc through the air. It just drops like a rock. She rips one of her sleeves and wraps the fabric around my neck. "Stay with me! Nurse! Guards! Someone!" Her voice sounds like it's coming from inside a seashell, yet I know she's yelling from the way her lips contort over her buckteeth.

"What the hell, Swanson? You said you wanted to make up," Nurse Celia's voice trills.

My ears ring, my palm throbs, and my neck aches, but what I feel most is the temperature warring within and outside of me: cold floods my veins while warmth streams over my skin.

"Aster! Aster!" Gill's freckles glow like the cinnamon sprinkles atop Ivy's favorite donuts. "Stay with me!"

I become fluffier, my body weightless, my mind empty like a helium balloon drifting toward the sky. The white room grows brighter, louder. Gill's eyes spin like those pinwheels I loved to blow on when I was a child.

Her eyes are red now. She's entirely red, from her thick ropes of hair, to her pale skin that glows as though it were on fire, to her hands that are wet with my blood. She's red like the dress Ivy wore in my dream. Like the sticky, soiled fabric of my gray jumpsuit. Like our last name.

Redd.

Ivy's suddenly there, small and distant, sitting on Celia's desk, swinging her legs like she used to on those tire swings. She watches as death heaves me away. She doesn't move. She just stares, her expression blank, emotionless, like the last time I saw her and tried to hold her hand.

"I gave up my future so that you could have one," I tell her, but she doesn't hear me because the blood makes me sound like I'm gurgling.

Perhaps my life ending will allow hers to truly begin. One less person to make plans for, one less hospital bill to pay with the loan she took out on *her* apartment and with the money she made from the sales of her quilts. I hope she's forgiven me for sending one to *The Masterpiecers*. I hope she knows it was a coincidence. A sad coincidence.

The shadow fades as the body steps into the sun.

FIFTY-FOUR

Ivy

"How much longer do we have to wait?" I ask Cara, who's sitting in my tent, bouncing her sneakered feet.

"Until I get orders to get you to the reception room," she says.

"Can you at least get me a magazine?"

She shakes her head.

"A book?"

Again she shakes her head.

"*Ugh*," I grumble, flopping onto my back in the silver gown Amy has laboriously buttoned me into. "This is so boring!"

"You're going to mess up your hair," Cara says.

"Like I care."

"*I* care. If I bring you down with a lopsided hairdo, I lose my job. I don't want to lose my job."

"It's your last day," I say. "And possibly the last year of this show with all that's happened."

Josephine arrived with a lawyer this afternoon. When our assistants took us back to our quarters, making sure there was absolutely no contact between Chase and me, a grim-faced Dominic and a nervous Brook exited the gallery with her. As if this show hasn't been splashed across the media enough! But more troubling—at least in my opinion—is the fact that Josephine's new right-hand woman is Lincoln. Should have known those two were kindred spirits. I'm dying to speak to Chase about it, hear what he thinks.

I drum my fingers, perplexed about the upcoming evening. The anticipation contracts my muscles and spouts blood through my veins at such speed that my heart feels like it's about to detonate. I roll up and start pacing the room.

Cara watches me. "I didn't think Ivy Redd ever got nervous."

"I'm anxious, not nervous."

"Chase didn't seem particularly anxious," she continues.

Is she trying to get a rise out of me? "Good for him." I look in the direction of his room. I wonder if his assistant has him locked in there with nothing to do as well. For a second, I think I see the outline of his body through the fabric walls, moving around the room, but it's just my shadow. Cara's right, though —Chase was totally self-assured when he left the gallery.

"We're a go," Cara says, readjusting her head mic.

I inhale so quickly that the air tears through my lungs, making me sputter. Cara unzips my tent and gestures for me to go ahead of her. Instead of walking, I freeze.

"You wanted out. You got out. Now let's go," Cara says, holding up the flap.

I quickly pat my hair down to make sure the braid swinging between my bare shoulder blades is as sleek as Amy intended it to be and that the gold chain she wove into it is in place. Finally, I step past Cara, into the empty grass hallway lined with the twinkling potted trees. I take them in—I take in everything around me, the makeup stations, the stone stairs, the vertiginous main hall, the Egyptian artifacts—because, whether I win or lose, this is my last night on the show, and probably my last time ever sleeping inside a museum.

Chase is waiting by the entrance of the Temple room. Sensing my presence, he turns to stare at me. Warmth battles the chill that's enveloped my body.

"Any day," Cara says, tapping her foot again. "There's only a couple million people waiting."

Chase rolls his eyes. I'm tempted to smile, but my lips just quiver limply. As I arrive at his side, he grabs my hand and laces his fingers through mine.

"Whatever happens, you were great," he says.

"Thanks." My voice is hoarse.

"And you're not a phony, Ivy. Your beauty and intelligence might be enhanced by all the makeup and nice clothes, but you weren't fabricated like some forgery."

My brows draw together. "Have you been drinking? Because if you have, then you've had way more fun than me."

Cara clears her throat. "That's enough talking," she says.

His black pupils throb. "I just hope you know the difference."

Surprisingly, all three judges are standing together on the raised platform between the temples, all in glimmering outfits. The guests also have selected glitzier attire for the occasion.

"Ready?" Chase asks just before we enter the room.

I glance at him and attempt to smile. I even try to answer, but no words come out of my mouth. He tugs me through the cavernous room underneath a shower of applause and music. Although Dominic is smiling, there is no cheer in his eyes. Josephine, on the other hand, appears truly content, her smile as sharp as the conical studs adorning the collar of her gold lamé dress.

I pull my hand out of Chase's the second we're on the platform. The spotlights trained on us are blinding, yet I can see Lincoln on the outskirts of the circle, her eyes as shiny as her sequin-heavy dress. I look beyond her at the sea of people staring. A wave of nausea arcs through me, so powerful that cold sweat begins trickling down my spine. I curl my fingers and dig my lacquered nails into my palms. Voices hum louder as the clapping dies out, and then the voices evaporate in turn, supplanted by the theme song.

When the final notes fade, Dominic takes the microphone. "We've made it," he exclaims, pumping his fist in the air victoriously. "After the most tumultuous show, we've made it! Through tears brought on by a great human loss, and through the strain of false rumors and bad publicity, we did it."

I pull my shoulders back. Chase's shoulders are also stiff, straining the shiny fabric of his tuxedo.

"I was afraid of letting down our final contestants, our sponsors who have so graciously funded us, and the network, which has been so very tolerant of our erratic schedule. I thank you...all of you...for your patience and support. I thank our viewers who have spent hours with us on the other side of their television screens, cheering and voting for our contestants. And last but not least, I want to thank the amazing team of people, the assistants, the camera and lighting crew, the museum, the insurance company and their guards, and the stylists without whom none of the magic of these past nine days could've been possible."

The crowd is still standing, stitched together like the pieces of my quilts, basking us in applause.

Dominic raises his palm in the air to ask for silence, which comes so swiftly it's as deafening as the uproar. "And now, for the moment of reckoning...Chase and Ivy have had no contact with each other, or anyone besides their assistants since the last time you've seen them."

Perhaps I'm imagining this, but his eyes seem to mist over as he looks at me. After what feels like an eternity, he turns back to his adoring audience.

"So, the way we're going to do this—so that their answers don't overlap—is have the finalists write down their responses.

Jeb will transcribe them onto the monitors displaying their faces."

Just as he says this, every screen lights up, alternately with my face and Chase's. Keeping his eyes averted from mine, Brook hands me a small tablet and an electronic pen.

"Go ahead," Dominic says.

Fingers shaking, I write my answer:

They are all fakes.

CHASE IS STILL WRITING which either means that he's very slow or that his answer is more elaborate. I tip my head toward one of the screens that is reflecting my own face back to me. My answer hasn't magically appeared yet, so I drop my gaze back down to the tablet and think so hard my brain begins to hurt. Suddenly, the conversation I had with Chase before entering the Temple room wallops me upside the head. I try smudging my writing with my thumb, but the tablet doesn't work like that. Too soon, Chase is handing his tablet over to his brother.

I got what Chase wanted me to get: that there's a difference between fake and forgery. I glance back down at the short line I wrote, and then back up at Chase's sharp profile. I can still win. All I need to do is add a few more words, a sentence. Dominic's instructions were to find the fake, and that's the Picasso—the only one that was tampered with to give the illusion it was real. The other paintings and statues were all counterfeited: erroneous sizes, too flawless, wrong materials.

But would I have come to this realization without Chase?

"Time's up," Brook says.

I'm still clutching the stylus. I place the tip on the tablet, the temptation so great it makes my fingers shake harder. But then I think of Brook and of his offer to represent me. And I think of the man at my table last night and his proposition to buy all of my pieces. And of how art dealing is Chase's calling and he won't be able to do it if he doesn't get into the school. And then I think of Aster and realize that it's time for me to go home and take care of her.

Without adding a single word, I transfer the tablet to Brook's empty right hand. He clicks on both tablets, and our answers materialize on the surrounding screens.

Mine will be wrong, but it's okay. These last few days were a dream. And like all dreams, there comes a moment when you must wake up.

FIFTY-FIVE

FIFTY-SIX

Ivy

When Dominic announces Chase is the winner of the third annual Masterpiecers' competition, I hoist up my brightest smile. Once Brook has patted his back, once Dominic and Josephine have shaken his hand, I walk over to congratulate him, but the crowd moves in, climbing onto the platform, crushing me, and Chase disappears in the sea of tuxedos and rainbow silks. People touch my arms, grab my hands, tell me how impressed they were with my performance. Some even give me their business cards. My breathing becomes shallower, like on the Brooklyn Bridge, and I hasten my search for Chase. He spots me, yet it's as though a wall separates us because we still can't reach each other.

"Even though you didn't win, I'm very proud of you, Ivy," Dominic says.

The somberness I noticed earlier is still there. Did he know I was going to fail? Or does it have to do with his meeting with the lawyer and Josephine?

I touch his sleeve as I thank him. He nods, then retreats into the crowd. In the mayhem, someone bumps into me. Lincoln.

"Losing sucks, doesn't it?" she says.

"Chase deserved to win."

She smirks. "Tell yourself that if it makes you feel better."

She once said we'd probably be friends if we weren't adversaries, but she's wrong. "So, you're working for Josephine now?"

"Yep. I reached out to her this morning before leaving. I offered to become her personal assistant against housing at the Masterpiecers and use of the facilities."

"And she accepted?"

"You know many people who turn down free labor? Besides, I had some information she wanted."

"You always have an angle, don't you?"

"It's not an angle, Ivy; it's an extra ace. I learned at a young age that the world is far from fair." Her eyes gleam like the coins in the basin girdling the temples.

"What's going on with Dominic?" I ask.

"I can't tell you, but you'll know very soon."

"Does it have to do with me?"

Her gaze skims mine, but settles on the person next to me.

"So you're working for the devil, now?" Brook says.

"If Josephine's the devil, what does that make you, Brook?" She gives him a strange smile. "Enjoy your evening. I know I will." She winks and leaves.

Neither of us speaks. Then I feel an overwhelming need to ask, "Did she really get eliminated yesterday because of...of what happened in your pool?"

He snorts. "Is that what she told you?" he asks, watching Lincoln cross the room toward Josephine.

I nod.

"She was eliminated because she was careless," he says, just as a fuchsia-clad Madame Babanina accosts him.

"Brook, dear, you look so handsome tonight," she says, not

bothering to address me. Perhaps if I'd won, I would have been of interest to her.

"So this is good-bye?" I ask Brook, hoping he'll mention his offer to represent me. He doesn't. Maybe he never meant to.

"I suppose it is," he says.

The notorious divorcee swings her head toward me, and her curvy bangs bob against her forehead. "Sorry for your loss," she tells me, snaking her arms around Brook's like vines. "Brook, dear, I have someone I'd like you to meet." She begins tugging him away. "He'd like to start a collection and I was thinking who better to advise him than—"

She stops chattering suddenly. Many people have gone quiet and are shifting, creating an aisle down which march a squadron of men and women in navy uniforms with yellow FBI insignias. Spearheading the cortege is Detective Clancy and Detective McEnvoy—in navy and yellow also.

"FBI," McEnvoy yells. The lights in the room flare up, making his silver hair look metallic. "Nobody move!"

When his gaze lands on mine, I take a step back and bump into another body. A pair of hands shoots out to steady me. "It's me, Ivy," Chase whispers. "Just me."

Clancy said she would see me again—is this what she meant? Did she come here to arrest me?

Suddenly, she stops. And it's not in front of me. "Brook Jackson, put your hands where I can see them."

Brook doesn't react.

"Hands up, Jackson, now," she repeats.

As a collective gasp echoes through the room, Chase's fingers harden, crushing my skin.

Slowly, Brook raises his arms.

"Austin, frisk him," Leah says.

"Is this a joke?" Brook asks, as McEnvoy pats him down.

"Do I look like I'm laughing?" Leah says.

"He's clean," Austin announces.

"Brook Jackson, you are under arrest for colluding with wanted criminals, trafficking stolen goods, and laundering money for the mafia."

"What?" he yelps.

Chase's hands slip off my arms and plummet limply against his sides. I catch one and squeeze it.

"Did you know?" I whisper.

"I knew he was up to something, but I didn't—I—" His voice cracks. He stares down at me, then at our hands, then squeezes back. "I didn't know he was working for the mob."

"This is fucking ridiculous," Brook thunders.

"Is it?" Josephine lunges out of the crowd toward him. She has something in her hands. An empty package. She waves it around. "You were using the Masterpiecers as a front! Using art for terrible things."

"What the hell is that?" he asks.

"It's *un paquet*. The package that your friend Troy Mann sent you. We had the handwriting analyzed and the paper dusted for prints. At first, I thought Ivy was trying to earn brownie points, sending us a quilt after she got in"—she looks my way—"but she didn't send the package. She didn't write your name on it. *Troy* did. And it's not the first you've received from him. What did he send you this time? Money? Drugs?"

Brook's left eye twitches as he glares back at Josephine.

"Ma'am, please step back," an agent tells her. When she doesn't, they pull her back.

"*Tu devrais avoir honte!*"

Jeb, who's handling one of the cameras, angles it toward Brook before whirling it back toward Josephine.

Her icy blue eyes glow like the flames atop candlewicks. "You are a disgrace, Brook."

"Ma'am," Clancy says, "calm down or we'll have to ask you to step out."

Jeb zooms in on Josephine's face. On the overhanging screens, I can see her skinny nostrils flare.

"Turn those goddamn things off before I arrest you for interfering with criminal proceedings!" Austin presses his palm over the lens. "This is a federal arrest people, not some episode on your fuckin' game show."

In seconds, all the video equipment is shut off, and the screens go dark.

"Read him his Miranda rights, Austin," Clancy tells her partner.

"Brook Jackson, you have the right to remain silent. Anything you say can and will be used against you in a court of law. You have the right to an attorney. If you cannot afford an attorney, one will be provided for you. Do you understand the rights I have just read to you?"

"Dominic, tell them this is a misunderstanding."

Slowly, hunched over like a very old man, Dominic walks away.

"With these rights in mind, do you wish to speak to me?" Leah asks Brook.

"I'm not speaking to you, or to anyone else here." Brook's jaw is ruddy and his hair, which is usually so well brushed, sticks out in places. "I want a lawyer. Chase, call Dean right away!"

"Dean Kane?" Austin asks.

"Yes!"

"Doubt Mister Kane can represent you as he'll be needing his own defense." Austin glances my way when he says this. "Once we catch him."

"What are you talking about?" Brook asks in a shrill voice.

Clancy comes toward me. "Ivy, why don't you come with me?" she says, her voice low.

"Wh-why?" I stutter.

She looks around. Agents are escorting the agitated audience outside.

"What happened?" I ask, trying to make myself heard over the din.

Her large brown eyes settle back on mine. "Your sister was attacked."

Is it possible to flatline when you're still alive? "Attacked?" I repeat stupidly.

Clancy nods.

"Is she..." I swallow thickly. "Is she alive?" I ask, as Chase winds one arm around my waist.

"She's in a coma," she says, before telling me how it happened.

At some point, I interrupt her. "I don't understand."

"What don't you understand?"

"Why did Dean order the hit?"

"To retrieve the diamonds Troy Mann hid inside your quilt."

"Diamonds?" *There was more than one?*

"Dean and Troy were working together. It's your sister who made the connection."

"But then that would mean—" I shoot my gaze toward Brook, the shock of my realization so violent that I'm unable to finish my sentence. "You didn't send Dean to help her," I yell at him. "You sent him to execute her!"

I launch myself toward him, but Chase holds me back.

"Let go of me," I scream.

"No."

"Let go of me right now or help me God—"

He still doesn't.

"Chase, please," I beg, my voice breaking.

"Did your sister take the diamonds, Ivy?" Leah asks.

"I don't know," I say.

Brook laughs, a dark, mean laugh. When I glower at him, he winks.

Leah turns toward her partner. "Take him away," she says, at the same time as Chase whispers inside my ear, "What do you want to do? Punch him? Then *you'll* get arrested." His fingers dig deeper into my waist. "He's not worth it, Ivy."

I'm trembling so hard that my teeth rattle.

"Ivy, our liaison back in Indiana, Officer Joshua Cooper—he's a friend of yours, isn't he?" I don't think I nod, but I must, because Clancy continues, "He's with your sister. He asked me to tell you that he'll stay by her side until you get back."

Her mouth moves some more, but my ears are buzzing so loudly I can't make out much of what she's saying. I do pick up four words, though.

"Might never wake up."

She insists on the *might,* but all I hear is the *never.*

Ivy

EPILOGUE

It's been three weeks, and still Aster is asleep. Every day I visit her, and every day, it tears me apart a bit more.

When I arrived at the hospital, I asked the nurse to shave my sister's hair off. The woman who attacked her hacked off strands, leaving half of her head bare and the other half covered with ugly dreadlocks. I heard her name was Gill Swanson. I've been tempted to pay her a visit, but I think I would strangle her if I were to meet her.

The heart monitor beeps, reminding me that Aster's still alive. I don't know if she can hear me, but I talk to her all the time. I tell her about my new project, making a quilt just for her. I tell her I'm using Mom's prized fabrics. I even tell her about the history of the cloth rolls. Her heart spiked when I mentioned they were gifts from our father, so I embellish the few stories Mom shared with me about our dad.

Her heart hasn't spiked since.

"Hey," a gentle voice calls out from the doorway of the hospital room.

I put down my needle and the strips of ochre satin I've just cut, and stare at the one person who's made the past weeks bearable. "Hey back. I missed you."

Chase crosses the room in four quick strides and deposits a kiss on my mouth.

"One week in, and you're already skipping school," I tease him.

He chuckles, but then he stares at Aster, and his laughter dies out. "Anything new?"

I shake my head sadly.

"She'll wake up. I can feel it," he says.

"Just like you felt I would win?"

"I never thought you would win."

"Aha! You finally admit it." I wink when I spot his jaw darkening with a blush. "You even tried to help me at the end, and I still didn't give the right answer."

"I wanted you to win. I really did. I knew my brother was going to be kicked off, which would've made room for me."

"How is he?"

"He keeps claiming how innocent he is, but I know he's not."

"I hope he'll survive prison better than Aster."

"You're too nice."

"He's not entirely evil, Chase. No one is."

He stares at me with that penetrating gaze of his that makes me feel as though no one else exists in the world, and then he digs into his jacket pocket for something. "This arrived for you. The nurse asked me to bring it up." He extricates a lumpy envelope with no return address and places it on top of the shimmery satin strips.

My name is printed on the front, along with the hospital's address. Cautiously, I slice the paper with my sewing scissors. When I spot a black velvet jewelry box inside, a chill shoots up my spine.

"Someone sent you jewelry?" Chase's voice is so loud that

I fear the cop stationed outside the hospital room will overhear him. Thankfully, the door doesn't open. "Should I be jealous?"

I lift my eyes to his face. The vein on his temple lobe is pulsing. He's not just jealous; he's angry.

"It's probably the family heirloom Kevin stole from me," I say in a low voice. I know now that it wasn't Kevin. It was Brook. I figured it out when he winked at me the day he was arrested. I'm surprised he hasn't told the police about the diamond yet.

"He stole something from you?"

I inhale a slow breath and nod. I hate that I'm lying to Chase, but what choice do I have?

"Did he send it from his grave?"

I lower my gaze to the velvet box. "His wife must've found it in his personal effects."

"Wouldn't she have assumed it was a gift he got her?"

Why must Chase be so smart? "Maybe Dominic told her they were looking for it, and she felt obliged to return it, what with all that's happened."

I stare at the box. It shimmies in and out of focus.

"Well, aren't you going to open it?" His usually calm voice sounds somewhat sharp.

I swallow. And then I click on the latch. And it's as excruciating as if I were pulling the trigger during a game of Russian roulette. The box unbolts and the lid rises. Silence hangs, thick and heavy like the rainclouds outside. Not only is the stolen diamond back, but it's been woven into an intricate setting that spells my name.

"I understand why she couldn't keep it," Chase says. "Although she could've removed the stone from its setting."

The brilliant rock winks at me, a scornful reminder of why I'm sitting in a guarded hospital room next to my sister's lifeless body.

"Here. Let me put it on you," Chase says, reaching for the box.

"No," I say quickly, snapping it closed.

He frowns.

I want to tell him the truth, but how can I explain it now that my name is linked to the diamond? "If Aster wakes up and sees it, she'll be sad. Mom never made her one."

I was wrong.

Brook *is* entirely evil.

NEXT UP:

COLD LITTLE HEARTS

ACKNOWLEDGMENTS

They say it takes a village to raise a child. It is the same for a book. It took an elite group of writers and beta readers to transform *COLD LITTLE GAMES* (previously titled: *The Masterpiecers*) into the novel you have just read.

I'd like to thank my sister, Vanessa, for giving me the idea for an art competition. I'd also like to thank her for going through the first draft, and the second, and the third. You're a real trooper! *Un grand merci* to Jacqueline whose keen eye tightened and sharpened my plot. Granted, I had to rewrite the entire thing, but wasn't it worth it? Theresea, my writing sidekick, my sounding board, my friend, thank you for your unceasing encouragement and your wonderful company. Thank you to Astrid and Marina for always being so positive about what I write. You girls keep me going. A big thank you to Katie Hayoz who is as terrific an author as she is a beta reader and a friend. Thanks to Elizabeth and Becky and Samantha and all of the other early readers who have consolidated my faith in Ivy and Aster's story.

Thank you to my husband for not begrudging my passion for writing. I love you. To my three wonderful children, I hope that one day, I will have made you proud. To my parents and my other two siblings, thank you for your enduring support. Without you, writing as a profession would still be a dream—and my website would still be an awful mess (right, Sam?). All my love to my extended family. I am very lucky to have so many extraordinary people in my life.

You can also follow me on oliviawildenstein.com or through my Facebook page https://www.facebook.com/owauthor/ for writing updates and publication news.

ABOUT THE AUTHOR

Olivia Wildenstein grew up in New York City, the daughter of a French father and a Swedish mother. She chose Brown University to complete her undergraduate studies and earned a bachelor's in comparative literature. After designing jewelry for a few years, Wildenstein traded in her tools for a laptop computer.

When she's not writing, she's psychoanalyzing everyone she meets (*Yes. Everyone*), baking up a storm, and attempting not to be late at her children's school.

Wildenstein lives with her husband and three children in Geneva, Switzerland, where she's an active member of the writing community.

Connect with the author:
oliviawildenstein.com
press@oliviawildenstein.com

www.ingramcontent.com/pod-product-compliance
Lightning Source LLC
Chambersburg PA
CBHW050615170726
48283CB00001B/260